House Secrets

Also by Mike Lawson

House Secrets

A Joe DeMarco Thriller

Mike Lawson

Grove Press
New York

Printed in the United States of America
Published simultaneously in Canada

ISBN-13: 978-0-8021-4480-5

Grove Press
an imprint of Grove/Atlantic, Inc.
841 Broadway
New York, NY 10003

Distributed by Publishers Group West
www.groveatlantic.com

10 11 12   10 9 8 7 6 5 4 3 2

To Gail—for everything—forever.

Acknowledgments

I want to thank all the people at Atlantic Monthly Press who worked so hard on this book and my last one, and in particular: Morgan Entrekin, Jamison Stoltz, Eric Price, Deb Seager, Jodie Hockesmith, and Sue Cole. Everyone at the company has been incredibly friendly, helpful, competent, and professional and I am very fortunate to be associated with such a fine publishing company.

Frank Horton, as always, for proof-reading and editing my manuscripts before they go to the publisher. Roger Hubbard, life-saver, for his artistic and computer skills.

Everyone at The Gernert Company—David Gernert, Stephanie Cabot, Courtney Hammer and Erika Storella—who have toiled so hard to keep me gainfully employed. I'm a lucky guy.

Prologue

———◆———

"Carl, goddamnit, don't bruise his neck!"

"I'm trying not to, but he's a strong little bastard."

"Shit, you're twice his size. Grab him by the hair, not the neck."

"That did it," Carl said after a minute. "I just saw a buncha bubbles come out."

"Yeah, well, hold him there a while. I don't want what happened in that movie."

"Movie?"

"You know, the one with what's-her-name, where she boils the rabbit."

"Oh, yeah. But what's that—"

"At the end there, don't you remember? When Douglas gets her in the tub? Bubbles comin' outta her mouth, eyes wide open, then like five minutes later the bitch pops up and tries to stab him."

"I don't remember that part," Carl said. "I remember the rabbit but . . ."

"Oh, for Christ's sake," Jimmy said. "Just hold him there."

"You got his keys?" Carl said.

"Yeah, I got the keys," Jimmy said. "What do you think I'm jigglin' here?"

Jimmy opened the door which led into the kitchen of the house. "Now where's his office, den, whatever?" He started through the kitchen but stopped when he heard the refrigerator door open. "What the hell are you doing?"

"Gettin' a Coke," Carl said. "I'm thirsty."

"Are you nuts?"

"I'm wearin' gloves. What's the big deal?"

Jimmy just shook his head. Carl, sometimes he just didn't know.

Two minutes later, they were standing in front of the safe. It had been behind a picture, a sailing scene.

"Why do they always put it behind a picture?" Carl said. "I mean, you know where it's gonna be."

"They put it behind a picture because it'd look pretty fuckin' ugly, just sittin' there in the middle of the wall," Jimmy said.

"Oh."

Jimmy spun the lock on the safe.

"How the hell did Eddie get the combination, anyway?" Carl said.

"He said something about a locksmith the guy used."

Jimmy swung open the door to the safe. Inside it were a bunch of little notebooks, the covers doodled on, the pages all ragged. Jimmy took out the notebooks, several at a time, and tossed them into his shoulder bag. Carl had said that the shoulder bag looked like a faggy purse, which it sort of did, but it was better than carrying around a shopping bag.

At the back of the safe was a wad of cash bound with a rubber band. Jimmy flipped through it. Maybe five grand. The guy's disaster money. He handed the cash to Carl and looked back into the safe. The only thing remaining, lying flat on the bottom, was a clear plastic sheet with little pockets containing coins. Jimmy didn't know anything about old coins but he figured these must be worth something or the guy wouldn't have put them in his safe—but he didn't touch the coin holder.

"That's it," he said, but then he noticed something under the coin holder. He lifted up the plastic and saw a flash drive for a computer. "Damn," he muttered, "almost missed that." He put the flash drive into his bag.

"Gimme the money." Carl handed him the cash and Jimmy tossed it back into the safe and closed and locked the door. Eddie had said not to take any money, or anything else but the stuff he'd told them. And if that's what Eddie said . . .

"Now let's find his laptop," Jimmy said "And any more of these flash thingamajigs."

Carl finished the Coke he was drinking, made a small burp, and put the soda can in Jimmy's man-purse.

"Okey-dokey," Carl said.

Chapter 1

———◆———

Mahoney was reclining near the pool, a big blue beach umbrella shading his head. His meaty right hand was wrapped around a frosted glass containing equal parts vodka and tomato juice. Clenched in his left hand, in the V created by two thick fingers, was a cigar. He wore white swim trunks with a red stripe down the side, and partially covering his broad chest and substantial gut, was an unbuttoned aloha shirt patterned with red hibiscuses. His hair was white and full, his legs were white, thick, and hairless, and his large bare feet were pale.

DeMarco thought he looked like a beluga whale that had crashed a luau.

"It's about time you got here," Mahoney said.

This complaint was typical of Mahoney. There he was—lying under an umbrella, drinking, doing nothing—while DeMarco had been forced to drive seventy miles in heavy traffic because his boss hadn't wanted to talk over the phone. Or maybe Mahoney just didn't want to *hold* the phone as this could have interrupted his drinking and smoking.

Nor did Mahoney offer DeMarco a seat or a drink. This breach of etiquette could have occurred because Mahoney was oblivious to the creature comforts of his subordinates—or it could have been because DeMarco looked impervious to such ailments as dehydration and heat stroke. DeMarco's forefathers were Italian and his features reflected his heritage. He was five foot eleven, with heavy shoulders and strong arms. He combed his dark hair straight back, and the first strands of gray were just beginning to appear at the temples. He had a handsome face, but a hard one, and if Francis Ford Coppola had been casting extras for *Godfather IV,* he would have hired DeMarco on the spot.

So DeMarco stood there in front of Mahoney's lounge chair, squinting into the midday sun. It was the first of September and the temperature was in the low eighties. As he waited for Mahoney to tell him why he'd been summoned, he glanced up at the large house in the background. DeMarco didn't know who had loaned his boss the use of the mansion with its pool and its magnificent view of Chesapeake Bay, but he suspected it was someone trying to curry his favor. DeMarco wondered if that same person had loaned Mahoney the woman he could see in the window.

The woman—lithe and tanned—was in her thirties and she was walking back and forth in front of a large picture window, talking on a cell phone. The only thing she was wearing was a black bikini bottom the size of a stripper's g-string. Her bare breasts, from a distance of fifty yards, were flawless.

Mahoney swiveled his thick neck to see what DeMarco was looking at.

"Yeah, she's a character," he said. "And in case you're havin' impure thoughts, she's not with me. She's the girlfriend of the guy who owns the house."

Impure thoughts—a Catholic sinner's expression—and DeMarco bet that Mahoney had been confessing to that particular transgression from the time he was a pudgy altar boy. But was he lying about the woman? DeMarco didn't know. He doubted if God knew. And the fact that Mahoney could lie so nimbly was not surprising: he was a politician. John Fitzpatrick Mahoney was the Speaker of the United States House of Representatives, third in line for the Oval Office if both the president and vice president were unable to serve. A truly terrifying thought in DeMarco's opinion.

"Hey! Stop looking at her tits and pay attention," Mahoney said.

DeMarco reluctantly shifted his gaze back to Mahoney's blue eyes—the red-veined eyes of a dedicated drinker.

"There's a guy," Mahoney said, "an old buddy of

mine, an ex-congressman from Virginia. His name's Dick Finley and he retired about ten years ago. Anyway, a week ago his son died in some kinda weird accident and Dick wants somebody to look into it."

"Does he need a lawyer?" DeMarco asked. "I mean is he planning to sue somebody?"

DeMarco had asked the question not because he cared about the answer but because he had just looked up at the mansion again—and he wanted to keep looking. The young woman was still on the phone, but this time she saw DeMarco staring at her. She turned to face him so he was treated to a full-frontal view, and then she smiled and wiggled her fingers at him. She was so firm nothing else wiggled. He bet Mahoney was lying.

Mahoney snorted in response to DeMarco's question. "If he needed a lawyer, Joe, I wouldn't have given him your name."

DeMarco was offended though he knew he had no right to be. He had a law degree—had even passed the Virginia bar—but he had never practiced law. He was too busy doing other unsavory things on Mahoney's behalf.

"It sounds like what he needs," Mahoney said, "is somebody to turn over a few rocks and see what crawls out."

There you go, DeMarco thought. That was his job description: rock flipper and bug crusher. Not very flattering but accurate enough.

Chapter 2

Retired congressman Richard Finley lived in Colonial Beach, Virginia, not far from the Chesapeake Bay mansion where DeMarco had met Mahoney.

Finley answered the doorbell wearing a sun-faded red golf shirt, khaki pants, and scuffed Top-Siders. He was short, in his eighties, bald and tanned, and had the kind of neat round head and small-featured face that looked good without hair on top. He smiled at DeMarco when DeMarco introduced himself but the smile didn't reach his eyes. Finley's eyes looked hollow and haunted, as if he'd been punched in the gut by fate one too many times.

He led DeMarco onto a deck that looked out over the beach, said how much he appreciated DeMarco coming, and asked if he wanted a beer. As Finley was popping the tops on two Coronas, DeMarco commented on the view.

Finley glanced over his shoulder at the water as if he'd forgotten it was there. "Yeah," he said, "I bought this place for my wife and kids to come in the summer. And for my grandkids if I ever had any, which I never did. Now my family's all dead so I guess I'll just donate the place to some charity when I'm gone."

DeMarco almost screamed: No! Give it to me! But instead he nodded his head solemnly.

"My wife, breast cancer killed her, and my other boy, he died in Vietnam—God curse John Kennedy for that. And now my youngest son is dead. We had Terry when I was forty-one. I never thought for a minute that I'd outlive him."

"I'm sorry," DeMarco said.

"But with my wife and my oldest boy, at least I knew *why* they died. With Terry, I don't know what happened. And that's why I called John, to see if he knew somebody who could . . . I don't know, poke into things."

Dick Finley explained that his son, Terry, had been a reporter for the *Washington Post* and two days ago his body had been found in Lake Anna where Terry had a home.

"They said he'd been out in his kayak and had fallen overboard and drowned. But the story doesn't make sense."

"You don't think he drowned?" DeMarco said.

"He drowned," Dick Finley said. "The autopsy was definitive on that. And the water they found in his lungs came from the lake."

"Then I don't understand," DeMarco said.

"It's a long commute from D.C. to Lake Anna, and Terry was a workaholic. The day he died, I know he left the *Post* about eight, so he wouldn't have gotten to the lake until at least nine-thirty. So why would a guy go kayaking at nine-thirty, ten o'clock at night? I asked the police that, and they said there was a full moon that night, but I still don't buy it. And the other thing is, Terry got that kayak five, six years ago. He was always getting interested in some new thing—biking, kayaking, rock climbing—and then after a couple of months he'd lose interest. The only thing he cared about was work. What I'm saying is, I don't think Terry'd been in that boat in two or three years, maybe longer."

"But his body was found in the lake, near the kayak," DeMarco said.

"Yeah, but there's other stuff. Like Terry's laptop is missing. That laptop was *always* with him. If he wasn't carrying the thing, it was close by—in his car, on his desk, wherever he was. I asked the sheriff where his computer was, and at first he said he didn't know. Two days later he calls back and says that Terry had filed a report with the D.C. cops before his death saying it had been stolen."

"And you don't think it was?"

"No. I talked to Terry the day he died, that morning. If his laptop had been stolen, he would have told me. He'd have been going *nuts* to find it. And the sheriff said that Terry reported the theft over the phone, not in person. So who knows who really filed the report?"

"I see," DeMarco said.

"And that's not all," Finley said. "Terry was working on something, something he said was going to win him a Pulitzer. He wouldn't tell me what, but he said when he filed his story the dome was gonna come off the Capitol. Now to tell you the truth, I didn't think too much of that. Terry was always working on some story he said was gonna be big, but usually wasn't. But then he goes and dies, and now I don't know. You want another beer?"

While Finley was getting his beer, DeMarco looked down at the beach and noticed a pudgy, middle-aged man walking a small dog. He watched as the guy tossed a stick of driftwood into the water. The stick looked heavy and was as long as the dog, but the dog—poor, dumb creature that it was—charged into the water after it. A wave crashed into the animal and it disappeared for a moment, then it reappeared with the stick in its mouth. The dog fought its way back to the beach and brought the stick to the man, who immediately tossed it again, farther out this time. DeMarco felt like going down to the beach and throwing the stick into the water and making the pudgy guy go fetch it.

After Finley handed him his beer, DeMarco said, "Do you think there might be something in your son's house that would give me an idea of what he was working on?"

"Maybe you can find something, but I looked a couple days ago," Finley said. "I went all through his desk, even looked in his safe to see if he'd put something there, but all that was in the safe was some cash and some old coins he'd collected." Finley smiled then, but it was a sad smile. "The coins were like the kayak," he said. "Terry bought 'em ten years ago and probably hadn't looked at 'em since then. But if you want to look in his house, I'll give you the keys."

"That'd be good," DeMarco said. "I'll take a look later if I think I need to."

"I did find one thing that I can't explain," Finley said, and he reached into his shirt pocket and carefully removed a wrinkled piece of paper and handed it to DeMarco. The paper was water-damaged and torn. It was a cocktail napkin from a place called Sam and Harry's, a bar in D.C. that DeMarco went to quite often.

"That was in Terry's wallet," Finley said. "His wallet was in his pants when he died and it got wet, of course. All the cash and credit card slips were all stuck together and I tore that when I tried to separate it from the other stuff. That's all of it I could salvage."

DeMarco studied what was written on the napkin for a moment but could make no sense of it. "You think what's written here might be related to whatever he was working on?" he said.

"I don't know," Finley said. "It looks like he was just doodling on that napkin—Terry was a real doodler—but I don't think he would have put it in his wallet if it wasn't important. Look, the only thing I know for sure is that he didn't fall out of a damn kayak at ten o'clock at night."

Chapter 3

"Old man Finley's a good guy," the sheriff said. "I liked him when he was in Congress and I still like him. But he's wrong about Terry. There wasn't anything suspicious about his death."

The Louisa County sheriff was in his forties, well-muscled and tanned, and on the credenza behind his desk was a picture of him and a boys' baseball team. Two of the kids in the picture were clutching a good-sized trophy. DeMarco hoped the sheriff was as good a cop as he was a coach.

"We didn't find any signs of a struggle," the sheriff said. "His house wasn't ransacked and he definitely drowned in the lake. The lake's got some kind of algae in it which is pretty distinctive, and the medical examiner found it in his lungs."

"You don't think it's strange that he was kayaking in the dark?" DeMarco said.

"It wasn't that dark. There was a full moon that night and the lights from other houses on the lake would have provided more light. But there's something else, something we didn't tell Mr. Finley."

"What's that?"

"Terry's blood alcohol level was .18 at the time of his death. We think he had a few drinks after work, came home with a pretty good buzz on, and decided to go for a little moonlight paddle. Drunks have bad judgment. And their coordination and sense of balance aren't too good either. Have you ever been in a kayak, Mr. DeMarco?"

"No. Been in a canoe, but not a kayak."

"Well, sometime you oughta try to get *in* one. What I'm saying is, the toughest part of kayaking is getting in and out of the damn boat without tipping it over, and if you don't believe me, try it. Then try it again after four drinks."

———◆———

DeMarco called the *Washington Post* and spent five frustrating minutes navigating his way through a particularly annoying voice mail system before he was finally connected to Reggie Harmon's phone.

"Reggie, my man," DeMarco said, "I'm in the mood to buy you a big salad for lunch."

"A *salad*?" Reggie said, as if he couldn't imagine consuming something so horrible.

"That's right, Reginald. A two-olive salad with martini dressing. Onions if you prefer."

"Ah, that kinda salad. Well, veggies are one of your four basic food groups, aren't they?"

"Yes, they are, my friend. Plus vodka's usually made from potatoes. Carbohydrates, you know. And if you have a twist in your second martini, you'll ward off scurvy."

"Where and when, son? A man my age can't afford to ignore his health."

"The Monocle. As soon as you can get there."

DeMarco hung up the phone. He should have been ashamed of himself, appealing to the late-morning cravings of an alcoholic to get information— but he wasn't.

DeMarco had called Reggie from his office, a small windowless room in the subbasement of the Capitol that seemed to have been designed to induce claustrophobia. He spent as little time there as possible, and the décor—or the lack of it—reflected this. The only furniture in the room was his desk, two wooden chairs, and a battered, four-drawer file cabinet. The file cabinet was a totally unnecessary item because DeMarco didn't believe in keeping written records; they could subpoena *him,* but not his files. At one point he'd had a couple of pictures on one wall that had been given to him by his ex-wife, but since they had reminded him of her unfaithful nature every time he looked at them, he'd finally taken them down. The pathetic part was that the bare space on the wall where the pictures had been still reminded him of her.

The Monocle Bar and Grill was located near Union Station, less than a fifteen-minute walk from the Capitol. DeMarco locked his office door and walked up the steps to the main floor of the building, to the rotunda, the space directly beneath the dome. He saw a page he knew leading a tour group: a smart-assed, jug-eared little bastard named Mullen. Pages had the professional longevity of butterflies, here one summer and gone the next, so DeMarco rarely knew their names—but he knew Mullen's. He had walked out of his office one day and saw Mullen smooching a girl page out in the hall, next to his door. Instead of acting embarrassed as he should have, Mullen had the balls to offer DeMarco fifty bucks for the use of his office. The kid would probably be president one day.

To reach the Monocle, DeMarco walked down First Street, past the Supreme Court. He looked up, as he always did, at the words EQUAL JUSTICE UNDER LAW carved into the stone above the building's sixteen massive marble columns. The high court was one of the few institutions in Washington that DeMarco still had any faith in, and he had this faith for a simple reason: the nine people who worked there had nothing more to gain. They were at the pinnacle of their profession, they had the job for life, and they didn't have to please anybody to keep the job. Those, he believed, were circumstances that tended to produce honest if not always wise decisions. But he was probably wrong about that too.

As DeMarco stepped inside the Monocle, the maître d' glanced over at him to see if his attire was appropriate, nodded curtly, then returned to his reservation list. The Monocle was a bit pretentious but then this was understandable: its clientele tended to be the legislative branch of government as opposed to the electorate, and the walls of the bar were covered with photographs of drinking politicians. It seemed like Mahoney was in half the pictures.

DeMarco saw Reggie Harmon sitting at the end of the bar, the only customer at eleven in the morning, his first martini half-gone. Reggie was sixty and he looked like a vampire that had been caught in a sunbeam. He had a pale sunken-cheeked face and dyed black hair plastered to a long, narrow skull. His shirt was two sizes too large around the collar and his thin fingers poked beyond the cuffs like claws.

As DeMarco sat down on the stool next to him, Reggie slowly swiveled his head in DeMarco's direction. His eyes were so red that DeMarco wondered if any of the reporter's blood reached his brain. Exposing too many nicotine-stained teeth in the grimace he called a smile, Reggie said, "What do you call a hundred lawyers buried in a landfill?"

"A good start. Reggie, that's the third time you've told me that stupid joke. You need to get some new material."

"Well, you could still laugh, just to be polite," Reggie said.

DeMarco just shook his head then pointed at Reggie's drink and held up two fingers for the bartender's benefit.

"What do you know about Terry Finley?" DeMarco asked.

Reggie drained his first martini. "The kid that drowned?" he said.

"Yeah, the kid that drowned." Finley had been forty-two when he died.

Reggie shrugged, then reached for the full glass the bartender had just placed at his elbow. He swallowed a third of the drink before saying, "What do I know about him? Well, he worked the political beat, of course."

"Why 'of course'?"

"The only reason he got the job was because his dad was a congressman. The schemers in charge figured a kid whose dad worked on the Hill would give the paper an edge."

"Did it?"

"No. Terry was an annoying, ambitious little shit, one of those guys who always thought he was gonna be the next Bobby Woodward, but he never tried to use his old man to get there."

"Was he any good?"

Reggie swallowed the remainder of his second martini; as an afterthought he reached for the olives from his first martini. At the rate Reggie drank, DeMarco was thinking that they should just hook up an IV bag to his arm.

"Only in his dreams," Reggie said. "A couple years ago he got everyone all excited when he said he'd discovered that this colonel over at the Pentagon was an al-Qaeda mole. The basis for his conclusion was that the guy—the Pentagon guy—was always meeting this dishy, Arabic-looking gal in these seedy hotel bars. Turned out the guy was just boffing the lady, who happened to be Egyptian, but was no more into Islam than the Pope. That was Terry: seeing a spy ring instead of two people fuckin'."

"Huh," DeMarco said. "Was he working on anything important before he died?"

"Maybe. I heard him and his editor going at it one day. Frank was trying to get Terry's ass up to the Hill to write about some political squabble, and Terry kept telling him that he didn't have time. He said he was working on the biggest thing since Clinton got a blow job."

"But you don't know what the story was about?"

"No. All I heard was Terry say that if Frank knew who his source was, he wouldn't be giving him chickenshit assignments."

"Shit. So now I have talk to this Frank guy to find out what Terry was working on."

"Well, unless you got a hotline to hell, you can forget that."

"What?"

"Frank's dead."

"Dead? When did he die?"

"A week ago, about two days after Terry."

"Jesus," DeMarco said. "Was there anything mysterious about the way he died?"

Reggie took his time finishing his last drink as DeMarco waited impatiently for his answer. Finally, he said, "Frank was sixty-three years old. He was five-seven, weighed two-fifty, and smoked unfiltered Camels. He thought high cholesterol was the name of a racehorse. The only mystery is that Frank didn't have a coronary when he was forty-three."

Chapter 4

———◆———

"Are you feeling lucky, punk?" DeMarco muttered, his lips twisted into an Eastwood snarl—then he fired the gun, a .357 magnum.

"Stop doing that," Emma said.

DeMarco ignored her and looked at the man-shaped paper target. There were five holes in it, and although no hole was closer than six inches to any other hole, all of his shots had hit the punk.

"Well, pilgrim, what do you think of that," he said to Emma, switching from Eastwood to Wayne.

"I think you're jerking the trigger instead of squeezing it," Emma said.

"Let's try the Glock now," DeMarco said. "I'm gonna use the two-handed, cop's grip this time."

"I give up," Emma said.

Emma was tall and slim. She wore her hair short, and it was colored a blondish shade with some gray mixed in. Her profile was regal, like a Norse queen on a coin, and her eyes were light blue, cool, and cynical. She was at least ten years older than DeMarco, maybe fifteen, but in such good shape that she would have run him into the ground had he ever been dumb enough to challenge her to a race. She was wearing jeans, a long-sleeved navy-blue pullover, and black Reeboks. Clipped to her belt was a holster and in the holster was an automatic with a worn grip.

DeMarco had decided it was time to learn something about firearms. He was a firm believer in gun control—meaning that the only people who should be allowed to have guns were cops and soldiers, and himself, of course, if he thought he ever needed one—but a few months ago he came close to being killed because he didn't know where the safety was on a weapon. So though he had no immediate plans to buy a gun, and hoped sincerely that he would never need one in the future, he figured a little basic education couldn't hurt. And there was another thing: he thought it'd be kinda fun to shoot a few guns, which it was.

So under Emma's less than patient tutelage, he fired three weapons that day: a 9mm Glock; a .22 automatic that Emma said was the firearm often preferred by professional killers; and the .357 magnum. He had wanted to shoot the Glock and the .357 because those were the guns they always mentioned in the movies.

DeMarco put a fresh target on the target-hanger, sent it down-range twenty yards, and picked up the Glock. He liked the way it felt. He spread his legs in what he considered to be a shooter's stance, gripped the gun in both hands, said "Freeze, asshole"—and pulled the trigger six times. When he finished there were six holes in the target, three of them bunched fairly close together in the paper guy's left shoulder. Other than the fact that he'd been aiming for the heart, not bad, he thought. Emma thought differently.

"Joe," she said, "if you're ever attacked, and if you have a choice between a bat and a gun, use the bat."

"Well, let's see you do better," DeMarco said.

Now why in the hell had he said that? It must have been all the gun smoke in the air, the fumes short-circuiting those brain cells that caused him to actually think before speaking.

Emma was now retired but she had worked for the DIA—the Defense Intelligence Agency. She was, however, a person who rarely, and then only reluctantly, talked about her past, and consequently DeMarco had no idea what she had done for the military for almost thirty years. He did know that by the end of her career she'd been a senior player in the intelligence community in Washington, and that early in her career she'd been some sort of spy. And there was one other thing he knew—he knew that she could shoot a gun.

She hit a button that pushed DeMarco's target ten yards farther away, pulled the automatic from the holster on her hip, and then, without appearing to take aim, she fired. BAMBAMBAMBAMBAM. Five shots fired so rapidly it was hard to distinguish one from the other. When the smoke cleared, DeMarco looked at the target.

The paper man had a two-inch-diameter hole where his nose had once been.

———◆———

Emma's reward for instructing DeMarco was dinner at a place of her choosing, and she surprised him by selecting a mid-priced restaurant in Alexandria that specialized in soft-shelled crab. She may have chosen the place because of the way they were dressed but DeMarco suspected that she was being kind to his wallet. Emma was rich; DeMarco wasn't. As they waited for their dinners, Emma sipped a glass of white wine and looked at the ragged, water-damaged napkin that Dick Finley had taken from his son's wallet.

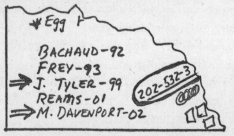

"So what do you think?" DeMarco asked.

"I would guess that these are people's names followed by a year, but who the people are and what the dates signify . . . well, your guess is as good as mine. As for the numbers, they look like a D.C. phone number minus the last three digits."

"Yeah, I figured that. How 'bout the 'egg'?"

Emma shrugged. "Maybe part of a shopping list, but I doubt it. He would have written 'eggs,' not 'egg.' And it looks like there's some word that comes after 'egg,' but I can't even make out the first letter."

"That's the best you can do? I thought in your old job you decoded encrypted messages."

"Not me," Emma said. "The people who do that sort of thing have PhDs and use really big computers. I did other stuff." This last statement was followed by an enigmatic smile. Emma had a really good enigmatic smile.

"Great," DeMarco said. "So that's it? You don't have any bright ideas about what I should do next?"

"As a matter of fact, I do," she said.

———◆———

"Emma," DeMarco whined, "why can't he just fax me the damn information? We're dealing with names on a *cocktail* napkin, for Christ's sake, not plans for a missile defense system."

"Fax you! You must be joking," Emma said. "Neil's so paranoid he never puts anything sensitive into a computer connected to the net, he doesn't even own a cell phone, and he never, ever sends information out on lines that can be tapped."

It was for this reason that Emma and DeMarco, the day after their session at the shooting range, were now sitting in a room on the Washington side of the Potomac River within sight of the Pentagon. Neil was an associate of Emma's from her days at the DIA and he called himself an "information broker"—which really meant that he hacked and bugged and spied, then sold whatever he acquired to the highest bidder. DeMarco had always found it disconcerting that a man with Neil's skills should have an office so close to the Pentagon.

Neil sat behind a cluttered desk in a chair engineered for his girth. He was in his early fifties and growing bald on top, but he gathered his remaining gray-blond hair into a thin ponytail that hung down from the back of his head like the tail on a well-fed rodent. As usual, he was dressed in a loose-fitting Hawaiian shirt, baggy shorts, and sandals. DeMarco had no idea what Neil wore when the temperature dropped, but as he rarely left his office, the issue was academic.

"Emma, you look lovely as always," Neil said.

"Thank you," Emma said. "And you look as if you've lost some weight."

DeMarco looked over at Emma to see if she was serious. Neil was the size of the Chrysler Building; if he lost a hundred pounds it wouldn't be apparent.

Neil, however, was pleased by the compliment. He beamed a smile at Emma and said, "Thank you for noticing."

DeMarco cleared his throat.

"Yes, Joe," Emma said, "we'll get to it in a minute. You know, it wouldn't hurt you to develop a few social skills, such as the ability to make small talk for more than sixty seconds."

"It's all right, Emma," Neil said. "I need to get going. Cindy and I are going dancing tonight."

Cindy was Neil's wife—and the fact that Neil had a wife and DeMarco did not was proof of God's dark sense of humor. But Neil *dancing*? The image that came to mind was the hippo in *Fantasia,* not Travolta in *Pulp Fiction*.

"Well, good for you," Emma said. "Maybe if Joe took his girlfriends dancing he might be able to keep one."

Neil smirked at Emma's comment then pulled an unlabeled manila file folder out of a stack of identical folders sitting on one corner of his desk. DeMarco didn't know how he knew which folder to select, but knowing how Neil liked to show off, he wouldn't have been surprised if the files were marked like a crooked deck of cards.

"To begin," Neil said. "We have five names, five apparent dates, and a partial phone number. The phone number I'm still working on. I've checked Finley's home and cell phone records but he didn't call anyone with a number matching the seven numbers on the napkin. He may have called the number from a public phone, in which case I can't tell who he called. So, since there are three missing digits from the phone number, and therefore a thousand possible phone number combinations, what I'm doing now is cross-checking those combinations against existing phone numbers to see if I can find anyone connected with what else I've learned. Which brings me to the names on the list. The obvious thing to do was to see if there was any common factor linking them. And there was." He paused, then said: "The common factor is Paul Morelli."

"Paul Morelli?" DeMarco said. "Do you mean *Senator* Paul Morelli?"

Senator Paul Morelli was, according to every political pundit on the planet, the man most likely to be the Democratic candidate for president in the next election.

"I do," Neil said. "In 1992, Marshall Bachaud was the district attorney of the fair isle of Manhattan. In January of that year, he was in a car accident which kept him hospitalized for twenty-six weeks and required three surgeries to rebuild various parts of his anatomy. Over the protests of many, the governor of New York appointed a young assistant DA named Paul Morelli as the acting district attorney until such time as Bachaud could resume his duties. As acting DA, young Morelli became a visible public figure.

"In 1996," Neil continued, "Morelli became the Democratic candidate for mayor of New York City. His opponent was a popular fellow with a good record named Walter Frey. Frey was the New York State attorney general at the time, and four months prior to the election he was accused of throwing a major case involving a company in Albany. Emails between Frey and the company were discovered, the emails indicating that Frey had been providing helpful information to the defendant's attorneys. Then, and although unrelated to the case, it was also discovered that Frey was having an affair with a young lady who worked for him. Frey eventually admitted to the affair but he claimed, and looked quite stupid doing so, that the young lady had been hired by someone to seduce him. And if you look at photos of Walter Frey, it *is* hard to imagine why the woman would have succumbed to his charms. Ironically, the affair damaged him more politically than the case-fixing accusations because Frey had always been such a big family values guy."

"Was he ever convicted of a crime?" DeMarco asked.

"No," Neil said. "The evidence was circumstantial at best, but it didn't matter because his reputation was destroyed by the press. And Paul Morelli became mayor."

Neil licked a fat finger and flipped to a new page in the file. "Now to Mr. Reams. In 2001, while still mayor, Paul Morelli decided to run for the Senate. Polls showed that he was the people's choice but the Democratic old guard in New York wanted David Reams. Reams was well-connected, came from money, and had served in the House. The thinking was that Morelli was young and his time would come, and that Reams had more experience and connections in D.C."

"Oh, I remember this," Emma said.

"Yes," Neil said. "One fine day, the police burst into a motel room on Staten Island and find Reams in bed with a sixteen-year-old boy. Reams claimed that he had no idea who the boy was or how he had ended up in the motel room. He said he must have been drugged and demanded that his blood be tested, which it was, and the results came back negative for narcotics. Reams was convicted because of the boy's age and served ten months. And Paul Morelli was elected to the Senate."

"What about Tyler and Davenport," DeMarco said. "What happened to those guys?"

"Those guys are women," Neil said.

Chapter 5

According to Neil, J. Tyler was Janet Tyler. Tyler had worked briefly for Paul Morelli when he was mayor of New York, which Neil discovered by searching W-2 forms provided by the city to its employees in 1999. M. Davenport was Marcia Davenport, an interior decorator who had apparently helped the Morellis decorate their Georgetown home when Morelli moved to Washington to begin his first term in the Senate. Neil's file on Davenport contained a copy of a check signed by Paul Morelli's wife and a billing statement pilfered from Davenport's home computer showing that she'd charged the Morellis $365 for her services.

But that was it. There were no news articles or police reports or any other public documentation on either woman to explain why they were on Terry Finley's list.

Since Davenport lived in Washington, D.C., and Tyler lived in New York, DeMarco decided to begin with Davenport. She was thirty-six years old, had been married briefly, but was now divorced. She had no children and lived in a condo on Connecticut Avenue not too far from the National Zoo. Riggs National Bank held the mortgage on her condo, her credit rating was excellent, and according to her tax return, she made seventy-two thousand dollars last year.

The concept of privacy evaporated when people like Neil booted up their computers.

The woman who came to the door was quite attractive in DeMarco's opinion. Blond hair; large, warm brown eyes; and a slight overbite that DeMarco thought was sexy as hell. She was small, no more than five foot four, but had a lush figure: relatively large breasts, a small waist, and a nicely rounded backside. She was wearing a white blouse and jeans, and she was barefoot—one of the advantages of working out of one's own home. A pair of reading glasses was stuck on top of her head and she was holding a piece of cloth in one hand, some sort of fabric sample, DeMarco guessed.

"Ms. Davenport, my name's Joe DeMarco. I work for Congress and I was wondering if I could speak to you."

"I'm sorry," she said, "but I'm really busy right now. So if you're conducting a poll or something . . ."

"I'm not a pollster. I need to talk to you about Senator Morelli."

At the mention of Morelli's name, Davenport inhaled sharply, her lips closed in a tight line, and the sexy overbite disappeared. DeMarco couldn't immediately categorize the look on the woman's face. Fear? Anxiety? Maybe anger. Whatever emotions she was feeling, fond memories of Paul Morelli were not included.

"What's this about?" Davenport said. She was crushing the fabric sample, but might not have realized it.

"May I come inside?" DeMarco asked.

"No. And I want to know why you're here."

That was a hard question for DeMarco to answer. He didn't want to tell her that he was there because her name had been found on a napkin in a dead man's wallet.

"I just want to know about your experience working for Senator Morelli," DeMarco said.

"Why?"

"I can't tell you that. It's a government matter relating to an investigation in progress."

For a minute, DeMarco thought that Davenport was going to refuse to say anything but then she said, "I never worked for the senator. I worked for his wife, and I only consulted with her twice." She hesitated a second, then added, "Things just didn't work out."

"What does that mean?"

"It means she didn't like my design ideas. Now I have to go," Davenport said and closed the door.

———◆———

DeMarco arrived at the Starbucks on Pennsylvania Avenue at exactly 2 p.m. and was relieved when the Speaker's limo arrived only five minutes later. It wasn't unusual for Mahoney to keep him waiting forty minutes—or to forget their meetings altogether.

He had called Mahoney right after meeting with Marcia Davenport and convinced his boss to meet with him before he left town. Mahoney was on his way to San Francisco to give a lecture at some convention, meaning that he'd adlib a twenty-minute speech, pocket ten thousand dollars, then spend the rest of his time in California touring Napa Valley wineries. And it didn't appear that he would be touring alone. When the Speaker's driver opened the rear door of the limo, DeMarco caught a brief glimpse of a shapely leg encased in black hose.

DeMarco had decided it was time to get Mahoney's advice. The connection between Terry Finley and Paul Morelli made him nervous. Morelli was not only a man in the political stratosphere, he was also a member of Mahoney's party. DeMarco, therefore, thought it prudent to let Mahoney know what he had learned before proceeding any further.

Mahoney ambled from the limo to the outside table where DeMarco waited. DeMarco was sitting outside because he knew that Mahoney would want to smoke, and would whine if he couldn't. He sat down heavily and reached across the table to take one of the two paper cups of coffee that DeMarco had purchased. He took a sip of the coffee, winced at the taste, and then dipped into his pocket for his flask, the small silver one embossed with the Marine Corps seal. The seal on the flask matched a tattoo on his right forearm, and when he spoke to veterans' groups his sleeves were always rolled up. He smacked his lips in satisfaction at his laced coffee and looked a question at DeMarco.

"Dick Finley thinks his son may have been killed," DeMarco said. If you didn't start out with a headline, you lost Mahoney's attention rapidly. DeMarco then told Mahoney about the napkin that had been found in Terry Finley's wallet and all the other suspicions Dick Finley had about his son's death.

When he told Mahoney what Neil had learned about the three men on Finley's list, Mahoney looked at his watch, then over at the limo, and then he said something that surprised DeMarco. "Shit, everybody knows about that stuff. Before Morelli was elected to the Senate, there was an article in the *Times,* or maybe it was in one of them tight-assed New York magazines. Anyway, the article said how Morelli was so fuckin' lucky that he oughta be buyin' lotto tickets instead of workin'."

"Maybe it wasn't luck," DeMarco said.

Mahoney snorted; not an attractive sound. "A guy gets in a wreck; another guy gets caught dippin' his wick into a secretary; and a third guy is nabbed for porkin' teenage boys. There's an old saying, son: Never attribute to malice something that can be explained by stupidity."

"Good point," DeMarco said, but he was also rather annoyed that Neil hadn't told him that everything he'd learned had been written up in a magazine.

"So you think I should drop this?" DeMarco said. "I can take it further, talk to some of these men, go up to New York and see this lady, but . . ."

"No, I'll tell you what I want you to do. I want you to go see Paul Morelli."

"You're kidding," DeMarco said.

"No. I may owe Dick Finley—he was a big help to me when I first came to this town—but I owe it to the *country* to let Paul know what's going on." Mahoney finished his coffee and said, "Morelli's the best thing to happen to the party since FDR— or me—and he's gonna be the next president of the United States. He's a good guy—maybe a great guy—so he needs to know that some reporter was trying to dig up dirt on him. And if Terry Finley really was killed, which I doubt, he needs to know that too. So I want you to go talk to him and tell him what you've learned. I'll call him and get you in. Now I got a plane to catch."

Chapter 6

DeMarco's illusions had been mangled so often by politicians that he thought he should qualify for handicapped parking—but he had to admit that he was pretty impressed with Paul Morelli.

Morelli hailed from a blue-collar family, the youngest of five children. He attended college on a poor-boy scholarship and according to legend, obtained his law degree studying twelve hours a day and doing charitable work in the time remaining. He apparently never slept. Ambitious, brilliant, and charismatic, he took to politics as baby eagles take to the air and became one of the youngest occupants of Gracie Mansion. And as mayor of New York, he was a grand success: crime dipped; no ugly scandals marred his term; labor unions refrained from untimely, crippling strikes. Then off to the Senate he flew, and the Senate, all the commentators concurred, was but a pit stop on his race to the Oval Office.

Certainly the way he looked wasn't a hindrance. He was a youthful forty-seven, his hair was a curly black crown streaked with just the right amount of gray, and he had a profile that plastic surgeons could use for a template. He was also tall and perfectly proportioned, and if he tired of politics he could model swimwear. But even his critics had to admit that he was more than a pretty face. He was a dazzling strategist, the consummate negotiator, and one of the most eloquent speakers to ever choke a microphone. And the things he spoke of, the causes he championed, the battles he fought were always so . . . *right*. The last Democrat with such magnetism had been a man named Kennedy.

When DeMarco rang his doorbell that evening, Morelli answered the door himself. He was dressed casually: an NYU sweatshirt, soft-looking beige slacks, and loafers. The sleeves of the sweatshirt were pulled up on his forearms, exposing strong wrists matted with coarse, dark hair. DeMarco felt stiff and overdressed in his suit and tie.

Morelli led DeMarco to a comfortable den, commenting on the warm autumn weather as they walked. Already in the den was a man that Morelli introduced as his chief of staff, Abe Burrows. Burrows sat in one of the two chairs in front of Morelli's desk and had a stack of paper in his lap that was six inches high. He nodded at DeMarco but didn't rise to shake his hand.

Unlike Paul Morelli, Burrows wasn't physically impressive. He was short and overweight, his gut spilling softly over his belt. He had fleshy lips, a lumpy potato of a nose, and thin sandy hair that was styled in a curly Afro in a vain attempt to disguise the fact that he was going bald.

"Abe and I were just going over a few things," Morelli said with a tired smile. "There just isn't enough time during the day and I'm going out of town tomorrow."

Morelli pointed DeMarco to the chair next to Burrows then took a seat in the high-backed chair behind his desk. Even dressed in a sweatshirt, Morelli looked like a man who belonged behind a big desk, giving orders, and DeMarco couldn't help but feel inadequate. Here was a guy just a few years older than him, yet while Joe DeMarco was a GS-13 in a dead-end job, Paul Morelli was going to be running for president.

"Would you like a cup of coffee, Joe?" Morelli said, and when DeMarco said yes, Morelli glanced over at Burrows. Burrows frowned at being drafted as DeMarco's waiter, but put the stack of papers aside and left to get the coffee.

"John Mahoney asked me to see you tonight, Joe, but he wasn't too clear on why. Do you work for John?"

"No, sir, not directly," DeMarco lied. "I'm just a lawyer who does odd jobs for Congress." To deflect Morelli from asking more questions about who employed him and what he did, DeMarco said, "By the way, sir, my godfather's done some work for you."

"Your godfather?"

"Yes, sir. Harry Foster."

"Well, I'll be darned," Morelli said. "Harry's a good man; I've known him for years." Then Morelli asked DeMarco a question that he thought was odd: "Are you and Harry close, Joe?"

"Uh, no, sir, not anymore. We were when I was a kid, but since I live here now and Harry lives in New York . . ."

"I understand," Morelli said. At that moment Burrows returned with coffee for DeMarco and the senator. Morelli thanked Burrows, took a sip from his cup, then said, "So, Joe, what can I do for you?"

"Mr. Mahoney got a call from an old friend, an ex-congressman named Dick Finley who retired about ten years ago. Finley's son just died and the police ruled the death as accidental, but Finley thinks his son may have been killed because of something he was working on."

"What did his son do?" Morelli asked.

"He was a reporter. He worked for the *Washington Post*."

"Oh, that guy," Burrows said.

"You knew him, Abe?" Morelli said.

"Yeah, I knew him," Burrows said, then made a face that led DeMarco to conclude that Burrows wasn't a Terry Finley fan.

"What makes Mr. Finley think his son was killed?" Morelli said.

DeMarco told him.

"Hmm. Sounds rather speculative. But then, I imagine Mr. Finley is quite distraught by his son's death. I assume he's also a rather elderly gentleman."

"Yes, sir," DeMarco said, but he was thinking that Morelli was very good. Without having said anything negative, he'd just implied that Dick Finley was not only out of his mind with grief but possibly senile.

"At any rate," Morelli said, "what does this have to do with me, Joe?" Before DeMarco could answer the question, the door to the den swung open and the senator's wife entered the room.

DeMarco had seen newspaper photos of Lydia Morelli posing at the senator's side at various Washington galas, but the photos hadn't captured her frailty. She was petite, no more than five-two, and painfully thin. DeMarco had read that she was five or six years older than her husband, but in the same room with him, their age difference appeared closer to a decade. Nonetheless, she was still an attractive woman with large, blue-gray eyes and blond hair cut in a style that framed good cheekbones. Unlike the senator, she wasn't dressed casually. She was wearing a beige-colored pantsuit, a pink blouse with a wide collar, and high-heeled shoes.

Lydia's eyes widened momentarily in surprise when she saw DeMarco sitting in the den but she recovered quickly, smiled at him, and said to her husband, "I'm sorry, Paul. I didn't know you had company."

"Hi," Morelli said to his wife. "Where've you been?"

Morelli had asked the question casually but DeMarco noticed a slight edge to his tone, as if he was annoyed that his wife had gone out or that she hadn't told him where she was going.

"Oh, I had dinner with an old sorority sister," Lydia said. She then raised her right fist into the air in a halfhearted manner, muttered "Go Alpha Pi," and walked over to an armoire on the far side of the room. When she opened the armoire, DeMarco could see that it was actually a liquor cabinet filled with bottles of booze, glasses, and decanters. "I'll be out of your way in just a shake," Lydia said, her back to the men as she looked into the cabinet. "I just want to make myself a drink to take into the tub."

DeMarco could see that the senator was somewhat embarrassed by his wife's behavior. When she had said "sister," she'd slurred the word slightly, and he noticed that as she walked toward the liquor cabinet she'd moved carefully, as if she was making an effort to maintain her balance. She'd obviously had several drinks with her sorority pal and was a bit tipsy.

Bottles in the cabinet clanked together loudly as Lydia searched for the one she wanted. A bottle of scotch clutched firmly by the neck, she turned and smiled at DeMarco again. "Aren't you going to introduce me to this handsome gentleman, Paul?" she said.

"Oh, of course," Morelli said. "Joe, this is my wife Lydia. Lydia, this is Joe DeMarco. Joe's an investigator for the House."

"Really," Lydia said. "Like a private eye?"

Burrows laughed, probably thinking that Lydia was making a joke, and she immediately shot him a look that wiped the smile off his face. DeMarco had noticed that she'd ignored Burrows when she entered the room, and judging by her reaction to his comment, it was apparent she didn't like the man.

Feeling the need to respond, DeMarco said, "No, ma'am. I'm just a lawyer. I'm . . ." Then he stopped. He didn't think he should be discussing the reason for his visit with the senator's wife, and Paul Morelli, immediately sensing DeMarco's discomfort, said, "Joe's just looking into a matter concerning a reporter, Lydia. Nothing significant."

Lydia arched an eyebrow and said, "Well, it would have been much more interesting if he'd been a hardboiled private eye. He looks like one."

"Lydia," Morelli said, his impatience evident, "we need to . . ."

"Oh, all right. I'm out of here. I'll let you boys get back to whatever you're doing." As she passed through the doorway, her right hip bumped the door frame slightly, and she muttered, "Oops."

Morelli stared at the open door for a moment, then looked at DeMarco and said, "I assume you know what happened to our daughter, our Kate. It's had horrible impact on us, particularly on Lydia. We're both still recovering."

Again, DeMarco couldn't help but be impressed with Morelli's diplomacy. Without saying anything derogatory, he'd just explained why his wife might have had a couple of drinks too many and had acted a bit silly in front of a complete stranger.

"Yes, sir," DeMarco said, "and I'm sorry for your loss."

DeMarco knew that Kate Morelli had actually been Paul Morelli's stepdaughter—Lydia's daughter from her first marriage—and that Paul had adopted her when she was less than two. She had been sixteen years old when she died in an automobile accident six months ago. DeMarco remembered a newspaper picture of the senator at his daughter's funeral, supporting his wife, tears streaming down his handsome face. The photo had been a portrait of the perfect family with the center gouged out.

Morelli shook his head, as if scattering memories he didn't want to recall, and said, "Where were we, Joe?" Then answering his own question, he said,

"Oh, yes. You were about to tell me what Terry Finley's death has to do with me."

DeMarco started to tell him about the three men on Finley's list—Bachaud, Frey, and Reams—and when he did, Abe Burrows erupted.

"Not this bullshit again," Burrows said. "You know, DeMarco, this stuff with those three guys happened anywhere from five to fourteen years ago. Fourteen years! But people still keep talking about it. These men, they all did something dumb, but just because their mistakes helped Paul's career there's always some asshole implying that Paul caused their problems. And the Republican Party . . . Those bastards have spent thousands, maybe millions, investigating these three incidents, coincidences, whatever the hell they are—and they spent the money because they were hoping to find something to pin on the senator. Like maybe he paid that little faggot to climb into bed with Reams."

"Abe," Morelli said, apparently not happy with his aide's choice of words.

"Well, it's such horseshit!" Burrows said. "And I'll tell you something else. I hate to speak ill of the dead, but Terry Finley . . . He was like one of those snappy little dogs you see. You know, those mutts about six inches high that are always straining against the leash, trying to get at you like they're pit bulls. That was Finley. He was always searching for the next big scandal, the next Watergate, the next Lewinsky—and he never found it. He worked at the *Post* fifteen years, and like you just heard, people like the senator didn't even know he existed."

"I can't confirm Abe's impression of Terry Finley," Morelli said to DeMarco, "but I have to agree with him about one thing: these allegations that I engineered the tragedies that befell those men is a subject that's not only baseless but one that's been completely discredited."

DeMarco had the impression that this was the way the two men worked together: Burrows was the one who made the violent, emotional frontal attack while Morelli came across as being cool and reasonable. Or maybe he *was* cool and reasonable.

"There were two other names on the list, Senator," DeMarco said. "Two women. A Marcia Davenport and a Janet Tyler."

"Who?" Morelli said. "Do you recognize those names, Abe?"

"No," Burrows said.

"Davenport is an interior decorator. You or your wife apparently consulted with her regarding this house when you first moved to Washington."

"Is that right?" Morelli said. Then he snapped his fingers, "Wait a minute. A small, blond woman?"

"Yes, sir."

"Right. I remember her now. She came to the house a couple of times, but as I recall, she and Lydia weren't able to work together. But that's all

I remember. I don't think I even spoke to the woman."

That pretty much matched what Marcia Davenport had told DeMarco.

"And the other woman?" Morelli said. "What was her name again?"

"Janet Tyler. She worked on your staff when you were the mayor."

"Well, shit," Burrows said. "The entire New York city government was part of the senator's *staff* back then."

"So you don't remember her either, Abe?" Morelli said.

"No," Burrows said.

"Joe, I'll tell you what," Morelli said. "Why don't you stop by my office tomorrow and Abe'll see what we have in our files on the Tyler woman. I mean, I'm just as curious as you are as to why her name would be linked to mine."

"Aw, come on, Paul," Burrows said. "This guy Finley, he's got a bug up his ass about his kid's death, but it doesn't have anything to do with us."

"Richard Finley was a distinguished member of Congress, Abe," Morelli said, "and his son died tragically. If we can do something to help make sense of what happened, I want to help."

DeMarco had to admit: he was pretty impressed with Paul Morelli.

Chapter 7

It took half an hour to set up the phone call.

Paul Morelli couldn't call the old man directly. He first had to call another man, and that man would tell the old man that they had to talk. He gave the middleman the number of a phone booth at the Guards restaurant on M Street in Georgetown. He had picked the Guards because it was close to his home and not usually frequented by the hordes of college kids who invaded every other drinking establishment on M Street. His other reason for selecting that particular place was that it had a phone booth—an actual booth where you could shut the door—and the booth wasn't too close to either the dining room or the bar.

He arrived at the restaurant wearing glasses with heavy black frames and clear lenses, a baseball hat, and a light jacket. The jacket wasn't necessary for warmth;

he wore it because he could turn up the collar to further obscure his face. He knew, however, that if anyone studied him closely he'd be recognized. He entered the restaurant and immediately proceeded to the phone booth. The bartender was engaged in a conversation with a good-looking brunette and barely noticed his arrival.

Two minutes later the phone rang.

"Your people may have screwed up with that reporter," Morelli said. "The reporter's father found a number of suspicious things about his son's death, and now there's a guy from Congress looking into it."

"What sort of things?" the old man said. His voice, as usual, was calm and completely devoid of emotion. Morelli had always admired this about him: he never allowed emotions to cloud his judgment. Emotions were counterproductive. Or maybe, he thought, the old man didn't have any emotions.

Morelli quickly told him about Dick Finley's concerns.

"None of that's significant," the old man said.

"True," Morelli said. "But your guys missed something. They didn't check Finley's wallet, and inside it were five names written on a cocktail napkin." Morelli quickly discussed the three men on Finley's list. The old man was familiar with the names so the discussion didn't take long.

"That's old news," the old man said. "You said five names. Who were the other two?"

"A couple of women, a Marcia Davenport and a Janet Tyler."

Morelli hadn't wanted to tell him about the women but finally decided that he had to. Dick Finley knew their names and now so did DeMarco and whoever DeMarco had talked to. Maybe even the police. The old man's ability to acquire information was incredible—his tentacles spread in all directions—and it was always possible that he might learn about Finley's list from some other source. But Morelli knew that he was on very dangerous ground here.

"Who are they?" the old man asked.

"Davenport's a decorator who did some work on my house here in D.C. Tyler was on my staff in New York."

"What do these women know?" the old man said.

"They don't know anything," Morelli said.

This was the only time Paul Morelli could recall ever having lied to the old man.

"I went through Finley's laptop and his note-books," Morelli said. "According to what was there, Finley had contacted these women because I'd fired both of them. I guess he was hoping that they'd have something negative to say, something that he could use, but they didn't, of course. Finley was grasping at straws."

"You sure?" the old man said.

"Yes. The problem isn't the list or the people on it," Morelli said. "The problem is that this investigator may be plowing the same ground that Finley plowed."

"And you still don't have any idea how Finley got the doctor's name or connected him to . . ."

"No. I don't know how he made the connection."

"So what do you wanna do? Do you want this investigator taken care of?"

For the old man it was that easy: You want somebody gone? No sweat.

"Absolutely not," Morelli said. "If something happened to him, that might get people really digging, people like the FBI. I just want him watched for a while. I think he'll give up in a couple of days, conclude there was nothing strange about Finley's death, but until he does I'd like him watched. What I don't want him doing is talking to the doctor."

"You know," the old man said, "the doc, he's been useful lots of times. But since we can't figure out how the reporter got on to him, well, I think maybe it's time . . ."

"Yeah, I think you're right," Morelli said. "But this investigator, let's just watch him. Oh, and one other thing: have someone come by and get Finley's laptop. I want it found someplace. Finley's father is suspicious because it's missing."

"You sure the computer's safe?"

"Yes. The important stuff was in a notebook, the one he had on him the night he died."

"Okay," the old man. "So what's this investigator's name?"

. "DeMarco," Paul Morelli said. "Joe DeMarco." Morelli thought about mentioning that DeMarco was Harry Foster's godson, but decided not to. He wanted to keep it simple for the old man.

The old man was silent a moment then he said, "We're so close, Paul. I never thought we'd get this far."

Morelli almost said: *I did*. But he didn't. Instead he said, "I didn't either, but we have, and we're going to make it. Thanks to you."

Chapter 8

DeMarco retrieved his mail from the box and the first thing he saw was a letter from Elle Myers. He hadn't seen her in almost six months, and the last time he'd spoken to her had been three months ago. He opened the envelope, read the short letter, and then just sat there for a long time thinking. It was ten minutes before he trudged slowly up to the second floor of his house.

DeMarco lived on P Street in Georgetown, in a small two-story townhouse made of white-painted brick. When DeMarco's wife divorced him she had left him his heavily mortgaged home but she took almost everything else he owned, including all the furniture. For nearly two years after her departure his will to refurnish the place had been sapped by her infidelity: she'd had an affair with his cousin. He eventually replaced much of the furniture she'd taken, and the first floor of his home once again looked as if a normal person dwelled there. But the second floor of the house, which consisted of two small bedrooms and a half bath, was still barren except for two objects: a secondhand upright piano and a fifty-pound punching bag that hung from an exposed ceiling rafter.

DeMarco had bought the piano on a whim at an estate sale. He had played when he was young and still remembered how to read music. He knew he'd never be able to play anything requiring real talent, but he figured if the music was slow enough, the grace notes rare enough, he might be able to entertain an audience of one. He also figured that he needed another hobby—something besides pounding the heavy bag. He and two friends had nearly broken their backs getting the instrument up the narrow stairway to the second floor of his house, and he decided, that day, that if he ever tired of playing it he would turn it into kindling before ever attempting to get it back down the stairs.

He played for an hour, pecking away at "Black Coffee," a blues song that Ella Fitzgerald used to sing. He mangled the song, his left hand even more ham-fisted than normal. As he played he thought of Ella singing—and of a time he'd danced with Elle.

He'd met her on a vacation to Key West. She was a school teacher who lived in Iowa and he liked everything about her—her looks, her sense of humor, the fact that she cared about teaching kids—but it had been impossible to sustain the relationship, her living a thousand miles away. He could have relocated—or she could have—but neither was willing to make that sort of commitment, to give up good jobs and begin life over in an unfamiliar place. They inevitably drifted apart. The letter he'd received said that she had gotten engaged, to a nice guy, a local fireman—but the whole tone of the letter was *oh, what might have been.*

So he played his piano and thought of Elle and felt sorry for himself. He imagined himself old and alone, feeding pigeons on a park bench on a bleak winter day. He could hear his mother bemoaning the fact that she had no grandchildren and never would. And he realized, being an only child, that the DeMarco line would end with him. Fortunately, before he could consider hunting down a knife to slash his wrists, the phone rang. It was Neil.

"That phone number," Neil said. "I have something for you, but I don't know what it means."

That was a very unusual admission coming from Neil.

Since Neil wouldn't tell DeMarco what he had found unless DeMarco had a phone equipped with an NSA-approved scrambler, DeMarco had to go to Neil's home to get the information. Thankfully, Neil lived less than two miles away.

Neil's wife was home with him, and unlike Neil,

she was a sweet, normal person. After exchanging their vows, she'd set about, as women usually do, changing her husband in various and subtle ways—and Neil didn't even know that he was being changed. At his office, Neil was pompous and condescending and liked to show off, but in his home, his wife in the kitchen and able to hear him, he tended to curb his more annoying habits.

"As I told you," he said to DeMarco, "I came up with every possible number combination associated with that partial phone number. I eliminated all the unassigned numbers, then identified who the remaining numbers belonged to. What I did was, I cross-referenced . . . Aw, never mind, I won't bore you with the details, but let me tell you it was a lot of work. Anyway, I found four people who were interesting. One was *extremely* interesting.

"The first is a woman named Tammy Johnson. She works at the Justice Department. I can imagine a number of reasons why a reporter might be talking to somebody at Justice about Paul Morelli, but the problem is that Ms. Johnson works in personnel. She handles things like health insurance and pensions, so I doubt that she was a hot source for Terry Finley, but I'll leave that for you to confirm.

"The second number," Neil said, "belongs to a gentleman who lives in southeast D.C. and goes by the curious name of DeLeon White. Mr. White is an independent pharmaceutical retailer."

Fuckin' Neil; his wife still had a lot of work to do. "You mean he sells dope," DeMarco said.

"Crack cocaine, to be precise. So maybe DeLeon sells crack to Morelli."

"I kinda doubt that," DeMarco said.

"Yeah, me too," Neil said. "It's the last two names that were most intriguing. The third phone number is assigned to a Michelle Thomas, a lady who works for a very high-end escort service."

"A call girl?"

"Oui. Now Terry Finley was single and I assume he had some sort of sexual outlet, but I doubt if he used Ms. Thomas's services."

"Why's that?"

"Because she's *way* out of his price range. Michelle Thomas is Neiman Marcus. Terry Finley was Kmart. But Paul Morelli, on the other hand, he could afford her."

"Yeah, that is interesting," DeMarco said. "The problem is that Paul Morelli's so damn-good looking that women would pay him to sleep with them. I doubt he's using hookers."

"One never knows," Neil said. "Now we come to the fourth number." Neil waited a dramatic beat then said, "The fourth phone number is assigned to Lydia Morelli's cell phone."

"What!"

"Could just be a coincidence. Tomorrow I'll pull the phone records for these four people and see if any of them called Terry Finley. According to Finley's records, he never called them."

———————◆◆◆———————

DeMarco returned to his place and immediately went to the kitchen and removed a bottle of vodka from the freezer compartment of his refrigerator. The vodka was made in Russia and there was a pretty green label on the bottle. It had cost fifteen bucks.

DeMarco had been experimenting with vodkas of late. Emma had introduced him to Grey Goose and he liked it, but it cost about thirty bucks a bottle. And in a bar, you could pay twelve bucks for a Grey Goose martini; they should say "stick 'em up" when they served you. Then one night he'd been channel surfing, and he caught a show in progress that was essentially about the ignorance of vodka drinkers. On the show they gave five people—all pretentious bozos who claimed a preference for high-end brands—six different vodkas to taste in unlabeled shot glasses. The vodkas ranged in price from top-shelf to bargain-basement, and, as could have been predicted, the drinkers couldn't identify their favorite brand and three of the five concluded that the cheapest booze was the best booze.

So DeMarco was on a holy quest. He was trying to find a vodka that tasted as good as Grey Goose but cost half as much. This brand—the one he'd just pulled from his freezer—wasn't it. It tasted like it had been drained from the crankcase of a Russian tractor.

He took his cut-rate vodka into his den. He had an idea. Neil had said that tomorrow he'd work his magic and see if any of the four people that he had named had called Terry Finley, but DeMarco thought there might be a quicker way to get the information. He called Dick Finley.

"Have you found something, Joe?" Finley asked as soon as DeMarco identified himself.

The ex-congressman sounded weak, but it was late and the man was old, so maybe he was just tired. The death of a son can make a man tired.

"Mr. Finley, did Terry have a cell phone?"

"Sure."

"Do you know where it is?"

"It's in a box on my dining room table. The police found it in his car and they took it, but they eventually gave it back to me. Why?"

That was good, DeMarco thought. If the phone had been on Terry's body it would most likely have been destroyed after being submerged in water for several hours. But that made DeMarco wonder why the phone was in Terry's car instead of on him. Dick Finley provided the answer without having to be asked.

"The battery on the phone must have been low," Dick Finley said, "because the cops said it was hooked up to one of those cigarette lighter chargers."

"Could you get Terry's cell phone, Mr. Finley," DeMarco said. "I want to see if Terry received a call from a certain number. You see, most cell phones keep a record of recent calls received and—."

"I know that," Finley said. "I'm not that outta touch with the modern world."

"Yes, sir. So could you get Terry's phone and check the call log."

"Yeah, hold on a minute."

It was more like five minutes before Finley came back on the line.

"Okay, I got the phone," he said.

"Good. Now get into the calls-received menu, see if there's any number that starts with two-oh-two, five-three-two, three."

"Is that the number that was on the napkin?" Finley asked.

"Yes, sir."

"All right, let me see if it's here. Damn it, these buttons are so small I have a hard time working them."

DeMarco waited impatiently.

"Here we are," Finley said. "Yeah. There's a number here that starts with those numbers. It's two-oh-two, five-three-two, three-two-three-one. That number's listed twice."

The phone number that Dick Finley had just read belonged to Lydia Morelli. When Finley asked him the significance of the number, DeMarco lied and said he didn't know. The last thing DeMarco wanted was for Finley to know that there was a connection between Paul Morelli and his son's death.

DeMarco thanked Finley and hung up, more puzzled than ever. He could understand Terry Finley calling Lydia: Finley was brash and ambitious, and from everything he'd learned, he wouldn't have been at all surprised if Terry had had the balls to call the senator's wife and question her about her husband's past. But why on earth would she call him? He was the sort of reporter that politicians and their spouses avoided like the pox.

One thing DeMarco was sure of: *he* wasn't going to call Lydia and ask her why she had phoned Terry. He wanted to, but he wouldn't. Paul Morelli was not only a powerful man, he was also the Speaker's friend. So for DeMarco to just pick up the phone and call Lydia—right after her husband had just said that he had no knowledge of the significance of Finley's list—would be a very dumb thing to do. But he really wanted to know why she'd called Terry.

DeMarco sipped some more of his drink. It felt like the muscles in his jaw were beginning to lock up, as if he was being partially paralyzed by the cheap Russian hootch. This made him wonder if Russia had an organization like the FDA, some watchdog group that ensured their vodka-makers didn't put gasoline additives in their liquor. The smart thing to do would be to pour the rest of the vodka down the drain before he was paralyzed completely.

He thought some more, but couldn't immediately think of a good way to approach Lydia about her calling Terry. Tomorrow he'd go see Abe Burrows and see what his records said about Janet Tyler—the other woman on Finley's list—and maybe he'd even take the shuttle up to New York to talk to her. He hadn't seen his mom in awhile, so the trip to New York wouldn't be a total waste. But that's all he'd do for now.

Decision made, he said, "*Za vashe zdorovye*"—the only Russian he knew—and recklessly poured the remainder of the vodka down his throat. He was still coughing when his phone rang.

"Yes," he croaked into the phone. His voice sounded as if someone had stepped on his larynx with a ski boot.

"Mr. DeMarco, this is Lydia Morelli. I need to talk to you."

Chapter 9

"Can you believe this bastard?" Carl said. "Every fuckin' light, he hits on the yellow."

"Yeah," Jimmy said. "You're gonna lose him. Get up on his ass. It's the morning rush. He sees the same car behind him for an hour, he won't think nothin' of it."

"Where's he goin' anyway?" Carl said. "I thought he worked at the Capitol."

Jimmy just shook his head. He loved Carl like a brother—you could put his crank in a meat grinder and he wouldn't talk—but he was always asking questions. Stupid questions. Questions Jimmy couldn't answer. Questions to which there were no answers. He was going to pull out the guy's tongue one of these days if he didn't quit it.

"And why are we following him?" Carl said.

That was *it*. "Because Eddie said to!" Jimmy

screamed. "For Christ's sake, you heard the same fuckin' thing I did. Eddie said follow this asshole and if he talks to anybody, find out who and call him. That's all I know."

"Yeah, but he shoulda told us why. It's like we're mushrooms: they keep us in the dark and—"

"Yeah, yeah, I've heard it before," Jimmy said. "And open your window. That goddamn smoke is killin' me."

They were approaching another intersection and again the light turned yellow just as this DeMarco guy reached the intersection.

"Goddamnit!" Carl said, and stomped on the gas pedal. The light turned red before their car was halfway through the intersection.

"We should have gotten a transmitter to put on his car," Jimmy said.

"Aw, we're okay," Carl said. Before Jimmy could respond, to tell Carl they *weren't* okay, Carl said, "Can you believe these houses, these friggin' embassies?"

They were on Massachusetts Avenue, in the section known as Embassy Row.

"I wonder if these countries pay for these places," Carl said, "or if *we* pay for them. I mean it would really piss me off if my taxes were paying for these fuckin' mansions."

Jimmy just shook his head. "Get up on his ass," he said again. "You're falling too far back."

And sure enough, at the next intersection, the damn guy hit another yellow light.

"Son of a bitch," Carl said, again accelerating to make the light, but the light was already red when he started through the intersection. The car that broadsided them was a cab. It hit the front right fender of the rented Taurus they were driving, spinning the Ford almost in a complete circle. Jimmy's airbag, the passenger-side airbag, exploded. Carl's didn't.

Carl and Jimmy stepped out of their car slowly, shaken, Jimmy gently touching his nose to see if it was broken. The airbag had slammed right into his face. The driver of the cab pried open his door with some difficulty, then came running toward them, his froggy eyes huge and insane behind the thick lenses of his glasses. He was a dark-complexioned man, and Jimmy guessed he was from Afghanistan, Pakistan— one of them Muslim places. The cabbie stopped a foot from Carl, pointed at the stoplight, pointed at the crumpled hood of his cab, and began screaming obscenities in a foreign tongue.

Carl hit the cabbie right between the eyes, breaking the guy's glasses.

"You terrorist motherfucker," Carl said.

Chapter 10

DeMarco looked in his rearview mirror and winced. The asshole that had been tailgating him for the last six blocks had just run a red light and had been broadsided by a cab. Served the dumb shit right. Five minutes later, DeMarco turned off Massachusetts and onto Pilgrim Road, driving into the shadow created by the National Cathedral's towering walls.

When he'd spoken to Lydia Morelli the previous night she'd said, "Let's meet at the cathedral, Mr. DeMarco. It's seems an apt place for a confession." He hadn't known what she'd meant by that statement, but when he'd asked which cathedral, she said, "Why, the National Cathedral, of course. Do you know another here?" DeMarco did—but it hadn't seemed like the right time to dazzle her with his knowledge of all the churches he didn't attend.

The National Cathedral was the sixth or seventh largest church in the world, and like the great medieval cathedrals of Europe, it had taken almost a hundred years to complete, its construction interrupted not by siege, plague, or famine, but by more mundane reasons like lack of funds and squabbling labor. But after a century of toil it stood magnificent, a home God must have been proud to show his friends.

Lydia had told him to meet her in the Bishop's Garden on the south side of the cathedral. DeMarco parked his car and hurried to the garden. He was ten minutes late but Lydia wasn't there. He cursed himself for his tardiness and wondered if she'd left already, but a more likely explanation was that she'd changed her mind and decided not to meet him at all. He took a seat on a stone bench, checked around one more time for Lydia, then looked upward.

The National Cathedral has three huge stained glass windows, called rose windows, each sixty feet in diameter and made from thousands of pieces of glass. From outside the church, they appear as large dull circles in the white stone walls—shards of dark glass set into ornate stone frames, no pattern evident, no hint of radiance or beauty given. Inside the cathedral, it was completely different. From the inside, the windows were marvels of form and color, as intricate as oil paintings. DeMarco didn't know why you couldn't see the pattern in the windows from outside the church. He suspected it had to do with the physics of light but maybe divinity played a hand in this phenomenon as well: you had to enter God's house to enjoy its wonders.

Fifteen minutes later he saw Lydia Morelli walking toward him. She was wearing a simple blue blouse, gray slacks, and low-heeled shoes. From a distance, she looked slim and elegant. Up close she looked weary and malnourished, and DeMarco wondered if she might be ill.

She took a seat next to him on the bench, breathing as if the short walk from the parking lot to the garden had winded her, and when she exhaled he could smell liquor on her breath. It was only nine-thirty a.m. It seemed that Lydia was indeed ill; her illness was alcoholism. DeMarco could understand a bit better now why her husband had seemed annoyed about her drinking.

Lydia closed her eyes until her breathing returned to normal then opened them and looked around, apparently checking to make sure no one was nearby. Impatient, DeMarco said, "Why did you want to see me, Mrs. Morelli?"

Lydia stopped scanning the area and looked directly into his eyes and said, "Because your life's in danger."

Whoa! If you want to get someone's attention, that's a good way to start a conversation.

"What are you talking about?" DeMarco said.

"I heard what you told Paul and the toady."

"The toady?"

"Sorry. My pet name for Abe. At any rate, I heard what you told them. I eavesdropped. After I left Paul's office, I stood near the door and listened." When she said this she smiled somewhat smugly, as if she was proud to have put one over on her famous husband.

"Terry Finley didn't die in a boating accident," Lydia said. "He was killed because he was investigating Paul."

"Mrs. Morelli, you need to tell me what you're talking about."

"What do you think of my husband?" she said.

"What do I think?" DeMarco said, confused by the question. "I guess I think he's a brilliant politician. Everyone says he's going to be the next president."

Lydia nodded as if agreeing with DeMarco, then said, "He's a monster. He belongs in a cage, not the White House."

DeMarco was almost too stunned to react. "Mrs. Morelli," he said, "I'm not sure where—"

"I'm the one who contacted Terry," Lydia said. "I'm the one who asked him to dig into Paul's past."

Jesus Christ.

"I heard Paul and the toady talking about him one day," Lydia said. "They were laughing, saying how he was this stubborn little journalist who never got it quite right."

Now *that* bothered DeMarco. Paul Morelli had said that he didn't know Terry Finley.

"But I asked around," Lydia said, "and I figured that Terry was exactly who I needed. I needed someone willing to do anything to make a name for himself, yet it had to be someone connected with a credible paper like the *Post* or the *Times*. I decided it was time for me to finally do something, and Terry was perfect."

DeMarco thought she may have selected Terry Finley for another reason: if she'd gone to one of the big-name reporters, they might have had more sense than to listen to her. But he still didn't know what the hell she was talking about.

"I'm not following this, Mrs. Morelli," DeMarco said. "What exactly did you want Terry to do?"

"I wanted him to destroy my husband."

DeMarco rocked backward. "Why would you—"

"I told Terry that someone had been helping Paul his whole career. A very powerful man."

"What man?" DeMarco said. Every time she opened her mouth he became more confused.

Lydia ignored the question. "What happened to those three men, those men on that list you found, was that they were set up. The man who was caught in bed with the teenage boy was drugged, just like he said. And the man who had the car accident . . . well, it wasn't an accident. Someone ran him off the road or tampered with his car."

"How do you know this?" DeMarco said.

"Because I just do. I don't have any evidence, something you could present in court, but I *know*. I know because I've heard Paul and Abe plan the downfall of other men who have gotten in Paul's way. People have been bribed and blackmailed and murdered to——"

"Murdered?" DeMarco said. He wondered if this woman might actually be mentally ill, some sort of schizophrenic with conspiracy delusions.

"Yes. Paul's never killed anyone himself, of course. Other people do the dirty work but he's the one who benefits."

Lydia started to say something else but DeMarco interrupted her. "Who do you think he had murdered, Mrs. Morelli?"

"Besides Terry, a man named Benjamin Dahl. Paul—this was when he was mayor—was trying to build a community center in the Bronx and Dahl had a piece of land that he needed for the project but Dahl refused to sell. I heard Paul on the phone one night talking about Dahl. I heard him say: 'This has gone on long enough. We need to do something.' Two days later Dahl had an accident in his house. He fell down a flight of stairs and broke his neck."

"That's it?" DeMarco said. "You think your husband had this man murdered because he said 'we need to do something'?"

"Yes."

"Well, maybe he was telling somebody to find a different piece of land, or to make Dahl a better offer or, or, to take legal action against him," DeMarco said.

"He wasn't," Lydia Morelli said.

DeMarco started to swear, then stopped himself. Swearing wouldn't help. "So," he said, as calmly as he could, "you wanted Terry Finley to find proof that your husband had committed crimes to advance his career."

"Yes."

"And you were feeding him information to help him."

"Not information. I didn't really have any. All I was really doing was *encouraging* him, pressing him not to give up, to dig deeper. And he found something. I don't know what, but the last time I talked to him he was excited. He . . ."

According to Dick Finley and Reggie Harmon, Terry was always excited.

". . . he said he'd found someone in New Jersey who could break things wide open. But he didn't tell me who the person was or what he knew. Terry was . . . I don't know, overly dramatic. Unnecessarily secretive. And two days later he was killed."

When Lydia made the last statement, she'd leaned in toward DeMarco, putting her face closer to his, and once again he could smell the booze on her breath.

DeMarco was thinking that he should just leave. He was talking to an alcoholic who obviously hated her husband—a description that probably fit more than a few women whose spouses worked on Capitol Hill—and it was a combination that made him doubtful of everything she was saying.

"What about the two women on Terry's list, Marcia Davenport and Janet Tyler?" DeMarco asked.

"Paul raped them." Lydia's voice was completely flat when she said this, just a simple, unemotional statement of fact: *Paul raped them*.

Oh, this just keeps getting better and better, DeMarco thought. "And how do you know this?" he said, making no attempt to hide his skepticism.

As Lydia told the story, the thin fingers of her left hand tugged unconsciously at a tendril of hair above her ear. DeMarco found it ironic that while she spoke of her husband sexually assaulting women the sunlight was glittering off the diamonds in her wedding ring.

Lydia said that the night it happened Marcia Davenport had come to the Morellis' house in Georgetown. She was there to take photos of the interior and to spend some time looking around to get ideas for decorating the place. Lydia said that after Davenport arrived, she left to meet a friend for drinks. The senator was home at the time, in his den. When Lydia returned home two hours later, she found Davenport sitting on the floor in Paul Morelli's den, backed into a corner. She was crying, her clothes were disheveled, and Paul Morelli was on the phone with Abe Burrows.

"But how do you know he raped her?" DeMarco said.

"She told me he did," Lydia said.

"She *said* your husband raped her? She used the word 'rape'?"

"No. She said, 'Help. He attacked me.' What else could she have meant?"

"Attacked" didn't necessarily mean rape, but DeMarco didn't say that. Instead he said, "Then what happened?"

"When Paul saw me he screamed at me to go up to my room and stay there. When I didn't move right away, he picked up a thing on his desk, a paperweight or something, and threw it at me. It hit the wall near my head. I don't know if he was trying to hit me or just scare me, but he was acting insane. And he was drunk."

DeMarco found it impossible to imagine Paul Morelli drunk and throwing things at his wife. It also occurred to him that Lydia Morelli had probably been drunk herself since she'd just returned from having drinks with a friend.

"Then what happened?" DeMarco asked.

"A few minutes later, Abe showed up at the house and he and Paul spent the next two hours in Paul's den with the Davenport woman. Then she left and

I never saw her again. And Paul would never tell me what happened."

"And Davenport never reported the, uh, attack?"

"No. Paul must have talked her out of it. Or he paid her not to tell. Or he scared her. I don't know what he did, but he did something."

"And you didn't call the police?"

"No. He's my husband."

DeMarco didn't know how to respond to that.

"And this other woman," he said. "Janet Tyler. How do you know he did something to her?"

A look of annoyance passed over Lydia's face, as if answering DeMarco's questions was irritating her. "This was when we were still in New York. He came home one night, all agitated. Paul's *never* agitated, and I could tell he'd been drinking. He'd just walked through the door, he hadn't even taken off his coat, when Abe showed up. I heard Abe say, 'Tyler's not going to be a problem,' and when Paul asked why, Abe said 'because of her fiancé.' Then they realized I was there and they went outside."

"That's it?" DeMarco said. "That's why you think she was assaulted?"

"No, there was something else Paul or Abe said, but I can't remember the exact words. It was a long time ago."

No shit. According to the dates on the napkin, it had been nine years ago. "But Tyler never reported being raped either, did she?" DeMarco said.

"No, but I know that's what happened," Lydia said. "I mean, I didn't at the time but after what happened to Marcia Davenport later and . . . well, then I put it together."

Before DeMarco could say anything else, she said, "Go talk to those women. That's what Terry did. And find out what Terry was doing in New Jersey. You need to get evidence against Paul. You need to get him!" She almost shrieked the words "get him" and as she did, she reached out and dug her finger-nails into DeMarco's forearm.

Christ, she was *nuts*, DeMarco was thinking, and at that moment he heard a noise behind him and he turned. Thank God. It was a priest, not a reporter. The priest was walking down the garden path, reading from a prayer-book as he walked, moving his lips as he read. He glanced at Lydia and could see the anguish on her face, then he turned his gaze toward DeMarco, his expression not accus-ing, just asking if they needed his help. DeMarco shook his head no. Lydia didn't need a priest; she needed a psychiatrist.

"Mrs. Morelli . . . ," DeMarco said, and then he stopped. He didn't know what to say.

"I know," Lydia said. "You can't believe it. You can't believe that the great Paul Morelli could have done the things I've said. Well, I'm going to tell you something about my husband, something that only Abe and I know."

"And what's that?" DeMarco said, having no idea what this woman might say next.

"Most of the time Paul is the most unemotional, calculating bastard you'll ever meet. Like why do you think he married me, a woman five years his senior and with a child to boot?"

"I don't kn—"

"He married me because of my father, because he thought my father could advance his career."

All DeMarco could remember reading about Lydia's father was that he'd been a judge, but he didn't know anything else about the man.

"Paul analyzes everything," Lydia was saying. "He never loses his temper. He never allows his opponents to rush him into doing anything prematurely, before he's had a chance to think things through. And he is, as you said, brilliant. Except when he drinks. Paul can't handle liquor. At all. Even small amounts. And he knows it and he hardly ever drinks, and whenever he does, at a party or a fund raiser, that little bastard, Abe, watches him like a hawk. But sometimes, for whatever reason, Paul gets drunk. Maybe it's the stress of the job. Or maybe the demons inside his head are *screaming* at him. I don't know. I don't know what triggers it. But when he drinks, and he's almost always alone when he does . . . well, then the genie comes out of the bottle and all Paul's sick urges coming spewing out."

This conversation was surreal. Here was this morning drinker talking about her husband's drinking problem. Meeting with her had been a huge mistake.

"The night he attacked Marcia Davenport," Lydia said, "Paul was in his den drinking and Davenport made the mistake of going in there."

"He drinks then he assaults women," DeMarco said. He was being sarcastic but Lydia Morelli didn't notice.

"Yes," she said. "And it's always the same kind of woman."

"What do you mean?"

"Go see Janet Tyler," Lydia said. "Talk to her. Follow up on Terry Finley's investigation."

DeMarco was completely frustrated. "Mrs. Morelli, why are you telling me all this?" he said. "I'm not a cop or a reporter. I'm just a lawyer. So even if what you're saying is true"—he almost added *and that's one big goddamn if*—"you're talking to the wrong guy."

"I told you why I'm telling you. I'm telling you because your life's in danger and I'm trying to keep you from getting killed like Terry. But I'm also telling you because you're an investigator. I heard Paul say that when I met you."

"I am, but . . ." DeMarco shook his head. "Look, you have to understand something: I don't have the clout or the authority to investigate your husband."

And he didn't. To investigate someone like Paul Morelli, special prosecutors were assigned: smart, ruthless, independent bastards with dozens of people on their staffs. But Lydia Morelli didn't care.

"You have an *obligation*," she said. "You have a job to do and you need to do it."

She rose from the bench and said, "I have to go. I have . . . I have an appointment."

With a bottle was DeMarco's immediate thought.

"And you have to do your job," she said again, and then she turned to go.

"Wait a minute," DeMarco said. "I have to know something."

"What?" she said, now impatient to leave.

"According to the dates on that napkin, Davenport was, uh, attacked in 2002, Tyler in '99. Why are you doing this now?"

Lydia waved the question away, as if she were shooing flies. "It doesn't matter," she said. "All you need to know is that I'm telling the truth. Now I have to go. Oh, and one other thing—if you tell anyone we had this discussion, I'll deny it."

With that pronouncement she walked away. She moved slowly, like an old woman, her back bent, her steps unsteady and weary, as if the knowledge she carried inside her head was weighing her down.

What the hell had he gotten himself into?

Chapter 11

Garret Darcy watched the man and woman in the cathedral garden through binoculars. The guy was dressed in a suit and tie but he didn't look like someone who worked in an office. He was a hard-looking bastard. A cop maybe? Or maybe a hood. Yeah, he looked more like a hood than a cop. Now that would be interesting.

It would be good if something interesting happened. It was great to be working again but following Ladybird was dull work. For one thing, she was so easy to follow. Not only was she a civilian but from what he'd seen, she drank quite a bit, not an activity that improved one's observation skills. But even if she'd been teetotaler and trained to spot a tail, she never would have seen him. Darcy could tail a ghost; he'd spent an entire career following people.

He sorta wished, though, that he'd been assigned to Big Bird. He couldn't help but wonder if Phil and Toby had been given the primary target because of Kosovo. He had screwed up one time, one damn time, and that had been years ago—but he bet that was the reason that he'd been given the wife instead of the man himself.

But what the hell. He was getting paid and it was easy work. Phil and Toby, they had to hustle to keep up with Big Bird because he was always on the move. Those guys, poor bastards, weren't sleeping more than five hours a day and when they did sleep, half the time it was sitting in a car. By comparison, Ladybird was a piece of cake. She stayed in the house in Georgetown most of the time and, as near as he could tell, spent most of her day watching TV and sipping drinks. When she did go out, she'd meet a girlfriend and have lunch and more drinks, and at night, unless she was accompanying her husband to some function, she was usually in bed by ten, at which point Darcy would head on home.

Today, however, was different, meeting this guy who looked like a hood in an out-of-the-way spot. He had to find out who the guy was. Maybe Phil and Toby knew already, but the boss, that tricky little shit, he liked to keep things compartmentalized. He'd ask Phil later if they knew the man, but for now, as soon as the hardcase and Ladybird quit blabbing, he'd follow the guy to his car and get a license plate number.

If he'd had a parabolic mike he could have heard what they were talking about but he didn't have one. That was the odd thing about this op. The boss didn't seem to have access to the kind of equipment they'd used in the past. No mikes, no tracking devices, no night-vision goggles. They even had to bring their own cameras, which in his case was a little low-budget, piece-of-shit Kodak digital. And when Phil had asked if they should try to get a bug into Big Bird's house, the boss had said no, not yet. Well, maybe that wasn't so surprising considering who Big Bird was. But this op—it was just a little bit off. The boss was up to something.

Now that was a laugh: that cagey bastard, he was *always* up to something.

Hey, what the hell, it was an easy gig. When he'd enlisted in the marines, before he'd started working for the boss—a million years ago it seemed like now—he and some guys had been bitching about sitting around doing nothing, waiting all the time. An old gunnie heard them griping and said: "Boys, you get paid the same for marching as you do for fighting."

And he was getting paid. He thought when he retired that he and Sharon wouldn't have any problem at all living off his government pension, but money ran through Sharon's hands like water. They'd whittled their savings account down to nothing. So quit bitching, he told himself. You get paid the same for marching as you do for fighting, and a dull job was better than no job, and it was definitely better than being in the middle of a shit storm like Kosovo.

Chapter 12

DeMarco turned in to Emma's driveway and parked his car.

Emma lived in McLean, Virginia, in a beautiful redbrick home, one that seemed much more expensive than she should have been able to afford on a retired civil servant's salary. But would Emma ever reveal the source of her wealth? Of course not. The Sphinx was more likely to sing to a camel.

He heard music coming from the house. Emma's lover, Christine, played a cello in the National Symphony and she often practiced at home, but DeMarco could hear sounds—or in this case *noises*—being made by more than one musician. DeMarco was not a classical music fan to begin with—give him that ol' time rock and roll—but this music . . . Well, it wasn't your typical, monotonous Beethoven / Mozart elevator music. It sounded like cats screaming in agony.

He rang the doorbell. The awful composition continued. He rang again and Emma answered the door, looking wild-eyed, like maybe she was the one torturing the cats.

"Thank God you're here!" she said. Not usually the reaction she had when she saw him. Turning her head, she yelled over her shoulder, "Christine, I have to go. Joe's here and he has a . . . an emergency." She didn't wait for Christine's answer and immediately closed the door.

"Take me someplace that has liquor and is sound-proof," Emma said.

"What's going on?" DeMarco asked.

"Christine's quartet."

DeMarco had forgotten that Christine moon-lighted with a small quartet. He'd heard them play once, an experience he'd repeat only if heavily medicated.

"They're working on a piece by some avant-garde Swedish composer. Or maybe he's Danish. Who cares? They've been playing this one passage for over an hour and I was thinking of shooting them all before you arrived."

———◆◆◆———

They didn't find a soundproof bar but they found one that was quiet enough, not even a CD playing on the sound system. Emma ordered a blue martini, curaçao liqueur mixed with lime and gin, the color of the drink almost matching her eyes. DeMarco spent a long time selecting a brand of vodka, discussing his options with the bartender, before finally settling on one made in Ireland called Boru. Who would have guessed that the Irish made vodka? And it was good, certainly better than the antifreeze he had in his refrigerator at home, but not cheap. Emma pointed out that cheap and good rarely went together, an axiom DeMarco was determined to disprove.

"So what do you think?" DeMarco said after he finished telling Emma about his conversation with Lydia Morelli at the cathedral.

"The first thing I think is that you had better take the part where she said you're in danger seriously. There are some strange things about Terry Finley's death, and the fact that Senator Morelli claimed not to know Finley bothers me."

"It bothers me too, but you have to remember that the person who told me that Paul Morelli knew Terry had booze on her breath at nine-thirty in the morning."

"Still, take it seriously. Has anybody been following you?"

"How would I know?" DeMarco said. Then he remembered the yahoos who had been broadsided by the cab. "Well, maybe," he said and he told Emma about the wreck. "But if those guys were tailing me, they were pretty inept."

"Oh that's right," Emma said, "all thugs belong to Mensa."

Ignoring the sarcasm, DeMarco said, "What's really bugging me is that I can't tell if Lydia is telling the truth, and if she is, why now? Why didn't she tell somebody all this stuff years ago?"

"You know," Emma said, "political wives are different from other women. Take Jackie Kennedy or Hillary Clinton, or hell, even Eleanor Roosevelt. They were all publicly humiliated by their womanizing husbands, but they stuck by them anyway. One reason could be love. There's nothing unusual about a good woman loving a bad man, and these men were charming, charismatic people. So maybe a politician's wife stands by her cheating husband simply because she loves him. But then there are other factors. Maybe these women, after all the sacrifices they've made, don't want to give up their positions. They want to be the first lady. Or it could even be that their motives are actually noble. They know that it would be bad for the country if they were to initiate a messy, public divorce."

"Okay, so political wives are different," DeMarco said. "And maybe up until now, Lydia's stood by this wonderful guy that she says is a murderer and a rapist because she loves him or wants to be the first lady or whatever. But if that's the case, what's changed? Why'd she contact Terry Finley and why's she telling me about her husband now?"

"I don't know," Emma said, "but her daughter died just a few months ago. That could have been the catalyst. The woman is obviously in pain, she starts drinking heavily, so maybe she's . . ."

"Nuts?"

"No, not nuts. Traumatized. So even though she's remained loyal to her husband for years, when her daughter died things changed, her priorities changed."

"In other words, she got religion," DeMarco said.

"Maybe not literally, but yes. At any rate, you need to pursue this. You need to find out if she's telling the truth."

"Emma, Mahoney thinks Paul Morelli's the second coming of JFK. If he knew I was running around trying to prove he was some kinda sexual predator, he'd . . ."

As usual, Emma wasn't listening. She said, "And who's this powerful person that's helping him?"

"I don't even know if there *is* a powerful person," DeMarco said. "And if there is, why not tell me who he is?"

"Maybe she's afraid of him," Emma said. "Telling you his name could put her in danger."

"But not telling puts *me* in danger," DeMarco said.

Emma sat there thinking, holding her martini glass by the stem, twirling it, making the blue liquid swirl in the glass. "That one guy, what's-his-name, Reams, the guy who claimed he was drugged? Neil said his blood was tested for drugs and came back negative. What if he really had been drugged? Who would have the influence to change the results of a police drug test?"

"Jesus, Emma, that's a hell of a leap."

"Maybe. At any rate, you need to go to New York and meet this woman, this Janet Tyler. And you need to find out what Terry was doing in New Jersey. Neil may be able to pin down a location using Finley's credit card or cell phone records."

"And what do you suggest I tell my boss?" DeMarco said.

"Don't tell him anything. Didn't you say he was in San Francisco with his latest mistress?"

"I was just kidding about that. I don't know if she's his mistress."

"She is," Emma said.

"And you would know this how?" It always bugged DeMarco that Emma never allowed a lack of data to prevent her from being absolutely certain of her opinion.

"Because John Mahoney's a scoundrel," Emma said. "I feel so sorry for *his* wife."

Chapter 13

Paul Morelli's office was located in the Russell Senate Office Building on the northeast side of the Capitol. The interior walls of the building are polished slabs of white and gray marble, and the doors to the senators' chambers are all brass and mahogany and an impressive eight and a half feet in height. The taxpayers house their senators in style, and Morelli's suite had a fireplace, rich antique furnishings, and a reception area filled with plaques and awards that the state of New York had bestowed upon its favorite son. A photograph of Morelli and the president was prominently displayed. The president appeared uncomfortable in the photo—he had the look of a man who knew he was posing with his replacement.

Morelli's receptionist was a woman in her fifties with a horsey face and watery eyes. When DeMarco asked to see Abe Burrows, she pointed wordlessly at an open door while blowing her nose loudly into a tissue.

Judging by his office, Burrows was a typical harried, overworked chief of staff. His small, messy room was overflowing with documents half-read or never-to-be read; his in-box was a Tower of Babel about to collapse; yellow call slips formed a large, untidy pyramid next to his phone.

DeMarco had known dozens of men like Burrows. They didn't have enough charisma to be elected as dog catchers but they were smart, hard- working, and fanatically dedicated. While their bosses were cutting ribbons and smooching babies, they stayed in the office until midnight, reading the fine print on the bills and making the deals that passed the laws. Politicians were often the hood ornament on the government's machine—people like Abe Burrows were the engine.

Burrows was on the phone when DeMarco entered his office, and DeMarco heard him say: "You tell your guy that Morelli won't give a shit about bridges in Mississippi until someone over there starts caring about Northeast interstates. Call me back when you got your head outta your ass."

He was short and overweight, had frizzy hair, and wore wrinkled clothes that fit him badly—yet DeMarco knew it would be a mistake to assume Burrows's appearance was an indicator of his character. Senators didn't select their chiefs of staff for charm and good looks; they picked them because they were harder than diamond-coated drill bits and usually just as sharp.

Slamming down the phone, Burrows looked at it and said, "Dipshit." Looking up at DeMarco, he raised his eyebrows in curiosity.

"Joe DeMarco, Abe," DeMarco said.

"Yeah, I know. What do you—"

"The other night, when you and the senator couldn't remember Janet Tyler, he told me to stop by here. He said you'd check your files."

"Oh, yeah. But I'm kinda busy right now. I'm . . . Aw, never mind. Hang on." Burrows hit a button on his desk and said into the speaker box, "Call George Burak. Tell him to pull the personnel file on a gal named Janet Tyler. She worked for the senator when he was mayor. Tell him to do it right away and call me back." Burrows disconnected the phone call without waiting for a response, then said to DeMarco, "Why are you wasting your time on this?"

DeMarco obviously couldn't tell Burrows what Lydia Morelli had told him. So he just shrugged and said, "Just being thorough. I told Dick Finley that I'd check out the names on that list, and Tyler's the last one."

"Good," Burrows said, then he ran his hands over his face, like he was trying to scrub away his fatigue. "You know, we're gonna start our run for the White

House sometime next year. And Paul will get the nomination, no doubt about it. But as soon as we declare, the Republicans are going to do everything they can to smear him. They already took a pretty good shot at him when he ran for the Senate, and they didn't find bupkus, but when he gets the nomination they'll pull out all the stops. They'll use anything to discredit him."

"I'm not trying to hurt the senator," DeMarco said.

"I didn't say you were. What I'm saying is that Terry Finley was bush-league. There was no way in hell a guy like him was going to find something wrong about Paul when the entire Republican Party and every conservative journalist in America can't do it."

Maybe they could if Paul Morelli's wife was helping them.

"I've been in politics all my life," Burrows said, "and Paul's the best I've ever seen. And I'm not saying that just because I work for him. He's the real thing, DeMarco. He's going to change this country."

Burrows's phone rang. He hit the speaker button and said, "Yeah."

"George is on line three, Abe," a disembodied voice said.

Burrows punched another button. "George?" he said.

"Yeah," George said. "What do you want to know about this Janet Tyler?"

"Who is she?" Burrows said. "Apparently she worked for Paul when he was mayor, but I don't remember her."

"You don't remember her because she was only with us two months. We hired her to help with some zoning study, but I guess she quit."

"You guess?"

"Well, we didn't fire her. The file only says secretary, Brooklyn zoning study, separated in '99. That's it. If we'd fired her ass, the file would have said so."

"And that's all you got?"

"Yeah. I even asked a couple of my guys about her, but they don't remember her either."

"Thanks, George," Burrows said and hung up. Looking at DeMarco, he said, "Okay, you happy now? You now know everything I know about Janet Tyler."

The phone call between Burrows and this Burak character hadn't sounded the least bit rehearsed. And the conversation that Lydia Morelli claimed to have heard between Burrows and Paul Morelli regarding Janet Tyler had happened eight years ago. It was possible that Burrows didn't remember the discussion—assuming Lydia was telling the truth, which was a big assumption. So who should DeMarco believe: the alcoholic or the politician? Now that was a tough choice.

"Yeah, I'm happy, Abe," DeMarco said. "Thanks for your time."

———◆———

Emma watched DeMarco exit the Russell Building, and smiled when his head swiveled to stare at the well-formed derriere of a young woman who was just entering the building. She had to find DeMarco a girlfriend, or even better, a wife. DeMarco was the kind of man who needed a wife.

Emma knew that he had fallen head over heels for a spunky FBI agent a couple of years ago, but then the woman had been transferred to L.A. And then he'd hooked up with some school teacher, and although Emma had never met the woman, she'd sounded nice. But the teacher lived in Iowa and she and DeMarco had drifted apart, and now she was marrying somebody else. Emma needed to find him someone local so he couldn't use distance as an excuse for not making a commitment.

The term "commitment shy" may have been a cliché, but in DeMarco's case it was valid. And the reason, Emma knew, was his ex-wife. His ex had been an adulterous airhead but for some reason he just couldn't get over her or get beyond what she had done. But DeMarco's love life—or rather his lack of one—would have to wait.

DeMarco had descended the steps of the Russell Building and was now standing on the corner of Constitution and Delaware. When a cab came into view, he waved it down and jumped in, and Emma, watching from half a block away, saw a dark blue Buick fall into place behind the cab.

DeMarco hadn't known it, but Emma had been parked near his house at five-thirty that morning. At seven, she noticed a car with two men in it pull up and park, and when DeMarco caught a taxi to the Russell Building, the car had tailed the cab—and Emma had tailed the car. Emma pulled out her cell phone. It was time to find out who was in the Buick.

The men following DeMarco were a block from the Russell Building when they were pulled over by the U.S. Capitol police. Emma knew that the female officer driving the patrol car would tell them that they had been seen "lurking" near the Senate Office Buildings and, times being what they were, the Capitol cops wanted to know what they were up to.

The officer made the men exit their car. They were big, beefy white guys in their late forties or early fifties and both had short dark hair, though one guy's hairline was receding. The one with the retreating hairline also wore glasses with heavy, black frames, the glasses being the main thing that distinguished him from his companion. For some reason, Emma could imagine these two at a hockey game, their faces painted, screaming in delight whenever a player was body-checked into the glass.

The policewoman patted them down one-handed, her other hand on her sidearm while she did, then looked inside the car but didn't search it. While she was inspecting the interior of their vehicle, the men slouched against the hood of their car, arms crossed over their chests, disgusted looks on their faces. After a brief discussion—and a lot of pissed-off body language—the men handed the officer their driver's licenses. She ordered them back into their car and returned to her vehicle. Emma saw the man with the glasses slam his hand down on the steering wheel in frustration. Ten minutes later, a long time to do a simple check on outstanding warrants, the officer left her patrol car and returned the men's driver's licenses. As the Buick departed, the driver stuck his arm out the window and gave the cop the finger.

The officer remained standing outside her patrol car until Emma drove up next to her. Emma powered down the passenger-side window of her car, exchanged a few words with the other woman, and the officer handed Emma the memory card from a digital camera.

Emma wasn't a particularly sociable person but she had friends everywhere.

The shuttle from Reagan National to LaGuardia arrived at ten-thirty, and by eleven-thirty DeMarco was standing in the hallway outside Janet Tyler's apartment. He rang the doorbell, and from inside the apartment, he could hear the commotion caused by a couple of kids responding to the bell and their mother telling them to settle down. He saw the peephole darken and then the door opened.

A woman he assumed was Janet Tyler was holding a little girl in one arm, the girl about two years old. Clutching the woman's knees was another little girl with big brown eyes and curly dark hair, and she was cuter than Shirley Temple. Tyler herself was slim and short, five-two or five-three, but unlike her dark-haired, brown-eyed daughters, she had blue eyes and blond hair. Her hair was tied back in a careless ponytail and there were food stains on her pink T-shirt. She had the frazzled appearance of a mother with two high-energy children born close to a year apart.

"Ms. Tyler?" DeMarco said.

"Yes."

DeMarco held up his identification and introduced himself.

"Congress?" Tyler said.

"Yes, ma'am. May I come in? I need to ask you a few questions about Senator Paul Morelli."

Tyler inhaled sharply, and DeMarco recalled that he'd gotten an almost identical reaction from Marcia Davenport. These women were afraid of Morelli.

"I . . . I don't have anything to say about the senator," Tyler said. "I only met him once."

"You worked for him when he was the mayor. I'd just like to know—"

"I'm sorry, but I can't talk right now. I have to get my daughter to the doctor's office."

The woman was a terrible liar. DeMarco was a good one.

"Ms. Tyler," he said, "if you don't talk to me today, you're going to be subpoenaed to testify before a congressional committee. You're going to have to fly to Washington and you may be there for several days, at your own expense, until the committee gets around to hearing your testimony. If you want to avoid all that, I'd suggest you talk to me."

Tyler struck him as a timid person, not all that sure of herself, and he felt like a heel bullying her. But he needed answers.

She closed her eyes briefly then said, "I have to get a neighbor to watch my girls. There's a café across the street. I'll meet you there in twenty minutes."

"These guys are connected somehow to the CIA," Mary Tollier told Emma.

When the U.S. Capitol police officer had taken the driver's licenses from the two men in the Buick she had photographed the licenses, then dusted them with fingerprint powder and photographed them again. Emma then took the memory chip from the cop's camera to a woman named Mary Tollier who worked at the DIA. Tollier had once worked for Emma, and thanks to Emma's influence, she had ascended the bureaucratic ladder, coming ever closer to that shatter-proof glass ceiling. Mary Tollier owed Emma.

"What!" Emma said. "Who are they and what do they do?"

"The answer to both questions," Mary said, "is I don't know. The names on the licenses are phony. I ran their fingerprints, got nothing from any of the databases, but half an hour later I got a call from a very rude man at Langley asking why I was running those particular fingerprints. We traded insults and hung up."

"Thanks, Mary. Oh, Mary, I just thought of something. You're a music lover. I have a friend in a quartet, and tomorrow they're playing some stuff by this marvelous new Swedish composer. I can't make it, and I was wondering if you'd like to have my ticket."

Emma would tell Christine that she had to use the ticket to bribe Mary to get information.

Emma knew she deserved to go to hell for what she'd just done.

———◆◆◆———

Janet Tyler entered the café twenty minutes later as promised, and saw DeMarco sitting in a corner booth. She had changed out of the Gerber-stained T-shirt and combed her hair and put on some lipstick. She was a pretty, young mom—and a very nervous one.

She took a seat across from DeMarco. "What's this all about?" she said.

"Would you like some coffee?" DeMarco said.

"No."

"Okay. I know you worked for Paul Morelli in 1999. You were involved in some kind of zoning study, but you quit after only two months. I want to know why you quit."

"I didn't like the job," Tyler said.

Terrible liar.

"I don't believe you," DeMarco said.

"I'm telling you the truth. I just didn't—"

"Did Paul Morelli attack you, Janet? Did he rape you?"

Tyler's eyes widened in shock but DeMarco

couldn't tell if she was shocked because he'd made an outrageous, untrue accusation against Morelli or if it was because he knew what Morelli had done to her.

"No," she said. "He never did anything to me. I just didn't like the job and I quit. Why are you asking these questions?"

Lydia Morelli had said something about Tyler's fiancé, something to the effect that her fiancé had been used to silence her. That had been eight years ago and Tyler had kids, so DeMarco assumed that by now she had married the guy.

"Who's your husband, Janet?" DeMarco asked.

"I'm not married."

"Then who's the father of your children?"

"That's none of your business."

"Janet, I work for the federal government. How long do you think it's going to take me to find out what I want to know?"

"You bastards," she said. "Why can't you just leave us alone? What are you going to do? Take my children from me? Deport their father?"

"Jesus, no," DeMarco said. And what was she talking about?

Tyler put her head in her hands and started sobbing, which made DeMarco feel even worse than he already felt.

"Janet," he said, "I'm not going to do anything to you or your kids. I just want to know—"

"My fiancé's name is Hussein Halas. He's a Jordanian national and we're not married because he hasn't been able to get a divorce from his wife. Now is there anything else you want to know?"

"I told you. I want to know if Paul Morelli did anything to you. And if he's blackmailing you in some way to ensure your silence."

"No," she said, but she didn't look at him when she said the word. "Can I go now?"

DeMarco couldn't think of anything else to say to make her talk. "Yeah, you can go."

Tyler immediately rose to leave, wanting only to get away from DeMarco as fast as she could. He felt like a thug leaning on her the way he had and because of this, he said, "And don't worry, Janet. I promise I'm not going to do anything to harm your family."

DeMarco had no idea if he could keep the promise he'd just made.

———◆———

"Did you check the fingerprints I sent you, Marv?"

"Yeah. Why are you asking about these men, Emma?"

"I'm not going to tell you."

"Well, shit, Emma. I can't just—"

"You know, Marv, maybe the media won't care. I mean, how long has it been? Ten years? Twelve? Yeah, maybe after all this time they won't care that you guys stole a suitcase of heroin from a DEA evidence locker and then traded it for Russian surface-to-air missiles. Now that wouldn't have been so bad, except maybe the part about stealing the dope, but then you gave the missiles to a terrorist and he used one to shoot down a helicopter carrying a Philippine politician. And the real bummer was, the politician was on our side. Oops."

"We didn't know he was a terrorist," Marv whined.

"I know. You went *way* beyond stupid on that one, Marv."

"You're bluffing, Emma. That op was classified then and it's still classified, and if you leaked that story, you'd go to jail."

Emma laughed. "Like you could ever prove I leaked it."

The phone was silent for a moment. "Okay, fine," Marvin said. "Their real names are Carl van Horn and James Suttel."

"Are they agents?"

"God, no. They're just a couple of mutts we used a few times."

"Used for what?" Emma said.

"You know, stuff. Stuff we didn't wanna be tied to. The last time it was a banker down in Haiti. He was funneling money to the wrong people and we tried to get the Haitian government to put a stop to it, but the banker was bribing too many people. So we sent van Horn and Suttel down there. All they were supposed to do was scare the banker a little, but van Horn, he bricked the guy's kneecaps. He said he needed the brick to get his attention."

"Good Lord," Emma said, shaking her head. The CIA just amazed her—and terrified her.

"Are they working for you now?"

"No, we haven't used them since Haiti. Look, these guys are basically hoods, Emma. They could be working for anybody. Now are you going to tell me why you're asking?"

"Of course not," Emma said.

———◆———

"Hussein Halas is trapped in the nine rings of immigration hell," Neil said.

DeMarco had called Neil after he spoke to Janet Tyler. He wanted to know more about her fiancé and Neil had worked his magic.

"He's been trying to get his citizenship papers for almost ten years but he can't because he has a wife back in Jordan. And the fact that he's a Muslim doesn't help. But the catch-22 is, he has to go back to Jordan to divorce his wife, but if he does that, they won't let him back into the U.S."

"But Immigration could probably deport this guy in a heartbeat if they wanted to," DeMarco said.

"Oh, you betcha," Neil said.

Chapter 14

Harry Foster claimed to be a political consultant—
it said so right on his office door.

But what Harry really was, was a guy who always
knew a guy who knew a guy. If you needed a politician on your side, Harry knew who was for sale. If
you wanted a building permit to slide through the
system, Harry knew where to apply the grease. Your
no-load brother-in-law needs a job? No problem.
Harry knew a guy at the union hall. To get things
done in New York you could play by the rules, but
if you wanted to win you hired an old-time, back-
room boy like Harry Foster.

Harry had helped Paul Morelli get elected mayor
of New York City.

Harry was sixty-five now and was one of those
people who looked better at sixty-five than he had
at twenty-five. He was a bit shorter than DeMarco,

slim and in good condition. His once black hair was now a handsome shade of silver, receding at the temples, giving him an attractive widow's peak. His skin was pockmarked from old acne scars, but a good tan maintained in a sun worshiper's coffin minimized this small blemish. His hands were manicured, his hair perfectly trimmed, and his face was scented with something rich and subtle.

You could still hear traces of Flatbush in Harry's speech but he had come a long way from Brooklyn. He and DeMarco were seated twelve stories above Fifth Avenue in an office fit for an urban prince, drinking coffee from bone china cups. Below them was Central Park in all its autumn glory, and from their height the view was unmarred by muggers, winos, and the great unwashed.

As DeMarco had told Paul Morelli the night they met, Harry was DeMarco's godfather. DeMarco's dad and Harry had known each other as boys—an Italian kid with iron fists and his Irish friend with a silver tongue. DeMarco's father made a wrong turn somewhere along the twisted road of life and became an enforcer for a mobster in Queens named Carmine Taliaferro. Harry took a different route, going to work for a crooked Bronx borough president, and ending up where he was today, rich and covered in a thin mantle of respectability.

Whatever bond Harry and DeMarco's father had formed as boys held them together in their later years.

Harry would occasionally visit DeMarco's boyhood home in Queens, and he and his dad would sit there in his mother's kitchen, drinking coffee, while Harry made jokes about the old days when the nuns used to twist their ears. And while they talked, DeMarco's mom would glower at Harry, as if it was his fault that her husband worked for the mob. And maybe it was.

Harry and DeMarco's dad remained friends until the day Gino DeMarco was cut down in his prime by gunmen from a rival gang.

"It's been a long time, Joe," Harry said. "What's it been? Almost two years?"

"About that, I guess. I'm sorry we don't get together more often."

"Hey," Harry said and shrugged. Men were busy.

"I was just visiting my mom," DeMarco lied, "and decided to stop by."

"And how is your lovely mother?" Harry asked, a wry smile on his face. They both knew DeMarco's mother's opinion of Harry.

"She's doin' fine. Hard as a hickory bat."

Harry laughed. "Ain't that the truth." He studied DeMarco for a moment. "You seem a bit antsy, son. Can I assume there's a purpose to this visit, something more than just dropping in to say hello?"

Though DeMarco's mother had never approved of him, Harry had been there for DeMarco when his dad was killed. He had sent him money on occasion when he was in college and had been a source of comfort when his marriage failed. Harry was the closest thing he had to a father, and now he wanted a father's advice.

"I need to ask you something about Paul Morelli, Harry."

"You want to talk about Paul?"

"Yeah. I like the guy but . . ."

"Well, shit, who doesn't," Harry said.

". . . but I've heard something about him and if it's true . . . Well, then maybe he's not who everyone thinks he is. You've known him a long time and I need your take on this thing."

"You're saying you've heard something *bad* about Paul?" Harry said, suddenly less relaxed, sitting up straighter in his chair.

"Yeah."

DeMarco wasn't about to tell Harry that he'd heard the bad thing from Paul Morelli's wife, but he did tell him about Terry Finley's death and Dick Finley's speculation that his son had been killed because of whatever he'd been investigating. Harry's reaction to the names of the three men on the bar napkin found in Terry's wallet was the same as Abe Burrows and Paul Morelli's—and John Mahoney's: what befell those men was nothing more than coincidence and if anything underhanded had taken place, it would have been uncovered by now.

"This isn't just about the men," DeMarco said. "There was a woman's name on the list. She lives here in New York and she worked for Morelli when he was mayor. I've been told that Morelli may have attacked this woman. Sexually."

Harry's reaction completely surprised DeMarco. "That golddigging bitch!" he said. "If she thinks she can pull this crap now, I'm gonna make her life a living hell."

DeMarco didn't know what Harry was talking about but before he could say anything, Harry added, "You're talking about Susan Medford. Right?

"Uh, yeah," DeMarco said. If Harry hadn't been so angry he might have noticed DeMarco's hesitation. But Harry was angry.

"It's her mother," he said. "Goddamnit, this has *got* to be coming from her."

"Harry, what are you talking about?"

"It was New Year's Eve, an office party, and shit, I don't know what the hell got into Paul. He had too much to drink and there was the stress of the Senate campaign, and I'd heard that things weren't going too good between him and his wife at the time. Anyway, for whatever reason, Paul gets sorta shit-faced, gets this little gal in his office, and tries to smooch her or something. I guess she'd never had her tit squeezed before by a drunken wop, and she gets all hysterical and runs out of the party. Her mother says the girl's blouse was half ripped off, but that was bullshit."

"He assaulted her, Harry, is that what you're saying?"

"No, goddamnit, he didn't *assault* her! Don't even say shit like that. Paul just got a little drunk and hit on her. Maybe he groped her a bit, but that's it."

"So what happened?"

"So what happened is her mother gets a lawyer. She decides she's going to sue the mayor of New York for sexual harassment, attempted rape, and any other fuckin' thing she can dream up. Fortunately, the lawyer she retained knows me and he calls me before the press gets wind of all this. We agreed to settle the outstanding mortgage on the mother's condo—the girl lives with her—and the girl, we gave her a hundred grand. For *damages,* her lawyer said, like her tit had been permanently bruised. And then we got the mother and the girl and the lawyer to sign papers that said if they ever, *ever* discussed the settlement we'd fuckin' own 'em."

"Jesus, Harry," DeMarco said.

"Hey!" Harry said, annoyed at DeMarco's judgmental tone. "We had to kill the thing. Paul still would have won the election but it would have been just like it was with Schwarzenegger, all that crap about him groping women. So we paid her off. But Paul sure as shit didn't rape her. And now you're telling me the gal—it's gotta be her goddamn mother—is telling people this.

"Well, I'm gonna call that bitch as soon as you leave and I'll tell her exactly what's gonna happen to her. That woman, the mother, she loves this place she has—got a view of the Hudson to die for—and I'm gonna tell her that she's gonna be livin' out the back of her fuckin' car if she reneges on the agreement she signed." Harry shook his head. "The thing is, even though Paul didn't do a damn thing to the girl, other than maybe try to smooch her, this is the last damn thing he needs right now."

"Has Morelli ever done anything else like this?" DeMarco said.

"Hell, no! It happened one damn time." Harry fumed, still agitated. "So who told you about this?"

DeMarco hated to lie to Harry, but he had to. "I can't say, Harry. You know, it's a lawyer thing. But what I can tell you is that the woman's name was just on this list and somebody I talked to, somebody who knew Terry Finley, said that he'd heard some kind of rumor about a sexual assault, but nothing specific, nothing that could be confirmed."

DeMarco knew that if Harry talked to Paul Morelli, Morelli would know that Susan Medford wasn't on the list. The twisted tales we weave.

"And so now what, Joe? Where are you going with this?

"I'm not going anywhere with it. I don't have any desire to cause Morelli a problem. You told me what happened, and that's the end of it."

Harry studied DeMarco's face for a bit before saying, "What time's your plane leave, son?"

"Four," DeMarco said.

"Come on. Let's go get some lunch, then I'll give you a lift to the airport."

———————◆◆◆———————

Harry called for his car and they drove to a restaurant in lower Manhattan. The name of the restaurant was written over the door in letters so faded they were almost illegible, and inside the restaurant, the hardwood floors were scuffed and worn, the tables small and wobbly. The blue checkered tablecloths had been laundered, but the stains of a thousand meals were evident.

A man in his seventies who spoke English with a heavy Italian accent came over and embraced Harry as soon as they stepped through the door. DeMarco noticed the waiters were all men in their late fifties or sixties with Mediterranean complexions. The restaurant wasn't crowded, only three other tables were occupied, and everyone—the owner, the waiters, the customers—were of a type: working-class Italians in late middle age or older. It was a place that catered to a thin slice of a particular generation, and when that generation passed, it too would pass.

The owner directed them to a table apart from the other diners, and they sat only a minute before they were served a carafe of strong red wine. They never saw a menu. Food just began to arrive, a different course every twenty minutes or so. DeMarco couldn't remember the last time he had eaten so well.

During lunch, Harry told stories about Paul Morelli.

"He gets things done, Joe, like you wouldn't believe. Most politicians, they don't know how to solve problems—they make speeches. But Paul, he's a genius. You need money to fix something, he finds sources. You need two parties to agree, he brings 'em together. I'm not bullshittin' you. I've never seen a guy that can make things happen like him."

This conversation was repeated throughout the two-hour lunch. Harry told stories of day care centers built, of old people taken care of, of businesses rejuvenated. He told of blacks and whites working together, of stingy old men donating their fortunes to charity.

As they were leaving the restaurant, the owner came up to Harry, embraced him again, and kissed him on the cheek.

"I just wanna thank you again, Harry, for what you did for my Gina."

"The only thing I did, Benny, was talk to Mayor Morelli."

Harry looked at DeMarco and said, "Benny's daughter needed a bone marrow transplant. The only acceptable donor was her brother, a complete thug, breaking rocks up at Attica. The kid was such a degenerate he wouldn't help his own sister. I mentioned this to Paul, just in passing, and he personally goes up to the pen and talks the kid into donating. Didn't promise him squat. After the kid's paroled, Paul gets him a job with the teamsters. He's been driving eighteen-wheelers for six years now, keeping his nose clean."

Saint Paul of the Big Apple.

<hr />

Harry waited until DeMarco disappeared inside the terminal at La Guardia, then pulled his cell phone off his belt. He flipped open the lid of the phone and his finger descended to punch the buttons, but then he stopped.

He really should talk to Paul about Joe. The fact that he was asking questions about Susan Medford wasn't good and if it had been anyone other than his godson, he wouldn't have thought twice about making the call. But Joe *was* his godson.

He also realized that he'd fucked up. Big time. Susan Medford had just been a name on a piece of paper, and Joe hadn't really known anything about her until he shot off his big mouth. Paul would really be pissed if he knew what he had done.

But still—he should call Paul.

He unconsciously began to flip the lid of the cell phone open and shut, open and shut, oblivious to the little clicking sound.

If Paul should find out later that Joe had visited him and he'd kept it to himself . . . well, that wouldn't be good. But what if Paul told him to go see the old man? He didn't think that was likely, but you could never be sure. Jesus, he didn't *ever* want to have to go see the old man about Joe. Joe was like a son to him.

Harry jerked in surprise when someone rapped on his car window, the sound like a man's wedding ring tapping the glass. It was an airport cop, telling him to get moving, to get off the parking strip. Asshole. What did he look like? Some rag-head suicide bomber?

He closed the cell phone and clipped it back onto his belt.

Joe was a good guy. He wasn't gonna be a problem.

Chapter 15

The pit boss had been chewing out one of his dealers for showing up late when he saw Eddie. Aw, shit. What was he doing here? He was alone at a five-dollar blackjack table and that's what he was betting: just five bucks a hand. He obviously wasn't here to gamble.

Eddie had to be the broadest man the pit boss had ever seen. Not fat, just *wide*. The damn guy's shoulders had to be a yard across, and his chest and waist weren't much smaller. He was like a big, square chunk of concrete on two stubby legs. But it was his hands that were scary: the size of catchers' mitts, the fingers like mangled sausages, all splayed and bent up funny, crisscrossed with thick, ugly scars. He'd love to know who had been tough enough to fuck up Eddie's hands that way, but he'd never ask. And he'd also bet—he'd bet every cent he had—

that whoever had done it was dead and had died very painfully.

Oh, no. Eddie had just looked at him and moved his head, a little get-your-ass-over-here motion. He wanted to talk. Christ, why'd *he* have to be on duty tonight?

He walked over to the blackjack table. "Stacy," he said to the dealer, "go powder your nose. Five minutes, no more."

Stacy stacked her cards and walked away without a word. She was like most of their female dealers, in her forties, still good-looking enough to turn a few heads but past her prime as a stripper. And like most dealers, the woman was a complete zombie. The cards would fly from her hands, and she'd tell the suckers whether they'd busted or not, and she'd pick up their chips if they lost or pay 'em if they won, but the whole time her mind was a zillion miles away, thinking about whatever these friggin' gals thought about while they worked.

"Hey, Eddie," he said as soon as Stacy was gone, "long time no see. What can I do for you?"

Please, please God, let him say he wants a hooker.

"You see that guy over there?" Eddie said. "At the twenty-five-dollar table, the guy in the green jacket?"

The pit boss turned his head slowly, like he was just casually taking in the room while they talked. "Yeah," he said, "that's the doc. He's in here all the time. Loser."

"Not tonight," Eddie said. "I want him to win big."

Aw, fuck.

"How much?"

"Ten, fifteen grand. That'll be enough."

"Okay." *Yes, sir, yes, sir, three bags full.*

The pit boss went back to his station in the middle of the blackjack tables, picked up his phone, and made a call. Five minutes later Ray was there, a man in his fifties, white shirt, little black bow tie like all the dealers wore—and fingers like a concert pianist. Ray was the best mechanic they had. Maybe the best mechanic on the boardwalk.

"Take over Dave's table," the pit boss said. "I want the guy in the green jacket to win ten grand."

"You got it," Ray said, eyes lighting up like a slot machine that had just paid off. Ray lived for this.

The pit boss spent the next two hours wishing he was someplace else. Anyplace else. He was pretty sure that he had just become an accessory to something, he didn't know what, but whatever it was, he was sure it wasn't good.

The doc let out another victory yell. The fuckin' guy, he thought he was magic tonight. If he only knew.

The pit boss looked over at Eddie. He was still sitting alone at Stacy's table, still betting just five bucks a hand. His eyes were focused on the doc, watching as the doc's stack of chips grew taller.

Chapter 16

———◆———

DeMarco had just returned from his trip to New York and was sitting in his den, a vein throbbing in his temple, reading an op-ed piece in the *Washington Post*. The evil bastard who'd written the editorial was urging Congress to raise the minimum retirement age for federal employees to sixty-five, spouting baseless nonsense as to how this would save the taxpayers big bucks. DeMarco concluded that if *he* were running things, the first thing to go would be the First Amendment. Before he could work himself into a state of quivering anxiety thinking about the possibility of working for Mahoney until he was sixty-five, the doorbell rang.

Opening the door, he discovered one of his neighbors. She had lived in the house on the right side of his for about six months but he couldn't remember her name. Ellen, Helen, something like that. He said hello to her and her husband when he saw them outside but that was as far as he chose to carry the relationship. She was a plump woman in her early thirties, normally pleasant and cheerful, but today looking as if she had been given a preview of Armageddon. She had a baby in one arm screaming its head off, the baby's face the color of a tomato. Her other hand had a firm grip on the upper arm of a truculent brat who appeared to be about ten.

"Thank *God*, you're home," she said to DeMarco. "I didn't know what I was going to do if you weren't."

"What's the problem?" he asked, knowing he didn't want to hear the answer.

"Wesley's really sick. He's got a temperature of a hundred and four and I've got to get him to the emergency room. I called my normal sitter to take care of Stanford but she's out of town and my sister can't get here for an hour. So could you please, *please* watch Stanford until my sister gets here? I just have to get this baby to the hospital."

DeMarco's mind raced as he tried to think of an excuse even remotely sufficient for turning away a woman with a feverish infant. He considered telling her he was a paroled pedophile.

She saw his hesitation and said, "Just for an hour. Please. Until my sister gets here. I'd take Stanford with me but he catches colds really easily, and I'm afraid he'll get the flu sitting in that waiting room with all those sick people."

"Sure," DeMarco said, "I'd be happy to take care of, uh, Stanford for an hour."

"Oh, thank you so much, Mr. DeMarco. I can't tell you how much I appreciate this."

"It's Joe, and it's quite all right, uh . . ."

"Allison. Allison Webster."

"Right. Allison."

Thrusting Stanford at him, she said, "My sister's name is Joyce. She's on her way."

After she left, he and Stanford stood inside his foyer, staring at each other. DeMarco wasn't sure if Stanford was big or little for his age—he was short. He had reddish brown hair and distrustful-looking, tiny blue eyes. His fists were clenched.

DeMarco broke down first and said, "So what do they call you? Stan?"

"No. My name's *Stanford*. Stan's a guy that works at a garage."

Great. An elitist midget.

When DeMarco didn't say anything else, Stanford said, "So what do you wanna do?"

"Fly to Iowa and see my ex-girlfriend."

"Huh?" Stanford said.

"Never mind. I don't wanna do anything. What do you wanna do?"

"You gotta computer?"

"Yeah."

"You got any games on it? You know, Spider-Man, Donkey Kong, something like that?"

Donkey Kong?

"No," DeMarco said, "I don't have anything on my computer except a tax program."

"How 'bout Nintendo. You got Nintendo hooked up to your TV?"

"No, but I have cable."

"Big deal. Everybody's got cable."

"Look, kid, this isn't a day care center. I don't have any toys; I don't have any games. I have a TV, a punching bag, and a piano. Take your pick."

"*You* have a piano?"

It irked him, the kid sounding so surprised.

"Yeah," he said.

"Steinway?"

"Yamaha."

Stanford snickered. He'd been there less than three minutes and he was already getting on DeMarco's nerves.

"Well, since there's nothing better to do, I guess I could practice for my recital."

DeMarco looked skyward, Job incarnate. He could imagine the brat banging out a two-fisted version of "Beautiful Dreamer" for a solid hour.

"Yeah, that sounds like a good idea," he said. "Make some productive use of your time. It's up the stairs, second floor. And don't touch anything else up there unless you ask first." He didn't know why he had said that; there wasn't anything else up there to touch except his punching bag.

"My mom says you're a grouch."

"I am. Go play the piano."

As Stanford started up the steps, DeMarco said, "By the way, did your piano teacher tell you what pianissimo means?"

Stanford smirked again and nodded.

"Good. Practice pianissimo."

DeMarco poured a drink to get through the next hour and sat back down to finish reading the paper. He had just raised the glass to his lips when the music began. Brahms, Beethoven, one of those guys. And the kid was good—and playing from memory. DeMarco knew he wouldn't be able to play like that if had three hands. He consoled himself with the possibility that Stanford was an idiot savant.

He spent the next hour listening to the music, dwelling on the many facets of Paul Morelli. According to Lydia, someone powerful was helping her husband's political career and that person had possibly killed Terry Finley when he began to investigate the senator's past. Furthermore, per Lydia, Paul Morelli was a sexual predator, a fact that neither woman on Finley's list was willing to confirm. But then Harry had inadvertently told DeMarco that Morelli had done something to another woman, this Susan Medford. But what had he done? Tried to kiss her? Groped her? Or was it something worse?

DeMarco was skeptical of everything Lydia had told him. She had no facts, she drank too much, and she was obviously still distraught over her daughter's death. And not only was he skeptical, but allegations that Paul Morelli had conspired to ruin the careers of the three men on Finley's list had been investigated by people smarter than both DeMarco and Finley. DeMarco was convinced that that was a dead end.

The rational part of him—he couldn't remember if that was the right or left side of his brain—said that Harry was probably right, that Morelli was a good man who may have strayed once or twice, and Lydia's view of her husband was distorted by alcohol and a loveless marriage. But from somewhere deep inside his skull, from that atrophied little nodule that responded to intuition and emotional radiation, a voice was saying that Harry had it all wrong. DeMarco was still trying to figure out what to do when his phone rang.

"There's a dark blue sedan parked fifty yards from your house," Emma said. "The two men in it followed you this morning when you went to the Russell Building."

"You're kidding," DeMarco said.

"Does it sound like I'm kidding? Leave by your back door and meet me at Paolo's." Paolo's was a restaurant in Georgetown within walking distance of DeMarco's house.

"I can't leave just yet," DeMarco said, and explained the situation with young Stanford.

"A woman asked *you* to babysit her child? She should be reported to social services." Before DeMarco could pretend to be offended, Emma said, "Then as soon as the kid leaves, sneak out your back door. Leave the lights on and the TV blaring."

Stanford's aunt arrived a few minutes later, and as the boy was leaving, DeMarco said, "Stanford, you have a lot of talent. I enjoyed listening to you play."

"Ah, any dope can play a piano. You oughta see me play Nintendo."

———◆◆◆———

"The kid's leaving," Jimmy said. "But the woman who picked him up ain't the same one who dropped him off."

He and Carl had seen the first woman knock on DeMarco's door, a baby in her arms, the little red-headed shit at her side. DeMarco had talked to the woman, then the redhead went inside DeMarco's place, and the woman and the baby took off in a cab. And now some other woman comes and picks up the kid. It looked like the neighbor had just asked DeMarco to watch her brat for a while. Jimmy wasn't sure, but that's what it looked like to him. The good news was they'd actually have something to report to Eddie. No way in hell was he going to tell Eddie that they'd lost this guy twice in two days.

"I wonder why that broad left her kid with him," Carl said.

"I dunno," Jimmy said.

"And where the hell was he all day?"

Here we go again, Jimmy thought. The questions. And if that wasn't enough, his nose still hurt where that airbag had whacked it. Those airbags were dangerous.

"You know," Jimmy said, "instead of asking stupid questions all the time why don't you think about what we're gonna do if Eddie says to take care of this guy. And open your goddamn window! How many times do I have to tell you? That fuckin' smoke just kills my sinuses."

Carl rolled his eyes, but he opened the window. "We could do a hit-and-run," he said after a bit. "That'd work."

"Nah, too risky these days. I mean if you do it out in the country, that's okay. But in the city, forget it. They got cameras everywhere. Like that wreck yesterday. Who'd a thought there'd be a camera at that intersection?"

"Yeah. Good thing we got fake IDs. My insurance rates are already through the roof."

"So you got any ideas," Jimmy said, "other than a hit-and-run?"

"No, I guess not. You know, it'd sure be nice if once in awhile we could just *pop* these assholes. Always tryin' to make these things look accidental is a pain in the butt. How 'bout you, you got any ideas or you just gonna run down my ideas?"

"Yeah, actually I do," Jimmy said. "You know how his garage is attached to his house?"

"It's under the house."

"I know," Jimmy said. "It's *attached.*"

DeMarco's garage was in the basement of his home. When he entered his driveway, he drove downward, under the first floor of the house. Adjacent to the garage, on the basement level, was a room that contained DeMarco's washer and dryer, the furnace, and the water heater.

"Anyway, remember today," Jimmy said, "when we went inside? Well, his bedroom is right over the garage."

"So?"

"So we go in there and we drill a couple of holes in the garage ceiling, which is his bedroom floor. We drill the holes so they come out under his bed. Say we do that tomorrow. Then whenever we get the call from Eddie, we wait until he falls asleep and we go in the garage and start his car. Maybe we leave the door between the garage and the rest of the house open for good measure."

"You gotta be shittin' me," Carl said.

"No. The reason I thought of it was a couple months ago out in Idaho, Oregon, one of them places, this guy and his wife killed themselves that way. I mean an accident, not suicide. The guy left the car runnin' in the garage, they went to bed, and they woke up dead. Carbon monoxide."

"The guy left his car runnin' all night?"

"Yeah. Motors on these new cars are so quiet you can't even hear 'em."

"But won't he wake up when we start the car?"

"Maybe, but if we wait until he's snorin' away, he probably won't hear it. And if he does . . . well, then I guess we'll just smother him or something and stick him back in bed."

"What if the car runs out of gas?"

"Now that's a good point. We bring along a couple cans of gas and top off the tank before we start the car."

Carl sat there a minute, thinking about Jimmy's idea. He started to light another cigarette, but stopped. He didn't want to have to listen to Jimmy bitch anymore about his sinuses.

"I don't know," Carl said. "You really think they'll buy he left his car on?"

"Hey, I told ya. They did with that couple in Montana."

"I thought you said it was Idaho."

"Montana, Idaho, what's the fuckin' difference!"

———— ◆ ————

DeMarco saw Emma inside Paolo's, seated at the bar. She was talking to a beautiful woman with long, chestnut-colored hair in a low-cut formal dress, the lady looking as if she'd just escaped some black-tie affair. The woman—it was probably because of the way her hair was styled—reminded him of those fifties movie stars, someone like Rita Hayworth or Ava Gardner. When Emma saw him and excused herself, DeMarco could see that the woman was disappointed.

He and Emma took seats at a table near the front of the restaurant that had just been vacated by another couple. DeMarco thought of making a crack about women hitting on Emma in bars, but decided that wouldn't be smart. Instead he said, "So who do you think is following me?"

"I know who's following you," Emma said. "They have IDs with the names Jerry Fallon and Tim Reed, but their real names are Carl van Horn and James Suttel. They're bottom feeders who freelance for the CIA."

"The CIA!"

"Yeah."

"Holy shit. So maybe Lydia was referring to some big shot at Langley when she said someone powerful was helping her husband."

"Maybe. There are people at the CIA capable of doing anything."

"You think Colin Murphy might be involved?"

Murphy was the current director of the CIA.

"No," Emma said.

"Why not?"

"Because these incidents that helped Morelli's career began back in 1992. Since that time, there have been seven or eight directors of the CIA and Murphy wasn't at the agency until two years ago."

"So if it's not Murphy then it's gotta be one of the old guard over there, one of the career civil servants who's been there forever and is high up the food chain."

"That's possible. But it's also possible these two men aren't working for the CIA at all. Like I said, they freelance. Anyone could have hired them. What did you learn in New York?"

DeMarco told her.

"So the man's a rapist."

"Wait a minute. My godfather just said—"

"Nonsense. You know what Lydia told you and it sounds like her husband's blackmailing Janet Tyler using her fiancé, and he probably silenced Marcia Davenport in some similar way. And now this godfather of yours . . ."

Emma said "godfather" like Harry Foster was Vito Corleone.

". . . confirms that Paul Morelli can't keep his hands to himself."

DeMarco shook his head. "It's not that cut and dried, Emma, and you know it. All the evidence against Morelli can't even be called circumstantial. It's too unsubstantial to be called circumstantial."

DeMarco thought that was pretty clever; Emma didn't.

"You need to talk to Lydia again. You need to find out who's helping the senator and why she's coming forward right now."

"Emma, can you even imagine Mahoney's reaction if he knew I was running around trying to prove Morelli's a criminal?"

"I don't care about Mahoney's reaction."

"Of course you don't. You're rich, you're retired, and you have a pension."

"That's irrelevant," Emma said.

"For you it's irrelevant," DeMarco said.

When DeMarco just sat there, Emma poked his leg under the table with her foot. "Well, what are you waiting for? Call Lydia. Set up a meeting."

"Are you nuts?" DeMarco said. "What if her husband's there?"

"Her husband's in Miami. He's the keynote speaker at the National Hispanic Business Association convention. And he's delivering his speech in Spanish, I might add."

"How do you know this?"

"Because I read more than just the sports section of the *Washington Post*," Emma said. "So go on. Set up another meeting with Lydia."

DeMarco didn't move. He did not want to get cross-wired with Mahoney over this.

"Joe, we're talking about a man who may become the next president of the United States."

Goddamnit, she was right. As usual. DeMarco pulled out his cell phone and started to punch in Lydia's number, but Emma said, "No, use the pay phone."

Lydia's phone rang a long time before she answered, and then it took DeMarco quite a while to set up a meeting for the next day because she was drunk. In fact, it had sounded to him as if she was on the verge of passing out.

He returned to the table. "She was wasted," he said to Emma. "She could barely talk."

"Maybe alcohol is the only way she can find peace," Emma said.

"Yeah, and maybe she's a delusional lush."

"But she agreed to meet you?"

"Yeah, tomorrow morning. She said her husband wouldn't be back until four so at least I don't have to worry about running into him. Which reminds me: I do not want those two CIA guys, or whoever the hell they are, to see me talking to her."

"Oh, I think I can help there," Emma said.

Chapter 17

They watched DeMarco exit his house and then stand on the sidewalk until a cab arrived.

"Here we go," Carl said, starting the car.

"Yeah," Jimmy said, "and do not lose this cluck today. We've lost him twice in two days, and there's no way in hell I'm telling Eddie we lost him a third time."

"You got that right," Carl said. He turned the wheel to the left, to pull away from the curb, but before he could a FedEx truck parked next to him and prevented him from leaving.

"What the fuck!" Carl screamed. He looked over at the FedEx driver, a big black son of a bitch. The guy was reading the address on a package. Carl rolled down his window, waved his arms at the driver, and when the guy didn't see him, he pressed down on the horn. The driver glanced over at him and made a just-a-minute gesture, then went back to reading the address.

"You motherfucker!" Carl screamed.

"Son of a bitch!" Jimmy yelled and he yanked open his door. "I'm gonna get the number on that cab," he said, and took off running down the street.

No way, Carl thought, was Jimmy gonna catch that cab on foot, all the weight he was packing. Carl had to get this son of a bitch to move his truck. He threw open his door, the door banging hard against the side of the FedEx truck, then he pounded on the truck with his fist.

"You black motherfucker!" Carl screamed, "Move this fuckin' truck!"

"What did you say?" the FedEx driver said, looking at Carl, his eyes going all big.

Oh, shit, Carl thought. He hadn't meant to say that. And this guy was *huge*.

"I said, move this truck," Carl said. "Right now. It's an emergency."

"I'll move this truck when you apologize for disrespectin' me, you fat, four-eyed . . ."

"Thank you, Andre," Emma said, and handed the FedEx driver a hundred-dollar bill folded so that he couldn't see the denomination.

"I can't take money from you, Emma, everything

you've done for us. And anyway, I enjoyed it. 'Specially after that bastard started calling me names."

"It's not for you," Emma said. "Buy your wife some flowers. When's the last time you gave her flowers?"

Sheesh, Andre thought. It's like all these women took some sorta make-you-feel-guilty class.

Chapter 18

DeMarco met Lydia Morelli in Georgetown, on the walking trail that runs parallel to the C&O Canal. In years past, mules had walked along the banks of the canal towing barges from Washington to ports as far inland as Cumberland, Maryland. The canal still had a number of working locks, and for all DeMarco knew it still served some useful function, but whether it did or not, it was a pleasant place to walk.

Lydia was already there when DeMarco arrived, sitting on a wooden bench and staring vacantly down at the water trickling along the bottom of the canal. She was wearing a camel-hair trench coat over a white cable knit sweater and dark slacks. When she saw DeMarco, she stood up and walked toward him. She looked terrible: puffy, dark bags under her bloodshot eyes, her complexion sallow.

It appeared as if she'd spent the night battling the invincible bottle and the bottle, as always, had won.

"Good morning," DeMarco said, "and thank you for agreeing to see me."

Lydia just nodded and took a pack of cigarettes from the pocket of her coat. Her hands trembled when she lit the cigarette, and when she exhaled the smoke, DeMarco could again smell a slight odor of alcohol on her breath. She wasn't drunk, maybe she'd only had one drink, but with the exception of Mahoney, DeMarco tended not to have much confidence in people who had bourbon for breakfast. They started to walk down the path, DeMarco feeling hulkish beside her, being so much taller and broader than she was.

"Mrs. Morelli, I need to know—"

But she interrupted him before he could complete the sentence. "I can tell you're not too sure about me but I can also see you're starting to have some doubts about Paul. You wouldn't have asked to see me if that wasn't the case."

She may have been an alcoholic but she was intuitive and she wasn't stupid.

"Maybe," DeMarco said, "but I need to know more. I need to know who's been helping your husband and I need to know why, after all this time, you've decided to destroy his career."

"You don't need to know *either* of those things," Lydia said, her voice testy. "They're irrelevant. The only thing that is relevant is that a corrupt, evil man is going to become president if you don't do something to stop him."

DeMarco stopped walking and took hold of her arm and spun her around, gently, to face him. "I don't believe for one moment that this is about your concern for the country," he said. "There's something personal going on here, something between you and him. And you've known about the things he's done—or the things you *think* he's done—for years. So why are you doing this now and who's helping him?"

Lydia shook her head. "I'm not going to give you his name."

"Why not?"

"Remember when I told you that Paul only married me because of who my father was?"

"Yes."

"When my father went down in flames . . ."

DeMarco didn't know what she meant by that.

". . . Paul was afraid, even as bright as he is, that he would never make it big in politics. But then, because of me, the devil danced in."

The devil?

Lydia saw the expression on DeMarco's face. "I didn't mean that literally, Joe. I'm not a religious fanatic. Nor am I demented." She paused, then added, "But maybe if I were religious, none of this would have happened.

"But his name isn't important. And the reason it's not important is that you'll never get to Paul through him. He never does anything personally, and you'll never find a connection between him and Paul. What you need to do is concentrate on the women Paul attacked. That's your best shot."

This wasn't making sense. Why wouldn't she name this guy? She had said that it was because of her that Paul had met the man, but so what? Was she worried if she named him she'd implicate herself in some way? Maybe Lydia's motives were self-serving and had nothing to do with her husband.

'Are you afraid of this man, Mrs. Morelli, is that why you won't tell me his name? Are you afraid he might kill you if he found out?"

Lydia started to shake her head no, but then she said, "Maybe he would kill me. I don't know. Sometimes monsters eat their young."

Christ, another cryptic, useless comment. He didn't know if Lydia Morelli just enjoyed being dramatic, if she was being intentionally evasive—or if she really was insane. But he did know that she was making him angry.

"Goddamnit, I need some help here! I need to know who this guy is to protect myself. And two men have been following me, men who freelance for the CIA, and I need to know why."

"The CIA?" Lydia said, and then she laughed, although DeMarco didn't know what he'd said that was funny. "I can assure you he isn't connected with the CIA," she said. "So I don't know who's following you, Joe, or why."

Before DeMarco could argue further, she said, "Just focus on Paul. Talk to those women on Terry's list. Make them admit that Paul attacked them."

"I did talk to them, Mrs. Morelli, and they claim your husband didn't do anything to them."

"They're lying. Talk to them again. Make them agree to testify against him."

This was hopeless; the woman had a one-track mind. And she was telling him no more than she'd already told him at the cathedral.

"Mrs. Morelli, you're asking me to help you destroy one of the most admired politicians in the country—a man *I* admire—but you have no evidence, you won't tell me why you hate him, and you won't tell me who's helping him. And now I'm in danger. I'm not pursuing this any further."

"Terry Finley wasn't afraid," Lydia said.

Terry Finley was an ambitious megalomaniac with delusions of grandeur, is what DeMarco almost said, but he didn't. Instead he said, "Well, Terry was a braver man than I am." And that was probably true as well. "Mrs. Morelli, either you give me some details, or I'm leaving."

At that moment, two college-aged girls, one blond, one brunette, wearing T-shirts and sweatpants, jogged passed DeMarco and Lydia. Their long hair was tied in ponytails that swished back and forth across their backs in rhythm to their strides, and they were chatting and laughing as they passed, not the least out of breath as they ran. DeMarco imagined that Lydia Morelli had been like those girls at one time—healthy and happy and carefree—but now she walked next to him carrying the grief of her daughter's death, her hatred for her husband, and secrets she wouldn't or couldn't share. He felt sorry for her but it was time for him to go. She wouldn't help him and he couldn't help her.

"Goodbye," DeMarco said. "Call me when you have something to say." And he turned to leave.

"Wait!" Lydia said.

DeMarco turned back to face her. "What?" he said.

"My husband, he . . . I need a drink."

The last thing she needed was a drink, but maybe some booze would get her to open up. "There's a place close to here," DeMarco said.

They'd just reached the point where the canal intersected Wisconsin Avenue, and there was a set of wooden steps leading up to the street. They ascended the steps and walked half a block to the corner of M Street and Wisconsin Avenue, to a restaurant called Nathan's. In the evening the bar would be filled with young hustlers trying to score and impress, but at eleven a.m., they had the place to themselves.

The waiter who served them was typical of Georgetown—a college student who considered himself too bright for menial labor. His body language made it clear that their presence was a major inconvenience, and when Lydia ordered a bloody mary, his expression conveyed his youthful disdain for old drunks who couldn't wait until noon to start destroying their livers.

DeMarco looked nervously over at the door, hoping no one would come in and see him with her. He did not want Paul Morelli to know that he was secretly meeting with his wife. Lydia just sat there, fidgeting, until the waiter finally brought her drink.

"Now talk," DeMarco said. "Straight answers. No more nonsense about devils and monsters."

Lydia ignored him. She grasped the glass in both hands and gulped down half her drink, then sat back in her chair and closed her eyes. The alcohol seemed to calm her and some of the tension left her face. She opened her eyes and looked directly into DeMarco's, and said, "Paul molested my daughter. His stepdaughter."

DeMarco didn't know if she was telling the truth, but the image of Paul Morelli forcing himself on a sixteen-year-old girl made him cringe. And Lydia noticed his reaction and she seemed pleased, as if thrilled by the look of revulsion on his face.

"Yes," she said. "And that's not all. My daughter didn't die in a car accident. She committed suicide. She didn't miss a turn that night. She drove her car at full speed into a bridge abutment. There wasn't one skid mark. She made no attempt to stop. The bastard killed her."

DeMarco started to say something, not sure exactly what—to say he was sorry, to ask how she could be certain—but before he could say anything, she said, "So you were right, Joe. This is personal. It's very personal." She reached for her drink again but with less urgency than she'd displayed before.

"I don't think Paul's ever had an ordinary affair," she said. "I don't believe he's ever snuck off to a motel room with a secretary for a sweaty afternoon between the sheets. Normal men do things like that.

"But my husband doesn't allow himself to have affairs. He knows such behavior could ruin his career. In fact, he has enormous self-control. He's a cold, calculating son of a bitch with a heart of stone." She paused dramatically, then added, "Except when he drinks."

DeMarco inadvertently glanced down at the half-empty glass in front of her.

"Yes, I know," Lydia said. "The pot calling the kettle black. But when I drink, the only one I hurt is myself. When Paul drinks, he assaults women."

"Mrs. Morelli, you've already told me this," DeMarco said. "What I need to know is—"

But Lydia didn't care that she was repeating herself. "Paul likes backing a frightened woman into a corner," she said, "and forcing her to submit. He likes to dominate, to . . . to violate. It's just his little thing, his *kink*. He's a sick, twisted shit."

Realizing she was speaking louder than she intended, she took a breath to calm herself, then stopped to light a cigarette. Her hand was shaking so badly that DeMarco finally took the lighter and lit the cigarette for her.

"Thank you," she said with a small, embarrassed smile. "I guess I'm not in the best shape, am I?" She took a deep drag on the cigarette and a long ash hung on the end of it for an instant, then crumbled into her lap unnoticed.

"I'll tell you something else," Lydia said, "as demeaning as it is for me to admit it. After the first year we were married, my husband and I rarely made love. But on occasion, he'd . . . he'd just . . . I don't even know how to describe it. He wouldn't even take off his clothes. He'd push me down on the floor, the bed, wherever, and he'd be angry, brutal. It was like he was trying to punish me. But you know what? I never complained, and I didn't complain because I'm sick too. I still loved him, in spite of everything I knew he'd done. I loved him until I understood why Kate died."

"Mrs. Morelli, what makes you think he molested your daughter?"

"Don't you understand what I've been telling you? Who would be a better victim for him than a shy, teenage girl?" she said.

"But how do you know?"

Lydia was wearing a watch on her thin left wrist, one with an expandable metal band. As she talked she twisted the watch band and DeMarco could see the metal digging into her flesh, leaving deep red marks in her skin. He couldn't tell if she was oblivious to the pain—or if she welcomed it.

"I don't know when it started. I missed all the symptoms that were so obvious after the fact. Kate had always been a quiet, thoughtful girl, but she became moody. Her grades dropped. She started having screaming tantrums over the smallest problems. I attributed the change to hormones. I was so stupid.

"Oddly enough, it was me she was hostile toward. Around Paul she was always silent, a typical sullen teenager. But with me, she was constantly angry, always lashing out at me. I realized later that she thought I knew what was going on and blamed me for not stopping it. The night she died she became completely hysterical. I had to go out of town unexpectedly. My aunt was sick. Anyway, Kate said she wanted to go with me and I told her no because the next day was a school day. Well, she went absolutely berserk, screaming, crying, carrying on like a two year old. But, God forgive me, I didn't take her. It wasn't until after she was gone that I realized that she'd acted that way because she didn't want me to leave her alone with him."

This was all just too nebulous, DeMarco thought. "Did your daughter ever tell you directly that your husband was molesting her?" he said.

Lydia's eyes flashed. "No, goddamn you, she didn't. But I know! A mother knows!"

She burst into tears and then got up suddenly, knocking her drink off the table, scattering ice cubes across the hardwood floor, and rushed to the restroom. The waiter saw the overturned drink and with a look of disgust came over to clean up the spill.

Smirking, he said, "Are we having a little problem here?"

Irritated at the kid's undeserved sense of superiority, DeMarco said, "Shut up and mop up the mess. Then bring her another."

The waiter hesitated a second, thinking about telling DeMarco to go to hell, then realized what a mistake that would be. He was a condescending little shit but he wasn't stupid.

"Yes, sir," he said, managing to put a snide twist into the "sir."

At least now DeMarco understood Lydia's hatred for her husband, but understanding what motivated her didn't necessarily make him believe her. Drunks are emotional and irrational. It was possible that she'd become so saturated with the bitterness of a bad marriage and the delusional effects of alcohol that she had misinterpreted words and actions that were completely innocent. Her daughter's moodiness may have indeed been caused by teenage hormones, and the absence of skid marks at the crash scene could have been completely consistent with the accident. Maybe the girl had been fiddling with the radio or talking on a cell phone. He just couldn't be sure. And then, of course, there was the fact that he really didn't *want* to believe her. He just couldn't imagine Paul Morelli doing the things she had accused him of.

Ten minutes later Lydia Morelli returned from the restroom. Her eyes were red from crying and her mascara had washed away, making her face look even more haggard and vulnerable.

"I'm sorry," she said. "I just . . . I just lose it sometimes."

"It's all right," DeMarco said. "You're under a lot of stress."

She studied DeMarco's face for a moment, and her eyes registered her disappointment. "Yes, I am under a lot of stress—but I can tell you're not convinced that I'm telling the truth."

"It's just that—"

"I have money, Joe," she said desperately. "I'll pay you anything you want."

"Mrs. Morelli, this isn't about money. The problem is that there's no way to prove that your husband's done any of the things you've said."

He had almost said: there's no way to prove that you're telling the truth.

Lydia bit her lower lip, struggled to maintain her composure—and failed. "What the hell am I supposed to do?" she said, her voice rising to a shriek. The snotty waiter looked over in annoyance.

When DeMarco didn't answer, she grabbed his wrist, her fingernails biting into his skin. He thought of a sparrow clinging to a tree branch in a hurricane.

"Tell me. What should I do?" she repeated. "Should I just go to the White House with him, knowing what he did to my daughter?"

"I don't know what you should do, Mrs. Morelli. Maybe it would be best if you left him."

He didn't know what on earth had possessed him to say that but her answer surprised him.

"It wouldn't be enough," she said.

DeMarco realized then that she was so warped by hatred that she didn't consider divorce in terms of her own well-being, but only in terms of the damage it would do to her husband.

"I know him," she said. "He'd make himself out to be the victim. The public would sympathize with him and before long he'd be on the cover of *GQ*, the most eligible bachelor in America."

She searched DeMarco's face again and when she didn't find what she was looking for, her features sagged in resignation. "You're not going to help me," she said.

"Mrs. Morelli, I need to know the name of the man that's—"

"Nobody will ever help me," she said softly, speaking more to herself than DeMarco.

Goddamnit, he needed to get her to talk about the mystery man. He needed to find out who was tailing him and why. But Lydia wasn't through. "Maybe it's time I helped myself," she said.

"What do you mean?" he asked, not liking her fatalistic tone.

"I'll go to the press and tell them about my daughter. Tell them everything Paul's done. I've thought of doing it before, but I didn't have the guts." Her lips compressed into a determined line. "And the papers will believe me," she said. "*They* won't ask for proof. I'll look like the spineless fool I've always been, but it'll sure as hell ruin him."

"Mrs. Morelli, maybe you should give this a bit more thought," DeMarco said. What he meant was: maybe you ought to wait until you're sober before deciding to become a media spectacle.

"Oh, to hell with you," she said, and without another word, rose from the table. She bumped into a chair, stumbled slightly, regained her balance, and walked from the restaurant. DeMarco made no attempt to stop her. He just sat there, watching through a window until she was out of sight. When she was gone, he caught sight of his reflection in the window. He averted his eyes, not enamored at all with the view.

He felt like beating the shit out of the snotty waiter.

Chapter 19

It was the same guy Ladybird had met at the National Cathedral.

Garret Darcy knew his name now. It was DeMarco. He'd gotten the name using DeMarco's license plate number and later found out that he'd also met with Big Bird. But no one could figure out what the guy was doing. He meets with Big Bird one night, then the next day he meets with Ladybird, then Phil and Toby see him go into the Russell Building, to Big Bird's office, and now here he was meeting with Ladybird again at the canal. What the hell was his angle?

All they knew about him was that he was a lawyer and he worked for Congress. But that was it. His visits to Big Bird's house and office, those may have been legit, like maybe he had some sort of political business with the man. Meeting with Ladybird, though, at these out-of-the-way spots, that didn't make sense. He was pretty sure the guy wasn't diddling her—his body language was all wrong for that—but what they were talking about, he didn't have a clue.

Darcy took out his cell phone and called his employer.

"The man from the cathedral, he's meeting with Ladybird again." They didn't have a code name for DeMarco yet but the boss knew who he meant. "They met down by the C&O Canal and now they're sitting in a joint called Nathan's in Georgetown. She's drinking, as usual. The guy, he's just sitting there, mostly listening, not saying much. You want me to follow him this time or stick with her?"

The boss hesitated, apparently thinking things over. Darcy had the impression that he was pissed because he didn't have the assets to follow them both. This operation was definitely low-budget. "Yes, follow him," he finally said.

"You know," Darcy said, "if I had a parabolic mike I could have heard what they were talking about when they were at the canal."

"I know that!" he snapped, and hung up.

Now that was unusual, the boss losing his cool. The stakes had to be pretty goddamn high for that to happen.

Chapter 20

DeMarco called Mahoney's office. He was informed that the Speaker wouldn't be returning from San Francisco until that evening and then would proceed directly to the Greek Embassy to celebrate some sort of United States–Greek trade agreement. DeMarco assumed that a trade agreement meant that the two countries had agreed to lower tariffs on each other's products, but the only Greek imports he knew of were olive oil and ouzo. It was probably because of the ouzo that Mahoney had supported the agreement.

Since he had the time, DeMarco returned to his office and turned on his computer. He wanted to know more about Lydia Morelli. And the remark she'd made about monsters eating their young particularly puzzled him. When she'd made the comment, he thought she was referring to the powerful man who had been helping Paul Morelli but her words made it sound as if the man was in some way related to her. Could she have been talking about her father?

He didn't know, so he started Googling. He knew that Neil could have done the research better and faster, and would have been able to access databases that DeMarco couldn't, but Neil was expensive—and annoying—so DeMarco ventured into cyberspace on his own, pecking at his keyboard with two blunt, unskilled fingers.

Paul and Lydia Morelli's families had been covered extensively in the media. Morelli's father had been a diesel mechanic, his mother a homemaker. All his siblings were alive and all had middle-class jobs. Morelli appeared to have no blood connections to powerful people in either politics or the business world, and, being a politician with an Italian surname, he had been thoroughly investigated for connections to organized crime. Obviously none had been found.

Lydia's parents were higher up the social ladder than Morelli's. Her father had been a federal judge and her mother, who had inherited old money, could best be described as a socialite though she had worked off and on at various art galleries. Lydia had no siblings, nor did her father. Her mother had a sister who edited children's books.

Lydia's father's career had ended in disgrace when he was accused of fixing a case involving a rich man's son. He was never convicted of a crime but he resigned from the bench, and most assumed his resignation was the result of a plea bargain with the prosecution. In other words, the prosecutor had a case that could drive the judge into bankruptcy with legal costs, and the publicity would certainly ruin his reputation, but they didn't have strong enough evidence to assure a conviction. Five years after retiring, the judge died of cirrhosis and his wife died a few years later of ovarian cancer.

Paul Morelli was Lydia's second husband. Her first husband had been a man named Peter Brent, a white-bread corporate accountant who collapsed at the age of thirty while jogging. He and Lydia had been married barely long enough for him to sire a child, and Paul Morelli had married Lydia when her daughter Kate was less than two. Speculation by one of the cattier New York gossip columnists was that Morelli had married Lydia because of her father's connections— connections that evaporated when the judge resigned in disgrace. This was what Lydia had meant when she said her father had gone down in flames.

Lydia's family history was mildly interesting and somewhat tragic, but DeMarco saw no evidence of anyone in the picture so powerful that he could have helped Paul Morelli's political career, particularly in the way Lydia had described. He couldn't find a monster.

Most of the one hundred guests at the Greek Embassy understood that embassy affairs were but an extension of their workday, another opportunity to politic or lobby or spy. Not Mahoney. To him a party was a party, and he was one of only ten people dancing, his partner a thirty-something blond displaying an eye-popping amount of cleavage. As DeMarco watched his boss dance, he was surprised, as always, at how light Mahoney was on his feet when wooing a potential conquest.

The waltz ended and DeMarco caught the Speaker's eye. Mahoney did not look pleased at the interruption. He bowed to his dance partner, kissed her hand, and then made an irritated motion for DeMarco to meet him on an outdoor balcony. The young lady he had been waltzing with stood for a moment on the dance floor after Mahoney departed, seemingly stunned motionless by his charm. DeMarco couldn't fathom it.

Mahoney was firing up his cigar as DeMarco stepped onto the balcony.

"Can't smoke inside anyplace anymore," Mahoney groused. The cigar finally burning, giving off its expected stench, he said, "So now what's so fuckin' urgent it couldn't wait until tomorrow?"

"Lydia Morelli was Terry Finley's source. She's trying to destroy her husband because she believes he molested her daughter and drove her to suicide."

"What the hell," Mahoney said, and his eyes

stopped tracking the women in the room and focused on DeMarco.

"And I'm being tailed by two goons who may or
may not work for the CIA."

Mahoney stared at DeMarco a moment then said
exactly what DeMarco had expected him to say: "I'll
be right back. I need a drink for this. Here, hold
this," he added, handing DeMarco his cigar, the tip
all nasty and gooey.

After Mahoney had returned with his drink,
DeMarco told him everything that Lydia Morelli
had said. Mahoney didn't say anything at first. He
just stood there puffing on his stogy, frowning,
looking out from the balcony. DeMarco followed
Mahoney's line of sight and could see he was staring at the steeple of the National Cathedral, the
place where DeMarco had first met with Lydia.

"I'm not buying any of it," Mahoney said at last.
"I think Lydia went off the deep end after her kid
died, started hitting the sauce, and decided everything was her husband's fault. All this stuff about
some powerful guy helping Morelli and him assaulting women . . . I mean, come on! And the rape thing
is the dumbest part of the whole story. You've seen
Paul. Do you think a guy that looks like him would
have to force anybody?"

"Yeah, but these women . . . They acted strange,"
DeMarco said. "They were afraid of Morelli, I could
tell when I was talking to them."

Mahoney shrugged. "Who knows what happened between him and those gals. Maybe he did screw 'em. And you said the one had a boyfriend. She probably doesn't want him to find out that she slept with Morelli."

Mahoney clearly saw no relationship between infidelity and a man's ability to govern, and DeMarco could understand why.

"What about the guys following me?" DeMarco said.

"I dunno," Mahoney said, "but I tell you one thing for sure: they ain't workin' for the CIA. After 9-11 and Iraq, those clowns over at Langley are doing everything they can to stay under the radar. No way they'd get involved in any of this stuff: Terry Finley, Morelli, following you. Uh-uh, no way."

"So who hired the guys following me?"

"I told you, I don't know. And for all you know, they could be following you for some reason *not* connected to Terry Finley."

That was possible, but DeMarco didn't think so. No, his being followed was in some way connected to his investigation into Finley's death. Which reminded him. "And what do I tell Dick Finley?" he said.

"Nothing. You don't say anything to him yet. If you were to tell Dick that you thought his kid was killed and his death was in some way related to Paul . . . Well, Dick's not in office anymore but that doesn't mean he still doesn't have connections. You tell him any of the stuff you've told me and his next phone call will be to the fuckin' crew at *60 Minutes*. So you tell Dick nothin', and if he asks, you say you're still lookin' into things."

"So what *do* you want me to do? Somebody probably killed Terry and they probably killed him because he was investigating Morelli."

Mahoney shook his big, white-haired head. "Joe, Terry Finley is not the priority at this point. Morelli is."

"Yeah, but . . ."

"I'm gonna give Paul a call tomorrow and tell him what his wife told you."

"You can't be serious!"

"Hell yeah, I'm serious. Lydia Morelli's a drunk that's come unglued. I'm sorry about what happened to her daughter but it's affected her judgment. I mean, Jesus, Joe. None of this crap makes sense. Paul having people killed, molesting his stepdaughter. No, the woman's sick, poor thing, and her husband needs to know."

DeMarco realized something significant then. John Mahoney had never struck him as a man given to hero worship, particularly if the hero was a politician. Mahoney had been in politics forever and had seen his brethren commit every crime and perversion imaginable. But for some reason—and DeMarco could understand this because he too had initially been awed by Morelli—Mahoney had placed the senator on a pedestal. DeMarco had been half-joking when he told Emma that Mahoney considered Morelli the reincarnation of JFK, but now he was beginning to believe that this was really the case.

There could also be another reason why Mahoney was such a strong Morelli supporter: maybe Morelli had promised Mahoney the vice presidency, or a cushy ambassadorship to someplace like Ireland where he could attend parties and drink Guinness and play golf into his twilight years. Whatever the case, when it came to Paul Morelli, John Mahoney had a blind spot big enough to obscure an elephant.

Mahoney finished his drink and set the glass on the rail of the balcony—and the glass fell two stories into the bushes below. Mahoney didn't notice.

"I'm glad you came to me with this when you did," Mahoney said, and thumped DeMarco on the back. "You did the right thing. Now go home; I'll take care of it."

And with that pronouncement, Mahoney flipped his burning cigar into the same bush where his glass had landed. Then DeMarco watched as the Speaker arranged his face into its best devil-may-care Irish smile and plowed his way through the ballroom crowd, directly toward the Greek ambassador's buxom wife.

Chapter 21

Emma wore faded jeans, a down vest over a long-sleeved shirt, and to protect her knees, she had on pads, the sort skateboarders wear. On her head was a large-brimmed straw hat and on her hands were thick, cloth gloves. In her right hand was a machete.

When DeMarco had arrived at her home, she'd been on her knees in her backyard, tugging and hacking at some aggressive, quick-growing vine. The vine appeared to have tunneled beneath a neighbor's fence and was now strangling one of Emma's fragile plants. DeMarco knew that Emma employed gardeners—with the size of her yard, she needed professional help—but she was not above personally defending her territory when leafy predators invaded.

She stopped attacking the vine long enough to hear what Lydia Morelli had told DeMarco, and then listened in dismay to Mahoney's reaction to

Lydia's story. Now she stood, the machete hanging from her hand, glaring at DeMarco. The knee pads and vest, combined with the straw hat, made her look like some sort of bloodthirsty Asian warrior.

"Damn it all, Joe," she said. "Lydia tells you that her husband molested her child and instead of helping her, you tell Mahoney. Jesus! I just feel like, like . . ."

DeMarco thought for a moment—probably his imagination—that she was beginning to raise the machete.

"Emma," he said, "I work for Mahoney. He's my boss."

"What the hell does that have to do with anything?" she said.

DeMarco knew she was serious; he was convinced that Emma had never compromised a principle in her life.

"So why are you here?" she said. "Are you looking for advice? Asking for absolution? What?"

"No, I'm not asking for absolution, goddamnit," DeMarco said. She was starting to piss him off.

"Then what?"

"I don't know," DeMarco said. And he didn't. He didn't feel right about dropping the investigation but at the same time he couldn't really be sure that Lydia's accusations were true. The way she drank, the lack of evidence, her bitterness toward her husband . . . it was impossible to be certain.

And if she *was* telling the truth, she was holding things back, not telling him enough so that he could help her or protect himself. So maybe he wasn't looking for absolution as Emma had put it, but maybe he was looking for someone to say that it was just possible that Mahoney was right and that Lydia's story was the product of a disturbed and addicted mind.

He had obviously come to the wrong person.

"Aw, forget it. I'll see you later," he said.

She didn't answer. She turned her back to him, dropped to her knees, and began to hack again at the offending creeper.

DeMarco thought he could hear the vine scream as he walked away.

———◆———

"I tried to get to you last night," Garret Darcy said to his boss, "but you didn't answer your cell phone."

"I couldn't," the man said, sounding annoyed that the hired help would question his availability. "So why did you call?"

"Yesterday, after he met with Ladybird at the canal, he went back to the Capitol, to his office I guess."

"So?"

"Then he went to the Greek Embassy. That's why I tried to call you last night."

"The Greek Embassy?"

"Yeah," Darcy said. "There was some kinda party goin' on there. I could see guys in tuxes and gals in gowns goin' in and out, but De . . . but the guy from the cathedral, he wasn't dressed like he was there for the party. Anyway, he was at the embassy maybe fifteen minutes then he left."

"Hmm."

Hmm? What the fuck did *hmm* mean?

"Do you think he could be working for the Greeks?" Darcy said, meaning that maybe this DeMarco guy was some sort of mole in Congress. But that would be really weird. Probably the last time the Greeks had spied on anybody had been during the Trojan War.

"I doubt it," his boss said, and if anyone would know who was spying on whom, he would. "So is that it?"

"No," Darcy said. "This morning he went to see a woman in McLean."

"Who's the woman?"

Garret Darcy told him.

"Are you sure? Absolutely sure?"

"Yeah," Darcy said. "Do you know who she is?"

"Oh, yes. I do indeed."

Chapter 22

Frustrated by everything connected to Terry Finley and his damn list, DeMarco decided to go to a driving range and hit a bucket of balls. Hitting golf balls was just as therapeutic as hitting his punching bag, but much less sweaty. DeMarco knew the object of going to the range was to improve his game but sometimes he just liked to take a big ol' driver and smack the balls as hard as he could. Most of his shots sliced or hooked, but DeMarco had good upper body strength and every once in awhile he'd drive the ball straight, about two hundred and fifty yards, like he'd been momentarily possessed by Tiger Woods.

He had just flung his golf bag into the trunk of his car when his cell phone rang. Cell phones were a curse, an infinitely long chain tethering a man perpetually to his job. He looked at the caller ID display. It was Dick Finley calling. Shit. What the hell was he supposed to tell the guy?

"Hello, Mr. Finley," DeMarco said.

"They found Terry's laptop," Dick Finley said. "He'd left it at this bar, the same place where that napkin came from. You know, the napkin that had the names written on it."

"Sam and Harry's?" DeMarco said.

"Yeah. It's there now. The manager just called me. He said Terry forgot his computer there one night and a bartender put it in the back room where the employees change, but then the bartender goes on vacation without telling anybody about the computer. Anyway, the bartender gets back from vacation today, sees the laptop's still there, and he calls the *Post*. The *Post* told him to call me."

So Terry's laptop hadn't been stolen by some killer as Dick Finley had thought. The reporter had had too much to drink, forgot his computer, and the next day when he discovered it was missing, he filed a report with the police saying it had been stolen—just like the Louisa County sheriff had told Dick Finley. And maybe the sheriff was right about everything else associated with Terry's death, including the fact that it had been an accident.

"The reason I called," Finley said, "is I was wondering if you could pick up the computer and take a look at what's in it?"

Shit. "Sure, I can do that," DeMarco said.

"If there isn't anything there connected to Terry's death, just . . . I don't know, just give it to somebody."

"You sound pretty tired, Mr. Finley. Are you feeling okay?"

"Yeah. I'm just old. So have you learned anything yet?"

"No, sir," DeMarco said, and to keep Finley from asking more questions—and so he wouldn't have to tell the man more lies—he added, "But I'll get over to that bar right now and get the laptop."

———◆◆◆———

So instead of doing something healthy, like whacking golf balls, DeMarco went to Sam and Harry's. He liked the place. It was dark and cool and quiet— it looked the way bars were supposed to look—and the bartenders had a tendency to overpour, experience showing that bigger drinks produced happy drunks which in turn produced bigger tips.

DeMarco got a beer—he didn't feel like experimenting with another brand of cheap vodka—and retrieved Finley's laptop from the bartender on duty. He found a table near an electrical outlet and plugged in the power cord for the computer. There were hundreds of files on the laptop, some going back years, including one that looked like a novel that never got beyond the third chapter. Most of the files were rough drafts of stories Terry had written but some contained interview notes and background material on subjects that he'd researched. He found only one file related to Paul Morelli.

In the Morelli file were references to past articles on Reams, Bachaud, and Frey, the three men on Terry Finley's list, but nothing that pointed to Morelli being guilty of anything specific. There were also large blocks of text that appeared to have come from past stories written about Morelli. It appeared that Terry Finley had found the stories on Internet sites and copied them into his computer. Terry had also talked to a lot of people. Most of the people he had interviewed were people related to the incidents involving Reams, Bachaud, and Frey. For example, he'd talked to the cop who had found Reams in bed with the teenage boy and the motel manager of the place where the incident had occurred. But nothing in Finley's notes shed any new light on the events that had taken place all those years ago, and nothing pointed to some powerful man helping Paul Morelli commit crimes.

Janet Tyler and Marcia Davenport were both mentioned in the file. Finley had found that Marcia Davenport had done some decorating work on Morelli's home and that Janet Tyler had worked on a zoning study in New York, but that was it. It appeared that all Finley had managed to do was confirm that both women had a prior association with Morelli but there was nothing to indicate that Finley suspected

Morelli of assaulting the women. Lydia Morelli's name was not mentioned at all.

It occurred to DeMarco that Finley's laptop wasn't necessarily up to date. Most reporters wouldn't use a laptop for taking notes when they interviewed people. Finley probably recorded his raw notes in a notebook or a tape recorder then later transferred whatever he'd learned to his computer. But no notebook or tape recorder had been found on Terry's body or in his house, according to both Dick Finley and the police reports that DeMarco had seen. Finley's notebooks were probably in his office at the *Post*, DeMarco figured, and his bosses had most likely already looked through them.

DeMarco glanced at his watch. It was too late to go to the driving range. He noticed a very attractive brunette sitting at the bar by herself playing with her BlackBerry. He decided to go up to the bar and order another beer.

Chapter 23

"Why the hell would he put his clubs in the trunk then go to a bar?" Carl said.

Jimmy didn't bother to answer. He just sat there, staring at the entrance to Sam and Harry's, wishing this damn job was over, wishing Carl would just shut the fuck up.

They'd gotten rid of the Buick and were now driving a Ford Explorer. Carl was blowing his cigarette smoke out the window, having just endured another lecture from Jimmy on secondhand smoke. Carl had said that Jimmy was more likely to get cancer from the exhaust fumes of passing cars, but he rolled down the window and it was probably a good thing he did. Jimmy was in such a shitty mood today, the way everything had been going, that he would have put the butt out in Carl's ear if he hadn't.

Today they were parked on a corner where they couldn't get blocked in. If they had to, they could drive right up over the curb. It was good to have a four-wheel-drive SUV with big tires. No fuckin' way were they gonna lose this jamoke again.

"Will you look at this guy," Carl said.

"Huh? What guy?" Jimmy said.

"This guy comin' down the block."

Jimmy looked over to where Carl was pointing. There was a middle-aged man with a dog walking toward them. The dog was about the size of a squirrel and had a pink bow on its head. The man wore a pink shirt with epaulets on the shoulders—the color of the shirt matching the dog's bow—and his pants were so voluminous in the thighs that it almost looked as if he was wearing a skirt. On his feet were espadrilles and on his head was a small cap that looked like a little kid's baseball cap because it had such a short bill.

"And they wonder why they get beat up," Carl said.

Before Jimmy could tell Carl that he was an idiot, his cell phone vibrated and he jumped like he'd been goosed. Friggin' cell phones. He opened the phone and listened for a moment then closed it.

"That was Eddie," Jimmy said. "He said we can quit followin' this guy."

"Thank God," Carl said.

"But he's on his way down here. He wants us to pick him up at National."

"Why's he comin' here?" Carl said.

Jimmy shrugged. "Says he's got something else for us to do, but he didn't say what."

"I just hope he's not pissed at us, the way we fucked this up. I mean, Eddie's definitely a guy I don't want mad at me."

"You got that right," Jimmy said. "I heard when he was in prison he broke a guy over his knee."

"He what?"

"This guy, he did something, and Eddie picks him up—grabs him by the balls and the throat with those fuckin' hands of his—and he snaps the guy over his knee like a *stick*. Broke his back."

"Jesus," Carl said.

"But he's not pissed, at least he didn't sound like it. He just said he had something else he wanted us to do. Maybe he wants us to clip this DeMarco asshole instead of just followin' him. Whatever. Anyway, quit worryin' and let's go get something to eat."

"Sure. Where you wanna go?"

"There's a place over in Arlington, on Wilson Boulevard. A place called Mario's. They make the best Philly cheesesteak you ever tasted."

"Yeah, that sounds good," Carl said. "Can you get a beer there?"

"No, it's more like a drive-in."

"Well, shit. Don't you know a place where you can get a cheesesteak *and* a beer?

Chapter 24

———◆———

Emma was sitting in her living room, staring at the burning logs in her fireplace. She'd just had a fight with Christine over something absurdly trivial, and Christine was at the other end of the house, avoiding her. She knew she should go apologize, and later she would, but not now. Now she just wanted to stare into a fire that was overheating the room.

DeMarco was the reason she'd had the fight with Christine. The fight hadn't been about DeMarco but he was the one who had put her in such a rotten mood. Emma was convinced that Lydia Morelli was telling the truth and that DeMarco and his devious boss were turning their backs on the poor woman. Maybe *she* should call Lydia and . . .

The doorbell rang. Emma wondered if Christine had called up a friend to go out with. Or maybe it was DeMarco coming back to annoy her further. She got up, reluctantly, and walked to the door.

Emma had never been introduced to the man standing on her porch but she knew who he was. His name was Charlie Eklund. He worked for the CIA. Standing behind Eklund was another man, a blocky, muscular man, who was scanning Emma's neighborhood with hard, watchful eyes. It appeared that Eklund had a bodyguard, and she immediately wondered why he would need one.

Charlie Eklund was in his seventies. He was small and slender, about five-seven. He was wearing a blue suit with a red sweater-vest, the vest making him look both old-fashioned and avuncular. He had carefully combed white hair and an unremarkable face, no feature being in any way particularly distinctive. The expression on his face was pleasant, and seemed as if it might be perpetually so, as if he was just too much above the fray to allow anything to disturb his good humor.

Emma had no idea what Eklund did for the Central Intelligence Agency. All she knew was that he'd been at Langley forever, and that his job title changed frequently. And the titles he had always contained phrases that made it sound as if he had power but not too much power, titles such as Assistant Deputy Director for something or other. But you could never tell by his title exactly what he did or what he was responsible for or who he reported to or who reported to him. All that was known was that he attended the important meetings—meaning those meetings that had to do with budget and manpower and the CIA's span of control.

Throughout his long career, Eklund had always stayed in the background and his fingerprints had never been found on anything. He had never been mentioned in the press or called before Congress to explain his part in some botched CIA venture, to explain why something had gone so horribly, awfully, publicly awry. CIA directors came and went; senior staffers were fired and replaced and retired; but Charlie . . . Charlie was always there.

"I thought we should have a little talk," he said to Emma.

Emma didn't answer.

"May I come in, please?"

Emma didn't answer.

"Very well," Eklund said, the pleasant expression still on his face, his eyes now twinkling, maybe with amusement but possibly with malice. Charlie Eklund's eyes made it hard to tell.

"What is the DIA's interest in Senator Morelli?" Eklund said.

"I don't work for the DIA," Emma said. "I'm retired."

"You're retired," Eklund said, "but sometimes you help them out, like you did in Iran a couple of years ago."

Emma wondered how he knew about Iran but didn't ask. Instead she said, "Why do you have people following Joe DeMarco?"

"Peterson told you the truth," Eklund said.

Peterson was "Marv," the man Emma had spoken to at the CIA about James Suttel and Carl van Horn.

"Or I should say that Peterson was *dumb* enough to tell you the truth," Eklund said. "Fortunately for him, he was smart enough to tell me that he had talked to you—but I'm still thinking of sending him to one of the Stans for his wagging tongue."

Eklund meant somewhere like Afghanistan, Uzbekistan, or Turkistan.

"So you're saying that Suttel and van Horn are not working for you," Emma said.

"Yes. I just *did*. It's as Peterson told you: they worked for us occasionally in the past but. . . . You've heard the old expression about not using a sledgehammer when all you're trying to do is drive a nail? The duo of Suttel and van Horn are a sledgehammer. They have an admirable flair for violence but they lack the finesse required for most operations, so we no longer engage them."

Eklund appeared to be telling the truth—but Emma knew that meant nothing.

"Now do you think we could possibly have this discussion sitting down?" Eklund said. "I have problems with the veins in my legs. Standing for long periods can be rather painful."

"So sit on the sidewalk," Emma said. "I don't like you coming to my home. I don't want you in my home. Why are you here?"

"I told you. I want to know what your interest is in Senator Morelli."

Emma said nothing.

"And why has your associate, Mr. DeMarco, been meeting with the senator's wife?"

Now *that* told Emma something. Suttel and van Horn had not followed Joe to his meetings with Lydia, which meant that someone else had, someone working for Charlie Eklund.

"I don't know what you're up to, Eklund but—"

"Call me Charlie. Please."

"—but if you start interfering with my life, or Joe DeMarco's, I will go to the media just as I told Peterson and tell them what happened in the Philippines."

"I don't care," Eklund said, making a dismissive gesture with one small hand. "Go to the media. *Run* to the media. That incident's ancient history and the principals involved no longer work at the agency. And the man who was director at the time . . . What was his name? It'll come to me in a minute. They come and go so often it's hard to keep track, but whoever he was, he's dead. I mean the story would embarrass us, of course, but we'd just say it happened before we reformed ourselves. Don't you know? We're the new, reformed CIA."

"Are you protecting the senator in some way?" Emma said.

"Protecting him?" Eklund said. "Now that is amusing." Eklund paused momentarily before adding, "And rather interesting that you'd suggest such a thing."

Emma wondered if she had now inadvertently given something away. You had to be very careful when sparring with Charlie Eklund.

Eklund stared at Emma for a moment. She stared back. "I can see we're not going to reach an accommodation this evening," he said. "I guess I should have come better prepared to this meeting."

Meaning he should have come with something to force Emma to cooperate.

"No we're not and yes you should have," Emma said. And she closed the door in Charlie Eklund's face.

Chapter 25

Blake Hanover was dying of lung cancer.

Hanover's apartment was in a decaying brown-stone in a low-rent part of the District. He had re-tired from the CIA as a GS-15, but Emma suspected that his three divorces had reduced his income to such a degree that he was barely able to afford the shabby one-bedroom unit in which he lived. He sat in a stained Barcalounger wearing a brown bathrobe, yellow pajamas, and brown slippers. A clear tube coming from a small green tank pumped oxygen into his nose. He was hairless from chemotherapy; his complexion was waxy and sallow; and his bald head was speckled with large, ugly liver spots. In his right hand he held a handkerchief and he would periodi-cally cough into it. The handkerchief was spotted brown with dried blood.

When Emma met Blake Hanover twenty years

ago he'd been a burly, blond-haired, chain-smoking spy. A cynical, jaded spy. He'd been the agent in charge of a joint CIA-DIA operation, and the operation, because of Hanover's ruthless tactics, had needlessly destroyed the life of a young Chinese female spy. Emma despised Hanover and she imagined the feeling was mutual. She would never have come to him for help except that she knew he'd been treated poorly by his old outfit.

Five years ago, at a time Hanover had expected to be retired with honors, feted with speeches and gold watches and plaques, the CIA had needed a scapegoat for an operation that had gone badly off-course. Hanover was the chosen goat. Emma doubted that he had been a particularly loyal employee to begin with, but after what had happened to him, she imagined all his feelings toward his old employer would be bitter and bad. Plus he was dying—something she had not known before she came to see him—and thus he might be even more inclined to tell the truth. Encroaching death often has that side effect.

"So why do you want to know about Charlie boy?" Hanover said.

"We've crossed paths," Emma said. "Or maybe I should say we've crossed swords."

"Ooh, too bad for you," Hanover said, and he laughed, and then the laugh turned into a series of coughs, and with each explosive hack his wasted body rose slightly off the chair.

"What did you do to piss Charlie off?" Hanover asked when he could breathe again.

"Does it matter?"

Hanover thought about that. "No, I suppose not. What do you want to know?"

"I want to know what he does at Langley."

Hanover's parched lips twitched in amusement. "I guess you could say he's an accountant. And a rainmaker."

"An accountant?"

"Yeah. Charlie hides the money. He's been hiding the money for years and he's very good at it and that's probably why he's been there so long."

Emma knew what Hanover meant. Congress gave the CIA millions of dollars each year and much of that money was earmarked for specific things. What Eklund apparently did was divert the money to wherever the CIA desired to spend it. For example, say Congress gave the agency several million to hire and train Arabic-language interpreters but the CIA preferred to spend the money tracking down nuclear stockpiles in Russia. The CIA had a tendency to do this, to decide that they knew better than anyone what their priorities should be. It was apparently Charlie's task to cook the books, to show how the Company had spent the dough trying to recruit Arabic speakers, yet alas, in spite of their diligence, they'd only been able to hire a score of translators with all the money they'd been given.

"And when Congress doesn't give us enough to do everything we want," Hanover said, "Charlie's good at finding other sources."

Like stealing drugs and trading them for hand-held surface-to-air missiles as they had done for that operation in the Philippines, Emma thought.

"But he's involved in all kinds of things," Hanover said. "He pokes his nose into ongoing ops, helps plan future ops, analyzes the intel we get. He's like a damn spider. Most times he just sits there, watching what's going on, but every once in awhile he'll crawl out on his web and *eat* something."

"I don't understand," Emma said.

"Now there's a first," Hanover said, but before Emma could say anything, he added, "What I mean is, don't let Charlie's twinkly-eyed ol' grandpa act fool you. If you've pissed him off, he just might eat you next."

"Can you think of a reason why he would be interested in a particular senator?"

"Which senator?

"It doesn't matter. Let's just say that he's showing an abnormal interest in a certain senator. Why would he do that?"

Hanover shrugged. "I can think of a number of reasons. The senator could be bitching about something we did . . ."

It was interesting, Emma thought: the man was retired and he'd been treated badly before he retired, but he kept saying "we" as if he was still working for the agency. Maybe he was more loyal than she thought.

". . . or he could be messing with the Company's budget—now that would really get Charlie's goat—or maybe he works on the Senate Intelligence Committee and he's asking the wrong questions." Hanover paused. "You know, Charlie's so old that he actually knew Allen Dulles. All this crap going on now after 9-11, setting up this intelligence czar to run the show, playing mother-may-I with Congress every time we wanna take a shit, forcing us to play with every pissant cop shop in town—that kind of stuff would bother Charlie a lot. And if this senator is twisting the Company's tail . . . Well, Charlie wants it the way it was in the old days, when nobody knew what the hell we did."

Emma knew Judy Powell in the most mundane way: they had been neighbors for more than a dozen years.

"Administrative assistant" usually meant a woman was a mere secretary but the title made her role sound more important than it really was, as well as less sexist than it really was. In Judy Powell's case, however, the term "administrative assistant" was dead-on accurate. She had worked for some of the most important people in Washington for over thirty years, and because she was so talented, what she did went far beyond answering phones and making travel arrangements for her boss. She currently worked for Senator Michael Sandoval, chairman of the U.S. Senate Select Committee on Intelligence.

Emma knocked on Judy's door.

"Emma!" Judy said, delighted to see her. Judy liked Emma for the same reason Emma liked Judy: they were both extremely bright, capable people. Judy was a large woman and comfortable with her size. She liked who she was. She dressed well, her hair was carefully styled to suit her round face, and her makeup was always perfectly applied. Her husband worked at the National Archives but Emma had no idea what he did and doubted that she ever would. Henry Powell spoke less than any man Emma had ever known.

Emma had been at Judy's home one time discussing the gardening service they both employed. Service had gone downhill, and she and Judy were discussing the situation, trying to decide if they should find another outfit or just beat on the current one to make it shape up. Judy had asked her husband his opinion. He'd lowered his newspaper, made a little beats-me gesture with his face, then resumed his reading. Judy had said, "Well, thank you so much for contributing, Henry." To Emma she'd said, "Henry almost said a complete sentence to me two weeks ago. I asked him, 'Henry, are you still passionately, madly in love with me?' You know what he said? He said, 'Yep.'"

Emma had suspected at the time that Henry was indeed still passionately, madly in love with his wife.

After they settled into Judy's kitchen, Emma said, "I have a favor to ask. A big one."

"Okay," Judy said.

"What is Senator Morelli's position on the CIA?"

Emma needed to understand why Eklund was interested in Morelli but subjects discussed in Senate Intelligence Committee meetings were often classified, and thus Emma couldn't simply get a copy of the Congressional Record to find out what Morelli might have done to annoy folks at Langley. But as Judy attended many of these meetings with her boss, she would know. Asking Judy to tell Emma what was said in those meetings, however, was something she shouldn't do—and both women knew this.

Before Judy could say anything, Emma said, "I don't want specifics, Judy. Nothing classified. And I wouldn't be asking if it wasn't important."

"I already knew that," Judy said. Judy was very bright. She took a breath and said, "On the committee, there are essentially two types of senators. The first type is the if-I-don't-know-it-can't-hurt-me type. They don't *wanna* know what the CIA is gonna do. This way if the agency screws up they can't be held responsible, but after the fact, they can call in the director and beat him up on C-Span. The other group wants to know exactly what the spies are doing and they're willing to be responsible if things go wrong. Senator Morelli falls into the second camp. He wants Langley on a very, very short leash. He wants them conducting absolutely no operations that haven't been cleared in advance by the committee. The CIA naturally finds his position rather restrictive, and considering the number of operations they conduct, impractical. They've made lots of noise about how their ability to respond quickly to emergent issues in the field would be jeopardized by such a requirement. Senator Morelli also wants to know exactly where they're spending their budget. The CIA has a tendency to spend a lot of money on things they claim they can't talk about, which means that no one really knows what happens to all the dough they get. Senator Morelli's favorite word when it comes to Langley is 'transparency.' He wants the agency, its operations and its budget, clear for all on the committee to see."

"Has a man named Charlie Eklund been in some of these meetings where Senator Morelli has expressed this opinion?"

Judy's smart eyes glowed. "Oh, yeah. Little Charlie just sits there in the back row, always a smile on his sly, white face."

"What'll happen if Morelli becomes president?"

"Who knows?" Judy said. "The relationship between a president and the CIA is a whole lot different than the relationship between a senator and the

CIA. My guess is, though, that Senator Morelli means what he says. He's going to have the DCI seated at a little desk right outside the Oval Office so he can keep an eye on the guy."

———◆◆◆———

Emma walked slowly back to her home but she didn't enter the house right away. Instead she took a slow tour of her yard, examining the grass and the trees and various thriving shrubs. She made sure that the wicked vine she had dismembered the other day hadn't begun a counterattack.

If Judy was correct, Paul Morelli was not a friend of the CIA. And if Blake Hanover was correct, Charlie Eklund would be no friend of Morelli's. The problem was that Morelli and Eklund were both capable of making it appear that they felt one way about an issue when in fact they felt just the opposite.

After fifteen minutes, Emma concluded that it was impossible for her to know what Eklund was up to. All she knew for sure was that this thing with Terry Finley and Paul Morelli had gone to a whole new level.

She opened the back door to her home and smelled something wonderful cooking in the kitchen. It appeared Christine was no longer mad at her. At least one thing was right in her world.

Chapter 26

———◆◆◆———

Two days after DeMarco met Mahoney at the Greek Embassy, the *Washington Post* reported that Lydia Morelli had been admitted to Father Martin's, an upscale alcohol rehabilitation facility in Havre de Grace, Maryland.

The fact that the senator's office had informed the media of Lydia's situation wasn't in any way remarkable. After Betty Ford had set the precedent, it had become quite common for the rich and famous to call a press conference whenever it was time to pry the monkey off their backs. The other reason for telling the media was the pragmatic, political one: they'd find out eventually, so why not get credit for being open and honest.

But in the case of Lydia Morelli, DeMarco knew there was another reason for releasing the story: if you were Paul Morelli, and you found out from a

little bird—or in this case a big, white-haired bird—
that your wife was thinking of going to the press
and telling ugly tales of murder and molestation,
you might like it firmly established that she's a
mentally unhinged alcoholic who's not to be taken
seriously.

DeMarco didn't know if Lydia had admitted herself to Father Martin's or if she had been committed
by her husband—but he did know he was not going
to dwell on the situation any longer. After his last
meeting with Mahoney, DeMarco had concluded
that whatever Paul Morelli may have done, his actions
belonged in that same hopper with world hunger,
global warming, and all those other problems too big
for him to solve. And to hell with Emma.

And at just that moment, as if she'd been peeking
in through a window into his skull, DeMarco's cell
phone rang and the caller ID said it was Emma. He
didn't want to talk to her, but he answered anyway.

"Hi," he said.

"Did you see the *Post* this morning?"

"Yeah, but—"

"No, I don't mean the article on Lydia. Look on
page three of the local section. Where are you?"

"My office," DeMarco said.

"Meet me at the Library of Congress in half an
hour," Emma said and hung up. If her voice had
been any colder, the phone would have frozen to
DeMarco's ear.

DeMarco pulled the *Washington Post* out of his trash can and flipped to the local news. The article was halfway down the page, a single paragraph. It said the bodies of two men had been found in a car in southeast D.C. The men had been shot in the back of the head, two bullets each. The paper called the execution "gangland style," whatever that meant. The men were identified as Tim Reed and Jerry Fallon, the false names used by Carl van Horn and James Suttel. The article noted that the area in which the men had been found was known for its drug activity, the implication being that van Horn and Suttel had been there trying to score or deal dope and someone had killed them.

The Thomas Jefferson Building of the Library of Congress is across the street from the Capitol, a two-minute walk from DeMarco's office. The Library of Congress bears no resemblance to your typical, municipal book-lender. There are three-ton doors made from gleaming bronze, vaulted ceilings, and marble floors. The nation's premier book depository bears a closer resemblance to a cathedral or a pagan temple than it does to the library down the block.

DeMarco found Emma standing beneath four large paintings by an artist with the odd name of Elihu Vedder. Mr. Vedder's paintings depicted, according to a brochure that DeMarco had once read, "the effects of good and bad government," two of those negative effects being "Anarchy" and "Corrupt Legislation." DeMarco had always thought there wasn't enough wall space in *any* building to depict all the effects of bad government.

"Why'd you want to meet here?" DeMarco said.

"Because it's close to your office. Somebody was following me this morning. I lost him, but if somebody's following you, I was hoping to spot him when he came in here looking for you."

"Somebody's following us?"

"Yeah," Emma said. She paused before she added, "The CIA is involved in all this and they may be following both of us."

"I thought you said van Horn and Suttel weren't working for the CIA. And who in the hell killed—"

"I know what I said, but things have changed." Emma then told DeMarco about Charlie Eklund's visit.

When she said that Eklund knew that DeMarco had met with Lydia Morelli, DeMarco said, "But Suttel and van Horn didn't follow me to those meetings."

"I know that," Emma said. "Which means somebody else did, and they reported back to Eklund."

"So what the hell's going on?"

"Before we get to that, let me tell you something else I learned," Emma said, and she told DeMarco about her conversation with Judy Powell, explaining how Paul Morelli appeared not to be the CIA's number-one fan. "So here's what could be going on," Emma said.

There were two possible scenarios, according to Emma. In scenario one, the CIA—or Charlie Eklund personally—was worried about what Paul Morelli might do to the CIA after he became president. So Eklund had assigned people to watch Morelli, hoping the senator might do something stupid—have an affair, hire a hooker, meet with the wrong people—and when Morelli became president, Eklund would walk into the Oval Office, plop his photographs onto Morelli's new desk, and say, "Play ball."

Scenario two: Eklund had really been helping Paul Morelli his whole career and Morelli's public attitude toward the CIA was just a head-fake. In this case, when he became president he'd let the CIA do whatever their dark, small hearts desired, and in turn, Charlie Eklund would continue to solve all of President Morelli's problems that couldn't be solved by more conventional means. In scenario two, maybe the CIA had been watching Lydia because her husband was afraid she might tell the media all the things she knew about him.

In both of Emma's scenarios, Suttel and van Horn worked for Eklund, which meant Emma's pal Marv Peterson and Charlie Eklund had both lied to her.

"But why would they kill these two guys?" DeMarco said.

"It's a rather big deal, Joe, the CIA spying on a senator—or spying *for* a senator. Eklund could have had them killed because we identified them and he was afraid they'd talk."

DeMarco sat there a moment trying to digest all this.

"Lydia was positive the man helping her husband didn't work for the CIA," DeMarco said. "She knows him personally."

Emma shrugged. "I don't think it would be all that hard for people as bright as Paul Morelli and Charlie Eklund to fool Lydia."

"Maybe not," DeMarco said, "but I think there's a third scenario. I think it's possible that Suttel and van Horn were working for someone *other* than Eklund, but Eklund is watching Morelli for the reason you said, hoping Morelli would do something the CIA could later hold over the senator's head."

Emma nodded. "You're right. That's possible too. But then why were Suttel and van Horn killed?"

"Because after you identified them, their boss, whoever he is, decided they were a liability."

"But if their boss wasn't Eklund, how would their boss know?" Emma said. "The only people who knew I had identified van Horn and Suttel were Marv Peterson and Charlie Eklund of the CIA. And you, of course."

"No, one other person knew," DeMarco said. "Mahoney. He knew because I told him I was being tailed by these ex-CIA goons. So it's possible that Mahoney told Morelli, and whoever Morelli talked to decided to take them off the board."

DeMarco looked up at the Elihu Vedder painting titled "Anarchy." The central figure in the painting was a mad, nude Medusa standing on the ruins of what appeared to be a government building. She held a torch in her hand as if she was about to set the city—presumably Washington—on fire. Maybe not a bad idea, he thought.

"This is just a fucking mess," he said. "We have Lydia saying her husband's Satan incarnate. We have this Eklund guy, who may or may not be Paul Morelli's pal. We have two dead thugs, and we don't know who they were working for or who killed them or why. And we have Lydia Morelli in a dry-out clinic because she's either a delusional drunk who needs help or because her husband locked her up to keep her from talking to the press. Oh, and we have one other thing: I have a boss who thinks Paul Morelli walks on water."

DeMarco stood up.

"Where are you going?" Emma said.

"Boston. Mahoney's sending me up there."

"Why?" Emma said.

"Just a little job involving one of his staff. No big thing. But Mahoney could be trying to get my mind off Morelli. I don't know. What I do know is that I work for the guy and I'm going. So you can sit there and get pissed at me, but this whole thing is *way* over my pay grade. I'm in no position to take on a United States senator, the Speaker of the House, and some scheming little prick at the CIA. The only thing I was asked to do was find out if there was anything funny about Terry Finley's death."

"Which there was," Emma said.

DeMarco didn't know what to say to that. So he left.

Chapter 27

Mahoney maintained a small staff in Boston and the lady who ran his Boston office—a stout, sixty-something, gray-haired woman with an impressive bosom—had been with Mahoney for years. Her name was Maggie Dolan and DeMarco was convinced that she had a multiple personality disorder. One minute she would be the soul of sweet compassion, hugging a grandmother who'd lost her Social Security check, and a minute later she would be cursing like a blue-water sailor at some idiot who wasn't marching to the beat of Mahoney's drum.

Maggie had called Mahoney to report a problem. The Speaker had forced her to hire a Harvard kid to work for her part-time, the kid's dad being a guy with big bucks and lots of influence. Maggie said that last week the kid had started acting screwy: showing up late for work, leaving early, looking as if he hadn't slept or eaten in days. He was a basket case, Maggie said. She had talked to the kid but he wouldn't tell her what was bugging him.

One of Maggie's personalities wanted to fire the Harvard boy's useless, pampered ass but she knew that might cause Mahoney a problem with the kid's rich daddy. Maggie Number Two said she was really worried about the poor child, afraid he might be planning to slash his wrists, and she couldn't bear to have that on her conscience. She'd told Mahoney she wanted to borrow DeMarco to find out what was going on, so Mahoney had loaned him to her.

DeMarco followed the Harvard kid for half a day and watched him walk around, head down, literally talking to himself, looking as if his dog, his cat, and his parakeet had all perished in the same fire. About every five minutes the kid would pull out his cell phone and call somebody who apparently never answered. This prompted DeMarco to call a lady named Alice, a gambling addict that he had on retainer. Alice worked for a phone company. Alice discovered that the Harvard kid called two phone numbers with almost equal frequency, sometimes as many as ten times a day. One of the numbers belonged to a woman named Patrice Hamilton and her residence was a dormitory at Harvard. The other number was for the Harvard bookstore.

DeMarco crossed Harvard's famous campus to reach the bookstore, periodically checking over his shoulder to see if anyone was following him. If anyone was, he couldn't see them. As he walked he also examined the kids who attended Harvard. He figured they had to be fairly bright to have been admitted to the place, but they all looked pretty ordinary to him, especially the boys. The majority of the boys wore wrinkled clothes, and judging by their hair, appeared as if they'd just gotten out of bed. Those who weren't hungover were running because they were late getting to wherever they were supposed to be. The girls were neater, more mature, more focused, seeming as if they were actually attending college to learn instead of drink.

DeMarco entered the bookstore and asked a saleswoman if Patrice Hamilton worked there. Yes, she did. DeMarco then asked if Patrice was there at that moment and was informed that she was, at the back of the store, restocking a shelf. He wandered to the back of the store and saw a stunning young woman putting barcode labels on books. She was tall and slim and had the face of a cover girl. She was also black.

DeMarco watched Patrice for a couple of minutes while pretending to look at a rack of sweatshirts, and while doing so, had one of those rare moments of inspiration, as if he'd just gotten a telegram from

God. He walked outside the store, called his friend Alice at the phone company again, and asked her to see if Patrice Hamilton had called people belonging to certain related professions. Yes she had, Alice said.

The lovely Patrice had called an ob-gyn twice and Planned Parenthood once.

DeMarco reported back to Maggie Dolan. "The kid's girlfriend is pregnant," DeMarco said. "And she's black."

DeMarco, cynic that he'd become, cynic that Mahoney had made him, figured the kid was pulling out his hair because the girl refused to get an abortion and he was going to have to tell his Beacon Hill parents that they were about to become the grandparents of a child of color. DeMarco realized there were other possibilities, other scenarios that put the Harvard rich kid in a better light, but he didn't care. Now that Maggie Dolan knew the basic problem, one or more of her personalities would help the boy resolve it.

DeMarco arrived home that night feeling about as low as he'd felt in a long time. He thought about calling Elle in Iowa to congratulate her on her upcoming marriage, but he knew that was a bad idea. He really wanted to tell her how he wished that things had worked out differently between them—and she'd most likely say that if he really felt that way, he should have done something about it. No, calling her wouldn't make him feel any better and would just make Elle feel bad too. She didn't deserve that. She deserved to marry her fireman.

So instead of picking up the phone he picked up a bottle of vodka, one made in Hungary, and tried not to think about anything at all. Not Elle, and not Paul and Lydia Morelli either. He found out that the more vodka he drank the more he thought about all the things he didn't want to think about, so he finally just went to bed.

Chapter 28

The next morning, DeMarco stepped out of his house wearing nothing but sweatpants and a T-shirt. It was a bright, crisp, gorgeous autumn morn. It was not possible to be depressed on a day like this, he told himself. He stood for a moment on his porch, feeling the sun on his face, and exercised a homeowner's prerogative to scratch his belly while surveying his small domain. Spotting his newspaper lying ten feet from the door, he tiptoed through the damp grass in his bare feet and retrieved it. He slipped the rubber band off the paper and flipped it open to the front page.

The headline screamed: SENATOR MORELLI SHOT, WIFE KILLED.

DeMarco's brain spat out the news of Lydia's death. It couldn't instantly reconcile that a week earlier she had been living, breathing, angry—clutching his forearm with her thin fingers, begging him to help her—and was now forever silent, beyond all help.

He sat down in shock on the top step of his porch to read the paper. The lead article said that a man had broken into the senator's Georgetown home and had shot Lydia once in the head as she lay sleeping next to her husband. The shot woke the senator. The man then shot Paul Morelli in the left shoulder but the senator was able to wrestle the gun away from the intruder and kill him. The policemen who responded to Morelli's 911 call said that when they arrived at the scene, they found the senator unconscious, holding the phone in his hand. Morelli was currently at Georgetown University Hospital in stable condition. His doctor said there was a possibility he might end up with some permanent damage to his left arm, though so far the prognosis looked good.

Lydia Morelli's killer was an eighteen-year-old African American named Isaiah Perry who had a juvenile record for armed robbery. Juvenile records were supposed to be sealed, but the *Washington Post* had more willing sources than the CIA. Before his death Perry had been a part-time janitor at the Senate Office Buildings and it was likely that Paul Morelli had met his wife's killer. The police suspected Perry was in the process of robbing the Morelli home when the shootings occurred, but they were still investigating.

Other articles in the paper discussed Morelli's phenomenal career, the near certainty of his being the Democratic Party's next candidate for president, and his stepdaughter's tragic death. The brief biography of Lydia Morelli provided more information about her father than about the woman herself. It noted that the week she was murdered, Lydia had been staying at Father Martin's for treatment and that she had left the clinic for the night to attend a function with the senator.

Still reeling from the news, DeMarco went inside his house to see if there was any coverage of the incident on television. Before he could turn on the set, the phone in his den rang. The caller ID said it was Emma. He didn't want to talk to her, to have her make him feel worse than he already felt, so he didn't answer the phone and Emma didn't bother to leave a message. He started toward the television set a second time but again the phone rang. Goddamnit, she was persistent. This time he picked up the phone and said hello. A gruff voice said, "Get over to my office."

<hr />

Maybe because it was the weekend Mahoney wasn't dressed in a suit. He was wearing khaki pants, a gray sweatshirt, and penny loafers with baggy white socks. A Red Sox baseball cap sat atop his big, white-haired head. He looked like a guy you might see sitting in a Back Bay bar drinking boilermakers at nine in the morning. But he wasn't that guy.

"Check out what happened to Lydia Morelli," he said without preamble.

"What do you mean?" DeMarco asked.

"What do I gotta do, start drawin' you road maps now? Find out what the hell happened, anything not reported in the papers."

"Do you think Morelli—"

"I don't think nothin'. Just do what I tell you. Make sure everything's on the up and up."

DcMarco looked into Mahoney's bloodshot blue eyes. He couldn't believe it. Mahoney had called Morelli to tell him about his wife and now Mahoney's *conscience* was bothering him. DeMarco had always suspected that if John Mahoney had any conscience at all, it had to be the size of a quark—one of those invisible particles a zillion times smaller than an atom, so small physicists had to divine their presence.

"Well what are you waitin' for? Get goin'," Mahoney said.

DeMarco rose to leave, stunned by the implications of what Mahoney was surely thinking. As he was leaving, Mahoney said, "Joe."

DeMarco stopped and turned back to face his boss. Mahoney's eyes lacked their normal twinkle, the one that said life was but a game.

"You pull out all the stops on this thing. I gotta know."

This was as close as Mahoney would ever come to saying that he might have screwed up.

◆◆◆

DeMarco felt a sudden desire for a drink—and for altitude. He drove to the Marriott Hotel on the Virginia side of the Key Bridge. The hotel had a restaurant on the top floor that provided a panoramic view of the District. One of the things DeMarco disliked about Washington was that there are no towering vistas, no mountain bluffs, no lofty lookouts, where a man can sit and view his environment and reflect on his place in it. One needs height to enhance perspective, and right now he desperately needed perspective.

He took a table near a window and ordered a bloody mary from a waitress who moved like a zombie on Prozac. When the drink arrived, he had a sudden overwhelming urge for a cigarette. He gave in to the urge, went to the hotel gift shop, and bought a pack of smokes that claimed to have less tar than a dewdrop. He had stopped smoking after he started dating Elle. She wasn't a smoker, and after their third date, she began giving him the usual sermons the righteous reserve for the less righteous. Quitting smoking for a woman was, in his opinion, the most romantic thing a man could do. But now he had no woman, so he could be as foul-smelling and unhealthy as he wanted to be.

As he smoked his cigarette—it tasted like shit—
he gazed out on a landscape famous for conspiracy
and deceit. The discriminating suites of the Watergate
were in plain sight across the river. As far as DeMarco
was concerned, the Watergate complex was a national
monument, as significant as the Lincoln Memorial,
because it was a permanent reminder to the gullible
that corruption could reach the upper tier. Due south
of the Watergate, across the Potomac, was the Pentagon. He grimly recalled those days when the generals
juggled the body count to keep the game from being
called on account of darkness. And then there was the
Capitol's shimmering white dome. The list of villains
who had hung their hats beneath that structure was
too long to recall at a single sitting.

The whole damn town disgusted him.

He was angry. He was angry at himself because
he hadn't helped Lydia. He was angry at Mahoney
for initially refusing to accept the possibility that
Paul Morelli might be anything less than perfect.
And, of course, he was angry at Paul Morelli because he knew in his heart, if not his head, that at
least some of what Lydia had said about him had
to be true.

But it was Lydia Morelli who made him the an-
griest. She had burdened him with her allegations
against her husband but had been so evasive that he
couldn't be positive about anything she had said. He
had been ready to let her disappear into the back

passages of his mind, ready to convince himself that everything she had told him was nothing but rum-soaked fantasy, and then she had to go and get herself killed—leaving DeMarco lugging a stinking carcass of guilt like the Ancient Mariner and his damn bird.

Why didn't she just go to the press as she had threatened? Probably because it was just that—an empty threat—something she ranted about when she drank, then lost her resolve the next day when greeted by daylight and her perpetual hangover. Or maybe she didn't go because her husband, after a helpful phone call from Mahoney, imprisoned her at Father Martin's clinic before she could.

And so now she was dead. Conveniently dead. And because of Mahoney's once-in-a-millennium attack by his microscopic conscience, DeMarco now had orders to go mucking about in something way too big for him to handle. Shit. Shit on 'em all.

Too impatient to wait for the slow-moving wait-ress to reappear, DeMarco walked up to the bar to order another drink. The television over the bar caught his eye: the screen was solid blue with a white banner warning that a special news bulletin was imminent. A reporter appeared next, dressed in his man-in-the-street look in a belted trench coat, and he announced in grave tones that he was speaking live from Georgetown University Hospital.

The bartender stopped wiping glasses and walked over and joined DeMarco as he gazed up at the set. The reporter informed them that Senator Morelli, who had been admitted to the hospital only ten hours earlier, was being released momentarily, alive and well. The bullet had passed through his left shoulder without causing significant damage. He'd been given three pints of blood, a few bandages, and was being released at his own insistence. The reporter rehashed the circumstances of Morelli's injury and his wife's death, and before he had to start repeating himself, the senator exited the hospital.

Serious-looking guys in suits, Secret Service agents or plainclothed U.S. Capitol cops, surrounded Morelli as he slowly made his way through a crowd of reporters and hospital personnel blocking the entrance. Judging by the number of white coats in the vicinity, it appeared the entire hospital staff was there to wish the senator Godspeed. Abe Burrows was at Morelli's side making irritated get-away gestures at the reporters.

Morelli motioned for his bodyguards to give him some room so he could address the media. He had a black sling on his left arm and bandages covered his shoulder. He was wearing a white sleeveless T-shirt that showed off his lean physique. A borrowed jacket was draped over his shoulders. He looked tired, his face somewhat gaunt, as would be expected of a person who had recently lost a lot of blood. Yet even haggard and unshaven, he was still handsome, still photogenic, still marvelously appealing. A good part of the population—the female part—realized that they were looking at a man who was not only rich, handsome, and powerful, but also now single.

In his remarks to the press, Morelli stated that his beloved wife's death was just one more heartbreaking reminder of America's failure to deal with drugs, poverty, and gun control. As grief-stricken as he was, he had to put aside his personal tragedy and focus, with more vigor than ever, on legislation that would keep others from experiencing the loss he was now feeling—the loss he would always feel.

And he was so good that for a moment even DeMarco believed him.

Chapter 29

Detective Lieutenant David Drummond was in his mid-fifties. He had a broad chest, heavy shoulders, and Popeye forearms. His white hair was thick and crew-cut—a drill sergeant's bouffant. His hands looked as if they'd been used to drive concrete pilings, the knuckles misshapen and knobby, and his nose appeared to have stopped several heavy objects moving at full speed. DeMarco looked around the office for a trophy celebrating Drummond as the one-time heavyweight champ of some D.C. precinct, but didn't see one. Maybe the cop was just clumsy, but that wasn't a theory he was eager to test.

Drummond's office contained a battered gray metal desk and two wooden chairs. The windows were fly-specked and as transparent as brick. The walls, originally white, were now yellow from the smoke of a million cigarettes exhaled under stress.

Drummond's muscular forearms rested on the desk, his hands squeezing a chipped coffee cup. On the corner of the desk was a picture of him and a fragile-looking, middle-aged woman posing on a swing in a rose garden gazebo. The woman held one of his oversized paws in her two small hands—King Kong held in check by Fay Wray.

"So," Drummond said. "Emma said you wanted to talk about the Morelli shoot-out. What do you wanna know?"

"Are you in charge of the investigation?" DeMarco asked.

"No. But I'm the only one in the department willing to talk to you, and the only reason I'm willing is because Emma called me."

DeMarco wondered how it was that Emma had any influence over a D.C. cop. His best guess was that Drummond hadn't always been a cop, but with Emma anything was possible. "I appreciate you taking the time, Lieutenant," he said.

"Yeah, right. So what do you wanna know?" Drummond said again.

"Details. Whatever wasn't printed in the *Post*."

Drummond hesitated. "I'm not too comfortable giving you a lotta inside dope on a case this hot. How do I know you're not gonna run off and blab to the press?"

DeMarco smiled and said, "If I do, you can beat me up."

Drummond smiled back but it wasn't a friendly smile. What big teeth you have, Grandma, DeMarco thought.

"Maybe where you come from, pal," Drummond said, "you think that's a joke. Where I come from, it's a distinct possibility."

Drummond stared hard at DeMarco for a second, then relaxed, putting spit-shined, ankle-high boots up on the edge of his desk. "The papers pretty much had it all," he said. "This yahoo Perry breaks a window in the back door of the senator's house, sneaks up to the bedroom, and puts one round through Lydia Morelli's temple. The senator wakes up when he hears the shot and the kid plugs him in the shoulder. The senator grabs the scumbag—he wasn't all that big—tries to wrestle the gun away from him, and the kid gets plugged through the heart. Morelli wasn't trying to kill him—or so he says. And I say if he was, who cares?"

"But why did he want to kill the senator?"

"You know he was a part-time janitor at the building where the senator worked?" Drummond said.

DeMarco nodded. "I saw that in the papers."

"Well, according to Morelli's aide, that guy Burrows, the senator caught Perry trying to steal a calculator from his desk the day of the shooting. The senator told the kid he was going to have to report him. We figure the bastard tried to kill Morelli to keep from losing his job—which is the most that would have happened to him. Or maybe Perry thought he might end up going to the can, but I doubt it. Those people know the system plea-bargains everything."

Those people?

"Why would he steal a calculator?" DeMarco asked.

"Shit, I don't know. To hock it, maybe."

"What kind of calculator was it?"

"One of them handheld jobs. They probably give one to all those senators to keep track of the national debt."

DeMarco ignored Drummond's attempt at humor. "Hell, Lieutenant, these days you can buy a top-of-the-line calculator for fifty bucks. Banks give 'em away when you open a savings account. I'll bet you couldn't get ten bucks for one in a pawnshop."

Drummond shrugged his shoulders. "Who knows what the asshole was thinking? Burrows said that when Morelli walked into his office the kid was just putting the calculator in his pocket. Maybe that was just the first thing he grabbed. Maybe he was planning to go through the whole room looking for small things to boost, petty cash, whatever he could find."

"Seems like an odd thing to risk your job over," DeMarco persisted.

"Or maybe he was some sorta kleptomaniac," Drummond said. "Like that movie star. Why would a movie star shoplift a hat? Who knows why people steal."

"Did Perry have a record for shoplifting?" DeMarco said.

Drummond frowned. DeMarco's interrogation was starting to irritate him. "I don't know, but I do know that I don't give a shit. What difference does it make if he was a shoplifter or not, or if he was going to hock the calculator or not?"

"How 'bout motive, Lieutenant? Don't you think the threat of losing a job is a pretty weak motive for killing two people in cold blood?"

DeMarco's tone was a bit sharp and Drummond responded accordingly. "Motive my ass! I could come up with a million motives. Isaiah Perry was a punk from a family of punks. His older brother's a pusher and a suspect in at least one murder. I think little brother just decided to join the family business." Slapping one thick palm on the surface of the desk, he concluded, "I don't give a shit about motive!"

DeMarco decided not to press Drummond further on the subject of motive. He asked a few questions about Isaiah Perry's criminal record, the armed robbery he'd committed as a juvenile, then another thought occurred to him.

"Why would he shoot Lydia Morelli first?"

"What are you getting at?" Drummond asked.

"If you were going to shoot two sleeping people, Lieutenant, wouldn't you shoot the man first, the one more likely to take away your gun and shoot you with it?"

"Maybe I would and maybe you would, but maybe this kid wasn't as smart as us. Or maybe it was dark in the bedroom and he couldn't tell who he was shooting first."

Before he could ask another question, Drummond said, "You're asking some funny questions, pal, and I don't think I like where you're going with 'em." He studied DeMarco a moment, his eyes narrowing with suspicion. "Are you trying to cause the senator problems? Is that your game?"

DeMarco decided it was time to disengage from this discussion.

"No, Lieutenant. I knew Lydia Morelli and I'm just disturbed by her death."

Drummond pinned DeMarco with his hard, cop's eyes. "Yeah, well I'm going to be real fuckin' disturbed myself if you use anything I told you to hurt Morelli. I like that guy. I liked him before this happened, but now that he shot this little prick, I like him even more."

Chapter 30

Paul Morelli had flown to New York ostensibly to consult with a doctor about his arm, a sports-medicine specialist whom he'd used in the past. There were any number of doctors in Washington he could have seen—several had even called and offered to see him for free, hoping to become his personal physician when he moved into the West Wing—but Morelli said he had confidence in the Manhattan physician.

His real reason for coming to New York was to meet with the old man.

He finished with the doctor at five p.m. No worries about the arm, the doc had told him, and then he gave Morelli a set of exercises to keep things from stiffening up. Morelli would follow the exercise regimen religiously. He went back to his room, rested for an hour, then took the stairs down to the parking garage. The nine-story descent was no problem at all. Harry Foster was waiting for him in the garage, parked in a handicapped parking space. Morelli didn't approve of this but said nothing.

Harry would drive him to the meeting. If he was seen with Harry, that wouldn't be a problem. He'd just say he'd been consulting with Harry on the upcoming campaign. He glanced at his watch. He had to be back at the hotel in two hours to meet some people for drinks but he had no idea where Harry was taking him or how long it would take to get there because the old man, as paranoid as ever, hadn't set the location for the meeting until the last minute.

The meeting place, fortunately, turned out to be a nearby office building in Manhattan. Harry pulled into the underground parking garage and handed Morelli a key to a room. The office building was used by lawyers, accountants, and other professionals. Most of the people who worked there had left for the day, but if Morelli should run into someone, there were plenty of legitimate reasons for him to be in such a place.

He got off on the sixth floor, looked down the hall, and didn't see anyone. It was so quiet on the floor that he wondered if anyone worked there at all. He wouldn't have been surprised if the old man had picked a suite of offices that had just been vacated. Morelli walked down to room 623 and slipped the key in the door. Eddie and the old man were already there.

Eddie, as usual, was standing off to one side, in a corner, near a window. He was like a massive rock: silent, unmoving, and strangely ominous. Morelli had always wondered how Eddie had gotten the scars on his hands. They weren't burn scars and seemed too wide to have been made by a knife blade. It almost looked as if his hands had been mangled—slammed in a car door or smashed with a hammer—then surgically rebuilt. They were functional but not quite human, like hands that Frankenstein might have sown onto the wrists of his monster.

The old man rose from the chair where he'd been sitting. He moved slowly forward, his face solemn. Neither he nor Morelli were huggers, and the two men shook hands, Morelli making sure he didn't squeeze the old man's hand too hard.

The old man looked as he always did: his soft white hair was carefully combed, his complexion burnished bronze, his stern face hinting at his potential for brutality. He was wearing a brown suit, a white shirt, and a wide green tie. Morelli bet the suit and tie were at least fifteen years old. The old man had enough money to buy his own chain of clothing stores but he had stopped caring about being fashionable years ago.

"How are you?" the old man asked.

Paul nodded his head, feigning a sadness he didn't feel. "Okay. And you?"

The old man shook his head. "You know, I hardly knew her. It's not like when Kate died, but . . ."

"I know," Morelli said. "I haven't slept since it happened. I should have taken better care of her. I should have been a better husband."

The old man nodded. "I know how you feel. When my wife died, I felt the same way."

They said nothing for a moment, both thinking of wives lost, neither feeling any real remorse.

"This kid, this black kid," the old man said. "Is there anything more than what the papers said?"

"No. He was just some young guy who worked in my office."

The old man shook his head. "I guess it goes to show: no matter who you are, no matter how powerful you are, you can't protect yourself from fate."

"The thing is," Morelli said, "we have an alarm system for the house but we never set it at night when we were there. We just used it when we went out. If I'd just set the damn alarm . . ."

"Yeah," the old man said, "but back to the black. You're sure he's not connected with anyone?"

"Yes. He was just a kid. Maybe he belonged to some local gang, I don't know, but he certainly wasn't working for anyone with a political agenda."

"Okay, as long as you're sure. We've come too far, Paul. We're too close. If there's anything I need to do, anything, you need to tell me."

"You know I will," Morelli said.

They sat in silence for a minute, the only sound in the room the old man's labored breathing. "Did you ever figure out why those women were on the reporter's list?" the old man said.

Goddamnit! He *had* to get the old man's mind off that subject but lying to him was so terribly dangerous. The old man had killed men just because he suspected they were lying.

"Just what I told you before," Morelli said. "The one woman, the one who lives in New York, she worked for a while on a zoning study when I was mayor and we fired her. She just wasn't competent. I think this reporter figured we may have fired her because she saw something and objected to it. I don't know if you remember this, it was quite a while ago, but the zoning study was done to help some people you knew in Brooklyn and you put some pressure on the borough president at the time. Anyway, this woman, she didn't know anything about that. She just worked on the project for a couple of months, not doing anything important. But the reporter didn't know this; he was just hoping that someone who'd been dismissed would talk to him."

The old man nodded. "And the other woman, this decorator?" he said.

"Same thing. Lydia hired her and later fired her. I guess she wasn't a good decorator. I don't know.

But this reporter, he must have talked to her for the same reason. She was in my house for a few days, and maybe he thought she might have heard something or seen something, and if she was angry about being fired, maybe she'd talk. Finley was grasping at straws," Morelli concluded, "running around talking to people I'd fired, hoping they'd have something to say."

"That must be a pretty long list, people you've fired," the old man said.

"You know, not really," Morelli said. "I've been lucky with most of the people I've hired, and when they get fired, Abe usually does it. That's what's so odd about this woman in New York. I don't think I even met her when she worked for me."

"Good," the old man said after a moment. "So we're done with the reporter?"

"Yeah," Morelli said. "Although I still don't know how he caught on to the doctor."

This was a lie too. Lydia had told Finley something, he didn't know what, that had led him to the doctor. But with the doctor and Lydia both gone . . .

"And this investigator you wanted us to watch? You want me to get somebody else on him? And this time Eddie'll make sure whoever it is won't get spotted."

"No, he's not going to be a problem," Morelli said. "He has no leads to follow."

Not with Lydia dead—but he couldn't say that.

Chapter 31

It took DeMarco twice as long as it normally would have to reach the public-housing project in Alexandria where Isaiah Perry had lived. It took him that long because he didn't know if he was being followed by either Charlie Eklund's people or people who might be working for Paul Morelli. So he wasted time and gas and drove down quiet streets and took turns he didn't need to take, and several times he waited until the light was almost red before driving through intersections. It occurred to him as he drove that if the CIA was involved they might have attached some tracking gizmo to his car, but if that was the case, there wasn't anything he could do about it.

The buildings in the housing project were boxy, two-story quadplexes made of pale brick and were as appealing as army barracks. Patches of playground grass, optimistically planted between the buildings, had become scorched-earth battlefields littered with sharp-edged bits of debris. The hunter-green paint applied to doors and window frames hung in tattered strips and the only touches of vibrant color throughout the complex were fluorescent swirls of militant graffiti.

DeMarco knew that public housing was part of someone's well-intentioned plan: a helpful hand held out to the needy, a cheap place to live until they could get back on their feet, until all those other obliging federal programs could boost them into the ranks of the middle class. But good intentions aside, the reality was that these places were spawning beds for misery, lightning rods attracting grief. They tended to concentrate the poor's problems, and like radioactive atoms, densely packed, the occupants too often reached a critical mass.

He found the address he wanted, shut off the motor, but remained seated in his car, not sure that he wasn't wasting his time. The papers had said that Isaiah Perry had been convicted as a juvenile for armed robbery, but the cop, Drummond, had begrudgingly told him what the papers had failed to state: that Perry had been fourteen at the time of his arrest, convicted as an unarmed accomplice, and given a suspended sentence. The actual armed robber had been Isaiah Perry's older brother, Marcus, the drug dealer that Drummond had mentioned.

But other than the one suspended sentence, there were no other blemishes on Isaiah's record. There had been no drug busts, no car thefts, no series of small escapades leading inevitably to murder. Isaiah Perry had been no Jesse James, and considering the environment in which he had been raised, having just a single brush with the law seemed a remarkable achievement. It was so remarkable, in fact, that DeMarco couldn't understand how he had gone from unarmed accomplice to cold-blooded killer with no record of crime in between.

He got out of his car and walked up the cracked sidewalk toward the door of Perry's home. There were two young black men sitting on the porch of the adjacent apartment. One of the men wore farmer's-bib overalls, a maroon turtleneck sweater, and a brimless leather cap. The other man was wearing a black Oakland Raiders hooded jacket that reached mid-thigh, black sweatpants, and black, high-top Adidas tennis shoes with the laces undone. The hood of the Raiders jacket was pulled up, obscuring the man's face. He looked like Darth Vader dressed for a trip to the gym.

Leather Cap was talking intently but quietly to the man in the Raiders jacket, who sat looking down at the ground, saying nothing in return. Leather Cap noticed DeMarco at that moment and stood up. He was at least six-two and very broad, and the dark scowl on his face looked like a storm cloud about to burst.

"You lost, Jack?" he said to DeMarco.

"No," DeMarco said. "I'm here to see someone."

Leather Cap glowered at him, but DeMarco ignored him—or tried to. The man was hard to ignore; his hostility was tangible.

DeMarco knocked on the door to the Perry residence and when he did, Leather Cap said, "Hey! What the fuck you doin', beatin' on Miz Perry's door? You another reporter? You best get your ass on outta here before I kick it up through your neck."

DeMarco suspected that Leather Cap was a friend of the Perry family, angered by the media's coverage of Isaiah's death. DeMarco could sympathize, but if he didn't do something this situation was liable to escalate to ugly. It was time to bring Big Brother into play. He stared coldly at Leather Cap while he slowly took out the half wallet that held his Congressional ID. He flipped the wallet open, á la cop, and said: "Guys, I'm federal. If I have to get a squad of blues over here to do my business, I will." He thought that sounded pretty good: it didn't have the élan of "Make my day," but it showed a certain streetwise grit.

The man in the Raiders jacket had not said anything to this point, but now he stood. He was even bigger than Leather Cap, at least six-five. Maybe the Raiders gave him the jacket as a bribe not to hurt their players.

"My mom ain't home," he said. "What do you want?"

DeMarco couldn't see the man's face clearly. The hood of the jacket created a shadow, effectively hiding his features, and his eyes were covered by wraparound sunglasses with black lenses.

"Are you Marcus Perry?" DeMarco asked.

"Yeah. So what?"

"Mr. Perry, I'd like to talk to you and your mother."

"Fuck for? I ain't done nothin'."

"I'd just like some information about your brother."

"Got nothin' to say to you. You cops don't know your ass from a hole in the ground. And my mother's over at her church, hidin' from the press. You bother her, and we will kick your ass."

DeMarco elected not to correct the man's mistaken assumption that he was a cop.

"Mr. Perry, you might find this hard to believe, but I just might be on your brother's side."

DeMarco didn't know what subconscious twinge had made him say that; the only side he was on was his own. Apparently Marcus Perry was of the same opinion.

"On his side! What the fuck's *that* mean?"

"What can it hurt to talk to me?" DeMarco said quietly.

"You don't have to talk to him, man," Leather Cap said to Marcus. "Tell him to get his ass on outta here."

Marcus didn't say anything for a moment as he studied DeMarco through the opaque lenses of his sunglasses. Turning to his friend, he said, "It's okay, bro. Let me see what this fool wants. If I don't talk to him, he'll just come back and bother Ma." Leather Cap started to say something, but Marcus said, "Go on. It's okay. I'll catch up with you later, over at your place."

Leather Cap nodded and reached up to put a hand on Marcus's shoulder. "I'm here for you, man. Any way you want. You know that."

Marcus simply nodded.

Leather Cap glowered at DeMarco as he walked away.

DeMarco said, "The reason I'm here is—"

"Let's get out of here," Marcus said. "I don't want you here if my mom comes home."

They got in DeMarco's car and drove into the kinder, gentler part of Alexandria, down King Street toward the waterfront. They passed ice cream parlors and trendy boutiques and bars called "pubs." The commercial quaintness of the area was a foreign landscape compared to the housing project only a few blocks behind them. While DeMarco drove, Marcus Perry sat silent and motionless in the car. His huge form filled the interior of the vehicle, his head almost touching the roof, his broad shoulders extending beyond the boundary of the passenger seat. With the hood of his jacket obscuring his profile, he was a brooding, hostile presence—an alien predator cruising a boulevard of fluff.

Marcus directed DeMarco to a bar two blocks off King Street, a place more run-down than those on the main boulevard. It was only ten in the morning, but several black men sat at the bar drinking beer and bourbon, smoking, staring glassy-eyed at the television set above the bar. Playing on TV was a Martha Stewart rerun, Martha giving clever homemaker tips on Thanksgiving table settings. DeMarco didn't know why the set was tuned to that particular channel but he suspected the television could have been showing Redskins cheerleaders, naked and mud wrestling, and the men at the bar would have had the same dull expressions on their faces.

Marcus and DeMarco took seats at a table as far away from the bar as they could get, and the bartender immediately walked over to take their order. The bartender was at least six-nine, and had the lanky, easy stride of an ex–basketball player.

"Sorry to hear about your brother, man," he said to Marcus.

Marcus nodded and said, "Give me a black jack on the rocks, Tommy."

The bartender arched an eyebrow in surprise. Apparently Marcus Perry wasn't normally one of his booze-for-brunch clients.

"You got it," he said. Looking down at DeMarco from his great height, the bartender said gruffly, "And what do you want?"

"Coffee, please," DeMarco said.

"Don't have no coffee."

DeMarco looked pointedly over at the full pot in the Mr. Coffee behind the bar.

Marcus said, "It's all right, Tommy. Bring him some coffee."

Marcus pulled back the hood of his jacket and took off his sunglasses, giving DeMarco the first good look at his face. His hair was cut in a lopsided flattop, very close on the sides, and he had a small diamond stud in his left earlobe. His skin was a dark chocolate-brown, his nose broad with flaring nostrils, his jaw strong and jutting. Heavy eyebrows and deep-set eyes made him look menacing.

The bartender returned with Marcus's whiskey and DeMarco's coffee. He slammed the coffee cup down on the table in front of DeMarco, spilling half the liquid from the cup.

DeMarco waited until the bartender left, then said, "Mr. Perry, my name's Joseph DeMarco. And I'm not a cop. I'm a lawyer."

"You said you was a fed."

"I am. I work for the government, for Congress, but I'm a lawyer."

"Aw, now I get it, you piece o' shit, you think you can sue somebody and make yourself some money."

DeMarco shook his head. "I'm not suing any-body. I'm not that kind of lawyer."

"Then why do you give a shit what happened to my brother? This some kinda political thing? You trying to cause that senator some kind of problem."

DeMarco hesitated. He couldn't tell Marcus he was investigating his brother's death because Ma-honey had told him to, so instead he gave the most honest answer that he could think of: "This isn't about politics. It's about finding out what really happened and why. I've talked to the police about what your brother supposedly did, and there're just some things that don't make sense."

His voice heavy with sarcasm, Marcus said, "What! You don't believe my brother, armed robber, biggest bad-ass in town, didn't shoot that old lady? Hell, everybody *knows* that wild nigger did it."

DeMarco didn't say anything. Words wouldn't penetrate the shield of Marcus's distrust.

Marcus eventually broke the silence, saying, "I don't know what you're playin' at, Jack, but m'little bro didn't kill nobody. I don't give a shit what that senator says."

Marcus Perry was a very tough young man with a shell around him as hard as armored plate, but it suddenly dawned on DeMarco that he was grieving for his brother. He was ashamed to admit it, but he realized that if Marcus had been a white college kid instead of a black gangster, it would have occurred to him earlier that the man was feeling the same sorrow anyone would feel at the loss of a cherished younger brother. No wonder Marcus Perry and his friends didn't trust people like him.

"Talk to me about your brother," DeMarco said softly. "Please."

Marcus just sat there giving DeMarco a flat, streetwise stare. He was convinced that there had to be some self-serving reason for DeMarco's being there.

"You need to trust me," DeMarco said. "I'm probably the only white man in Washington that doesn't think your brother's a cold-blooded killer. But if you don't talk to me, no one's ever going to know the truth."

Marcus continued to stare at DeMarco for another minute, then said, "Okay. I think you're bullshittin' me, but I'll tell you anyway." He took a sip of his drink, then pulled a deep breath in through his nose and began to talk.

"Isaiah never did a damn thing wrong, his whole life. He worked at that dumb-ass janitor job, and he did it while he was still goin' to school. He wasn't no drop-out like me, and he was gettin' goddamn straight A's too. You think I'm lyin', you ask the school. He was goin' to college next year, said he was gonna be an engineer. And he woulda done it too." Shaking his head, he added, "This thing's killin' my mother."

Tears started to glaze Marcus's angry dark eyes, but he quickly looked away and lit a cigarette to give himself time to regain his composure. DeMarco was thinking that Marcus Perry probably hadn't cried since he wore diapers.

"What about the armed-robbery conviction?" DeMarco asked.

"Total bullshit. I'm the one who robbed that store. Isaiah and me comin' home from school one day—he only fourteen, I'm sixteen, and I'm high—and we go in this damn bodega. Isaiah was just lookin' at the comic books or some such shit, and I go up to the old spic behind the counter and flash my nine. On the way out I tell Isaiah, come on. He didn't even know I'd ripped the place off. I told the cops that when they arrested us, but they didn't believe me. They know you got two niggers in a store, they both robbers."

DeMarco was surprised to hear that Marcus was only two years older than his brother. But he was old beyond his years, no more a kid than DeMarco.

"Did Isaiah have any other scrapes with the law?"

"Are you fuckin' deaf? I just told you, he was a good kid. He never did nothin'."

Trying to keep his tone neutral, DeMarco said, "Mr. Perry, according to the police your brother tried to steal a calculator from the senator's office, and the senator caught him. The police think your brother tried to kill the senator to keep him from reporting the attempted theft."

"That's horseshit!"

The customers at the bar glanced over at Marcus when he shouted. The bartender said, "He givin' you a problem, man?"

Marcus shook his head at the bartender, and said to DeMarco, "Isaiah wouldn't steal shit, 'specially some fuckin' calc-lator. Hell, he already had a calc-lator. Had one with a jillion damn buttons on it that did graphs and shit. So why would he steal one from that man's office?"

It was the same question DeMarco had asked Drummond. "The police think that he planned to hock it," DeMarco said.

Marcus started to spit, then realizing where he was, he said, "How much money you think you get hockin' a fuckin' calc-lator? I'm tellin' you that story's bullshit."

"It may be, but can you explain what your brother was doing in the senator's house that night?"

Marcus hesitated. Whatever he had to say next, DeMarco could sense he was reluctant to say it. DeMarco had to get him to talk.

"Mr. Perry, do you want your brother to go to his grave with people believing he was a thief and a killer? So please. Talk to me. Tell me why he was at the senator's house?"

To give himself time to think, Marcus took another sip of his drink, wincing as the liquid seared his throat. Finally he looked directly into DeMarco's eyes, and said very quietly, "He was sellin' him a gun."

"What!"

Marcus exploded. "Fuck you, you motherfucker! I knew you wouldn't believe me."

Marcus rose to his feet. "Wait a minute," DeMarco said. "I'm not saying I don't believe you. I was just shocked, that's all. Sit back down. Tell me what you're talking about."

Marcus sat down slowly, still bristling, but continued with his story.

"One night Isaiah's cleanin' up this office and this dude—not the senator—some other guy— starts talkin' to him, askin' Isaiah if he can get him a piece."

DeMarco interrupted to ask when this had occurred. Marcus said it was three days before his brother died, while Lydia Morelli was at Father Martin's. When DeMarco asked if he knew the name of the man who had talked to his brother, Marcus said he didn't know, only that Isaiah had called him a "kinky-haired little white dude."

Abe Burrows.

According to Marcus, Burrows had explained to Isaiah that because of the stance his boss had taken on gun control, he couldn't just walk into a store and buy a gun. The media might find out. But he wanted one for home protection, and figured Isaiah could help him out.

"Isaiah said the dude was cool about it at first, shuckin' and jivin' with him, but when Isaiah says he can't help him, he turns mean. Says just maybe somethin' gets stolen from his office, people gonna think Isaiah the nigger janitor done it—him havin' a record and everything."

"He knew your brother had a record?"

"Yeah. Thought juvie records was sealed, but this guy works for a senator. Could probably find out anything. Anyway, the little prick squeezed Isaiah. Squeezed him *hard*. Lets him know that if he don't get him a gun, he ain't gonna have the privilege of moppin' all those white men's floors."

Marcus glared at DeMarco as if he had invented bigotry.

"But my brother, he didn't want to lose that job, so he came to me for help, asked me to get the gun for him. Isaiah said it had to be a .22 or .25, nothin' bigger. The guy insisted on that. Gun I got for him was a piece of shit, but I figured anybody wanna pussy gun like that wouldn't know the difference."

"But why did he go to Senator Morelli's house?"

"Didn't know it was the senator's house. It was where the dude told him to go. Gave him the ad-dress, said to bring the gun after midnight, and come alone. I didn't think nothin' about that. Just figured the guy didn't want his neighbors to see Isaiah."

Marcus started to say something else, but he didn't. He shook his head sadly, lit another cigarette, and said, "And that's it. Next mornin' the police tell m'mom that Isaiah'd been killed—but I knew he'd been set up, somehow. He didn't kill that white woman and shoot that senator."

"Did you tell the police about your brother delivering a gun to the senator's house?"

Marcus barked a harsh laugh. "Yeah, right. Fuckin' cops ain't gonna believe anything I say."

DeMarco remained silent, trying to decide what to say next. He didn't want to call Marcus a liar, but he had his own doubts about the gun story.

"You don't believe me either," Marcus said, as if reading DeMarco's mind.

Before DeMarco could respond, Marcus said, "Fuck you, you dago piece of shit. Get outta here. Go on."

"Look, Mr. Perry—"

"I said get the fuck on outta here!"

Chapter 32

———◆———

Sharon was packing, humming to herself, happy as a damn lark. If she only knew, Garret Darcy thought.

Charlie Eklund had told Darcy that he wanted him to take a little vacation. A little bonus, the sly bastard had said. He'd even given him an extra five grand so Darcy and the missus would be able to do it up right.

It was all bullshit. Charlie boy was putting him on ice. He wanted him out of D.C. and not someplace where somebody could find him easily.

After Ladybird had entered that drunk tank in Maryland, Eklund had jerked Toby and Phil and him all over the place. One day he'd be following Big Bird and the next he'd be tailing DeMarco and sometimes that broad Emma. Now that was a joke. Whoever the hell this Emma gal was, she was good. She had to be a pro. Every time he'd been assigned to tail her, she lost him in about ten minutes. He would have been embarrassed except she lost Phil and Toby too, and Eklund, hell, he even laughed when he said he'd lost her.

But what he'd seen the other night—and what he'd heard—that was the kind of thing he hadn't wanted to see and hear at all. Why did *he* have to be there that night? Why couldn't it have been Toby or Phil? Eklund—that prissy little shit—he'd made people disappear before, and making a retired agent like Garret Darcy vanish, a guy with no official status . . . well, that wouldn't be a chore for ol' Charlie at all. And the funny part was, when the time came, it'd probably be Phil or Toby who would take him out.

Phil had put the bugs in place. With Ladybird at home, Eklund hadn't wanted to take the chance of getting caught installing the bugs. But when she went into rehab, and with Big Bird always out of the house, he had Phil plant the bugs. Phil put them in Big Bird's den, the living room, the kitchen, and the master bedroom, and then rigged them to a voice-activated tape recorder hidden behind the electric meter outside the house. It had been Darcy's job to pick up the old tapes every night and put in new ones.

That night, he'd been sitting there in front of Big Bird's house, waiting for all the lights to go off so he could get the tapes—and that's when it all went down. He'd seen it all and the bugs had heard it all. He'd even managed to get a couple photos on his little piece-of-shit Kodak. The photos weren't very clear, but they were apparently clear enough, because when Eklund saw them . . . Hell, Darcy bet the last time Charlie Eklund had been that happy was when Jack Kennedy died.

He'd been forced to wait a couple of days to pick up the last tapes, the important ones, and he was glad the forensic guys hadn't found the recorder when they were gathering evidence at the house. The bugs they never would have found, not unless they started ripping walls apart, but they could have spotted the recorder if they'd looked hard enough. Fortunately—or maybe unfortunately—the forensic weenies spent all their time up in the master bedroom, not outside the house.

And then he'd been dumb enough to listen to the tapes after he picked them up.

When Eklund asked him if he'd listened to them he'd said no, but he could tell that the little shit knew he was lying. And that's when he got his "bonus": the keys to the place near Lauderdale, the envelope with the extra cash. Yeah, what a peach of a boss ol' Charlie was.

He felt like telling Sharon to forget Florida, that they were going to Mexico. Or maybe Canada would be better, but it was so fuckin' cold up there. He knew a guy that could get them clean IDs, and his brother could sell the house for him and get the money to him some way. The problem was how would he get his pension check? If he sent in some change-of-address form to get his pension mailed someplace else, Eklund would be able to follow it right back to him.

"Honey," Sharon called out from the bedroom, "where'd you put your swimming trunks? The red ones, not the ones with the flowers on them."

His swim trunks. Jesus. He wondered what she'd say if he said: Babe, we're not gonna be doin' a lot of swimmin' because I saw something that I wish I hadn't and now this sneaky old fuck at Langley is probably gonna kill me. So, doll, we're gonna have to change our names and move to Nova Scotia and get jobs in a cannery so we don't starve to death.

Yeah, he wondered what she'd say if he told her that.

"I think they're in the bottom drawer," he said, "where my long johns are. And maybe you oughta pack the long johns too."

"What?" Sharon said.

Chapter 33

———◆———

Emma parked in front of the school—an unappealing three-story lump of brown brick—and was immediately appalled by the institutional grimness of the place. There were security screens over the lower-floor windows, cameras on the corners of the building protected by wire mesh, and a uniformed guard standing by the main entrance in a parade-rest position, a radio and a nightstick visible on his belt. The place reminded her of a prison, minus the machine-gun towers. The guard was watching a group of teenage boys who probably should have been in class, but were just sitting and smoking, laughing and talking loudly. She suspected the guard preferred them outside the school rather than inside where he'd have to deal with whatever mayhem they might cause.

She was here because DeMarco had asked her to verify something, something that she could have done with a couple of phone calls, but that she'd eventually decided to do in person. She wouldn't have normally helped DeMarco with a task as simple as this, but she knew that he was in way over his head, dealing as he was with Morelli and the CIA.

Emma nodded to the guard as she entered the school, and he nodded back, but kept his attention on the cluster of boys.

As Emma walked down a hallway past rows of dented lockers, she reflected back on how much she had hated high school. She had despised the cliques and the peer pressure to conform. She had been bewildered by the fads and disgusted by the simian antics of the boys—boys not much different from the ones in front of the school, only white and wealthy. And in those days, she had been confused by her sexuality and that may have been the most difficult part of all. But at the private school she had attended, the strongest drug she'd been exposed to was marijuana and if any of her classmates had been armed, she certainly never knew it. There'd been no guards, no metal detectors at the doors, no fear of a misfit with an automatic weapon massacring his tormentors. Compared to the school that Isaiah Perry had attended, her high school had been safer than a cloistered nunnery.

She found the vice principal in an office where one window was patched with plywood. The principal wasn't available; he was testifying in court. The vice principal, a woman named Beatrice Thompson, was a heavyset African American with the eyes of a combat veteran, one who had been left on the front line for far too long.

Emma could imagine Thompson leaving college, teaching certificate in hand, filled with hope and optimism and the desire to do good for her people. Now, twenty-five years later, she was beyond exhaustion. There had been too many children raised without fathers, too many children whose role models were kingpins of drugs and violence, too many children who believed the only honest way out involved a ball. Thompson's job was holding back the tide with a toy shovel, and she had realized years ago the futility of it. But still she tried, God bless her, still she tried.

"He was a terrific kid," Thompson said. "Headed for college, without a doubt. Great SATs, great grades, involved in all the right clubs."

"Did he have a calculator?" Emma asked.

"Of course. He needed one for an advanced math class he was taking. The school bought it for him."

"So why would he steal one?"

"I don't know," she said.

She should have said, *He wouldn't!* Why didn't she defend him? Emma wondered. Why did she, of all people, simply accept that Isaiah Perry had done what the papers had reported? Emma knew the answer: it had happened too many times before—a kid who seemed to have walked miraculously unharmed through a minefield of disadvantage and then falls within sight of the promised land.

This woman, this good woman, needed a different job, a job that would restore the optimism of her youth.

"Can I ask you one more thing?" Emma said.

"What?"

"How did Isaiah do it? How did he manage to do so well in school when so many others fail?"

The teacher smiled—a smile sadder than lilies on a grave. "His brother. His big brother, the drug dealer, helped him. Made sure he got to school. Made sure nobody messed with him. Made sure he stayed away from the gangs and the dope. Marcus came to a parent-teacher conference one time when Isaiah's mother couldn't make it; he scared the shit out of the teachers."

Emma walked down the steps of the school, head down, as she rummaged in her handbag for her keys. She heard a cry off to her left. The boys she had seen sitting outside the school when she arrived were now playing basketball. The basketball hoop didn't have a net and the backboard had a half-dozen holes in it that Emma was certain had been caused by bullets. Just as she glanced over, she saw a kid who couldn't have been more than five foot eight soar through the air and dunk the ball. It was as if he had steel springs in his skinny legs. The expression of pure delight on the boy's face as he hung from the rim delighted Emma.

She glanced away from the game and over to where her car was parked and was immediately less delighted. Charlie Eklund was standing next to her Mercedes. His bodyguard was standing a few paces away, head moving, as if looking for clear lines of fire.

"Why do you have a bodyguard?" Emma said when she reached her car.

"A year ago," Eklund said, glancing over at his man, "we decided that the demise of a certain South American cocaine cartel would benefit the political aspirations of a certain ambitious colonel. We succeeded in destroying the cartel, but unfortunately its leader managed to remain alive. That hadn't been part of the original plan. Well, this gentleman, this cocaine mogul, had a reputation for ruthlessness and he demonstrated it by killing our colonel and his family in a most gruesome manner, but more importantly, he somehow found out that I was personally involved in his troubles. And then, as luck would have it, the fellow disappeared and we can't find him. It's been six months and I suspect he might be dead, but I'm not certain, and until I am . . ." Eklund's head tilted in the direction of his bodyguard.

"Beautiful," Emma muttered. "And what are you doing here?"

"We—"

"Will you quit saying 'we.' The CIA isn't involved in whatever you're doing. This is *your* op, Charlie. For some reason you have been keeping Senator Morelli under surveillance and now you're watching Joe DeMarco—and me."

Eklund's eyes crinkled when he smiled. "Whether it's me or the agency," he said, "we—excuse me, I— I want you to stop what you're doing."

"And what exactly do you think I'm doing?" Emma said.

"Right now you and your friend are investigating the death of Lydia Morelli and I want you to stop. Immediately. I want this little drama to play out without any outside interference. Now is that clear enough for you?"

Emma studied Eklund for a moment before saying, "You had people watching Paul Morelli the night his wife was killed. Didn't you, Charlie?"

Eklund didn't respond but his eyes were both bright and flat at the same time, like the shiny plastic eyes they use in cheap dolls.

"I'm assuming," Emma said, "that you're here to make a threat, to tell me what's going to happen if I don't do what you want."

"Correct," Eklund said. "It's such a pleasure dealing with smart people."

"So get on with it."

"Very well. You have a friend, that lovely young woman who lives with you, the one who plays the cello. She travels a lot. We were just talking about drugs. Don't you think it would be unfortunate if the next time she traveled a large lump of heroin was found in her suitcase?"

Emma took a step toward Eklund but he didn't back up. He just craned his neck upward to look at her.

"And your friend, DeMarco, by virtue of his birthright, has links to organized crime. I can think of a number of ways to exploit that situation."

Emma lowered her head so her face was an inch away from Eklund's.

"Charlie," she said, her voice almost a whisper, "do you think your bodyguard is good enough to keep *me* from killing you?"

After lunch, DeMarco went back to his office and found two messages on the answering machine. The first message was from Emma relaying what he'd already suspected, that Isaiah Perry was a good student with nothing but positive prospects. Emma's message ended with the cryptic statement that Charlie Eklund of the CIA had just spoken to her again. She said she'd tell DeMarco later what Eklund had said, but for a while she wasn't going to be able to help him with his investigation. Instead, she said, she had to find a way to pry Eklund off their backs.

The second message was from a congressman who had confided to the Speaker that he was afraid his son was using drugs, but couldn't be sure. Mahoney had given him DeMarco's number.

DeMarco was surprised Mahoney had drummed up a new job for him when he had just told him to investigate Lydia Morelli's death, but then he realized that Mahoney might have spoken to the congressman before his current assignment. The other possibility, of course, was that Mahoney didn't care how many jobs he gave DeMarco simultaneously. He thought about just ignoring the congressman's call for a few days, but since he didn't know what to do next about Lydia, he figured he might as well go talk to the man about his kid. He also figured that if he was being followed, this extracurricular mission might confuse a tail—and it'd be damn nice to have someone beside himself confused, if only for a little while.

Half an hour later he was seated in front of the congressman's desk, pretending to take notes while the politician talked. The congressman was a big, florid man from Ohio with arms like a stevedore's, and DeMarco knew that he'd been a college football star twenty years ago. On Capitol Hill he had a reputation as a comer—decisive, insightful, aggressive. A real political linebacker. But when he talked

about his son, all his poise deserted him. His hands
fluttered nervously and his eyes looked everywhere but
at DeMarco. Although confident he could run the
nation, he didn't know what to do about the four-
teen-year-old boy he had sired. He gave DeMarco a
picture of his kid, told him where the boy went to
school, and looked relieved when DeMarco left his
office.

The campus of the prep school looked like a small
Ivy League college. The boys wore blue blazers and
striped ties. DeMarco saw the congressman's son
and another boy come out together when the bell
rang. They were both blond and clean-cut, and had
that superior, to-the-manor-born air about them.
They were America's future, God help us.

Instead of getting on the private bus that was taking their classmates home, the two teenagers caught
a city bus and rode into downtown D.C. DeMarco
followed them into a J.Crew store and watched as
they shoplifted a pair of gloves.

For the next hour they stood on a street corner,
obviously waiting for someone. While they waited,
DeMarco thought: So now what? What was he going
to do, now that he knew Isaiah Perry was most likely
not a thief or a killer?

At six o'clock, DeMarco watched the congressman's kid shake hands—twice—with a skinny, fur-
tive Hispanic man wearing a cowboy hat. When he
and his buddy went into the restroom of a fast-food

restaurant, DeMarco followed and heard them snort cocaine.

As the boys were waiting for the metro to take them back to Chevy Chase, a question occurred to DeMarco that had nothing to do with the yuppie brats he was tailing. How did Isaiah Perry get from the project where he lived in Alexandria to Georgetown? The police report said nothing about finding a car belonging to Isaiah near the senator's house. The Metro didn't have a stop in Georgetown, at midnight bus service would be problematic, and people didn't normally take a taxi to commit a double murder.

DeMarco told Emma about his latest insight into Lydia's murder and she told DeMarco about her conversation with Charlie Eklund.

They were sitting at Emma's kitchen table. DeMarco, a man who liked to cook, loved Emma's kitchen. It was large, bright, and spacious, and contained every culinary gadget known to modern man. From the back of the house Christine could be heard playing her cello. DeMarco recognized the piece she was playing, which meant it wasn't the highbrow stuff she normally played. Considering what he and Emma were discussing, a requiem of some sort would have been more appropriate.

"So Eklund is protecting Morelli," DeMarco said.

"I think he is now," Emma said. "But I think you were right before when you said that van Horn and Suttel weren't working for Eklund, that they were working for this powerful man that Lydia spoke of."

"Great," DeMarco said. "So now Morelli has two people helping him."

"Yes. And Eklund is threatening to do things to you and Christine if we don't stop looking into Lydia's death. So I have to find a way to . . . to neutralize him."

"What do you want me to do?" DeMarco said. "Back off for a while?"

"No. You can't do that." Emma paused. "I think we have one thing going in our favor. I'm pretty sure—no, I'm positive—that what Eklund is doing has not been sanctioned by CIA management. This means he doesn't have teams of people helping him. He may have paid a couple of guys to watch the Morellis—freelancers like Suttel and van Horn, or maybe retired agents—but I'm pretty sure he doesn't have fifty people involved in this and they aren't using satellites to track us. This is Charlie's op, not Langley's."

"How does that help us?" DeMarco said.

"It helps because Eklund's manpower is limited and if you make the effort, you can probably lose whoever might be following you."

So DeMarco, who had never been trained on how to avoid being followed by spies, left Emma's house and once again made erratic high-speed turns and darted down alleys and peered continually into the rearview mirror as he tried to shake a tail he couldn't see. And all the time he drove he wondered what sort of things Charlie Eklund might be planning to do to destroy his life.

Chapter 34

———— ✦ ————

DeMarco had not enjoyed visiting the Alexandria housing project during daylight hours. He liked it even less at night.

He parked his car under the only streetlight still burning on the block, then exited and locked his car, and walked up to the Perrys' front door. He knocked, waited a minute, then knocked again. The door was finally opened by a stout black woman in her fifties wearing a faded pink bathrobe. She had a seamed, work-worn face and the skin beneath her eyes was smudged gray from fatigue. Her dark eyes recorded a lifetime of grief, poverty, and bad luck.

In her arms was a little boy, no more than two years old. He had on pajamas covered with cartoon pictures of jumping bunnies and sucked a pacifier as he looked at DeMarco. His eyes were huge, innocent, and curious, and unlike the woman's, the baby's chubby features showed no concern. He wasn't old enough to know that unexpected callers in the night usually brought bad news.

"Yes?" the woman asked.

"I'm sorry to bother you so late, ma'am. Are you Marcus Perry's mother?"

"Yes. Who are you? Another reporter?"

"No, ma'am. I'm looking for Marcus. Is he home?"

"You the police? What's he done now?"

"I'm not with the police either, ma'am. I'm a lawyer. I have some business with your son."

"Business? You a customer of his?"

"No, ma'am. I just need to talk to him. It's important."

She studied DeMarco, the look of disgust on her face making him squirm. She apparently thought he was buying dope from Marcus.

"Please, ma'am, can you tell me where I can find him?"

"At this time of night," she said, "he's usually with his trashy friends at this club in the District."

DeMarco asked her for the name of the club.

"It's . . . I can't remember. Here, take this baby," she said, thrusting the infant at him. "There's a matchbook somewhere in the kitchen."

DeMarco awkwardly held the little boy and they looked at each other in silence, inquisitive brown

eyes gazing into cynical blue ones. The kid reached
out once and squeezed DeMarco's nose, then finding nothing else on his face worth playing with, resumed staring and sucking on his pacifier. Mrs. Perry
came back with a book of matches from a nightclub,
and handed it to DeMarco as she took the baby from
him. DeMarco thanked her and turned to leave.

"Hey," she said. "When you see him, you tell him
that that girl he hired to look after his son didn't
change his diaper all day. Now this baby has a nasty
rash from sittin' in his own shit. You tell him the
little bitch was so high on crack when I got home,
she didn't even know me. You tell him that, ya hear?"

She slammed the door in DeMarco's face before
he could answer.

———————◆———————

Rap music, soothing as a jackhammer, assaulted
DeMarco's ears when he entered the dance club. His
eyes adjusted to the dim light, and he saw he was
the only white person in the room and that every
head was turned in his direction. He instantly felt
the vulnerability of being different.

He peered through the smoky darkness until he
found Marcus Perry seated with a young woman
at a table in the farthest corner of the room. He was
dressed in more formal attire than when DeMarco
had last seen him. Gone was the hooded Raiders

jacket and unlaced tennis shoes. He was wearing a double-breasted black suit over a white silk turtle-neck sweater. There were gold chains around his neck and the scant light in the room was captured momentarily, then scattered, by the diamond stud in his ear. Tonight he would fit right in at the best clubs in town—unless they noticed the gun in the shoulder holster.

The young black woman with him was a long-necked beauty with the profile of a Nubian queen. She was wearing a tight red dress cut low enough to show a magnificent cleavage, and short enough to expose flawless legs. Marcus's lovely companion didn't appear very happy, though; she was look-ing out at the room, a bored expression on her beautiful face, tapping long-nailed fingers impa-tiently on the table top.

"Mr. Perry, I need to talk to you again," DeMarco said.

Marcus ignored DeMarco, not even bothering to look at him. He raised a glass slowly to his lips, took a sip, then set the glass down carefully next to a half-empty bottle of Jack Daniel's. He had the slow-motion movements and glassy-eyed look of the very drunk.

Before DeMarco could repeat himself, the young woman said to Marcus, "Honey, I'm gonna go on over and sit with Regina while you talk to this man. I'm sorry about your brother—you know that, sugar—but I don't know why you asked me out tonight. You ain't said two words since we been here. Come over and get me later, if you want. Okay?"

Marcus didn't respond. He continued to sit, facing straight ahead, eyes focused on an invisible horizon. The young woman gave a small, disgusted shake of her head and rose from her chair. She stood next to DeMarco, and looked down at him; in high heels she was well over six feet tall. DeMarco could feel heat coming from her body as if there was a small furnace burning inside her loins.

"I'd be real careful if I was you, mister," she said to DeMarco. "This thing with his brother has made him mad-dog crazy. He already beat on one man tonight who didn't do hardly nothin'."

Great. DeMarco took the woman's seat across the small table from Marcus.

"How'd you find me here?" Marcus asked, still not looking at DeMarco. His words were slurred and spoken so softly that DeMarco barely heard him.

"Your mother told me you'd be here."

Marcus barked a humorless laugh.

"Bet she was damn happy about that too."

"She wasn't."

DeMarco told Marcus what his mother had said about the babysitter.

"Gonna break that little bitch's head," Marcus muttered darkly.

"The reason I wanted to see you tonight was—"

For the first time, Marcus looked directly into DeMarco's eyes. "You think I don't give a shit about my son, don't you?" he said. "You think he's just another crack baby, got a dead hooker for a mother, a drug dealer for a father. Ain't that right?"

That was exactly what he thought, but DeMarco didn't say anything.

"Well, you're wrong. I married that boy's mama. And she wasn't no doper and she wasn't no hooker. She didn't OD or die from AIDS, or any o' that shit. She got cancer, this lymph thing. I love my son."

"I'm glad to hear that, Mr. Perry. But it's your brother I want to talk about."

"I already told you everything I know."

"No you didn't," DeMarco said.

Marcus's eyes narrowed ominously, and remembering the young woman's warning, DeMarco wished he had thought of a more diplomatic way to call Marcus a liar. He was dangerous enough sober; when he was drunk and ravaged with grief, antagonizing him could be fatal.

"Did your brother have a car?" DeMarco asked.

Marcus paused before speaking, his face suspicious. Knowing DeMarco could verify his answer, he finally said, "No. Why you askin'?"

"I think you know why. You drove your brother to the senator's house the night he was killed. Didn't you? Earlier, when you talked about delivering the gun at midnight, you said, '*I* didn't think nothing about that.' You drove him, didn't you?" DeMarco repeated.

Marcus shifted in his seat, sitting up straight, growing larger before DeMarco's eyes.

"You trying to make me an *accomplice,* is that what you're doin'?"

"No. I don't think you're an accomplice. I think you're a witness."

Marcus nodded his head slowly, unconscious of the gesture, but he didn't say anything.

"Tell me what happened. Please."

Marcus still didn't respond.

"Mr. Perry . . ."

"Yeah, I drove him. I sat in the car when he went in the house. He said he'd only be a minute. Anyway, he goes in the house—I couldn't see who let him in—and about five minutes later I hear two shots. About two minutes after that, I hear another shot. I didn't know what to do. I knew something had gone wrong, but I didn't want to go chargin' into that house, not in that white neighborhood. So I sat there waitin' for Isaiah to come out, prayin' he'd come out, but this white guy comes out of the house instead. I seen him clear. Short, dumpy dude with kinky hair. I was about to get out of the car and grab the little fucker—ask what happened to my brother—but then I hear all these sirens screamin' up the block and I got the hell outta there."

DeMarco could see now that it wasn't just grief that was tearing Marcus Perry apart—it was guilt. He felt personally responsible for what had happened to his younger brother, and was questioning his own courage for not having done something when he heard the shots.

"So now what?" Marcus asked defiantly. "You gonna run to the cops and tell 'em I helped my brother shoot that lady? You can't prove shit."

"I'm not going to do anything, Mr. Perry. But *you* need to do something. You need to tell the police what really happened."

Marcus shook his head slowly. He'd started to speak when his eyes focused sharply on something behind DeMarco. DeMarco turned to see what he was looking at, and saw the young woman in the red dress dancing with a man. Every move the woman made was an act of seduction. With her body, she couldn't help it; she would have looked seductive cleaning fish.

DeMarco turned back to face Marcus and saw he was still focused on the woman and her dance partner. There was a small, cruel smile on his face.

"You need to talk to the police," DeMarco said again.

"What do you think would happen if I went to the cops?" Marcus said, still looking at the woman. He faced DeMarco then. "Well, lemme tell you. They'd think I was there helpin' Isaiah, that I was his driver, but like *getaway* driver. No way in hell they'd believe he was deliverin' that man a gun."

DeMarco argued with him briefly, urging him to go to the police, but he knew Marcus was right. With his record, no one would believe that he wasn't involved in the killing.

"No, I'm not gonna talk to the police," Marcus said softly, "but I am gonna set things right. Yeah, I'm gonna set things right."

He wasn't talking to DeMarco; he was making a promise to himself.

"Don't be a fool," DeMarco said. "Paul Morelli's a United States senator, not some drug runner over in Southeast. If you want to do something, go to the police."

Marcus stood up, rising slowly to his six-foot-five-inch height. DeMarco stood to face him.

Marcus glanced over at the woman on the dance floor again, then looked down at DeMarco. There was a sheen of tears glazing his eyes. He reached out with his long arms, placed his hands on DeMarco's shoulders, then leaned down so their faces were almost touching. He grinned at DeMarco, the grin incongruous with the bright tears in his eyes.

"You're really full of shit. You know that?"

Marcus stepped around DeMarco and began to walk slowly toward the dance floor, toward the woman in the red dress—and the man dancing with her. DeMarco left the club quickly. He didn't want to witness the mayhem that was about to occur.

Chapter 35

Blake Hanover was wearing the same yellow pajamas that he had on the last time Emma had seen him. He sat in his Barcalounger and the green oxygen tank on the floor next to his chair hissed like Eve's serpent as it helped him breathe. He looked so much worse than he had on Emma's previous visit that she wondered if he was wearing the same clothes because he didn't have the strength to change them.

The apartment smelled of an old man dying.

"I need your help with Charlie Eklund," Emma said.

Hanover smiled, and Emma could see that even that took an effort. And she knew why he was smiling: she knew how ironic it was that she was coming to him for help. But Hanover didn't have the strength to make a sarcastic comment. All he said was, "Why?"

"It's a long story, Blake," she said. She realized immediately that she had never called him by his first name before. "But the bottom line is that Eklund's helping a man become president, and the man he's helping is a murderer."

"They don't usually become murderers until *after* they become president," Hanover said.

Maybe he wasn't as weak as Emma thought.

"But how can I help?" Hanover said.

"I need a way to control Eklund. I need leverage," Emma said.

"Good luck with that," Hanover said. "You're not going to find anything funny with his finances. Charlie's rich. He was born into money. And if he decided to steal money . . . Well, a guy who's able to hide the CIA's money trail from Congress and the GAO wouldn't have any problem at all hiding his own money.

"And if you're thinking of sex as a hook, you can forget that too. I truly believe Charlie's asexual. He's never married, and as far as anyone knows, he's never had a bunch of girlfriends. For years folks thought he might be gay, but there's no evidence of that either. What I'm saying is that even when Charlie was young, sex didn't seem to be a priority, and at the age he is now, I'm sure it's not one. So if you were thinking of getting him using sex or money, you're going to have to go a different way."

"Any suggestions?"

Hanover just sat there for a minute saying nothing, seeming to focus all his energy on getting his next breath. He finally said, "All I know is that the only thing that Charlie Eklund cares about is the CIA. The Company's his whole life. If you want to get him off your back you need to go after what he cares about."

Hanover opened his mouth, to say something else, but then started coughing—a raspy, wet, horrible sound. Emma went to his kitchen and filled a glass with tap water. She held the glass to Hanover's parched lips and he took a few small sips then motioned for her to remove the glass.

"Blake," Emma said, "do you have anyone to help you?"

Hanover shook his head.

"Do you want me to call someone? I can arrange for a nurse to take care of you. I'll pay."

Hanover shook his head again. "Hospice is coming in the morning," he said, "but I'm thinking, what's the point of dragging this out? There's an old .45 in the night table next to my bed. Do you think you could get it for me?"

"I can't do that, Blake. I'm sorry."

Hanover laughed. "I didn't think so. I just thought it'd be fun to ask."

As Emma drove, she thought about what Blake Hanover had said, that the only things Charlie Eklund cared about were his job and the CIA.

And then something occurred to her—something she could do to put Eklund back in his box.

She pulled her cell phone off her belt, then changed her mind. She doubted Eklund was monitoring her calls, but why take the chance? She turned in to a gas station that had a functioning pay phone and made a call. An hour later, positive that no one was tailing her, she was having coffee with two men at a bowling alley in Arlington.

Mike Koharski was in his sixties, gray-haired and stocky. He was an ex–navy chief who had spent twenty years on nuclear subs, and usually wore long-sleeved shirts to cover the tattoos he'd gotten during a shore leave he couldn't remember. The second man was Sammy Wix. Sammy looked like a cross between a troll and a jockey, so short and homely that little kids were delighted by the sight of him. Mike and Sammy were partners in a detective agency, one that rarely made a profit because they were notoriously picky about their clients.

"I need a man tailed," she told them. "And you need to be careful," she added. "He has a very nervous bodyguard."

Tit for tat, Charlie, she said to herself after she finished giving Mike and Sammy their instructions.

Emma's next call was to DeMarco. "What's the name of your reporter friend, the one who works at the *Post*?"

"Reggie Harmon," DeMarco said.

"Is he a good reporter?" Emma had asked.

"He drinks," DeMarco said.

"Good," Emma said.

Then Emma called four people she knew, four people who were not only friends but people who owed her in ways both personal and professional. What she asked of these four people she would never have asked had the stakes not been so high. One was a woman who worked for the president's national security adviser. Another was a man who worked as a high-level analyst at the National Security Agency. Another was a senior FBI agent who attended daily joint-intelligence meetings with the CIA and Homeland Security. The fourth person was a CIA section head, a married woman with whom Emma had once had an affair when they were both young. The last phone call bothered Emma the most, and she suspected that after this the woman would probably never speak to her again. But she had to ask.

What she asked of these four people was this: she wanted a current item that, if made known to the public, would be embarrassing to the CIA but would not in any way compromise national security or any vital ongoing CIA operation. That's all.

Reggie Harmon entered the church and looked around. He wasn't a Catholic and he didn't know what confessionals looked like or where they were located in the church. Then he saw the three small doors on the east side of the church. The doors were about halfway down the rows of pews and one of the doors had an unlit, amber-colored light bulb above it. He entered the door closest to the altar as he'd been told.

It was dark inside the confessional, dark enough that it made him nervous. He reached for the flask in his pocket and took a drink, the vodka a burning comfort as he swallowed. He'd just returned the flask to his pocket when a small panel slid open. There was a wire-mesh screen where the panel had been, and he could see the shape of a face on the other side of the screen but he couldn't make out the person's features.

If he'd been a Catholic, Reggie didn't think he'd have liked the idea of confessing his sins in such a place.

"Mr. Harmon?" the person on the other side of the screen said.

"Yeah," Reggie said.

"I have some information for you."

"Who are you?" Reggie said. He couldn't tell if he was speaking to a man or a woman. The person was using some sort of device to disguise his or her voice, and sounded the way people did who'd had their voice boxes removed. Reggie, a smoker as well as a drinker, didn't like the sound at all.

"All you need to know is that I work for the CIA. In your story you can call me a highly placed official at the agency."

"But how do I know you are?" Reggie said.

"Because of what I'm about to tell you," the person said.

The following day, on page A3 of the *Washington Post,* was a one-paragraph article. According to the *Post,* "a highly placed source at the CIA" had informed *Washington Post* reporter Reginald Harmon that a CIA agent had been deported from Jakarta, Indonesia, the previous day for attempting to bribe a member of the Indonesian cabinet. When Mr. Harmon contacted the Indonesian ambassador in Washington, D.C., Mr. Yussef Kalla confirmed the story and stated that the Indonesian government was "extremely disturbed" that an American intelligence operative would do such a thing. Mr. Kalla said he would be meeting with the secretary of state to discuss the incident. White House press secretary Gerald Hoffman said that he was not aware of the incident until contacted by the *Post* but was certain the president would be discussing the situation with CIA director Colin Murphy.

Chapter 36

———— ◆ ————

Packy Morris was the chief of staff for the junior senator from Maryland. Unlike Abe Burrows and most other senior Senate aides DeMarco knew, Packy didn't have a perpetually harried look about him. His casual air may have stemmed from a what-me-worry attitude toward life in general, but in all likelihood it was because his daddy owned half of downtown Baltimore. Packy Morris did not consider unemployment a significant threat.

Packy was six-seven and weighed over three hundred pounds, and the pounds were soft and flowing: if muscle was there, it was far, far below the surface. He had short dark hair that he combed forward and a fleshy, hooked nose. He always made DeMarco think of a jaded Roman emperor wrapped in an enormous white toga, thumb pointed downward, delightedly condemning a bleeding gladiator to death. Of late, Packy had taken to wearing red suspenders and bow ties, the suspenders looking like racing stripes on an eighteen-wheeler, the tie almost hidden by his many chins.

When DeMarco entered his office, Packy's size-fourteen feet were resting on his desk and he was leaning back in his chair reading the sports section of the *Baltimore Sun*. He looked over the top of the paper at DeMarco and said, "I think the Ravens should invest their money in science. With the millions they've squandered on players, some egghead could have built them a bionic man by now. Like that movie *Robocop*. They could make Roboguard or Roboend. Something that wouldn't be on the disabled list half the fucking season."

"Are you still betting on the Ravens, Packy?"

"I'm not betting; I'm donating. I'm declaring my bookie a charitable institution on my taxes this year."

"Tell me about Abe Burrows, Packy."

"Brother Abe, my colleague in legislative servitude?"

Packy was a magnet for gossip; he gathered it to his bosom like a miser collected gold.

"Yeah. What's your take on him?"

"Why are you asking?

"Just curious."

"Just curious?" Packy repeated, his shrewd eyes narrowing. When Packy's eyes narrowed, they disappeared into creases of fat.

"Yeah," DeMarco said.

"Are you going to tell me *why* you're curious?"

"No."

"Gee, what a sweet deal. I help you—you tell me shit. How can I refuse?"

DeMarco didn't say anything.

Several years ago, an unscrupulous lobbyist—an oxymoron, to be sure—had been hired to prevent Congress from passing a particular law. The lobbyist decided that one way to better ensure that he met his client's objective was to blackmail certain legislators who were undecided on how to cast their vote. He hired several young women who were much better-looking than your average curbside hooker to lure the chosen lawmakers to their beds, and then used a hidden camera to photograph them in positions they wouldn't want their wives to see.

DeMarco had been assigned by Mahoney to extricate one congressman who had been trapped in the lobbyist's snare, and in the course of doing so, he came across photographs of Packy Morris. In the photos Packy was naked—a sight that still gave him nightmares—and he was sandwiched between two nude women whose faces had been made up to look like the actors' in the musical *Cats*. DeMarco didn't know why the lobbyist had compromising photos of Packy but he suspected it had to do with the fact Packy's father was absurdly rich. He gave the negatives to Packy—and made no comments on sexual fantasies involving felines—but Packy had never been quite sure that DeMarco hadn't kept a set of the pictures for himself.

"Okay," Packy said, "but let me ask one thing: Whatever you're working on, does it have anything to do with my favorite senator from Maryland?"

DeMarco raised his right hand—a gesture made by perjurer and truthsayer alike—and said, "I swear, Packy, I am doing nothing that will touch your boss."

Packy's eyes narrowed again as he attempted to measure DeMarco's capacity for deceit. Skeptical, but apparently satisfied, he said, "The Cisco Kid and Pancho. Morelli's the hero, of course, but he needs his Pancho, and Abe Burrows plays a very nasty Pancho."

"What do you mean?"

"You've seen Morelli—all sweetness and reason, nary a harsh word for anyone. Well, before Morelli ever gets to the bargaining table, Abe runs around town stabbing people in the back and banging them over the head. We all play hardball up here, Joe, but Abe's a pitcher that doesn't just brush back the batters—he throws right at their heads and likes it when he beans 'em."

"What's their personal relationship? Are they close, are they friends? Is Burrows loyal to Morelli— I mean in more than an employer-employee sort of way?"

Packy thought for a moment, his lips moving as he speculated, as if he were chewing something very small with his large front teeth.

"Are they friends? No. But Burrows loves Morelli."

"Loves him? You mean he's gay?"

"No. Abe loves him platonically. He worships the ground Morelli walks on, and Morelli doesn't even know Abe's alive."

"Do you have some basis for this insight, Packy?"

"Nothing empirical. Just a feeling I get when I see them together. You don't think of senator and aide—you think of husband and subservient, adoring wife. And there're stories," Packy added, eyes twinkling, now enjoying his role as gossip spreader.

"What stories?"

"Oh, like once in New York, before Morelli became mayor, a cop stopped his car one night because the car's all over the road. Burrows paid a thousand-dollar fine and lost his license for being under the influence. The cop who made the arrest said Burrows was driving, but the cop's partner, six months later, said that Burrows was sober as a judge and Morelli was so shit-faced he could hardly talk."

"So Burrows took the fall for his boss?"

Packy shrugged.

"How far would Burrows go for Morelli, Packy?"

"I thought I made that clear." Packy hesitated a beat then added, "Abe would die for him."

Chapter 37

———◆———

"Look," Reggie said, "do we have to keep meeting here? This place gives me the creeps."

"It's a *church*," the person on the other side of the confessional screen said. "How could a church give you the creeps?"

"I don't know, but it does. It seems, I dunno, sacrilegious or something doin' this here."

"Humph," the person said. "Is your tape recorder on?"

"Yeah," Reggie said. "It's too fuckin' dark in here to take notes"—and then immediately wished he hadn't cursed inside a church.

———◆———

A front-page article in the *Washington Post* reported that the CIA had announced the discovery of an al-

Qaeda training facility in Nigeria three months ago. Nigerian president Joseph Mbanedo vehemently denied that his country was harboring terrorists, but the U.S. ambassador to the United Nations had pressed for economic sanctions against the West African nation. Yesterday, a highly placed official at the CIA informed *Washington Post* reporter Reginald Harmon that closer analysis of satellite photos by the National Reconnaissance Office revealed that the suspected terrorist-training facility was in fact a soccer field used by members of a Methodist missionary church located a mile away. CIA spokesperson Marilyn Seely said that the error had already been reported to the President's national security adviser, Stephen Martell, and that diplomatic efforts were underway to address the error.

———————◆———————

Sammy Wix, the jockey-sized detective whom Emma had assigned to follow Charlie Eklund, said, "Every morning on his way to Langley, he stops at this Starbucks about six blocks from his house. He likes mochas. He gets out of his car—him and that big square-headed bodyguard of his—and they go inside and he gets his mocha. He's usually there at about seven, give or take five minutes."

"Thank you, Sammy," Emma said.

———————◆———————

Reggie didn't know what the hell was going on, but his source at the CIA hadn't steered him wrong yet. In fact, the bastard, whoever he was, was turning Reggie into a star. He'd even slowed down his drinking a bit, with all that had been going on lately.

His source had told him to go to this Starbucks in Falls Church. At about seven a.m., a black Lexus would arrive and a little white-haired guy and a big tough-looking guy would get out of the Lexus and go into the Starbucks. Reggie was to wait until they came out of the Starbucks, which they did about five minutes later.

As the white-haired guy was descending the steps, Reggie stepped in front of him, and when he did, the tough-looking guy reached into his coat and Reggie saw the automatic in the shoulder holster. Holy shit.

"Excuse me," Reggie said, "are you Charles Eklund?"

The white-haired guy made a little it's-okay gesture to the other man and said, "Yes."

"My name's Reggie Harmon, Mr. Eklund. I'm a reporter for the *Washington Post*. I was wondering if you had any comment on the recent articles I've written discussing major CIA blunders in West Africa and Indonesia. I don't know if you saw the articles, but—"

"No, I have no comment," Eklund said. "Now if you'll please excuse me." And Eklund stepped around Reggie.

"Hey, wait a minute," Reggie said, and he started to follow Eklund but the galoot with the gun placed a hand in the center of Reggie's chest and shook his head.

Reggie just stood there as the Lexus drove away, rubbing his chest where the man had touched him.

Chapter 38

"Reggie," DeMarco said into the phone, "do you think you could get a copy of Paul Morelli's schedule for the week before his wife died?" DeMarco could have obtained the schedule himself, but at this point he thought it prudent to keep his interest in Morelli hidden.

The reporter said, "Morelli? What the hell are you into, Joe?"

"I can't tell you, Reg."

"Yeah, well, I'm kinda busy these days. I don't know if you've noticed, but I've tagged the CIA twice in two days."

Great, DeMarco thought, now Reggie had an ego.

"Look, Reg," DeMarco said, "you do this for me, and if what I'm working on pans out, I'll give you the whole thing on exclusive. I swear."

This was a blatant manipulation. It was highly unlikely that anything DeMarco was doing would come to a publishable conclusion.

"But what are you working on?" Reggie asked.

"Reggie, just trust me," DeMarco said, glad Reggie couldn't see him rolling his eyes. "What I'm into is a whole lot bigger than the CIA's not being able to tell the difference between terrorists and soccer players."

The phone went silent for long time. Reggie was either pondering DeMarco's offer or he had slipped into an alcoholic coma.

"Okay, Joe," he said, at last. "I'll give it a shot."

"What you could do is pretend you're writing a—"

"DeMarco, I don't need you to tell me how to get information. I'm an old drunk, not a young imbecile."

They hung up after agreeing to meet at a bar in Union Station at five.

<hr />

The bar was on the main floor of Union Station. It was a nice open place with a subtle Southwestern theme—subtle if you overlooked the four ten-foot red-plastic chili peppers hanging from the ceiling. Sunlight streamed in through tall windows, and in case the windows didn't provide enough illumination, there were small lamps placed along the bar for those patrons who wanted to see what they were drinking. Reggie instantly despised the place.

"What the hell are we doing in this yuppie spawning bed?" he said to DeMarco. "The lights in here are so goddamn bright you can see every broken vein in my nose."

"It was convenient, Reg."

"Its liquor license should be shredded. Bars should be dark and smoky. Brass and mahogany. Faded photos of old boxers on the walls."

Before Reggie could offer further insights on the décor, DeMarco asked, "Did you get the senator's schedule?"

"Child's play."

Reggie reached into a pocket and removed a sheet of paper. DeMarco snatched it from him and began to study it.

"If you tell me what you're looking for, maybe I can help," Reggie said.

DeMarco ignored him. The newspapers had said that the night Lydia Morelli was killed she had been temporarily released from her rehabilitation at Father Martin's to attend a function with her husband. The paper hadn't said what the function was, and DeMarco was curious as to how she had behaved with her spouse the last night of her life. On the date of the murder, the senator's schedule said: "7:30 p.m., Jasco Dinner."

DeMarco borrowed Reggie's cell phone—the battery on his was dead—and called Madeline Moss, a socialite he'd had a brief fling with following his divorce. Madeline attended formal affairs six nights out of seven, and even if she hadn't been invited to the event on Morelli's schedule, she'd still be able to find out what DeMarco wanted to know. After chatting briefly with her—yes, it had been a long time; yes, he did remember the good times—he sicced her like a society bloodhound onto the trail of "Jasco Dinner."

While waiting for her to call back, DeMarco perused the rest of Morelli's schedule, and while he did, Reggie swilled booze at an alarming rate and badgered DeMarco to find out what he was working on. If he hadn't given Reggie's cell phone number to Madeline, DeMarco would have ditched him, leaving him to pick up a bar tab that was rapidly approaching three figures.

Nothing on the schedule caught his eye. Morelli had had speaking engagements almost every night that week, addressing such diverse groups as the AMA, a construction company convention, and the Air Line Pilots Association. He spent his days on Capitol Hill in a series of normal committee meetings, except for one day when he took the shuttle to New York to meet with some constituents up there. He returned from New York that same day in time to dazzle the docs at the AMA dinner. He also attended a luncheon for a new exhibit at the Smithsonian, visited the emergency ward and pediatrics section of a D.C. hospital, and had his hair trimmed. Every other morning he played squash at a club that would have refused DeMarco membership. Morelli was a busy man—just looking at his schedule made DeMarco tired.

The one thing he did learn was that Morelli had apparently not been terribly concerned about his wife because he hadn't bothered to visit her at the clinic, except for the day he had picked her up to attend the Jasco function. He had simply packed her off for a week to keep her from talking to the press, then ignored her until the night she died.

Madeline finally called back and told DeMarco that the event in question had been an affair honoring Ellen Jascovitch, a do-gooder of Mother Teresa proportions who had devoted her life to battered women, homeless kids, and other charitable endeavors. Certainly a worthy event, DeMarco concluded, but nothing that sounded so important that it was necessary for Morelli to interrupt his wife's treatment. Speaking in her catty, gossip-spreading hiss, Madeline informed him that Lydia Morelli had not attended the function. The senator had called the hostess personally and said his wife was "indisposed." Madeline interpreted this to mean that Lydia had somehow managed to fall off the wagon in the short time between leaving the clinic in Maryland and the time of the dinner.

After DeMarco thanked Madeline for her help and swore her to secrecy—a promise he knew she was genetically incapable of keeping —he looked over at Reggie and saw that the reporter's gaze was fastened onto a woman at the other end of the room. The woman was in her fifties, slightly plump, the skin under her jaw sagging a bit. Her hair was henna-colored and she wore too much green eyeshadow. She looked like a feminine version of Reggie—a once good-looking woman who had seen too much of life from the viewpoint of a bar stool.

Reggie felt DeMarco looking at him, and without taking his eyes off the woman, he said, "I know that gal over there. We were in Chicago covering the same story, can't even remember what it was now, and she was there for some Texas paper. We started out trying to see who could suck the worm out of the tequila bottle, and by the time the evening was over we were back in her room tearing up the sheets. Goddamn, she was something then, Joe. Hotter than Houston burning."

Reggie shook his head and said, "I never saw her again after that one night."

DeMarco could tell the sight of the woman brought back bittersweet memories for Reggie, and he didn't think the memories were all of high-voltage sex. Reggie was thinking back to those days when he had a fire in his belly that wasn't caused by heartburn.

"Why don't you go over and say hello to her," DeMarco said.

Still looking at the woman, Reggie said, "Ah, hell, she'd never remember me. And the way I look now, I doubt she'd want to be reminded that we once danced the nasty."

"Time didn't stand still for her either, Reg. What have you got to lose?"

Reggie was silent a moment, then he said, "Hell, you're right." Rising from the bar stool, he checked his reflection in the mirror, straightened his tie, and patted down his thinning hair. Flashing his stained teeth at DeMarco, he said, "There's a reason the ladies call me Charmin' Harmon, DeMarco. Watch closely, lad, and learn."

DeMarco crossed his fingers as Reggie approached the woman. She looked up, startled when Reggie said her name, then put her head close to his as he talked to her. Suddenly the woman gave a Texas whoop and threw her arms around Reggie's skinny neck. They talked a few minutes, then the woman gathered up her things and they left the bar, going, DeMarco imagined, to some place where the lighting was softer and kinder to them both.

It pained him to admit it, but DeMarco was jealous of Reggie—the old lush was with someone and he was not. He looked around and saw there were couples everywhere. Couples walking hand-in-hand. Couples gazing into each other's eyes. Couples doing everything but coupling. The only unattached woman he could see was a bag lady pushing a shopping cart overflowing with treasured trash; there clearly wasn't room for him in her life.

Not ready to go home to an empty house, DeMarco ordered another drink from a passing waitress and forced himself to look at Morelli's schedule again. In reviewing the schedule a second time, his eyes locked onto the visit Morelli had paid to D.C. General Hospital, his goodwill tour of the pediatric and emergency wards.

Chapter 39

Emma watched as Charlie Eklund, followed by his bodyguard, came toward the picnic table where she was seated. Eklund took mincing steps, raising his feet high, as if trying to keep the wet grass from damaging his expensive shoes.

Emma had picked Tuckahoe Park in Falls Church for the meeting, the park being halfway between her house and his. The reason she'd chosen the park, though, hadn't been for Eklund's convenience. It was instead because it was partially surrounded by thick woods and hiding in the woods were her friends Mike Koharski and Sammy Wix, each armed with a rifle. Emma doubted that Eklund—or more specifically, his armed bodyguard—would try to harm her, but as Clausewitz had said: you plan for your enemy's capabilities, not his intentions.

"Good evening," he said as he took a seat across from her at the picnic table. His bodyguard remained standing, far enough away that he couldn't hear the conversation. "Thank you for choosing a place where I can sit while we talk." He paused, then said, "May I assume that the reason we're meeting is that you now plan to threaten me."

"As you said, Charlie, it's good to deal with intelligent people. And you're right. I'm going to threaten you, and you are going to stop following me and Joe DeMarco, and you're not going to do anything further to aid Paul Morelli."

"I've never done anything to aid Senator Morelli," Eklund said.

Emma realized that that statement might indeed be true. "Maybe not," she said, "but you are willing to cover up the fact that he killed his wife."

Emma didn't know what Charlie Eklund knew regarding the night Lydia Morelli had died but she was certain that he knew something. He had had people following her, so he could have a witness who had seen Abe Burrows leaving Morelli's house that night, a witness who could contradict the story that Morelli had given to the police. Taking things a step further, he might even have bugged Morelli's home and heard everything that had happened.

Before Eklund could make a denial, Emma said, "You're a reprehensible little shit. You're willing to let a murderer become president just so you'll have somebody in the Oval Office that you can control."

"I think you're overestimating my influence," Eklund said, flicking imaginary lint off his trousers.

"Possibly. But what I know for sure is that you are not going to do anything to harm people I care about."

"And I'm not going to do this because?"

Emma opened her purse. When she reached into her purse, Eklund's bodyguard reached under his coat. Emma ignored him, but she hoped he didn't pull his weapon. That could get him killed. She pulled an envelope out of her purse and took three photographs from the envelope. The photos showed Eklund speaking to Reggie Harmon. They were standing in front of a Starbucks coffee shop.

"This week there have been two major leaks by a highly placed source at the CIA and those leaks have been very embarrassing to your director. The reporter who wrote those stories is the man in these photos, speaking to you right in front of the coffee shop where you stop every morning on your way to work."

"Ah," Eklund said. "So you think you can convince my director that I was Mr. Harmon's source."

"Yes. The reporter won't reveal his source but he will tell people he met with his source at a Catholic church two blocks from your house—and that he's met with you."

"And you think those two facts and these photos are enough? You might not be as bright as I thought," Eklund said, his small mouth turned up at the corners, his bright little eyes hard as flint.

"Oh, but I am, Charlie. I asked myself a question, one I should have asked earlier. I asked: Why would you take this kind of risk? Why would you go off on your own, unsanctioned by the agency, and have people watch Senator Morelli? At first I thought it was simply because you didn't want an anti-CIA president in the White House, or if you had one, you'd want to be able to control him in some way. But I think this isn't about you protecting Langley from the White House. I think this is about you protecting yourself."

"Myself?" Eklund said.

"Your job is your life, Charlie, and you're way past retirement age. The friends you once had at Langley have already retired or died and you don't have the influence you once had. I think you're on your way out. What you've been doing is trying to find something you can use to blackmail Morelli so if they try to make you retire, you can force him to intervene. Or maybe you're thinking even more ambitiously than that. Maybe you're thinking that with the right leverage, you can force Morelli to make you the director."

Eklund didn't say anything but he was no longer smiling.

"Whatever the case," Emma said, "I think your current director, who's just had his ass reamed out royally by the president, would love to have something like this, someone to blame all his troubles on. I think if Colin Murphy sees these photos he'll send your old ass packing and then he'll spread it all over the Hill that you're a media snitch, something that'll make it hard for you to get confirmed as DCI even if you do have Morelli in your pocket."

Eklund stared at Emma. There were now two bright red spots on his cheeks.

"Well, we'll just have to see about all that, won't we?" Eklund said, and with that he rose from the picnic table and marched away on short, stiff legs.

Chapter 40

At eight that evening, DeMarco found the doctor who had given Paul Morelli the tour of the emergency room. He was behind a door that said STAFF ONLY, stretched out on a sagging sofa, smoking a cigarette, flipping through an old swimsuit issue of *Sports Illustrated*. On the coffee table near the sofa was a can of Coke and a crumpled candy-bar wrapper. On the floor was another Coke can that the doctor was using for an ashtray.

DeMarco wanted this man for his personal physician.

The doctor was in his mid-forties. His hairline was retreating from a broad forehead and his full black beard was streaked with gray. He wore reading glasses, wrinkled green scrubs, and broken-down running shoes. He looked tired and grumpy.

"Dr. Mason?" DeMarco said.

Looking at DeMarco over the top of his glasses, the doctor said, "I don't care if you've got bubonic plague—get out of here. I've been on duty thirty-six straight hours."

"I'm sorry to bother you but it's important."

"I'll bet. So what are you? A whiplash lawyer or an insurance agent?"

"Neither. I work for the government."

"Then definitely get the hell out of here."

"Doctor, do you have any idea what percentage of this institution's budget comes from federal funds?"

"No," he said.

That was good, because DeMarco didn't either. "It's a very large percentage," DeMarco said.

"So what?"

"Well, the senator who sent me here tonight has this big budget-whacking knife. If I come home empty-handed, he'll call the head of this quackery and threaten to use it, and he'll blame all his threats on you."

The doctor smirked. He'd been working a day and a half without sleep; nobody in administration could make his life worse. DeMarco decided to try a different tack.

"Doc, they're easy questions. It'll only take a minute. Please. I have a wife and two kids at home that I'd like to kiss before midnight. Gimme a break."

The doctor studied him for a second, then said, "Aw, what the hell."

DeMarco couldn't believe it: a man hard enough not to bend in the face of intimidation but soft enough to respond to a pathetic cry for help. Maybe that's why he was a doctor.

Rising to a sitting position with a grunt, Mason said, "So what do you want?"

"Senator Morelli visited this hospital last week. He talked to you in the ER when he was here. What—"

"Your boss wants to know about Morelli's visit? That's why you're here?"

"Doc, politics is a funny game and nobody tells a grunt like me the rules. So anyway, what did you and Morelli talk about?"

Mason shrugged. "The usual stuff. How many patients we see a day, staff turnover, how long the patients normally have to wait. That kinda thing. Background, so he could take a poke at the health care system like everyone else."

"Did he ask you about gunshot wounds?"

The doctor was clearly puzzled by the question. "No," he said, "but while he was here, a resident was patching up a kid who'd just been shot. The senator put on a mask and watched him work for a while— interested in the procedure I guess."

"Could you tell me exactly where the patient was shot?"

The doctor lit another cigarette, blew smoke in the direction of the NO SMOKING sign, then jabbed an index finger at a spot near his left shoulder. "Here.

The bullet entered the pectoralis major, just below the clavicle. The kid was lucky; if the bullet had been a little lower it could have nicked a lung."

DeMarco didn't know what the pectoralis major was, but the place the doctor pointed to was exactly where Morelli had been shot. They'd shown a little anatomy picture in the *Post*.

"Did he ask any questions about the damage caused by the bullet?"

"Yeah, he seemed concerned about the patient."

"Did he ask to look at X-rays?" DeMarco asked. "You know, to get a better understanding of the wound."

"No. Why the hell would he do that? And he only spent five minutes talking to me; the photographers were all up in pediatrics."

Washington Harbour is a couple of blocks downhill from M Street in Georgetown. It's not a harbor—or a harbour—but a cluster of buildings, including a swanky hotel and half a dozen restaurants perched on the D.C. side of the Potomac River. The restaurants are built around a plaza paved with cobblestones, and in the center of the plaza is a fountain. Closest to the river is a bar with outdoor tables and Cinzano umbrellas, and you can sit there and watch crew teams training on the river. On a spring day it was a lovely place to sit and drink. On a cool fall night, the wind blowing, the plaza empty, the umbrellas put away, it was as lonely and as bleak as DeMarco felt.

DeMarco took a seat on a bench near the river and looked out across the Potomac. At eleven at night there wasn't much to see. The river was just a wide black strip separating the District from the twinkling lights of the homesteads on the northern Virginia frontier. Planes continuously taking off and landing at Reagan National Airport created a "V" of red lights in the sky. The trust people placed in air-traffic controllers was mind-boggling, DeMarco thought.

He knew what had happened to Lydia Morelli. He couldn't prove it, but he knew. His only task this evening, as he sat watching the planes land, was to organize his thoughts into a coherent string of words which might convince others.

Paul Morelli had killed his wife. The Speaker had told him she was going to the press and Morelli had confronted Lydia. He would have asked if it was true that she was thinking about telling the media some ridiculous story about him molesting their daughter. And at that point, DeMarco believed, Lydia's hate spewed forth like water from a broken dam.

She would have raged and screamed and Morelli would have tried to calm her, to charm her into believing that everything she thought was just a figment of her imagination brought on by booze and bereavement. But Lydia had finally been pushed over the edge, refusing at last to be charmed, and her husband would have concluded that he had to do something to stop her.

It would have been easy for a man of Morelli's influence to have the doctors at Father Martin's keep her away from phones and prevent her from having visitors; it may have even been standard practice to isolate a person with a severe addiction when first admitted. DeMarco suspected, however, that at the time Morelli placed Lydia in the clinic he had not decided to kill her; he had committed her to keep her away from the media and to give himself time to think. Lydia had told DeMarco that her husband was a man who never allowed himself to be rushed into premature decisions.

And when he did have time to think, Morelli must have realized the only way he could guarantee his wife's silence was to murder her, and that he had to act quickly. He knew he couldn't keep her incommunicado at Father Martin's indefinitely. He also decided at some point that he needed help, and concluded that Abe Burrows was just the man to help him. To involve anyone else would make him susceptible to blackmail for the rest of his life, but he knew, as Packy Morris did, that he could trust Burrows with his life. And if Lydia had told DeMarco the truth about the team of Morelli and Burrows, Burrows had been the senator's accomplice before, maybe not in murder, but in other sordid ventures.

So Burrows and Morelli put their bright heads together. They had conspired over more complex problems than the murder of a defenseless alcoholic, and it took them no time at all to conceive the less than original idea of having someone break into the senator's home and kill his wife, after which the senator would kill the intruder.

DeMarco believed that when Morelli saw the shooting victim in the emergency room at the hospital, practically unharmed by a small-caliber bullet, it all started to come together—and then Morelli came up with the truly brilliant part of his plan. Morelli knew that the likelihood of anyone's seriously questioning his version of his wife's murder was small—he was, after all, Senator Paul Morelli. But if he was *shot* during the bogus break-in, then no one would doubt he was a victim and he would be completely above suspicion. There was of course some physical risk—not to mention a hell of a lot of pain—but considering what was at stake—his career and ultimately the presidency—it was a risk he was willing to take.

The concept formed, all they had to do was find a disposable pawn to play the part of the evil intruder. DeMarco didn't know why they had decided on Isaiah Perry. Maybe Burrows had examined the

backgrounds of a number of low-paid personnel in
the Russell Building to find someone with a record
or connections to a criminal. Maybe they just selected
Isaiah because he was young and black. Whatever the
case, they found the perfect assailant, a young man
with a juvenile sheet and a brother known to the law.

To lure Isaiah to the senator's home, they con-
cocted the idea of Burrows buying a gun from him,
and Burrows set about immediately to blackmail
him into complying. They also came up with Isaiah's
motive—the story of Morelli catching him stealing
from his office. In retrospect, Isaiah's motive had
been the weakest part of their plan, but it had still
been good enough for the police.

As DeMarco sat there in the darkness, he could
see exactly how it had happened: The afternoon of
the murder, Morelli travels to Havre de Grace and
convinces the clinic staff that his wife needs to leave
for the night to attend the Ellen Jascovitch dinner—
which of course she never did. Morelli leaves Lydia
with Burrows while he attends the Jascovitch function, telling Burrows to let Lydia drink all she wants.
Burrows may have even spiked her drink with a sedative to keep her docile or put her to sleep. If evidence
of a sedative was found in her bloodstream during
an autopsy, the ME would think nothing of it, Lydia
being the certified addict that she was.

After the Jascovitch affair, Morelli returns home
and at midnight that night, Isaiah Perry approaches

the senator's door and tentatively knocks. Burrows, not the senator, opens the door; it would have been Burrows because all Isaiah's dealings had been with Burrows, and they wouldn't want to alarm the boy prematurely. Inside the house, Isaiah sees the senator for the first time, and Morelli, with his incomparable charm, immediately puts him at ease. He tells Isaiah the gun is really for him and asks to look at it. He compliments the young man, thanks him for performing such an unusual service, then under some pretext, gets Isaiah to follow him to the master bedroom. Once inside the bedroom, the senator—DeMarco was sure it was the senator and not Burrows: even Burrows might have balked at murder—walks up to Isaiah Perry, presses the gun against his chest, and shoots him through the heart.

Lydia Morelli stirs in her sleep but doesn't awaken because of the amount of booze she drank earlier in the evening. Morelli walks over to his wife's sleeping form, and without hesitation, shoots her in the temple. He wouldn't have hesitated because he had no conscience.

After the killings, he and Burrows survey the room and arrange a few things to make it look as if the senator and Isaiah had struggled for the gun. This explains the time lag between the first two shots and the last shot that Marcus Perry had heard.

Then came the hard part. The senator positions himself in the location where he supposedly was when Isaiah shot him. He hands the gun to Burrows, then assists Burrows by placing the barrel in the exact spot on his shoulder where the gunshot victim in the emergency room was wounded. DeMarco could imagine Burrows hesitating, unwilling to pull the trigger, until Morelli screams at him to get on with it. He could imagine the bullet burning through Morelli's shoulder, and Morelli overriding the pain with his incredible will.

After Morelli is shot, Burrows waits to make sure his boss doesn't pass out, dials 911 for him, then watches as Morelli tells the police to hurry, to come to his house, that his wife has been killed. After the call is made, Burrows rushes from the house, probably going somewhere nearby so he can call 911 again if the medics don't show up quickly.

Yes, Paul Morelli had killed his wife. DeMarco could see it all, exactly as it had happened—and he knew without a doubt that no one else would see it his way.

There was only one thing that DeMarco could not explain: If Morelli had a powerful ally who had committed crimes for him in the past, why didn't he use that same person to kill Lydia?

Chapter 41

Mahoney owned a thirty-two-foot sailboat that he moored at a marina near Annapolis. His wife, Mary Pat, was an excellent sailor and so was one of his daughters. When DeMarco was still married, Mary Pat had taken him and his wife out sailing once, on a day when the wind was gusting twenty knots, and Mary Pat had put the boat so far over on one side that the handrails had touched the water. She'd scared the crap out of DeMarco, but his ex, dimwit that she was, had thought it was a hoot.

Mahoney never went out on the boat with his wife. He claimed he got seasick as soon as it left the dock but DeMarco suspected that he too was terrified of Mary Pat's reckless seamanship. Mahoney only used the boat when he wanted to brood. He didn't take it out of the harbor; he would just sit on the deck with the boat tied to the pier and smoke cigars and drink and think. He and DeMarco now sat beside each other on canvas deck chairs, sipping Jamaican rum. There was a full moon over their heads and small whitecaps danced on the water.

"He murdered her," DeMarco said.

The Speaker closed his eyes and his lips moved in a silent curse. "What happened?" he said.

DeMarco told him. When he finished, Mahoney said, "Are you sure?"

Was he sure? He was sure O. J. had killed Nicole; he was sure Lee Harvey Oswald hadn't acted alone—and he was just as sure that Paul Morelli had murdered his wife. He couldn't prove it, but he was sure.

"Yeah," he said.

"But you have no proof?"

"No."

"So what are you going to do?"

"At this point I don't think there's anything I can do. But *you* can do something."

"Like what?" Mahoney said, his eyes narrowing with suspicion.

"Talk to the cops. I'll meet with them after you've talked to them, tell them everything I know, but I if I go to them on my own they'll blow me off."

But they sure as hell wouldn't blow off John Fitzpatrick Mahoney. No, sir. They'd reopen the investigation and find some physical evidence tying Morelli to the crime. They'd make Marcus Perry admit to seeing Burrows leave the house. They'd whack Abe Burrows with a rubber hose and make him talk. But it would take a big push from Mahoney.

The Speaker responded immediately. The brain inside his large, handsome head could calculate self-serving strategies faster than any computer. It didn't take him a nanosecond to reject DeMarco's suggestion.

"No way," he said. "If I go to the cops and tell 'em I think Morelli's a murderer, and if they can't prove it, my ass is fried. Can you imagine the fuckin' headline? Speaker of the House Accuses Presidential Contender of Murder. No goddamn way is that gonna happen, not with what you've got. No, you go to the cops on your own."

"It won't work!" DeMarco protested.

"You make it work, goddamnit!"

DeMarco just shook his head.

"You know if I go to the police," DeMarco said, "there's a good chance it'll get back to Morelli. Are you going to support me if he comes after me?"

"Of course," Mahoney said.

Of course, my ass, DeMarco thought.

"And there's something else you need to know," DeMarco said.

"What!" Mahoney snapped.

DeMarco could tell that his boss wanted this meeting over, that he wanted DeMarco to leave, but DeMarco didn't care. He launched into a discussion about Charlie Eklund conducting surveillance operations on Morelli, and van Horn and Suttel's deaths, and the unknown man who'd been helping Paul Morelli throughout his political career. As DeMarco talked, he could see Mahoney's frustration building. DeMarco's tale was complex—and John Mahoney didn't have the patience for complex tales. But what he did have was the ability to get to the core of an issue.

Mahoney stopped DeMarco mid-sentence by yelling, "Enough! Enough with all this bullshit about the CIA and some guy who's been helping Morelli. Forget all that crap and focus on one thing: focus on Morelli."

"Yeah, but—"

"Joe," Mahoney said, looking directly into DeMarco's eyes, giving him that look—the look he used to convince other politicians to follow his lead, the look he used to get young women to crawl into his bed. "Focus on Morelli. If we nail him, son, he's of no use to this CIA guy. And if we nail him, whatever he's done in the past and whoever's been helping him in the past becomes irrelevant. We gotta get *him*. We can't let him get away with what he's done."

DeMarco didn't bother to ask Mahoney why he kept saying "we" when he wanted DeMarco to do all the work and take all the risks.

DeMarco wanted to take Mahoney out on his damn boat and feed him to the fishes.

Chapter 42

Lieutenant David Drummond put down the newspaper he'd been reading and looked up at DeMarco in irritation. Before Drummond could speak, DeMarco said, "What I've got to say is going to shock you."

Drummond's expression of annoyance was instantly replaced by one of amusement.

"You couldn't shock me, pal," he said, "if you dropped your pants and showed me a rose where your dick's supposed to be."

"Okay," DeMarco said. "I believe Senator Paul Morelli, abetted by his chief of staff, Abe Burrows, killed Lydia Morelli and Isaiah Perry in cold blood." Judging by the way Drummond's jaw dropped, DeMarco figured that he had given the detective a jolt even without undoing his belt.

Drummond didn't say anything for a moment.

He just sat looking at DeMarco as if he was trying to measure his mental stability. Finally, he cleared his throat and said, "Say what you came to say, bub, but I'm telling you up front that I think you're a nut. If I didn't owe Emma, your ass would be out on the street already."

DeMarco took a seat in the wooden chair in front of Drummond's desk. He took his time telling what he suspected, making sure Drummond had a clear understanding of all the nuances, of all the things he had learned that had led him to his conclusion. While he was speaking Drummond sat with his hands steepled under his chin, staring at DeMarco, the only indication of his feelings a skeptical droop to his lips.

When DeMarco finished, Drummond leaned back in his chair and placed his thick boxer's hands behind his crew-cut head. He was completely relaxed—not looking at all like a man who had just been given the conspiracy murder of the decade.

In a voice dripping with sarcasm, he said, "Let me see if I got this straight. Lydia Morelli, who's blotto ninety percent of the time, convinces you that her husband, God's gift to America, molested his stepdaughter and drove her to suicide. The fact that the highway patrol ruled Kate Morelli's death an accident is a small detail which you've apparently decided to ignore. Then when Lydia is put in a dry-out clinic, which even you admit is something she needed, you think it's because she's threatened, half a year after her daughter's death, to go to the media and tell them all the nasty things her husband's done. Oh, and she's also going to tell some other secret— about this powerful man who's been helping Morelli his whole career—but you don't know who this guy is. Have I got it right so far?"

DeMarco felt a flush begin at the base of his neck and work its way toward his forehead, but he only nodded in response to Drummond's question.

"Let's see now, where was I? Oh yeah. After Lydia is killed by this little bastard—"

"Isaiah Perry didn't have a motive for killing anyone, Drummond. He didn't try to steal a damn thing."

Ignoring DeMarco, Drummond continued, "You go to see Marcus Perry, a dope-dealing, murdering punk, and he convinces you that his little brother was at Morelli's house that night because he was delivering the man a gun. Selling him a gun, for Christ's sake! And according to solid-citizen Marcus, his brother was doing this because nasty ol' Abe Burrows, who looks like the Pillsbury doughboy, said he'd lose his job if he didn't."

"He was an eighteen-year-old kid, Drummond! Burrows intimidated him."

Drummond continued as if DeMarco hadn't spoken. "Now when Isaiah Perry gets to the senator's house, you think that the senator kills him with the gun he was supposedly selling, shoots his wife in the head, then calmly sits there and lets Burrows blow a hole in his arm. Oh, I almost forgot. Burrows deliberately told Perry to bring a *small*-caliber weapon and it was during a visit Morelli made to a hospital to see a buncha sick kids that he learns enough about anatomy and gunshot wounds in five minutes to keep from blowing his arm off. Now did I miss anything?"

"Yeah. Marcus Perry saw Burrows leave the house."

"Marcus was the fuckin' getaway driver, you moron! And why would Burrows be there—so the senator could have a witness who could blackmail him for the rest of his life?"

"No, because Morelli wanted someone to help him handle Isaiah, and because he was afraid he might pass out after he was shot and he wanted someone there to call an ambulance so he wouldn't bleed to death."

"Tell me something, DeMarco, since it's your story: *Why* did the senator shoot himself?"

"Because he knew if he was shot during this so-called break-in, no one would suspect him of murdering his wife. You people sure as hell didn't. And he'd be a real American hero—not only did he blow away a bad guy, he was shot while doing it. When the presidency is at stake, Drummond, people are willing to take big risks."

"You're a fuckin' head case," Drummond said. There was no inflection in his voice; he was merely stating a fact.

"Marcus Perry described Burrows to me. How did he know what Burrows looked like?"

Drummond paused for a moment, smiled, then said, "He saw him on TV, when Morelli left the hospital."

The bastard had an answer for everything.

"Then how did Isaiah gain access to the senator's house?" DeMarco persisted. "I know the house has a security system."

"The senator said they only set the system when they weren't home. The kid broke the glass in the back door and came in that way."

"Maybe Burrows broke the glass before he left the house," DeMarco said.

"Horseshit."

"Goddamnit, did you people do *any* kind of investigation? Did you check Isaiah's hands for gunshot residue to see if he'd really fired a gun? Did you analyze the blood splatter to see if it was consistent with the senator's story?"

Drummond laughed and said, "Gunshot residue! Blood splatter! You been watchin' *CSI* on TV, DeMarco? You think you're Gris Gussom, or whatever the fuck his name is?"

The fact was that the only thing DeMarco knew about gunshot residue *was* what he'd seen on television. Ignorance wasn't an inhibitor, though, and he said, louder than he had intended, "Maybe if you watched TV you'd have some idea of how to investigate a murder."

Drummond stood up. Pointing a thick finger at DeMarco, he yelled, "You're out of your fuckin' mind! Your goddamn murder theory is nothing but conjecture based on the ramblings of a drunk and a low-life criminal who's related to the kid who got shot!"

While Drummond was yelling, DeMarco had stood, tipping over the chair he had been sitting in, and yelled back. "Don't any of you idiots find it amazing that this straight-A student, who's never been in trouble in his life, would try to kill a United States senator?"

They stood there glaring at each other. They had reached the point that men always seem to reach when they can't agree—screaming at the top of their lungs, stopping just short of beating their paws on their chests. To DeMarco, they were proof of why only women should be heads of state.

After a moment, Drummond closed his eyes and took a deep breath. The effort he exerted to regain his composure was tangible. He reopened his eyes, and said in a neutral, bureaucratic tone, "Mr. DeMarco, exactly what do you expect this department to do?"

"I want you to reopen the investigation into Lydia

Morelli's murder, but this time treat her husband as a suspect."

Drummond nodded his head and said, "Your expectations will be conveyed to my superiors."

DeMarco studied the cop's suddenly impassive face, then said, "You're not going to do a damn thing, are you?"

Drummond leaned forward, placed his big knuckles on the surface of his desk, and said, "I'm six months short of a full pension. Get the hell outta here and don't come back."

Chapter 43

The phone next to the bed jolted him awake. He glanced with one eye at the clock on the bedside table: 7:30 a.m. Inconsiderate bastard. He picked up the receiver and grunted hello.

"DeMarco, you *ASSHOLE*! You be in the senator's office at ten sharp. You got that?"

It was Burrows. DeMarco was screwed.

"What's the problem, Abe?" DeMarco said. He already knew what the problem was.

"You know what the goddamn problem is!" Burrows affirmed.

DeMarco thought of telling Burrows to go to hell but knew he'd eventually have to face the music. And he needed to know what Morelli knew. "I don't know what you're so upset about, Abe," he lied, "but I'll be there if that's what the senator wants."

"You better," Burrows said. "You *ASSHOLE!*" he screamed again as he hung up.

DeMarco didn't have to be clairvoyant to know why Paul Morelli wanted to see him. Detective Drummond, feeling the need to cover his nearly retired ass, had called his boss after DeMarco left. "Hey, you won't believe it," Drummond had said to his boss. "This fruitcake just came in with this crazy idea that Morelli popped his wife. What a hoot." Drummond's superior would have chuckled in agreement but the word would have gone up the ladder. Eventually, someone trying to wheedle his way into favor had called Morelli and said, "Just wanted you to know, sir. But not to worry, sir. We're not taking this wacko seriously."

If the damn Speaker had done what DeMarco had asked, if he had *personally* talked to the chief of detectives as DeMarco had wanted, this wouldn't have happened.

He was fucked.

When DeMarco arrived at Morelli's office in the Russell Building, two fit-looking young men in suits were sitting in the reception area reading magazines. They tensed when DeMarco stepped through the door and watched him as he walked over to the receptionist's desk to ask for Burrows. DeMarco noted their wary eyes—then saw the flesh-colored devices in their left ears and the almost-invisible white cords running from the earpieces down into the collars of their suit coats. He thought they might be Secret Service agents, but as Morelli wasn't officially running for president yet, they were more likely plainclothed U.S. Capitol policemen. The Capitol police routinely provide protection for members of the House and Senate, and in this case DeMarco suspected that they may have been worried that someone associated with Isaiah Perry—a young black man who came from a gang-infested neighborhood—might decide to retaliate for Isaiah's death. Whoever they were, they were a couple of serious-looking bastards.

Burrows came out of his office as soon as the receptionist informed him of DeMarco's arrival. He looked as he had the last time DeMarco had seen him: baggy pants, a rumpled blue shirt with a tail hanging out, and a badly wrinkled tie. With his frizzy, white man's Afro and disheveled clothes, he looked like the last clown out of a circus Volkswagen— except for his eyes. Why hadn't he noticed those eyes before?

When he saw DeMarco, Burrows's face mottled red and his jaw clenched with suppressed rage. He started to say something to DeMarco, then stopped and turned to the bodyguards. "Check this guy over," he said. "Make sure he's not wearing a wire—or a gun."

Both men immediately got to their feet, and one of them put his hand inside his coat, ready to draw his weapon if necessary.

"Oh, for Christ's sake, Abe," DeMarco said, "I don't have a—"

"Keep your hands still, sir," one of the men said to DeMarco.

The other bodyguard ran his hands over every inch of DeMarco's body, probing at his crotch, running his fingers through his hair. By the time he nodded to Burrows to indicate he was satisfied, DeMarco's face was crimson with embarrassment.

"Let's go," Burrows said to DeMarco. "The senator's waiting."

"Mr. Burrows," one of the bodyguards said, "if you believe this man's a security risk, we should sit in on your meeting."

"No, he's not going to do anything," Burrows said. "He's dumb, but he's not that dumb."

DeMarco clenched his teeth. He felt like bouncing Burrows off the wall for that last remark, but if he did, the security guys would have him down on the ground and handcuffed in about two seconds. So he controlled his temper and followed Burrows to Morelli's office, recombing his hair with his fingers as he walked.

Morelli was standing in front of a window offering his profile to DeMarco. He was posed in a campaign-poster shot, the dome of the Capitol forming a perfect backdrop for the perfect candidate. The black sling was gone from his arm and so was the wan, drawn look he had exhibited leaving the hospital. To DeMarco he looked handsome and fit and presidential—and not the least bit grief-stricken.

The only testimony to his wife's passing was the black armband he wore on the right sleeve of his suit coat. The suit itself was gray with a light blue pinstripe and the maroon handkerchief in the suitcoat pocket matched the color of his tie. As Lydia had said, he'd soon be on the cover of *GQ*—America's most eligible bachelor.

The senator turned his head slowly and looked at DeMarco for several seconds without speaking. His dark eyes were unreadable, his face expressionless. Finally, he pointed to a chair in front of his desk and said, "Please take a seat, Joe."

Turning to Burrows, Morelli said, "Abe, when do I have to be at the White House?"

"Twenty-five minutes, Senator. The car will be out front in fifteen." Pointing at DeMarco, Burrows added, "I had him checked for wires. He's clean."

Morelli acted as though he hadn't heard Burrows and took a seat behind his desk. Burrows took a position off to DeMarco's right, leaning against a wall, too agitated to sit.

Morelli waited until silence strained the atmosphere in the room to the point of explosion before finally saying, "Why did you go to the police with that story, Joe?"

DeMarco hesitated. He couldn't say it was because Mahoney had told him to.

Before Morelli could respond, Burrows launched himself from the wall and screamed into DeMarco's face, "Listen, you dipshit! We know every word you told that cop. Now answer the senator's question."

"Control yourself, Abe," Morelli said to Burrows. To DeMarco, using the same soft tone he'd used before, he said, "But Abe's right, Joe. Being evasive isn't going to help. It's going to make me angry—and you don't want to make me angry."

Burrows's open rage was less frightening than Morelli's restrained manner. Abe was a string of firecrackers going off next to DeMarco's ear; the senator was a grenade—and when it detonated it was going to splatter DeMarco all over the room.

To hell with it, DeMarco thought. "I had information," he said, "that I felt the police needed to hear. It was my obligation to tell them."

"I see. So you were just doing your duty," Morelli said, nodding his head as if DeMarco's response made sense.

"Duty, my ass," Burrows said. "This prick is—"

Morelli raised a hand to silence Burrows. "Do you really believe I molested my daughter and killed my wife, Joe? Do you?"

Looking at Morelli, it did seem inconceivable that this handsome, confident, president-to-be could possibly have done anything so horrible.

"I only know what your wife told me, Senator," DeMarco said.

"And when did you talk to Lydia?"

"The day after I visited your house. She called me."

"But why would she call you?"

"I don't know," DeMarco said. "Maybe because she knew I was an investigator." There was nothing to be gained by telling Morelli that Lydia had contacted him because she wanted him to pursue Terry Finley's investigation. All he knew for sure was that the world had been punched inside-out: Morelli had murdered his wife and DeMarco was the one being interrogated.

"And you actually believed her allegations," Morelli said, shaking his head in disbelief that anyone would be so gullible.

"She was convincing."

"Joe, you must have known that Lydia had a severe drinking problem." There was a studio portrait of Lydia and her daughter prominently displayed on the corner of the senator's desk. He looked over at the photograph and said, "God rest her soul, but she was a very confused person."

In the photograph, Lydia's face was turned toward her daughter's, and a gentle, motherly smile curved her lips. Kate Morelli had her mother's blue eyes and an impish grin that broke DeMarco's heart.

"And, Joe," Morelli continued, "what on earth possessed you to spout all that nonsense about Abe being at my house and that poor boy selling a gun?"

DeMarco was tired of squirming—and he was damn tired of a runt like Burrows screaming in his ear. "Marcus Perry, Isaiah's brother, told me." He looked over at Burrows and said, "Marcus was parked outside your house that night, Senator. He was a witness." DeMarco had told this to Drummond so he wasn't telling Morelli anything he didn't already know.`

Morelli's only reaction was a small negative shake of his head as if amused that DeMarco would be foolish enough to listen to Marcus Perry, but Burrows said, "Witness, my ass! Marcus Perry is a goddamn drug dealer." Trying to sound sarcastic, but not quite able to pull it off, Burrows said, "And what else did Marcus tell you, DeMarco?"

When DeMarco ignored Burrows, keeping his eyes focused on Morelli, Burrows said, "Answer my question, goddamnit!"

DeMarco started to get out of his chair—he wasn't going to put up with any more crap from Burrows—but before he could stand completely, Morelli said, "Abe, go see if the limo's out front yet."

DeMarco realized immediately that Morelli wasn't concerned about what DeMarco might do to Burrows; he just wanted Burrows out of the room, afraid that in his agitated state, his aide would let something slip. Abe was a liability and the senator knew it. DeMarco wondered if Abe knew it.

"But, Senator . . . ," Burrows said.

"Abe, go check on the car. Now, please."

Morelli waited until Burrows shut the door behind him, then said, "You've made some very serious accusations against me without a shred of evidence, Joe, and I'm extremely upset. The police don't believe you, of course; in fact they're worried that you're mentally unstable. I suspect they've already notified the Secret Service and the Capitol police."

Great. Now he was on the Service's wacko-assassin list. That goddamn Mahoney.

"And I hope you're not thinking about going to the press with these wild theories of yours."

DeMarco didn't say anything but he was wondering if he shouldn't bring up Charlie Eklund and the fact that Eklund's people might have seen something the night Lydia died. He finally decided not to. DeMarco didn't know what Eklund knew, but he did know that Eklund wasn't an ally. So he just sat there as Morelli continued to threaten him.

"Because if you did go to the press," Morelli said, "you should know that I'd litigate you into abject poverty. In fact, I imagine I have enough influence in this city to make your life miserable without taking any direct action against you. I don't have to hire a single lawyer; all I have to do is whisper my displeasure into a few ears."

This was like Mike Tyson challenging his girlfriend to a fight. Morelli had DeMarco outweighed and outclassed, and they both knew it.

Trying to maintain a semblance of dignity, DeMarco said, "I informed the police of your wife's accusations because I felt I had an obligation to do so. I've done everything I intend to do."

And he realized, at that moment, that what he had just said was the complete truth. He was in so far over his head he wasn't going to have anything more to do with Paul Morelli, no matter what Mahoney said.

Morelli stared at DeMarco as he considered DeMarco's response. Finally he said, speaking almost in a whisper, "Joe, who put you up to this?"

Now DeMarco understood the reason for this meeting. It wasn't to find out what DeMarco knew—or even to threaten him. Morelli had called him here to find out if there was someone with *real* power behind him—and DeMarco was not about to tell him. The possibility of the Speaker's taking his side against Morelli was slim, but a slim chance was better than no chance at all.

"No one put me up to anything, Senator."

"You did this all on your own? Is that what you expect me to believe?

"Yes, sir"

"I don't think so."

Apparently Morelli couldn't picture DeMarco without a master holding his leash.

"Who do you work for, Joe?" Morelli asked again.

"No one, Senator. My office is independent."

This made Morelli smile. "Joe, you're a GS-13. There's no such thing as an independent GS-13 in D.C."

DeMarco didn't answer.

"John Mahoney referred you to me. Do you work for John?"

Oh, shit.

"No, sir," DeMarco said. "I've done some work for the Speaker in the past but I don't report to him. He just asked me to talk to Dick Finley."

Morelli thought about DeMarco's response for a moment, then nodded his head. "Yes, John's a friend. He'd never try to bring me down in such an underhanded manner. So it must be somebody else. Did some Republican put you up to this?"

Now that was rich: Morelli acting like the Republicans were the root of all evil when he was the one who had killed to stay in power.

"No, sir," DeMarco said. "It's like I told you, my position is independent of any politician or political party. I'm just a lawyer who exists to serve the members of Congress."

"You haven't served me very well, have you, Joe?"

There was nothing he could say to that.

Morelli looked at DeMarco for a moment, then rose slowly to his feet and walked back over to the window where he had been posing when DeMarco entered the room.

"Do you know why I'm going to the White House this morning?" Morelli said, glancing up at the Capitol's dome.

"No."

"The president can't get his welfare reform plan through Congress. It's not a bad plan but he can't get the legislature to . . . embrace it. I'm going to the White House to tell the president how to sell his plan."

He shook his head in dismay, thinking of the president's incompetence.

"And do you know what I'm doing this afternoon?"

"No."

"I'm meeting with select members of the House and Senate to introduce the most sweeping gun-control legislation this country has ever seen. I guarantee you that within ten years gun-related crime in this country will be reduced so drastically that you'll think you're living in Switzerland. And do you know who's going to be sitting beside me when I introduce this bill?"

DeMarco shook his head. He had no idea why Morelli was telling him all this, but anything was better than being grilled about who his boss was.

"Some of the most influential members of the NRA," Morelli said. "I'm going to call it Lydia's Bill—you know, like the Brady Bill—and the tragedy of my wife's death will be the wellspring of something glorious."

DeMarco realized Morelli was being completely sincere: he was proud that he was able to use his wife's murder to produce legislation that would keep others from being killed. He had taken cold pragmatism to a new level; stone had more conscience than he did.

Morelli fixed his dark eyes on DeMarco, and for a moment DeMarco felt the magnetic pull of his personality. "Joe, you must believe me," he said, "when I tell you I can create a new American reality. A reality that we will be proud to pass on to our children."

Paul Morelli was absolutely certain that he was fated to rule the nation and nothing but good would come of his ruling. He saw visions that others were too small and too dull to appreciate—and God help those others if they got in his way.

"I feel we're at a dangerous crossroads, Joe. This great country, myself . . . and you. You don't want to choose the wrong path; there's too much at stake. Now tell me who you're working for."

"Senator, it's like I said, I—"

"Joe," he interrupted, "I don't have time for this." For the first time Morelli's control slipped—just a bit—and the cold fury behind his soft-spoken words was naked and frightening.

He walked over to the chair where DeMarco was sitting, leaned down, and placed his hands on the arms of the chair. His face was only inches from DeMarco's, so close his black eyes were lasers boring into DeMarco's brain.

"You must understand," Morelli said. "I will allow no one to stop me. No one!"

His eyes pinned DeMarco to the chair.

"Do you understand, Joe?"

DeMarco nodded his head. Here was this politician in a suit—not some outlaw biker with a chain in his hand or some hood armed to the teeth—and Paul Morelli was scaring the crap out of him.

Burrows came back into the office at that moment. "Senator, we have to get going," he said. "The car's out front and so's the press. They must have heard about your meeting with the president."

Morelli ignored Burrows. He remained in the same position for what seemed an eternity, his face close to DeMarco's.

"Do you understand?" he said again in that same soft voice.

DeMarco nodded.

Apparently satisfied, Morelli straightened up and said, "I hope so, Joe. I really do."

Burrows handed the senator his topcoat and helped him into it. Turning to DeMarco, Morelli said in that same even, reasonable voice, "I'll find out eventually who put you up to this but regardless of who it was, I think you should plan on leaving Washington. It would be in your best interest. Don't you agree?"

DeMarco nodded again. He was starting to feel like one of those head-bobbing Kewpie dolls on the rear-window ledge of a car.

"Then thank you for coming today," Morelli said and turned and left the room.

Burrows started to follow his boss out of the office, but then he turned and made his hand into a pistol—thumb raised, index finger extended—and shot an imaginary bullet through DeMarco's brain. Abe Burrows didn't look like a clown anymore.

DeMarco stood alone in the center of Morelli's office, numb and disoriented. He had just been told to leave town by a man who would soon be the most powerful man in the world—the next president of the United States. He looked out the window. The sight of the Capitol's dome, instead of assuring him that he was safe, protected by law and its many servants, merely added to the unreality of his circumstance.

Chapter 44

DeMarco left Morelli's office and found himself behind the senator's entourage as they made their way toward the main entrance of the Russell Building. The group made a reverse flying wedge as it approached the doorway: the two bodyguards from the reception area were walking together, slightly ahead of the senator; the senator and Burrows walked side by side, their heads close as they conversed; a second aide was directly behind the senator, carrying a heavy briefcase. And then came DeMarco, trailing a few paces behind Morelli's party, like a reluctant goose on a southbound flight.

Morelli exited the building and was stopped immediately on the landing, just beyond the doorway, his way blocked by a reporter and her cameraman. The reporter was a twenty-something brunette wearing a short skirt to show off her legs and large-framed glasses to convince her audience that she was a serious journalist. Her gray-bearded cameraman looked bored, clearly wishing he was someplace else; it had been a long time since he'd found a politician worth filming.

At this point, time shifted into slow motion.

The reporter was asking Morelli something, pushing the microphone toward his face, but DeMarco didn't hear what she said because over the senator's shoulder, at the bottom of the steps, near the curb, he could see a man in an Oakland Raiders jacket. It was Marcus Perry.

Marcus began to ascend the steps toward the landing where the senator was standing. His face was expressionless, his eyes fixed on Morelli. There was a gun in his right hand, held down, partially obscured by his right leg.

Morelli's bodyguards were looking around nonchalantly, checking the limo parked at the curb, checking the legs of the reporter. They were looking everywhere but at Marcus Perry.

Marcus started to raise his right arm.

DeMarco screamed, "Marcus, don't!"

Marcus ignored him. The center—and end—of his universe was Paul Morelli.

One of the bodyguards looked back to see why DeMarco was shouting, but the other guard saw the gun in Marcus's hand. Marcus was now halfway up the steps, less than thirty feet from Morelli. The guard who saw that Marcus was armed scrambled frantically beneath his jacket for his own weapon, but at that moment Abe Burrows shoved past the man, knocking him off-balance.

Burrows stepped in front of Morelli and held up his hand to stop Marcus from coming any closer. DeMarco didn't think that Burrows was trying to shield the senator; he didn't think that Burrows had even seen the gun in Marcus's hand. Burrows was simply trying to keep him from bothering the senator during the press conference. Abe was used to running interference for Morelli—it was something he did automatically, like helping him into his coat. Abe's final act was a gesture of spontaneous help-fulness for the person he most adored.

Instead of Macus's bullets hitting Morelli, the first one struck Burrows in the chest, the second one in the throat. Some of the blood from the second shot sprayed onto the second aide's face, but miracu-lously, not a drop touched Paul Morelli.

Morelli didn't move—not one inch. He didn't duck or turn to run back inside the building or take any other action to avoid being killed. Because DeMarco was behind him, he couldn't see the ex-pression on Morelli's face, but that evening on the news he would see it as they played and replayed those moments. Morelli just stood there on the landing, looking down the steps at Marcus Perry with as much emotion as a man would display surveying the morning sky for rain.

How he could have done that—stood there fearlessly, not the least concerned for his own safety—may have been the clearest sign of Paul Morelli's megalomania. Or he may have had the presence of mind to know that a camera was focused on him, and he was determined not to look like a coward. But DeMarco didn't think that was it. DeMarco thought that Morelli was unafraid because he knew, without any doubt, that some poor black kid with a gun had no more chance of derailing his destiny than the autumn leaves drifting down from the trees.

Before Marcus could fire a third shot, weapons bloomed in the hands of both bodyguards. The weapons were some kind of small machine guns, Uzis or Mac-10s. Whatever the hell they were, they fired bullets at an incredible rate. DeMarco didn't know how many bullets hit Marcus. He seemed to stand there forever, jerking like a spastic puppet as round after round struck him in the chest.

When the shooting stopped, time resumed its normal pace. The female reporter was lying on the ground sobbing. The aide who'd been splattered with Abe Burrows's blood was running his hands frantically over his body, not sure if he'd been hit or not. The two guards, guns smoking, were breathing so hard they were almost hyperventilating.

The senator stood a moment surveying the carnage, then stepped over Burrows's body and helped the reporter to her feet. Burrows clearly was of no more use to him; the reporter had some potential value. One of the bodyguards, being less pragmatic than Morelli, knelt down and checked Burrows's pulse, although it was obvious the gesture was a waste of time.

DeMarco walked past them all, down the steps to where Marcus Perry lay. His eyes were open, staring up blindly at a pewter-colored sky.

Marcus had had no plan at all. He had simply driven to the Russell Building hoping to catch Morelli outdoors. Maybe it hadn't occured to him that the senator would have a security detail—or maybe it did, and he just didn't care.

DeMarco knew the media would portray Marcus's attempt to avenge his brother's death as nothing more than a grisly continuation of the senseless cycle of violence perpetuated daily in the projects: you kill mine, I kill you, and on it goes. But DeMarco knew it was deeper than that. Marcus had genuinely cared for his brother, and he knew, as DeMarco did, that Paul Morelli would never pay for his crime. Unlike DeMarco, though, Marcus had had the courage to do something.

Within minutes of the shooting, the Russell Building was surrounded by flashing blue and red lights. Uniformed members of the Capitol police descended on the scene in droves, delighted to have something more exciting to do than provide directions to tourists. Ignoring everyone around him, Morelli knelt dramatically at the side of his fallen aide and as he did the cameraman recorded his grief and the reporter talked into her mike. The pretty reporter was looking at Morelli with eyes that radiated something more than admiration, something just less than lust.

As DeMarco stood at the bottom of the steps near the spreading pool of blood that had drained from Marcus Perry, he looked up at Morelli and for an instant their eyes met. It may have been DeMarco's imagination, but he thought he saw the senator's lips briefly compress into a thin, self-satisfied smile. Morelli knew that with Burrows and Marcus both dead, there was no one left to contradict his story of Lydia's death.

Chapter 45

DeMarco walked away from the blood-washed concrete in front of the Russell Building and pushed his way through the gathering crowd. As he made his way across the Capitol's grounds, the spines of fallen leaves snapping under his feet sounded like gunshots. He stopped when he came to a quiet spot where he could talk and pulled out his cell phone.

To get quickly past Mahoney's secretary, DeMarco told her he was the president's chief of staff.

"Billy, me boyo," the Speaker said jovially when he answered the phone.

"It's me," DeMarco said.

"What the fuck?" the Speaker responded.

"Turn on your television. Channel 4," DeMarco said.

Momentarily he heard the sound of the television and Mahoney saying "Jesus Christ" several times. Then Mahoney said into the phone, "Hey, that's you. What the hell are you doing there?"

"The cops ratted me out to Morelli," DeMarco said. "I went to see them yesterday, to try to convince them that they needed to reopen the investigation into Lydia's death, and they told the senator. This morning he called me to his office and said he was going to litigate me into the poorhouse if I continued to pursue this thing. Then he told me to leave town."

"That dumb son of a bitch," Mahoney said.

"Morelli?" DeMarco said.

"No, that black kid," Mahoney said, apparently still watching the television. "What the hell was he thinking?"

"Did you hear what I said?" DeMarco said. "Morelli told me to leave Washington."

"Yeah," Mahoney said.

Yeah, what? DeMarco waited for Mahoney to say something else, and when he didn't, DeMarco said, "But the real reason Morelli called me to his office was to find out who I was working for."

"Son of a bitch," the Speaker muttered. *Now* DeMarco had his attention. "So what did you tell him?"

"I told him I didn't work for anyone."

"Did he believe you?"

"No," DeMarco said. "And I'll tell you something else: with Burrows and Marcus Perry both dead, Morelli's untouchable."

The Speaker was silent for several seconds. DeMarco could hear the television set in the background. Finally Mahoney spoke.

"Goddamn, son," he said, "you've sure fucked this up."

DeMarco entered the Capitol and descended the steps to his subbasement office. He bolted the door, took the phone on his desk off the hook, and shut off his cell phone. He needed to think; he needed to figure out what to do next.

He ultimately concluded that the answer was: do nothing.

Like he'd told Mahoney, the likelihood of ever convicting Paul Morelli for murdering his wife was now zero with Marcus Perry and Abe Burrows both dead. In addition to the lack of witnesses, there was the fact that the cops were unwilling to even consider that a man of Morelli's reputation and stature could be a murderer. And with Lydia dead, it seemed equally unlikely that he'd ever be able to connect Morelli to this powerful man who had been committing crimes for years to advance Morelli's political career. Finally, it was also obvious from talking to the women that Morelli had raped—he now had no doubt that Lydia had told him the truth about what Morelli had done—that neither Davenport nor Tyler was likely to ever testify against their attacker.

Paul Morelli, it appeared, was bulletproof.

DeMarco also knew that he was worrying about the wrong problem. Forget Morelli. What was going to happen to *him*? Oddly enough, he realized that he wasn't afraid that Morelli would have him killed. Morelli wasn't a crazed serial killer— he was a pragmatic man. He'd only killed his wife because he could think of no other way to silence her. But he didn't need to kill lowly Joe DeMarco, a man with no clout or authority and not one speck of evidence that could harm him. So Morelli probably wouldn't kill him but he might make good on his promise to ruin DeMarco professionally and financially and run him out of town. And would John Mahoney be there to save him from Morelli? Yeah, right. DeMarco laughed out loud at that idea. Mahoney's only concern was that *he* not get into the crosshairs of the future president of the United States.

DeMarco considered what would happen if he lost his job. He may have had a law degree but he'd never practiced law. He could just see himself, at his age, applying for a position at some law firm and the firm asking what he'd been doing since college. Uh, well, he'd say, I bring envelopes stuffed with cash to a politician that I can't name. Thank you very much, the law firm would say. Don't call us, we'll call you.

He did a quick calculation. If he got a good price for his George-town house, and paid off what he owed on the mortgage, and considering what he had in savings, how long could he survive before he'd have to accept a job at McDonald's burning French fries? The answer to that question, as near as he could tell, was about two weeks.

So he would do nothing. He wouldn't investigate Paul Morelli any further and he'd just have to wait and see what Morelli was going to do to him.

———◆◆◆———

DeMarco got back to his house about five-thirty, went into the kitchen, and scrambled a couple of eggs. His lucky streak continued: most of the eggs stuck to the bottom of the frying pan. He took the eggs and toast he'd made—he could make flawless toast—and carried the plate into his den and turned on the television set. The evening news was just starting.

The lead story, naturally, was the assassination attempt. They showed the film clip of the shoot-out on Capitol Hill, the anchorman describing Marcus Perry's and Abe Burrows's deaths like an NFL play-by-play announcer. When the tape ended, the anchorman informed his viewers that they were now going live to a reporter who had the latest developments on the attempted assassination of the senator.

Monica Bradshaw, the attractive, leggy reporter who had been at the Russell Building that morning, came on the screen. "We are here in the home of Eloise May Perry," she said, "the mother of Isaiah and Marcus Perry. Mrs. Perry and her minister, the Reverend Jackson Knoll, met with Senator Morelli earlier in the day, and the senator has agreed to let us record an historic announcement this evening."

The reporter's face glowed with the adoration of a disciple; the only thing objective about her broadcast would be the pictures captured by the camera's inhuman eye.

Paul Morelli, Eloise Perry, and a man DeMarco assumed was the Reverend Knoll came into focus. Seated in Mrs. Perry's lap was Marcus Perry's son, sucking his pacifier. Mrs. Perry looked even more world-weary than the last time DeMarco had seen her, but he thought he saw something in her eyes, something he hadn't seen before: hope.

Morelli glanced affectionately at the baby, then faced the camera. "As you all know, my wife was killed by a young man named Isaiah Perry, and I killed Isaiah in self-defense. Then Isaiah's older brother, Marcus, died while trying to avenge his brother's death. As you can imagine, Mrs. Perry and I are both numb with grief and bewildered as to why our lives were destined to intersect in such a horrible way. I decided, however, that there *had* to be a way to make something good come out of so much tragedy.

"This afternoon I met with Mrs. Perry and the pastor of her church, Reverend Knoll. We joined our hands and hearts in prayer, searching for answers, searching for something that could be done."

The reverend nodded solemnly at the camera in agreement. Knoll was a slim man in his late sixties, with a high forehead, his head covered with tight white curls. His eyes shone as if he had just shaken hands with God.

"With Mrs. Perry tonight is this beautiful child." Morelli looked sadly over at the baby squirming in Mrs. Perry's lap and gave one of his tiny feet an affectionate squeeze.

"This is James, Marcus's son. James is an orphan. His mother died of lymphoma. I don't believe that Marcus and Isaiah Perry ever had much of a chance in life in spite of everything their good mother tried to do for them. They were raised without a father and Mrs. Perry had to work two jobs to support them. She admits that it was difficult for her to keep her sons, particularly Marcus, away from the bad influences that prey upon the underprivileged children of this country. And now Mrs. Perry is the sole source of support for her grandson.

"But it will be different for James—and for Mrs. Perry. I am establishing a trust fund in the name of my late wife, Lydia Grace Morelli, to provide for all James's educational needs, including college at the university of his choice. To allow his grandmother the time and resources to care for him, the trust will augment her income and Reverend Knoll has found her employment with an institution that will allow her to adjust her work hours to suit her grandson's schedule. This baby will have the opportunity that his father and uncle never had. "

The camera swung to Mrs. Perry. The reporter, Monica Bradshaw, asked her, "Mrs. Perry, do you have anything to say?"

Tears shining in her eyes and streaming down her broad face, Eloise Perry said, "I'm just so sorry . . . so sorry, for what my sons did to the senator. I just thank Jesus that he has the goodness in his heart to forgive."

DeMarco swore. Had he been rich enough to have afforded it, he would have thrown something through the screen of his television set. Since he wasn't, he simply turned off the television, stretched out on the couch in his den, closed his eyes—and tried not to think about anything at all. He must have fallen asleep because when the phone rang and he looked at his watch, he saw it was ten p.m. He croaked a hello into the phone.

"The Mayflower. Room 1016," the caller said and hung up.

Aw, shit.

The caller had been Mahoney.

———————◆———————

Room 1016 was a two-room suite.

DeMarco was seated in an uncomfortable, straight-backed antique chair. The Speaker's broad ass was flying solo in a love seat, and his large lumpy feet and thick hairless legs protruded from the bottom of a white bathrobe. The robe had the hotel's name embroidered on the chest.

Mahoney's mane of white hair was tousled and his cheeks were flushed. In his right hand he held a glass of bourbon, and on the table next to him was a half-empty bottle of Wild Turkey. That could explain the flush. A subtle scent hung in the air—the scent of perfume, the scent of a woman. That could also explain the flush. The door leading to the bedroom was closed.

"Did you see him on television," Mahoney said, "that grandstand fuckin' play he made with the Perry kid?"

DeMarco nodded.

"He doesn't miss a trick. How'd the son of a bitch set that up so fast?"

DeMarco shrugged. He didn't care that Paul Morelli could devise self-serving schemes at the speed of light.

The Speaker sat sipping his bourbon, a frown wrinkling his forehead. He looked angry—and his anger appeared to be directed at DeMarco.

"So what are you going to do next?" Mahoney asked.

"Do next?" DeMarco said, shocked that Mahoney would interrupt his carnal pleasures to ask this question.

"Well?" Mahoney persisted.

"I hadn't planned on doing anything next. The only chance I had was to get the police to reopen the case, which they're not going to do. And now even if they did, with Marcus Perry and Burrows both dead, they won't be able to pin anything on Morelli. I'm sorry, but I've reached a dead end."

The Speaker swallowed the remaining bourbon in his glass and put the glass down hard on the end table next to his chair.

"Sorry! Sorry don't cut it, goddamnit! You have to do something."

"Like *what?*" DeMarco said, not even trying to keep the frustration out of his voice.

"I don't know 'like what,' but something. I have an obligation here, Joe. A moral obligation to the American people."

This was pure bullshit. Mahoney wouldn't know a moral obligation if one bit him on the ass. But now DeMarco knew why he had been summoned to the hotel room: his boss had been fretting all day that Morelli would eventually figure out that DeMarco worked for him, and Mahoney knew that even he might not survive if Morelli decided to go after him. So DeMarco could imagine Mahoney—anxiety having interfered with the temperamental erectile function—leaving his bed, angry and unfulfilled, to summon his henchman. DeMarco was apparently the only pawn he had left on the board.

DeMarco opened his mouth to protest but when he saw the look on Mahoney's face, he stopped. Instead, he said, "Could I have a drink?"

Mahoney hesitated. DeMarco knew that Mahoney didn't want to share his booze; he probably had just enough left to last until it was time to go home to his wife. But Mahoney finally, reluctantly, nodded his head. DeMarco poured an especially large shot just to annoy him.

"Sir," DeMarco said, after the bourbon had warmed his gullet, "exactly what is it that you want me to do? I mean—"

At that moment the door to the bedroom opened. *Oh, boy!* DeMarco thought. At least he'd get to see who Mahoney was screwing. He expected Mahoney to call out, to tell the woman to stay where she was, but he didn't. DeMarco turned his head and looked over his shoulder. The woman who stepped from the room was wearing a white hotel bathrobe just like Mahoney.

It was Mary Pat, Mahoney's wife.

Mary Pat had short white hair, the shade almost a perfect match to her husband's. She was five foot five, slim and lovely. And although she was Mahoney's age, she looked ten years younger because she had none of her spouse's filthy, life-shortening habits. She didn't smoke, she rarely drank, she did her yoga and went for walks, and in recent years she'd become a vegetarian. She was going to outlive Mahoney by thirty years. The other thing that would contribute to her longevity was that she was one of the sweetest people DeMarco knew. He firmly believed that nice people lived longer than the not so nice.

"Why, Joey!" Mary Pat said. She always seemed delighted to see him, but she was probably just as delighted to see her mailman. "What are you doing here at this time of night?" Before DeMarco could answer, she turned to Mahoney and said, "It's no wonder he doesn't have a girlfriend, John, the hours you have him working."

Mahoney mumbled something inarticulate, his words muffled by the ice in his glass banging against his big square teeth.

What in the hell was Mahoney doing in a hotel room with his wife? DeMarco wondered. He soon found out.

"Did John tell you, Joe? They're resurfacing the hardwood floors in the condo, and the smell was just *killing* us. Really! Whatever they use on those floors, it just smelled toxic. So we decided to stay here in this lovely suite tonight." She laughed and said, "I feel like we're having an affair."

God, DeMarco loved Mary Pat.

She got a glass of water and said, "Well, I'll leave you two to whatever you're doing. And John, don't be too long. You need to get some sleep."

Mary Pat returned to the bedroom and closed the door and DeMarco turned back to face his boss. Mahoney was still scowling. He may not have been cheating on his wife tonight as DeMarco had thought, but he had brooded himself into a black state over Morelli.

DeMarco resumed his conversation with Mahoney where it had left off. "Look, I know you're frustrated," he said, "but at this point, what do you think I can do? I mean, do you expect me to—"

"I expect you to get *results*!" the Speaker shouted.

DeMarco didn't have the slightest idea what to do. He was trying to think of something to say when the

Speaker nodded his large head a couple of times as if he had just come to a conclusion about his employee.

"What did you do about Hanson's kid?" he asked.

Mahoney had changed direction so fast, it took DeMarco a few seconds to figure out who he was talking about. Hanson was the father of the preppie doper he'd followed the other day. Glad to change the subject, DeMarco told him he'd discovered the kid was using drugs and that he had reported back to the boy's father.

"I gave him the name of a good counselor," he concluded.

Mahoney's lips twitched in a brief, scornful smile. "Most of your cases are like that, aren't they?" he said. "A couple hours of easy work with no risk involved."

DeMarco didn't say anything. Apparently Mahoney had chosen to forget how DeMarco had almost been killed twice while in Mahoney's service.

"Yeah," Mahoney continued, "half the time you don't even go to your office. You got it made, don't you?" Mahoney paused then added, "Son, it's time to earn your keep."

DeMarco sat there speechless, trying to think of something to say to this hypocrite, something to dissuade him, but he knew it was hopeless.

With some effort, Mahoney pushed his bulk up from the love seat and padded on splayed feet over to where DeMarco sat. He took the glass of bourbon

out of DeMarco's hand; he'd only taken a single sip.
The son of a bitch was going to finish what was left
in the glass.

Placing his hand on DeMarco's shoulder, Mahoney said, "You need to go someplace where you
can think, son. You gotta lotta thinkin' to do."

Chapter 46

The post was about three feet high. Emma placed her left foot on it, then bent from the waist, keeping her leg straight, and touched her head against her knee. She did this ten times.

The jogging trail was on the Virginia side of the Potomac River, and she was on the section near the Memorial Bridge. The Lincoln Memorial gleamed white across the river. The trail went from Washington all the way to Mount Vernon, about twenty miles. Emma ran this route sometimes when she prepared for marathons. She didn't know how far she was going to run today, but she thought she might go the whole way then call Christine to come pick her up at Mount Vernon. All she knew for sure was that she was about to explode, and running was the best cure she could think of.

She finished with her left leg, and had just placed

her right leg up on the post, when a voice behind her said, "Good morning." She turned her head. It was Charlie Eklund. His bodyguard was leaning against the front fender of Eklund's car.

"What do you want?" she said, but she continued with her stretching exercises.

"I've decided that we can stop threatening each other," Eklund said. "I have no need to follow you or your friend anymore, nor will I do anything to harm anyone you know. And you, in turn, will have no need to send photographs to my director."

Emma took her right leg off the post and turned to face Eklund. "Maybe I'll send them anyway," she said.

"No you won't. You know if you do then I'll do something to reciprocate."

Emma didn't say anything for a moment. She just stared at Eklund, so still, neat, and confident. The small breeze that was blowing didn't even ruffle his white hair.

"You think you've won, don't you? With Abe Burrows and Marcus Perry both dead no one can touch Paul Morelli for his wife's murder. You're thinking that even if I get you fired now, when Morelli becomes president, you'll go see him and be reinstated. You think you're going to be the next DCI, don't you, Charlie?"

Eklund smiled slightly, almost humbly, but his

eyes were bright blue buttons. "I do love this view," he said, looking across the river at the Lincoln Memorial. "You know what made Lincoln a great president? He was a very practical man. I'd suggest, my dear, that you become more practical."

Emma turned away from Eklund and began to jog. Yes, she'd run all the way to Mount Vernon. She'd run until she overcame the urge to break Charlie Eklund's tiny neck.

***

DeMarco couldn't start his lawn mower. He'd been pulling on the cord for about fifteen minutes, long enough that his shoulder was beginning to ache. The damn thing just wouldn't start.

Since he didn't know what to do about Morelli he figured he might as well get caught up on things around the house: wash some clothes, pay a few bills, and mow the damn lawn. He hated doing yard work, but unlike Emma, he couldn't afford to hire someone to do it for him. It'd been a month since he'd mowed the grass and he imagined his neighbors were beginning to turn up their little neatnik noses in disapproval. But now he couldn't start the mower. He was going to have to take the damn thing to Sears and get somebody to look at it, but he didn't want to take the time to do that today.

He walked across the street and knocked on George Carson's front door. George worked at the IRS, a fact DeMarco took shameless advantage of every April. He asked George if he could borrow his mower, then they spent the next fifteen minutes talking about how the Nationals were going to do better next summer. Hope springs eternal.

He had just begun to use George's gleaming, state-of-the-art mower—the thing was the Lexus of lawn mowers—when Christine and Emma drove up to his house in Christine's car. Emma got out of the car wearing a sweat-soaked T-shirt, shorts, and jogging shoes. He heard her tell Christine to come back and get her in fifteen minutes.

Emma took the time to admire George's mower, and for a moment DeMarco wondered if he should try to convince her how much fun it was to use, to see if he could Tom Sawyer her into mowing his grass, but he knew she'd never fall for it.

"You want some water or something?" he asked her.

He got a glass of ice water for her and a beer for himself and they sat down on the top step of his front porch.

"My boss," DeMarco said, "wants me to do something the entire Republican Party can't manage: he wants me to keep Paul Morelli from being elected president. What the hell am I supposed to do?"

"I don't know," Emma said.

It was so strange to hear Emma say that.

"The only thing I can think to do," DeMarco said, "is follow up on what Lydia told me: try to prove that Morelli assaulted those women or molested his stepdaughter or find whoever this powerful guy is who's been helping Morelli. But I think it's futile."

Emma snorted. "So now you're going to do what Lydia wanted you to do in the first place—now that's she's dead," she said.

That stung.

"I guess," DeMarco said.

Emma just shook her head. DeMarco could tell that she was just as upset and depressed as he was—and felt just as helpless.

"And this guy Eklund, what about him?" DeMarco said, and Emma proceeded to tell DeMarco about her most recent meeting with Charlie Eklund.

"It occurred to me while I was running this morning that Charlie is the least of our problems. Yes, he knows something that he can use to blackmail Morelli, and when Morelli becomes president, he'll use it to become DCI. But after that, my guess is that he won't be around for very long."

"Because of his age?" DeMarco said.

"No. Because Paul Morelli has a friend who helps him kill people, people like Terry Finley. I think the first time Charlie threatens Morelli he's liable to end up in a coffin."

"Huh," DeMarco said. "I hadn't thought about that."

Christine drove up at that moment, tapped the car's horn in a friendly beep, and Emma rose from the step.

"Hey! Where are you going?" DeMarco said. "We gotta figure this out."

"*You* gotta figure this out," she said. "I'm going home to take a shower, and then Christine and I are going Christmas shopping."

Christmas shopping? Who the hell went Christmas shopping in September? Christmas shopping was something you did on December twenty-fourth.

Emma stopped and examined George's lawn mower one more time before driving away.

Chapter 47

"Emma's mad at you," Neil said.

"Yeah, I know," DeMarco said. "Did you find anything on anybody in New Jersey?"

DeMarco, though he thought it was hopeless—and because he couldn't think of anything else to do—was once again backtracking Terry Finley's investigation to see if he could find anything that could be used to destroy Morelli. One of the things that Lydia had told him was that the last time she'd spoken to Terry, he had discovered something in New Jersey but he didn't tell her what it was. DeMarco, having no better idea, had sicced Neil onto that thin lead to see if he could come up with something.

"Yeah, I did," Neil said. "And it wasn't easy."

DeMarco didn't say anything; he was in no mood to stroke Neil's ego.

"You remember David Reams, the guy who claimed he was drugged when they found him in bed with that boy?"

"Yeah."

"Well, the man who signed off on the test that said Mr. Reams was drug-free was a man named Robert Bolt. Mr. Bolt is actually *Doctor* Bolt, a medical examiner and forensic specialist used by the NYPD. Three years after Reams was imprisoned, Bolt purchased a summer home at Egg Harbor, New Jersey. He selected Egg Harbor because it's a stone's throw from Atlantic City and the good doctor is a gambler—a bad one, judging by his last credit report. Anyway, he purchased the home for an amazingly low price."

"So you think Morelli—or whoever's helping Morelli—paid Bolt off with a summer place in New Jersey."

Neil shrugged. "I'm not sure, but it's the only connection I could find between Terry Finley's list and the lovely Garden State, and the only reason I found it was because I looked into Benjamin Dahl's death."

"What are you talking about?" DeMarco said.

Benjamin Dahl was the New Yorker who had refused to give up a piece of real estate that then-mayor Paul Morelli had needed for some civic project. Lydia had told DeMarco that Dahl had died by falling down a flight of stairs, but DeMarco didn't understand what the connection was between Dahl and this Dr. Bolt.

"Well," Neil said, "in Mr. Dahl's autopsy report, an assistant to Dr. Bolt noted a couple of details regarding Mr. Dahl's death that seemed inconsistent with a dive down the stairs. The good doctor, however, penned a note explaining why his assistant was incorrect and officially ruled Dahl's death an accident."

"What were the inconsistencies?"

"It doesn't matter," Neil said. "The point is that on two occasions it appears that Bolt, in his official capacity, may have aided Paul Morelli."

"So why didn't somebody spot this earlier?" DeMarco said. "I mean with all these investigations into Morelli's past conducted by Republicans and journalists, why didn't someone—other than you and Terry Finley—notice the connection to Bolt? And don't tell me they didn't because they weren't as smart as you, Neil."

"*A*," Neil said, "it was three years after the Reams incident that Bolt purchased the home in New Jersey. That's a long time between the event and the payoff, making the payoff less obvious and thus much harder for someone to spot. *B*, if the word 'egg' hadn't been on that napkin of Finley's and if Lydia hadn't told you that Finley was interested in someone in New Jersey, *I* never would have seen the connection. And *C*, in the case of Benjamin Dahl, nobody but

Lydia Morelli—who told both you and Terry Finley—knew that Paul Morelli was tied to Dahl's death."

DeMarco hated when Neil did one of his pedantic A, B, C recitations but he suspected Neil was right. Terry had found out about Benjamin Dahl from Lydia, and in his stubborn, plodding manner, had looked at everyone and every record connected with Dahl, and that's when he noted that Dr. Bolt was the forensic guy that had also signed off on Reams's drug tests. DeMarco wouldn't have been surprised if Terry had approached Bolt and tried to question him, and that may have been what got him killed.

"Do you have an address for Bolt?" DeMarco asked.

"I have two," Neil said, "but they won't do you any good."

"Oh, no. Don't tell me," DeMarco said.

"I'm afraid so. Three weeks ago Dr. Bolt had a phenomenal night at a blackjack table at the Resorts Casino in Atlantic City. The police report said it was so phenomenal that he bought everyone sitting at his table a bottle of cheap champagne. Anyway, he was mugged in the casino's garage, hit with a sap hard enough to crush his skull. The wit who wrote the police report said that Bolt committed suicide by tongue, meaning that a man who would brag to everyone within earshot that he had ten thousand dollars in cash in his wallet obviously had a death wish."

———◆———

DeMarco knocked on Marcia Davenport's door, waited a few minutes, and knocked again. She wasn't home. He left the apartment building and stood despondently on the sidewalk, hands in his pockets, pondering his next move. He realized quickly that he didn't have one. Then he looked across the street.

There were a number of restaurants across the street from Davenport's apartment building, restaurants with outdoor tables. In the summer, this section of Connecticut Avenue teemed with sidewalk drinkers. Although it was late September, it was a pleasant evening and there were a few customers outside, and DeMarco saw Davenport sitting at a table by herself. It was as if God had decided that he'd dealt DeMarco enough bad cards in recent days and felt it was time to give him a break.

"Hi, Marcia," DeMarco said when he reached her table. "Do you remember me? Joe DeMarco, from Congress?"

She was wearing a white V-neck sweater, a blue skirt, and high heels. The sweater clung to her figure and the V in the sweater was deep enough that DeMarco could just see the swell of her breasts. She

was a good-looking woman and it was easy to understand why Morelli had been attracted to her.

She looked up at DeMarco. "Yeah, I remember
you. And I don't have any more to tell you than the
last time we talked."

Her voice had a soft, dreamy quality to it, and
she didn't look as annoyed to see him as he'd expected, making him wonder how many drinks she'd
had. Hopefully enough that she would talk to him.

"May I sit down?" DeMarco said, then took a seat
before she could say no. "I was hoping—"

"You know," she said, "I had a really good day
today. I got a new client, a lady with money to burn
and a four-thousand-square-foot home that she
thinks needs a complete makeover. And on top of
that, just ten minutes ago, I gave my phone number to a really cute guy, a guy that I know is going
to call me. I should have known my luck wouldn't
last."

"Look," DeMarco said, "I'm not trying to screw
up your life, but with what's at stake here, I have to
insist on your help."

"With what's at stake?"

"The presidency, Marcia. Paul Morelli's going to
become the next president of this country if you
don't come forward and tell what he did to you."

Now that was pretty shitty, dumping the fate of
the entire nation on Marcia Davenport, but what
else could he do?

"I told you," she said, "he didn't do anything to me."

"I know what you told me and I don't believe you. Please, you have to . . ."

"Imagine, just for a minute, that you're a woman who's just been sexually assaulted by one of the most powerful men in Washington. You know it will be your word against his, and that he'll say it was consensual. But in the case of this particular woman, imagine that when she was in college she accused the son of the governor of her home state of date rape. The woman takes the governor's son to court and the boy's not only acquitted but his attorneys make the woman look like a trashy little gold-digger who was trying to extort money from the kid's dad. How much credibility do you think this woman would have, Mr. DeMarco? And then imagine this woman five years after this supposed assault, this assault that never happened. She seems to have gotten her life back together. Her business is going well. She's starting to trust men again. Do you think this woman would risk everything by accusing a man like Paul Morelli of a crime that she can't possibly prove?"

Davenport stood up. "Paul Morelli did *not* rape me. If I'm ever subpoenaed and asked to testify, I'll say he was the most wonderful man I've ever met. And I don't ever want to see you again."

Davenport was crying when she walked away and DeMarco couldn't possibly have felt any worse.

As DeMarco watched Davenport cross the street to her apartment building, he realized how much she looked like Lydia Morelli. In fact, she looked like Janet Tyler as well. All three women were short and blond, though Lydia had been thinner than the other two.

A waitress stopped at the table and asked if he wanted a drink. When she returned with his martini, she also brought him a bowl of those Goldfish crackers that are more addictive than heroin. DeMarco knew he wouldn't leave until all the little fish had disappeared.

He didn't know what to do. The doctor in New Jersey was dead and neither Janet Tyler nor Marcia Davenport would testify against Paul Morelli. The witnesses to Lydia Morelli's death were also dead and even if they hadn't been, the police clearly had no interest in investigating Morelli for his wife's murder. Charlie Eklund probably had information that could hurt Morelli, but he would never tell what he knew. So, no matter what the Speaker wanted, there was nothing else DeMarco could think to do. His ass was cooked.

As he raised his glass to his lips—a much too frequent exercise of late—DeMarco reflected on Paul Morelli's drinking habits. DeMarco just couldn't imagine the man that Lydia Morelli had described: a brilliant, calculating politician who has a few drinks then attacks women. But Davenport had all but confirmed that this was the case. And then there was the story that Harry Foster had told him: about the lady in New York, the mousy little thing who'd never had her "tit squeezed before by a drunken wop."

Drunken wops, DeMarco thought, and he raised his glass again.

Chapter 48

———◆◆◆———

DeMarco knew that Emma and Audrey Melanos had once lived together. Why they still weren't together he didn't know, but whatever had driven them apart hadn't diminished the love between them. DeMarco, an expert on failed affairs of the heart, could tell.

Audrey was younger than Emma, about DeMarco's age. She was pretty and petite, with a sun-kissed Mediterranean complexion and dark hair that reached the delicate nape of her neck. Her eyes were her best feature, a caramel brown that radiated a combination of compassion and intelligence. Or maybe intelligence wasn't the right word. *Wisdom* seemed more appropriate—wisdom borne of observation and empathy. It had been DeMarco's experience that Emma's lovers were rarely ordinary, and Audrey Melanos was no exception.

"I would have thought, Joe," Emma said, "that since Audrey was kind enough to fly down from New York to meet with you, you would have been on time for once in your life."

DeMarco suspected that Audrey hadn't flown down just to meet with him. He suspected she would have walked from New York to see Emma.

"I'm sorry," DeMarco said to Audrey. "I got stuck in traffic."

"You did *not* get stuck in traffic," Emma snapped. "It's nine o'clock at night and you live fifteen minutes from here. If you're going to make up excuses you could at least be a little more imaginative."

DeMarco was about to tell her that a wreck in Georgetown actually had delayed him, but before he could Audrey said, "It's okay, Joe. We just got here ourselves, only a minute ago. We were late too." DeMarco smiled over at Emma, delighted to have caught her in a fib. Naturally, Emma ignored him and pretended she was trying to catch a waiter's eye.

They were at the Washington Hilton, one of DeMarco's favorite places because of the piano player. He was a burly-looking guy with curly blond hair, and sitting behind his piano he looked as if he might have played football for some small college team. You didn't notice his legs until he stood up and hobbled away from the keyboard on his crutches. But whatever had happened to his legs hadn't affected his voice; his voice had a smoke-and-whiskey tinge that was perfect for melancholy love songs.

DeMarco had told Emma that he needed to talk to an expert on alcoholism and Emma had said that she had a friend who lived in New York who had a doctorate in psychology and specialized in addictive behaviors. If DeMarco had asked to speak to someone who specialized in lizard cancers, Emma would have had a friend who was an expert. In this case the expert just happened to be an ex-lover rather than someone who worked for an intelligence agency.

DeMarco, as Emma had noted, was not good at small talk—particularly when he was under pressure—but he made an effort. He thanked Audrey for flying down, asked if the flight had been okay, asked if—

"Oh for God's sake," Emma said, "just tell her what you need to know before you explode."

"Yeah, I guess I should," DeMarco said. "It's getting late."

"I'm in no rush, Joe, take your time," Audrey said. "And you," she said to Emma, "be nice."

DeMarco wanted to say Hah, take that!

"There's a man," DeMarco said. "A politician. He's very gifted, very intelligent. He does great, good things for our country. He is in fact an extraordinary politician."

Emma started to interrupt with some comment,

but Audrey looked over at her and managed to silence her with a look—and then she gave Emma's hand a squeeze to let her know everything was all right. DeMarco liked this woman.

"What you need to understand," DeMarco said, "is that the man I'm talking about is very rational, and he has enormous self-control. But on occasion, when he gets a few drinks inside him, and if he's alone with a certain kind of woman, he turns into a different person. He sexually assaults women."

"What do you mean by 'a certain kind of woman'?" Audrey said.

"The women he's attacked are physically similar. They're all short and blond, and most of them are kind of shy, not very self-confident. Anyway," DeMarco said, "a drink or two, and a switch flips inside this guy. Jekyll becomes Hyde—or Hyde become Jekyll—whichever one was the monster. Have you ever encountered such a personality?"

"Sure," Audrey said. "All the time. There's nothing unusual about a man who's normally rational— a good husband, a good worker—having a few drinks and turning into a sexual predator."

Before DeMarco could tell her she was missing the point, she continued, "Joe, alcohol is a mood-altering drug. It's not LSD, but it affects everyone in some way. Like you. When you drink you get melancholy. Am I right?"

How did she know that?

"I realize alcohol causes personality changes," DeMarco said, "but I'm talking about drastic personality changes produced by very small quantities of alcohol. Yeah, I get a bit blue when I drink, but it takes half a bottle and I don't get suicidal. It's a matter of *degree*."

"Yes," Audrey said, "and the degree to which alcohol affects different people depends on the individual. There are metabolic and genetic influences which come into play. Or he could be idiosyncratic or someone afflicted by pathological intoxication."

"*Pathological?* What are you . . ."

Audrey laughed at DeMarco's confusion, but it was a nice laugh, like the sound of silver bells tinkling. "What I mean is that he could have a reaction to alcohol that's almost allergic in nature," she said. "Like people allergic to penicillin or shellfish. For ninety-nine percent of the population, penicillin cures what ails them, but there's that one percent that goes into shock. The man you're talking about could have such a reaction. There are many documented cases, and usually people who have such reactions stop drinking after the first few experiences."

"I've never heard of it," DeMarco said.

Since Audrey wouldn't let her talk, Emma just rolled her eyes. Her message was clear enough though: the things that DeMarco had not heard of far exceeded those that he had.

"They even made a movie based on pathological intoxication several years ago," Audrey said. "It was called *Final Analysis* and starred Richard Gere and Kim Basinger. In the movie, Kim has a couple of sips of alcohol—cough syrup, actually—and then beats her husband to death with a dumbbell. Pathological intoxication has also been used, unsuccessfully I might add, as a defense in a number of criminal cases. The defense argues that the defendant had no more control over his actions than an insane person who commits murder or assault or whatever. I've testified twice for the defense in such cases, and the defense lost both times. Juries don't buy it, regardless of the scientific data. They can't believe that a couple sips of booze will affect a person so drastically since it's never affected them that way."

"Well, I'll be," DeMarco said, but he was distracted by the piano man. He was playing a medley from *Camelot* the way DeMarco had always wanted to play it. When he sang, in that whiskey-coated voice, the haunting lyrics of "If Ever I Would Leave You," DeMarco was reminded that his wife had left him in September. Elle's letter had arrived in September.

DeMarco shrugged off the music and gloomy thoughts of love lost. "So," he said, "the type of personality I'm describing—a normally-in-control, calculating individual who loses his self-control with just a small quantity of alcohol—is a possibility."

"Definitely," Audrey said. "The other possibility, of course, is that his sexual urges may have nothing to do with alcohol. I mean, alcohol may trigger them, but alcohol isn't at the root of his problem."

"What are you talking about?" DeMarco said.

"I'm saying some people have sexual urges that they can't control. Why would anyone molest children, for example? Morality aside, pedophiles know that if they're caught they'll become social outcasts and go to prison, yet they do it anyway. No rational person would be a child molester, yet they're often intelligent men. They do what they do because they can't stop themselves. And it's not just pedophiles that have these self-destructive urges. Why would a president of the United States, a brilliant man, a Rhodes scholar, have an affair with an intern *in* the White House? He knew what was at stake, not just the presidency and everything he was working for, but his legacy, his place in history. So why did he do it?"

"I don't kno—"

"Because he couldn't help himself. Even knowing the consequences, he couldn't stop. And that may be the case with this man you're talking about. In a certain situation, with a certain kind of woman, and with a little booze to loosen his inhibitions, he just can't stop himself."

The piano player segued into the theme song from *Camelot*. Images of JFK and Jackie as young Arthur and maid Guinevere didn't come to mind. Instead, DeMarco thought of sordid stories of Marilyn Monroe's death and Sam Giancana. Emma cleared her throat to gain his attention.

"Well," DeMarco said. "I guess I should get going. I appreciate you taking the time to see me, Audrey. I don't know what to do about this guy but I guess now I understand him a little better."

"Oh come on, Joe, use your head," Emma said. "Audrey just gave you the answer."

"You have an idea?" he said to Emma.

"Yes, but we'll talk about it later. Tomorrow. Right now you're going to leave so Audrey and I can catch up on old times."

"Emma," Audrey said, "you can be so rude sometimes. Joe hasn't even finished his drink."

"She can be rude all the time," DeMarco said. Then he raised his hands in a don't-hit-me gesture and said, "I'm outta here. And Audrey, thank you again for helping me even if I won't know how you've helped me until Emma tells me."

Chapter 49

———— ❖ ————

"You've got to be kidding!" DeMarco said.

"Not at all," Emma said. "It seems pretty straight-forward to me."

"Emma, I'm not the damn CIA. I don't have a bunch of trained agents hiding in my closet."

"There is no closet in this office." Looking around DeMarco's small, drab workplace, she added, "How can you stand working here?"

"You know what I mean," DeMarco said. "Your plan, it's just . . . It has too many moving parts. It's too complicated."

"Not if you plan properly."

"Isn't there some military saying about how after the battle starts all the plans fall apart?"

"I've never heard that one," Emma said.

Yes she had.

"And it'll be expensive. Where in the hell am I going to get the money for this?"

The corners of Emma's mouth turned up slightly, and then she answered his question.

DeMarco sat there stunned for a moment. "You know," he finally said, "he just might be crazy enough to do it."

"You'll never know until you ask," Emma said.

Emma rose, put on her coat, and opened the door to DeMarco's office. Standing half-in and half-out of the doorway, she said, "And by the way, it was the Prussian, von Moltke. He said, 'No plan of operations extends with certainty beyond the first encounter with the enemy's main strength.' But Mike Tyson said it better."

"Tyson? The boxer?"

"Yeah. He said, 'Everybody's got a plan—until you hit 'em.'"

Chapter 50

Sam Houston Murphy was dressed in a white shirt, a string tie, blue Levi's, and alligator-skin cowboy boots. He was six foot four, maybe six-six with the boots, and the shirt was stretched tight across a stomach the size of a kettle drum.

Murphy was in his sixties. He had a homely rubbery face, large ears, and a Bob Hope ski-jump nose. His dark hair, probably dyed, was a thick unruly shag with a Dennis-the-Menace cowlick at the rear. Your first impression was Texas shitkicker—until you looked into his eyes. His eyes were as hard as ball bearings.

DeMarco was sitting with Murphy near the pool of his San Antonio home. Fall was beginning to turn cruel in Washington, but here in Texas it was a sunny seventy-five degrees. Murphy's latest wife—a six-foot blond with the body of a Vegas showgirl—was swimming laps in the Olympic-size pool. Murphy's eyes followed his wife's form with obvious enjoyment as he drank coffee from a mug that said, LOVE ME, LOVE MY DOG. His dog, a bony-backed white mongrel with cataracts, lay sleeping on the tiles next to Murphy's chair.

DeMarco didn't like Murphy or his dog.

Murphy had been a senator for the last eighteen years but had decided not to accept another term because he was ready to make his run at the White House. He wasn't as popular as Paul Morelli but he was the best man the Republican Party had to offer at the moment. Some said he was the only one dumb enough to run against Morelli.

Sam Murphy was about as dumb as Lyndon Johnson or George Bush, Sr. He was born in a hardscrabble town in West Texas without a pot to piss in. He snagged a football scholarship from Texas A&M that garnered him permanent knee problems and a degree in petroleum engineering. He hit his first gusher six months after he graduated, the oil rights to the land bought with a federal grant he had been given to use for shale-formation research. He spent two decades turning barrels of oil into barrels of money, then veered into politics like a man genetically engineered to make deals in smoky back rooms. Three wives and twenty-some years later, he was one of the shrewdest politicians to ever hang a Stetson in the Senate cloakroom. If his opponent had been anyone other than Paul Morelli, Sam Murphy would have had a genuine shot at the Big House on Pennsylvania Avenue.

Murphy was this year's what-you-see-is-what-you-get candidate. His campaign theme was "Return America to the Americans." He would impose heavy trade sanctions to protect American industries and allow only German scientists and white Russian figure skaters to immigrate. He promised to abolish welfare in every form and declared that the best place for the homeless was a jail cell. He was a staunch supporter of capital punishment and believed that if every household had a gun, the judicial system would not be so overloaded. To a large segment of the working class, Sam Murphy was one of them: he drank Bud, drove a pickup truck, and liked blonds with big tits.

The private Sam Murphy was completely different from the public figure. He was pragmatic, insightful, and carefully picked his image and his issues. DeMarco knew he hated country-western music, preferred French wines to beer, and was usually chauffeured to appointments in a limo. He did like blonds with big tits, though.

While still looking at his wife, Murphy said, "Kinda surprised you wanted to see me, Joe Bob. Thought you was pissed at me."

DeMarco had made the mistake of making a crack in Murphy's presence once about every

Texan having two first names, and from that point on he was Joe Bob. DeMarco's middle name was not Bob.

"I still am, Senator," DeMarco said.

"Shit, you can call me Sam, son. Ain't a senator no more and don't want no truck with them that is. Now next time you see me you might be callin' me Mr. President, but until then, Sam'll be juss fine."

Three years ago the Speaker had assigned DeMarco to lend Sam Murphy a hand with a small problem. Why Mahoney was willing to aid a Republican, DeMarco didn't know, but Murphy had said that there was an administrator at NASA leaking bid information to contractors and turning a profit doing so. He told DeMarco he wanted to expose this scoundrel in the interest of God, country, and fair play. DeMarco was gullible enough to believe him, got the goods on the NASA guy, and he was duly sacked. That should have been the happy ending to a minor drama, except DeMarco read in the paper two months later that the administrator's replacement had awarded two large contracts to Texas companies. DeMarco didn't know how Murphy had pulled it off, but it was apparent that he had found some way to manipulate the system to his constituents' advantage. When DeMarco accused him of this, Murphy just winked and said DeMarco had better have a "whole shit pot full of evidence" before he went around making "slanderous" accusations against a

United States senator—knowing that DeMarco had no evidence.

Yes, DeMarco was indeed pissed at Sam Houston Murphy. Murphy believed in nepotism, cronyism, paybacks, and payoffs. He was the kind of politician who had made DeMarco cynical of all politicians—but he had never killed one of his wives.

Murphy inhaled sharply as his current wife pulled herself from the pool and stood for a moment in profile, as if posing for her husband and his guest. DeMarco had pocket hankies that contained more material than the bikini she was wearing.

DeMarco heard Murphy mutter to himself, or maybe to his dog, "Damn, ain't that somethin'." To DeMarco he said, "Well, since I know you ain't one of my fans, you gonna tell me what it is that made you fly all the way to God's country to see me?"

To make Emma's plan work, DeMarco needed somebody with money and clout. Sam Murphy had both in abundance. Plus, as DeMarco knew from previous experience, Murphy was a risk taker, the type that always bets the table-limit even when the odds were against him. He also knew where he stood in the polls, and DeMarco was hoping that he'd be willing to take a considerable risk to increase his chances of beating Morelli.

Mrs. Murphy glanced over at her husband and his guest, her eyes lingering briefly on DeMarco. She blew Sam a kiss then walked slowly away from the pool toward the house. Her sleek limbs glistened with water and the movement of her haunches made DeMarco think of a prowling feline.

"Sam," DeMarco said, "I know Paul Morelli has committed a serious crime but I can't prove it."

Murphy turned his eyes away from his wife's ass and looked at DeMarco.

"I know you, Joe Bob. If you're comin' to *me* for help, Morelli musta done somethin' God-awful horrible. You gonna tell me what it is?"

DeMarco did. While he talked, Murphy scratched the old hound's neck. Surprisingly, he didn't show any emotion when DeMarco discussed Morelli killing his wife and possibly molesting his stepdaughter. When DeMarco finished, Murphy said, "This thing about him and the booze—how it affects him—now that I think about it, there may be something to that. I remember being at functions with him and that aide of his, the tubby one who got killed, he'd count Morelli's drinks like he was Carrie Nation's brother."

"So you believe me," DeMarco said.

"You know, it don't matter if I do or not. I'd be a damn hypocrite if I said I wouldn't like to see Paul out of the race. And if he landed in jail, that'd just be icin' on the cake. But what is it you think you can do, son? I agree with the police. You ain't got shit for evidence—just a lotta coincidences strung together like beads on a cheap necklace."

"I can't get Morelli for murder, Sam. All I want to do is ruin his political career."

"Now that's a *noble* objective, boy, but like I said: How the hell you gonna do it?"

When DeMarco told him his plan, Murphy smiled broadly and said, "You gotta devious mind, Joe Bob."

Actually, Emma was the one with the devious mind.

"Yeah, I'm beginnin' to think right kindly toward you, son," Murphy said. "I'm not sure it'll work, but the most it'll cost me is three, four hundred grand. Hell, I'm gonna spend a *whole* lot more than that on TV ads."

Chapter 51

"Where were you yesterday?" Mahoney asked.

"Texas."

"Texas! What in the hell were you doin' there?"

"You don't want to know."

Mahoney sat a moment, studying DeMarco.

"Morelli?"

"Yeah."

Mahoney rose slowly from his chair, and while rubbing his lower back, walked over to a window in his office. The window looked out onto the National Mall. The Lincoln Memorial shimmered in the distance. Mahoney said he never tired of the view—Washington's obelisk, Lincoln's cube, Jefferson's temple—though it often made him feel sad and small, knowing he would never be included in the pantheon of democracy's giants.

"M'damn back's driving me nuts," Mahoney said as he gazed out the window.

Bedroom acrobatics or a drunken fall? Whatever the cause, DeMarco knew from previous experience that Mahoney wouldn't go to a doctor. He had to be bleeding before he'd go to one. What he would do was complain about his condition for the next three or four days to any captive audience, then visit a Korean masseuse he knew. His back would gradually improve after he visited the woman but DeMarco had always suspected that massage was a minimal ingredient in the healing process.

Mahoney turned back to face him, and the next three words that came from his mouth were three words that DeMarco had never heard him utter before.

"Joe, I'm sorry," he said, "about some of the things I said the other night, over at the Mayflower. It's just . . ." Mahoney shook his head instead of completing the thought.

He sat back down in his chair, moving cautiously. "There was this fella I went to high school with," he said. "He became a teacher. I really liked him, boosted his career when I got the chance, used to invite him over to the house when my girls were little. Then it turns out this guy's a child molester. I felt . . . hell, a whole buncha things. Sick. Mad. Used. I feel the same way about Morelli right now. It's driving me crazy."

"I understand," DeMarco said.

"So whatever you're plannin', I hope it works. But I gotta warn you: you better take him completely off the board. You leave him in play . . . well, you know."

DeMarco nodded.

Then Mahoney surprised him again.

"And, Joe," he said, "don't worry about Morelli runnin' you out of town. He ain't the fuckin' president yet."

Chapter 52

———— ✦ ————

"Five women work on Morelli's D.C. staff," Neil said. "Two came with him from New York and I would imagine are mucho loyal to him. Two others have been with him since he came to the Senate, and I would guess that by now these women would sacrifice their children to please him, he being the charmer that he is. Oh, and three of the four women I just mentioned have husbands who make good salaries and would therefore be less likely to be motivated by money."

"So tell me about the fifth one," DeMarco said. Why couldn't Neil ever just cut to the chase?

"The lady's name is Jackie Arnold. She's only been with Morelli six months. She used to work for a senator from South Dakota but when he lost his seat, she found a job with Morelli. One thing to bear in mind is that she's had considerable experience on Capitol

Hill; she's no virgin. After she lost her job with the South Dakota guy, and while she was job hunting, her bills added up. She currently owes Visa twelve thousand dollars and is only paying the interest on her bill. On top of that, she divorced thirteen months ago and her ex-husband is in arrears on child support. Most importantly, though, this lady lives in Gleedsville, Virginia, where her three-year-old daughter attends preschool. This means that Ms. Arnold just runs her ass *ragged*. She works long hours for Morelli, has a God-awful commute, and has all the attendant hassle of a single mother with a kid in day care who has to be dropped off and picked up and dealt with whenever the day care place is closed. This poor woman, I would assume, is fucking miserable."

———◆◆◆———

The bar was a political watering hole located on Pennsylvania Avenue, a couple of blocks from the Capitol, and its name was the same as its address: 701. Congressional staffers would gather there in small herds in the evening, talking louder than necessary, hoping everyone within earshot would think that they were the ones pulling the political strings. And sometimes, God help us, they actually were. DeMarco sat at the bar, hunched over a martini—this one made with a Ukrainian vodka—and watched as the recruiter talked to Jackie Arnold.

Sam Murphy had provided the recruiter. He was a fatherly-looking man with a tanned face, curly gray hair, and kind brown eyes. He was so smooth and charming you could imagine him bilking little old ladies out of their savings. He had contacted Jackie that afternoon at her office and offered to buy her a drink while he made his pitch.

He informed Jackie that he represented a think tank and that they had a vacancy on their staff. "Think tank," as those inside the Beltway know, is a euphemism for a group of intellectual whores, people with doctorates and government experience who prepare position papers for lobbyists and politicians. Smart people, in other words, who can argue both sides of any issue and often do so simultaneously. When the recruiter said the think tank was located in Leesburg, Virginia, five miles from where Jackie Arnold lived, her eyes lit up like she'd seen Jesus.

The job was irresistible. They were offering her 30 percent more than she was currently making to work in an office ten minutes from her home. Furthermore, the recruiter said, the firm paid day care expenses for all their employees and the day care facility was located only three blocks from the office. He didn't tell her that she would be the only woman at the company who had a child below the age of five.

There was one catch, the recruiter told her. Well, not exactly a catch, he said, but an *opportunity*. They wanted Ms. Arnold to introduce a young woman to

Senator Morelli and recommend that this woman replace her on Morelli's staff. If the young woman landed the job, Ms. Arnold would be given a five-thousand-dollar signing bonus.

"That lady's no dummy," the recruiter later told DeMarco. "She knew that getting your gal onto Morelli's staff was the reason we were offering her the job. She didn't say anything, but you could tell."

"But she agreed?" DeMarco said.

"Oh, yeah. The package I offered was just too good for her to pass up, so she pretended not to understand what was going on. But she did."

"What do you think she thinks is going on?"

"Oh, just the usual: that the Republicans are trying to place a mole on Morelli's staff so they'll be able to get some inside dope when he runs for president."

The apartments were next.

He needed two units in the same building, and one had to be a corner unit on the ground floor with lots of windows. It took him a day but he found a building on Capitol Hill with one vacant unit and one ideal corner apartment. The fact that the corner apartment was occupied wasn't a problem—not when a man had access to Sam Murphy's money.

The tenant currently occupying the corner unit was a sour-faced middle-aged woman who lived alone, and just by looking at her DeMarco could tell that she'd never experienced good luck in her entire life. One of Sam Murphy's many connections visited the woman. He fluttered his arms theatrically, and said that his film company wanted to use her apartment for one small scene in an upcoming movie. But even though the scene was small, the fake producer said, movies moved slower than Alaskan glaciers and they would need her place for at least three weeks, during which time they would put her up, all expenses paid, in one of the finest hotels in Hilton Head.

"The only catch," Sam's person told the woman, "is—"

"Aw, shit," the woman said. "Goddamnit, I knew there'd be a catch."

"The only catch is you have to leave next week. So if you can't get time off from work, then—"

"Hey! I can get the time. I can get the time. If that bitch doesn't let me go, I'll . . ."

So they had an apartment, near the Eastern Market Metro station, a corner unit just like DeMarco wanted, and then DeMarco rented the unit that was vacant.

❖

Now for the cop.

DeMarco called Sam Murphy, who called a guy, who called another guy, who called DeMarco. The guy who called DeMarco was a sergeant, one who worked in personnel. DeMarco told the sergeant what he wanted: a young hot dog, still in uniform.

"But he can't be bent," DeMarco told the sergeant. "I don't want somebody who's been investigated a dozen times by Internal Affairs. What I'm looking for is a guy who *might* be investigated by Internal Affairs at some time in the future. You understand?"

"I don't know. What do you want this guy to do?" the sergeant said.

DeMarco told him.

"Hey, that's not so bad," the sergeant said. "Hell, I don't think it's even illegal. I mean a lawyer might but—"

"Do you know someone or not?" DeMarco said.

"I know the perfect guy," the sergeant said.

———❖———

Maybe he wasn't perfect, but he was good enough. His name was Gary Parker. He was six-four, good-looking, blond, a little on the heavy side. By the time he was fifty he'd probably be a lot on the heavy side, but right now he looked to DeMarco like the man you'd want standing on the line next to you if you were trying to control a riot. When he met DeMarco, Parker wasn't in uniform; he was dressed in jeans, a black T-shirt, and a black leather biker's jacket. It was probably the jacket, but Parker immediately struck

DeMarco as cocky and overconfident—just right for what he needed.

DeMarco told Parker what he wanted him to do.

"Is that all?" Parker said.

"Yep."

"I don't get it."

"You don't need to get it," DeMarco said. "But what you do need to do is move into an apartment on Capitol Hill."

"What? There's no way I can afford a place on the Hill. I'm living in Springfield now."

DeMarco nodded; he knew that. "What if you had a job moonlighting at the Hooters in Tysons Corner, providing security, and the job paid a thousand a month?"

"Jesus!" Parker said. "And at a Hooters too?"

"Yeah, consider that a fringe benefit. At the end of the year it's up to you and Hooters' management if they want to keep you on, but for a year you'll be living on Capitol Hill, getting paid an extra grand a month, and have a fifteen-minute commute to work."

"And all I gotta do is . . ."

"Yep, that's all you gotta do," DeMarco said.

———◆———

Finding the photographer was simple, much easier than getting the cop. To find the right guy all he did was call his pal Reggie Harmon at the *Washington Post*.

Arnie Berg was short, middle-aged, had a scraggly mustache, hair that needed a trim, and a face pockmarked with old acne scars. He wore a blue sports coat with dandruff sprinkling the shoulders, brown corduroy pants, and Hush Puppies. Imagine a producer calling a casting agent and saying: "Hey, Morrie, send me a guy that looks like a sleazy paparazzo." The agent would send a guy who looked like Arnie Berg.

And you only had to be with Arnie five minutes to know that he had no shame and would do anything to make a buck. He was the one who would follow an aging actress, take pictures of her in a bathing suit, and the following week, on the cover of a tabloid would be a close-up of the woman's butt and a headline that read: STARS WITH CELLULITE.

DeMarco despised Arnie Berg—but that didn't mean he wouldn't use him.

Chapter 53

———◆———

She was in her early thirties. She was five foot four, had blond curls framing a sweet, heart-shaped face, dimples in her cheeks, and big blue eyes behind large-framed glasses. The glasses magnified her eyes into huge blue pools of innocence, making her appear more vulnerable than DeMarco suspected she really was. She also had a figure like Marcia Davenport's: large breasts in comparison to her small frame, hips that flared nicely from a twenty-two-inch waist, and legs that looked good in the short skirt she was wearing.

The first words that came from the sweet face were: "Well, *fuck,* are you going to let me in? It's colder than shit out here."

"Brenda Hathaway?" DeMarco said.

"Right. Now let me in before I freeze my ass off.

It was eighty fucking degrees in L.A. If I'd known it was gonna be so damn cold here, I would have asked for more money."

DeMarco picked up her suitcases from his porch, ushered her into his den, and poured her a brandy to ward off pneumonia. While taking the first few sips of her drink, she walked around the room, stopped by a print on the wall, and nodded as if she approved of it. One of DeMarco's many ex-girlfriends had given him the print. Slipping out of her shoes, she flopped down on the couch across from DeMarco's chair and put her feet up on the coffee table. Her legs were visible to the tops of her thighs.

"To show biz," she said, toasting DeMarco with the brandy snifter. "I understand you've got a part for me."

"Who told you about the job?"

"My agent, the useless shit."

DeMarco hoped Sam Murphy had paid the agent enough to ensure his silence. "What did your agent tell you?" he asked.

"He told me I was going to make fifty grand, and that I wouldn't have to screw a German shepherd to get it. He also said the publicity would jumpstart my career. I hope so; then I can dump him and find a real agent."

"Who talked to your agent about the job?"

"Geez, I don't know. Lighten up, will you. What is this? Fucking *I Spy*?"

"Brenda, I want you to stop saying 'fuck.'"

"Well, excuse *me*! What are you? Some kinda religious fanatic?"

"No. The role you're going to play doesn't have four-letter words in the dialogue. You're going to be innocent. Naive and demure. Everybody's kid sister. You need to start working on the part."

"You gonna wash out my mouth with soap or tell me what the part is?"

That almost made DeMarco smile.

"Two days from now—"

"You married?" Brenda asked.

"No."

"Gay?"

"No. Two days from now—"

"Divorced?"

"Yes."

"Why did you get divorced?"

"We had different priorities."

"What's that mean?"

"It means I don't want to talk about it."

"Do you have a girlfriend?"

"Not anymore."

She looked at DeMarco for a second, and turning serious for the first time, said, "Sorry. Looks like a fresh wound."

"Yeah. Now if you're through with the questions, here's the deal."

When he finished telling her what she had to do, Brenda said, "Fucking-A, this is heavy. Oops."

"Yes, it is heavy, Brenda. And it's risky. Are you sure you want to take the risk?"

"Do you have any idea how hard it is to get noticed in Hollywood?"

DeMarco shook his head.

"Well, thanks to plastic surgery, every woman out there has a perfect nose and perfect boobs. Getting a decent part is harder than winning the lotto. I'd do anything to break into the big time."

The heat of her ambition seared the air.

"And in case you're wondering," she added, "there's nothing man-made inside this body."

DeMarco spent the next hour with Brenda going over her role. She asked smart questions. Beneath the blond curls was a good mind. At ten o'clock, she yawned and said, "I think I've got the idea. It's been a long day, honey. Where am I staying?"

"Starting tomorrow, you'll be staying in an apartment on Capitol Hill. Tonight, you can stay here or I can find you a hotel room."

"I don't mind staying here."

DeMarco led her to his bedroom and said, "The bathroom's across the hall, and the sheets and towels are clean."

"This is your room, isn't it?"

"Yeah. I'll sleep on the couch in my den. It's a Hide-A-Bed."

She looked at him for a long heartbeat and said, "See you in the morning."

Fifteen minutes later he heard the shower running and tried not to think about what she would look like wet and naked. He read for an hour, then pulled out the Hide-A-Bed and tried to sleep. The reason he'd given Brenda his bed was that the Hide-A-Bed was as comfortable as an iron maiden.

At eleven-thirty the door to his office opened. He hadn't been asleep. He looked up at the open doorway and saw Brenda framed in the entrance, the light from the hallway behind her. She was wearing a short bathrobe that showed off her legs almost to her hips.

"I couldn't sleep," she said. "Still on West Coast time, I guess."

DeMarco didn't say anything.

She undid the belt of the bathrobe and shrugged the robe off her shoulders. She had a beautiful body.

DeMarco could tell when they were talking earlier that Brenda found him attractive—but he knew he wasn't irresistible. He suspected that she was just a young woman who liked sex and he wasn't repulsive and he was available. Going to bed with him may have been the equivalent, emotionally, of having a nice massage before falling asleep. And that was all fine by him.

Sliding under the covers, she said, "I promise—tomorrow I'll start working seriously on innocent."

Chapter 54

The event needed to be timed like a Flying Walendas trapeze routine.

Clayton Adams stood in the waiting room outside Paul Morelli's office, chatting with the receptionist, while watching the clock behind her desk. He was to wait exactly four minutes. As he waited, Jackie Arnold was inside Morelli's office with Brenda. By now Jackie had already told Morelli how bad she felt about leaving on such short notice and had introduced Brenda to the senator as an old friend. Adams checked the clock, flashed the receptionist a smile, and started down the hallway. He passed the open door to Morelli's office just as Jackie was beginning to discuss Brenda's experience and extol her many virtues.

Adams stopped abruptly, did a ham actor's double take, and said, "My God, is that you, Brenda?"

For ten years, Clayton Adams had been the Democratic congressman from the California district that included Burbank and part of North Hollywood. He could have served another ten years had he chosen to, but he was reaching his sunset years and concluded it was time to look out for number one. A year ago he'd left the House and joined a firm of political manipulators on K Street, and since he was making three times what he made in the House, his conscience didn't bother him a bit. And when Sam Murphy called and asked him to perform a small service—and said, "Oh, by the way, my cabin in Aspen's gonna be vacant in December"—one-time Democratic loyalist Clayton Adams agreed to tell a wee lie.

"Oh, Mr. Adams!" Brenda said, acting equally surprised.

"Paul, excuse me," Adams said, "but I just had to stop when I saw Brenda."

Morelli—still frowning, clearly annoyed that Jackie Arnold was quitting—said, "You know Brenda, Clayton?"

"Know her! This pretty little thing worked in my L.A. office for a while. Best gal Friday I ever had. How long were you with me, Brenda?"

"Six months," Brenda said.

"Paul, all I can tell you is, if you get a chance to hire this young lady, don't you dare pass it up. Well, I gotta run. Sorry again for interrupting. And

Brenda, it's so good to see you, sweetie. Call me later."

And the Flying Walenda caught the bar.

———◆———

While all this was occurring, DeMarco waited impatiently at the Monocle. Brenda was supposed to have met with Jackie at ten a.m., and DeMarco figured that by ten-fifteen she'd either get the job or she wouldn't. He figured her chances of getting it were maybe fifty-fifty. In addition to bribing Clayton Adams to provide a personal endorsement for her, Murphy had other folks supply Brenda with an impressive packet of references. But would it be enough? It was almost noon now, so he sat there stewing, wondering where the hell she was and what she was doing.

Brenda finally walked through the door thirty minutes later, gave him a little peck on the cheek, and wiggled onto the bar stool next to him.

"*Well?*" he said, as soon as she sat down.

"And it's nice to see you too, cutie," Brenda said. To the bartender she said, "A Manhattan please, and could I have two cherries?"

"Of course," the bartender said. She was so cute he'd have given her a bushel of cherries if she'd asked.

"Brenda, don't keep me in suspense," DeMarco said. "Did you get the damn job or not?"

Brenda reached into her purse and pulled out the temporary badge she'd been given so she could enter the Russell Building. "Say hello to the newest member of Senator Morelli's staff," she said.

"Thank God," DeMarco said. "So where in the hell have you been the last two and a half hours?"

"Getting my badge and meeting the folks in the office. And Jackie showed me some of the stuff she was working on. She's gonna stick around a couple more days to break me in. Oh, and I had a nice chat with the senator. It's a good thing I'm temporarily smitten with you, honey," Brenda said. "Paul Morelli is absolutely beautiful."

"Listen to me carefully, Brenda. Morelli is dangerous. Do not even try to play around with him."

"Ah, lighten up," she said, and gave his thigh a little squeeze.

After DeMarco and Brenda finished lunch, they drove back to DeMarco's place, picked up Brenda's luggage, and DeMarco helped her get settled into the apartment on Capitol Hill. When Brenda discovered silk sheets in the linen closet—which surprised the hell out of DeMarco considering the last tenant's appearance—the settling in took on a new meaning.

DeMarco liked Brenda Hathaway. She was quirky, fun, and bright, and he found himself enjoying her company both in and out of bed. She wasn't Elle Myers, and she wasn't going to be the next Mrs. DeMarco, but he would miss her when she left. He would miss her—but he wouldn't try to keep her from leaving.

Brenda's head was lying on his chest, her blond curls damp from their efforts. DeMarco was admiring the curve of her rump when the doorbell rang. He looked at his watch and cursed himself for not paying attention to the time. He jumped out of bed, ran to the front door, and looked through the peephole. It was Emma. Shit. He yelled through the door for her to wait, then ran back to the bedroom and told Brenda to hurry up and get dressed, and for Christ's sake, to comb her hair.

"Geez!" she said. "I could tell you weren't the type who liked to cuddle afterwards, but this is ridiculous."

"Hurry up," DeMarco said.

When he opened the door, Emma just stood on the stoop for a moment looking at him. She knew exactly what he'd been up to. And it wasn't just because of his tousled hair, or the fact that his shirt was half-untucked, or that he wasn't wearing a tie. Emma knew because . . . well, because she was Emma.

As she walked past DeMarco and into the living room of the townhouse she said, "Considering what's at stake here, I would have thought—"

"Aw, gimme a break," DeMarco said.

Before Emma could chastise DeMarco further, Brenda walked into the living room. Her clothes weren't disheveled like DeMarco's and her hair was in place, but she had that unmistakable, good-sex glow about her. She and Emma studied each other for a moment, Brenda wondering who Emma was, Emma inspecting Brenda like a side of beef.

"Who are you?" Brenda said to Emma.

"She's an associate of mine," DeMarco said. Before Brenda could ask more questions, he added, "Brenda, you need to buy some clothes suitable for a Senate aide. Why don't you go shopping now and meet me back here in about four hours."

Brenda's eyes narrowed and she opened her mouth to tell DeMarco to quit being such a bossy SOB, but before she could, DeMarco said, "And don't worry about the cost; you won't be paying for the clothes."

A minute after Brenda left, and just as Emma began to lecture him on the inadvisability of screwing the help, the doorbell rang again. It was Bobby Prentis, Neil's assistant. Bobby was a slightly-built young black man with rust-colored dreadlocks who rarely spoke. He communicated best, and most often, through keyboard and modem. From Bobby's small hands dangled two objects: a thin black leather briefcase and a medium-sized metal suitcase.

Emma and Bobby made a quick tour of the apartment, returning to the living room area where they started. The living room was adjacent to the kitchen, separated by a countertop used for informal dining.

"We want it to happen in this area," Emma said to DeMarco. "Make sure Goldilocks understands."

"Why—," DeMarco started to say, but Emma ignored him.

"Bobby, I want them no higher than this," Emma said, placing a hand on the top of a window frame, "and no lower than this," she said, touching the bottom of the window frame. "Understand?"

Bobby nodded.

"So put one here, one here, one over there, and one near the bedroom window, which I hope we won't need."

Bobby nodded. He set the two cases on the kitchen countertop, opened the black leather briefcase, and took out four video cameras that were not much bigger than packs of cigarettes. He opened the metal suitcase next, which was actually a portable hardware store, crammed with tools, fasteners, and wire. DeMarco was surprised Bobby had been able to lift the suitcase by himself.

As Bobby began to work, Emma said, "You have the cop lined up?"

"Yeah."

"And the photographer?"

"Yeah."

"Think they'll be able to keep their mouths shut?"

DeMarco shrugged. "I'm not too concerned about the cop; if he talks he'll get in trouble. It's the photographer who worries me."

"So have Murphy give him a tip," Emma said.

It took Bobby less than two hours to install the video equipment. When he was finished he nodded his head and left, having spoken no more than two sentences the entire time he was in the apartment.

DeMarco examined the places where Bobby had hidden the cameras. You could see them if you stood close to them and knew where to look, but a person casually taking in the décor would never spot them. Bobby's little spy shop in a box had even contained small vials of paint and he'd touched up the walls and molding wherever he'd made any marks.

Yes, Bobby was a professional when it came to things like this, as was Emma. DeMarco was not. As he stood there looking at the nearly invisible cameras he could imagine a million things going wrong. The batteries in the cameras would die; sunspots would interfere with the equipment; an electrical storm . . .

"Oh, yeah," Emma said, looking at Bobby's handiwork, a killer gleam in her eye, "we're gonna nail this bastard."

———◆———

Gary Parker, the cop, moved into the apartment building. He was delighted with his new digs.

DeMarco toured Arnie Berg around the apartment building. Showed him exactly where to stand. "No sweat," Arnie said.

Bobby, Neil's mute apprentice, gave DeMarco the keys to the surveillance van and showed him how to work the equipment. To make sure he understood, they did a dry run with Emma standing inside the apartment, talking for the microphones. The sound was crystal clear.

DeMarco called Brenda at Morelli's office to make sure that the senator's schedule hadn't changed.

"I caught him staring at my boobs when I stretched today," Brenda said. "I stretch a lot."

"Good. Keep him staring. But are you sure he's still on for Thursday, that his schedule's the same?"

"Yep. And speaking of schedules, I seem to be free tonight. How 'bout it, honey bunch? Wanna roll in the hay with a future movie star?"

He did.

———◆———

Wednesday night DeMarco met Sam Murphy in his suite at the Hyatt on Capitol Hill. Murphy was wearing the pants and vest from a black three-piece suit, the collar of his white shirt undone. He sat, relaxed, in an overstuffed armchair, his cowboy boots propped on the coffee table in front of him. His ugly dog lay on the bed, snoring. The critter smelled like a wet doormat.

"Well, Joe Bob, I'm all set to see the man tomorrow as planned."

"Did he agree to meet you in his office?" DeMarco asked.

"Yeah. Told him I didn't wanna meet no place public."

"What reason did you give him for the meeting?"

"Son, don't try to teach your daddy to suck eggs. I gave him a reason that made him feel good, one that made him think he had the upper hand."

"You gotta get some booze into him, Sam."

"Quit frettin', boy. I could get the Pope drunk and laid if I put my mind to it."

Sam Murphy looked over at DeMarco, his eyes flat and unsmiling and serious. "I'm gonna owe you one if you pull this off, Joe Bob. I want you to know I realize that."

"No, Sam, you will definitely not owe me one. If I had my way you wouldn't be running for president either."

Chapter 55

———◆———

Brenda was to wait until Sam Murphy left, then catch the senator just as he was leaving the office. DeMarco had told her it was important she meet Morelli in the hallway, and not inside his office. She was to tell him that she had missed her ride and would ask him if he would mind taking her to the Metro stop at Union Station, which was only a couple of blocks from the Russell Building. DeMarco was positive Morelli would offer to drive her home. He didn't like her being alone with Morelli in a car, but she was wired for sound and he would be directly behind her in the surveillance van.

At seven-thirty DeMarco heard Brenda over the headset: "Oh, Senator, I didn't know you were still here. I just came back to call a cab."

Goddamnit, Brenda, don't improvise. DeMarco was afraid Morelli might let her into his office to use the phone. Even worse, he just might let her take a cab home.

"What are you doing here so late, honey?" Morelli asked.

Honey? It sounded as though Sam Murphy had done his job.

"Well, you know," Brenda said, "being new and everything, I have to stay late sometimes to keep up."

"Where do you live?"

"By the Eastern Market Metro stop. I usually get a ride home from one of the other girls, but they all left early tonight. I was going to walk home—it's not that far—but when I went outside, I got scared. I don't like walking alone here at night, so I came back to call a cab."

DeMarco heard a long pause, then Morelli said, "Come on. I'll give you a ride."

"Oh, no. I couldn't impose on you like that, Senator."

Don't protest too much, Brenda.

"Darlin', it won't be any trouble at all. Let's go."

On the drive to Brenda's apartment, Morelli was the perfect gentleman. In fact, other than asking for directions, he hardly spoke at all, which made DeMarco worry that Sam Murphy hadn't gotten enough booze into the man.

Arnie Berg, the photographer, and Gary Parker, the cop, were in the surveillance van with DeMarco. They weren't able to hear Brenda and the senator

talking because DeMarco was listening to the trans-
mission through a headset. At this point, neither Arnie
nor Gary knew who they were about to encounter.

When they arrived at the apartment Brenda said,
"Senator, would you like to come in and have a cup
of coffee, or something? I don't mean to sound dis-
respectful, but I couldn't help but notice that you've
been drinking. I'd hate to see you get stopped by the
police on the way home."

Morelli didn't respond immediately and as the
silence grew, DeMarco sat in his car, muttering to
himself: Come on, you bastard, come on.

"Yeah, a cup of coffee might be a good idea,"
Morelli said at last.

"Get in position," DeMarco told his small team.
"And Arnie, when Gary tells you to give him the
camera, give it to him. And Gary, if Arnie doesn't
give you the camera when you ask for it, hit him with
your stick."

"Hey!" Arnie said.

"I'm serious, Arnie," DeMarco said. "If you don't
give Gary the camera, if you take off with it, I'll hunt
you down and kill you."

DeMarco wouldn't kill him, but he looked like
a guy who might. Arnie swallowed, his Adam's

apple bobbing. "I'll do what I said; you don't have to threaten me. But I wanna know who these people are."

"You'll find out soon enough. Now get in position."

Arnie and the young cop left the van. Arnie snuck up to the front window of Brenda's apartment, crawled behind some bushes, then pointed his camera at the interior of the apartment. The cop just stood on the sidewalk in front of the apartment building, fidgeting.

Over the headset DeMarco heard Brenda say, "Would you like tea or coffee, Senator?"

"You're sure a pretty little girl, Brenda," the senator said.

The phrase "little girl" made DeMarco's skin crawl.

"Thank you, Senator, but what would you like to drink?" Brenda's tone made it clear she was in no way encouraging Morelli.

"You live alone?" Morelli asked.

"Yes, sir."

"Have a boyfriend?"

"No, I just moved here. Now I've got some nice Darjeeling tea. How would you like that?"

"You must be lonely, a tiny thing like you, not having someone around to cuddle you. And I've seen you looking at me in the office."

The polished sophistication DeMarco had always heard in Paul Morelli's voice had disappeared completely. Drunken sailors approach hookers with more subtlety than he was displaying. The change in his character resulting from a few drinks was astounding.

"Yeah, I know what you want," Morelli said and after that neither of them spoke for a couple of seconds until Brenda said, "Senator! What are you doing?"

DeMarco checked to see where Arnie and Gary were. Arnie was still filming; the cop was still standing on the sidewalk.

DeMarco heard Brenda say, "Senator, stop," the words muffled, and the next thing he heard was a crash, as if a lamp had been knocked over, and then Brenda screamed, "Stop it, you bastard!" There was a panicky edge to her voice and DeMarco didn't think she was acting any longer.

DeMarco yelled to the cop, "Go, Gary, go."

As instructed, Gary yelled out to Arnie, "Hey! You with the camera! What the hell are you doing?"

And on cue, Arnie responded, "There's a girl being raped in there."

Gary ran down the walkway to Brenda's apartment and flung open the door. Brenda had been told not to lock it. Arnie followed Gary inside, his camera still recording.

Ten minutes later, Arnie and Gary reappeared with Morelli. DeMarco could hear sirens in the distance, coming in his direction. Gary had Morelli by the arm and Morelli's hands were cuffed behind his back. Arnie no longer had the video camera; Gary had confiscated it as evidence. Arnie was now holding a still camera with a flash and he was taking pictures as fast as the camera would take them.

Paul Morelli appeared to be in shock, his eyes glazed, his mouth slack-jawed. His hair was in disarray, a shirttail hung over his belt, and his belt was partially undone. The picture that would be on the front page of every newspaper in the country—a picture copyrighted to Arnie Berg—would be a classic. DeMarco watched the flash exploding on the camera like a strobe light, repeatedly freezing Morelli's dazed features.

At that moment a patrol car pulled up outside the apartment building and two uniformed cops got out. Gary escorted Morelli to the patrol car and placed him in the back seat. He then asked the two cops who had just arrived if they could go inside the apartment building, secure the scene, and get the victim. As the two cops walked into the apartment building, Gary walked over to the surveillance van and handed DeMarco the video camera that Arnie had been using.

Five minutes later, one of the cops emerged from the apartment with Brenda. She was clutching the lapels of a raincoat, holding the coat closed, presumably covering her torn clothing. Arnie's still camera captured the tears on her face. Brenda also managed a few words for her small audience: "It was terrible. He was like an animal."

And the Oscar goes to . . .

Brenda and the officer stood outside the building for a few minutes, the officer comforting Brenda, until a second patrol car pulled up to the curb. Brenda was placed in the second car. Ten minutes later both police cars left the scene, Morelli in one, Brenda in the other. The blue and red lights on the cop cars were flashing but the sirens were muted.

—◆◆◆—

Emma exited the car in which she'd been sitting and walked up to Brenda's apartment. She unlocked the door and ducked under the yellow crime-scene tape and entered the apartment. Ten minutes later she exited the apartment with the four cameras that Bobby Prentis had hidden and joined DeMarco in the surveillance van.

They studied the video recorded by Arnie and compared it to the videos recorded by the other cameras. The reason they'd placed the hidden cameras in the apartment was that they needed to make sure that they had at least one clear video of Morelli attacking Brenda. This was a one-take operation—they couldn't just hope that Arnie would be able to get an unobstructed view.

Emma and DeMarco watched together as Morelli backed Brenda against a wall. This happened just after he had said, "Yeah, I know what you want." Brenda responded by placing her hands against Morelli's chest and attempting to push him away, the camera a stark witness to her resistance. DeMarco winced when Morelli clamped his hands like a vice on both sides of Brenda's face and covered her lips with his mouth as she strained against him. She managed to say, "Senator, stop," but Morelli ignored her, continuing to kiss her while at the same time tearing clumsily at her blouse. He eventually pushed a struggling Brenda to the floor, knocking over a lamp as he did so, and the scene recorded by one of the cameras was perfect: it not only showed Morelli pawing at Brenda like some sort of deranged, out-of-control satyr, but it also showed the look of revulsion on her face.

Since DeMarco had told her what to expect, Brenda shouldn't have been surprised by Morelli's actions, but he was sure she was. She was like DeMarco had been in the beginning: incapable of believing, no matter what anyone said, that Paul Morelli could be anything other than a bright, shining knight.

After he had pushed Brenda to the floor, Morelli straddled her and she grimaced in pain as his knees pinned her arms to the carpet. With her arms immobilized, he began pulling up her skirt with one hand while he struggled to undo his belt with his other hand. It was while he was pulling up her skirt that Brenda had screamed "Stop it, you bastard!"

Brenda may have been acting up until that moment. She'd played the shy secretary in Morelli's office for two weeks, and when she invited him in for coffee, she was still in character. But when Morelli had her on the floor, tugging at her underwear, DeMarco could see the fear in her eyes and knew it was real. Just before Gary reached Morelli to pull him off Brenda, Morelli was recorded saying: "Come on, you little bitch. I know this is what you want."

Emma and DeMarco finally selected the camera that had the best view of the assault and Emma took the video cartridge from that camera and put it into Arnie's camera. Now all they had to do was get the camera back to Gary so it could be entered into evidence.

Forty minutes had elapsed since the cops had hauled Paul Morelli to the police station. Gary had been instructed to take his time processing Morelli and not to mention the video camera he'd taken from Arnie. Emma went to the police station, posing as an attorney waiting for a client. Gary had been instructed to go to the station's reception area periodically and when he saw Emma, she passed him Arnie's camera, the camera now containing the recording that DeMarco and Emma had selected. Gary then admitted the video camera into evidence.

While all this was occurring, DeMarco called his friend Reggie Harmon. He woke Reggie from his normal alcoholic stupor and told him to get down to the cop shop for the story of his career.

Per Reggie's story, which appeared on the front page of the *Post* the following morning, a tabloid photographer, Arnie Berg, just happened to see Senator Paul Morelli leaving the Russell Building with a good-looking blond. So, being the paparazzo sleaze that he was, Arnie followed the couple. No one was surprised by this. When the senator and the blond entered an apartment building, Arnie followed with his little camera and peered through the apartment windows, hoping to catch them doing something naughty. When Morelli assaulted Brenda, Arnie naturally kept filming but fortunately for Brenda, a young police officer, Gary Parker—who just happened to live in her building—was getting home from work. Officer Parker saw Arnie peeping through Brenda's window, at which point Arnie informed the cop of what was occurring inside the apartment.

And then Gary Parker just did his job.

Chapter 56

A week after his arrest, Paul Morelli met the old man at a card room, a windowless, concrete block structure near Newark, New Jersey. It was early, only nine a.m., and the card room wasn't open for business.

Morelli parked behind the building, near the rear exit. Another car, a big Lincoln, was already there when he arrived. He opened an unlocked door, walked down an unlit hallway, past the restrooms, and entered the main area of the card room. There was a small bar off to one side and eight green felt-covered tables filled the rest of the space. The tables had enough chairs for six players per table and on the tables were unopened decks of cards and stacks of poker chips locked up in Plexiglas cases.

The room was dark except for a single overhead light, a fake Tiffany-style stained glass lamp. The lamp hung over the card table at which the old man sat. Eddie was standing off to one side, almost invisible in the shadows, his huge, scarred hands just hanging at his sides.

The old man didn't rise to shake Morelli's hand as he usually did when they met. He just sat there, his black eyes boring into Morelli's as Morelli walked toward him. The old man, at that moment, in that lighting, with his seamed face and long, bony nose and his unblinking black eyes, reminded Morelli of some cruel, ancient bird of prey. Ancient, but still capable of ripping flesh from bone. He'd heard stories of how merciless the old man could be but until that moment it had never been so apparent in his features.

Morelli sat down and placed his hands on the table as if waiting for the cards to be dealt. In one night, Morelli had destroyed everything that they had worked for for fifteen years. Or that's the way the old man would see it. Morelli knew differently. Morelli knew that he'd just suffered a setback, but the game—his game—was far from over. But for him to succeed he needed the old man's help, and to get his help, he was going to have to tell him more lies. It was appropriate, he thought, that they were sitting at a poker table. Morelli was about to play for the highest stakes imaginable—his future, his life.

"How did it happen?" the old man said. His voice, as always, was low and calm. None of the emotions that he must be feeling showed.

"I'm not sure exactly," Morelli said. "It was a setup."

"I know *that*," the old man snapped, "but who set you up?

"Sam Murphy and that investigator we were watching for a while."

"You said the investigator was a nobody."

"He is, but Murphy helped him."

"But how did it happen? How did they get you alone with that girl?"

"I met with Murphy at my office the night it happened. He called and said he wanted to talk to me, about how we should both run clean campaigns. Anyway, we had a drink. You know I'm not a drinker, and I only had one drink. But after that drink, I started to feel odd, light-headed, woozy."

"Murphy spiked your drink?"

"Either him or the girl. She was in the office when Murphy came to see me. She's the one that poured the drinks for us. Anyway, right after the meeting, I agreed to give the girl a ride home. My mind wasn't . . . it just wasn't clear. It was like I was susceptible to suggestion. Anyway, she asked me to give her a ride and like a fool, I agreed. When we got to her place, she asked if I wanted a cup of coffee. Again I agreed. In fact, I thought the coffee might help clear my head." Morelli stopped and shook his head, as if astounded by how easily he'd been duped.

"Go on," the old man said.

"She gave me the coffee—or maybe it was tea—I can't remember. And the next thing I know she's up against me, her blouse is torn, and she's tearing at my clothes, at my belt. I tried to push her away, and I either fell or she tripped me. I don't know which. My mind was mush at this point and I was as weak as a kitten. The next thing I know, I'm on the floor, on top of her, and then this cop's in the apartment."

"So you didn't attack this girl?"

Morelli stared at the old man for a moment, pretending to bristle with resentment. "How long have you known me?" he said. "Have you ever seen me chase women?"

"But there's a tape of you attacking her."

"Have you been to a movie lately?"

"A movie?" The old man said, puzzled by the question.

"Yes. Have you seen what they can do these days with special effects? They can make people fly. They can put an animal's head on a man's body."

"So you think somebody doctored the tape?"

"Nobody saw that video for almost eight hours after my arrest, and the cop who arrested me, he didn't enter it into evidence until almost an hour after we arrived at the station. There was plenty of time to do something with that video." Before the old man could ask another question, Morelli said, "That tape isn't a tape of *what* happened. It's a tape of what they *say* happened. But the tape doesn't really matter."

"What? Why's that?"

"It'll never be admitted as evidence."

"You're saying you can beat this thing?"

Morelli shook his head. "No. I can't beat this. I mean, I'm not going to go to jail, but I won't get the nomination. That's not going to happen now."

The old man sat in silence a moment before he said, "So we're through. It's all over."

"No. This is a setback, but we're not through. I have a plan. In five years . . ."

Morelli had almost said *ten* years, but at the last minute he changed his mind.

". . . in five years, I'll be running for president. And I'll get elected."

"Five years?" the old man said.

Morelli knew what the old man was thinking. He was thinking: Will I live five more years? Will I be alive to see it happen? That's why Morelli hadn't said *ten* years. The old man was in good health—phenomenal health for his age—and he came from a family that lived long lives. In five years he'd be eighty-four. He'd live that long, or at least Morelli bet that that's what he was thinking.

"What's your plan?" the old man said.

Morelli told him. The old man didn't interrupt while he talked. He just listened—and analyzed. The old man was almost as bright as Paul Morelli.

When Morelli finished, the old man said, "It could work. But there's no way to speed it up?"

"No. Somebody else will be the next president. I'll have to wait until the next election."

"Okay," the old man said. His tone seemed to say: this had always been a long-range plan. What was five more years? "And Murphy and this investigator, what about them?"

"We'll deal with them eventually," Morelli said, "but not now. They're not the immediate problem. And Murphy, he won't be president either. He'll never get elected."

"What if he is?"

"Then we'll talk again."

Chapter 57

DeMarco watched the story unfold, learning only as much as the media chose to tell a stunned population. He made no attempt to contact Sam Murphy to get the insider's view. The month following the arrest, you couldn't turn on a television, open a newspaper, or walk by a magazine stand without seeing Paul Morelli's picture. Those who had once supported Morelli ducked the interviewers' questions; those that had never liked him said *I told you so*. Comparisons to every politician whose undoing had been a woman—Gary Hart, Ted Kennedy, and of course, Bill Clinton—were rehashed whenever the reporters ran out of things to say about Morelli.

The video of Morelli attacking Brenda was never seen publicly.

It was reported that a detective snuck into the evidence locker and made a copy of the video to sell to a television producer, but the detective was caught before he could leave the police station. DeMarco read that uniformed cops now guarded the evidence locker like it was King Tut's tomb, and he imagined that half the cops were being paid by Morelli to make sure the tape wasn't copied again, and the other half by Sam Murphy to make sure it wasn't destroyed. And although the public never saw the video directly, there were lawyers, judges, and cops who did, and these folks anonymously told the reporters what they'd seen. The end result was that even though very few people saw the actual footage of Morelli's crime, everyone knew, essentially frame by frame, what the camera had recorded.

Speculation that Paul Morelli had been set up began to spread as more facts became known—and the Morelli machine did the spreading. That Brenda was a former actress suddenly turned secretary was central to the argument. Then there was the fact that Gary Parker not only lived in Brenda's apartment building but had moved in just two weeks before the incident. And although no one was surprised that Arnie Berg had taken the video, the serendipity of Arnie—a guy who normally badgered athletes and entertainers—just *happening* to be near the Russell Building and being so eagle-eyed as to spot the little blond in Morelli's car . . . Well, *give me a break,* the Morelli rooters said.

Gary Parker had his picture taken with various Republicans who gave him awards. When asked about the coincidence of him arriving home just as Brenda was being attacked, Parker shrugged and said: "I was just lucky, I guess. And for that little gal, it's a damn good thing I was." Parker played the humble hero much better than DeMarco ever would have guessed.

Arnie, too, bathed in the limelight, a new icon to all his sleazy kind. It was one thing to catch Britney Spears looking fat and tacky on a trip to the grocery store but to bring a presidential contender to his knees—now that was good shooting indeed.

The spotlight focused on Brenda was the brightest—and for an aspiring actress, this was better than anything a Hollywood PR firm could have arranged. If there was a talk show she didn't appear on it had to be on Telemundo. She told the world that she had tried being an actress, but had never been able to land a decent role, so she had given up on her Hollywood dreams and moved to Washington to start a new life as a simple secretary. She couldn't believe her good luck when she was hired by Paul Morelli, a man she had always admired. That Morelli had attacked her . . . Well, she said, you can just never tell about people.

Paul Morelli was never tried, much less convicted, of a crime. His lawyers threw out legal roadblocks faster than firemen barricading a burning city block. They quibbled over the chain of custody for Arnie's camera. The delay in entering the camera into evidence, combined with the fact that a detective had made a copy of the video, led to speculation that the video had been doctored.

The lawyers argued that Morelli had been entrapped by a busty actress and a corrupt cop, as if he'd had no role in his own undoing. And the cup of tea that Brenda had made for Morelli became a huge point of contention. The teacup and its contents were never analyzed, and Morelli's lawyers claimed that the senator had been drugged and the cops, in their rush to judgment—as if the law was ever in a rush—had disposed of crucial evidence.

The attorneys even jousted over the nature of the charge itself. Per the U.S. Constitution, a sitting senator can only be tried for treason, a felony, or something called "breach of the peace." Morelli's lawyers maintained that no felony had been committed. They had the audacity to argue that if Paul Morelli was guilty of anything it was sexual harassment: a ripped blouse, they claimed, was nothing more than an overzealous fondle, no felony at all.

But the primary reason Morelli didn't stand trial was Sam Murphy's political acumen. Sam already had everything he wanted and he was afraid that a man as popular as Paul Morelli would never be convicted by a jury. And if Morelli was acquitted . . . well, hell, some people might actually think he was innocent. So Sam—and his money—convinced the judge that a trial would be a waste of time and that Morelli should be disciplined by the Senate, censured or expelled, whatever that august body felt was best. Yes, Murphy liked the situation *much* better the way it currently was: Paul Morelli had been tried, judged, and hung by the media—so why give the legal system a chance to reverse the decision?

———◆———

Paul Morelli maintained the lowest possible profile while all the lawyers sparred. He made only one public appearance, giving a statement to the press two days after his arrest, and it was the only time DeMarco had ever seen Morelli give a rambling, unclear speech. He couldn't decide if Morelli was so inarticulate because he was still shaken by his circumstances or if he was being deliberately confusing.

Something *strange* happened that night, Morelli said. The authorities were still trying to put the pieces together, and *he* was still trying to understand what had occurred. The implication was that he wasn't necessarily the one under investigation, and his words, his tone, his manner all hinted at dark conspiracies.

He reminded the audience of his years of brilliant public service, then talked about the strain he had been under lately—his wife's and daughter's deaths, his near assassination at the hands of Marcus Perry, the death of his close friend, Abe Burrows. He admitted that alcohol had contributed to his circumstance. He'd been drinking that night, something he rarely did, and had it not been for the booze and the stress he would never have allowed himself to be "lured into such a dangerous situation."

Looking like a man reeling from an awful, unfair beating, he concluded he needed healers, not jailers. He said he was packing himself off to Father Martin's, the same clinic where he had imprisoned his wife the week before she died.

It was a good performance. Morelli managed somehow to appear vulnerable if not the victim. DeMarco was sure there were many who felt sorry for him and some even gullible enough to believe he was innocent regardless of what had been reported and the credibility of the reporters. But as good as his performance was, DeMarco was sure it was not good enough. Too much damage had been done. Brenda Hathaway would be Paul Morelli's Chappaquiddick.

DeMarco watched the whole affair with an odd sense of detachment. He felt no remorse for ruining Morelli's career in an underhanded manner, but there was no sense of victory either, no glowing feeling that justice had prevailed. All he felt was relief: relief that it was over, relief that he was still employed, relief that he was still alive.

He never discussed with Mahoney how he had set up Morelli but on the day following Morelli's arrest there was a box of Davidoff cigars on the desk in his office.

It really bugged him that Mahoney had a key to his office.

Chapter 58

---◆---

The chapel at Arlington National Cemetery is not a large structure, but with only three people in it, it seemed cavernous and the words of the navy chaplain echoed throughout the nearly empty room.

Emma couldn't really explain why she had decided to attend Blake Hanover's funeral. She hadn't liked the man. She may have come because he had helped her while he was dying but she knew that wasn't the main reason. She suspected it was because the image of him dying alone and friendless in his apartment haunted her, and she found the idea of a funeral with no attendees almost as poignant.

But it turned out that there was one other attendee: Charlie Eklund.

The chaplain—a Catholic priest—was uncomfortable. He hadn't known Hanover and he didn't know what to say about the man. He read a brief history of Hanover's life, noting that he had been born and raised in Pennsylvania, served for four years in the marines, then spent another thirty years working for the CIA. "Mr. Hanover," the chaplain said, "is survived by two sons, David and Michael, who, ah, unfortunately were unable to be here today."

Now that was heartbreaking, Emma thought.

The chaplain looked at his small audience and said, "I was going to read a short passage from the New Testament but I was wondering if either of you had anything you'd like to say."

Emma shook her head.

"Yes, I would like to say something," Eklund said.

He walked slowly up to the front of the chapel. Hanover's ashes were contained in a simple, unadorned urn, resting on a small folding table. When Eklund spoke, he looked directly at Emma. He would have looked at her if the chapel had been filled with people.

"Blake Hanover was not my friend," he said, "but he spent his life in the service of his country and he deserves to be recognized for his service, and that's why I am here today. Blake was proud that he worked for the CIA, as I too am proud. A fickle and ignorant media reports only the failures of America's greatest intelligence service. The successes are not reported because they cannot be reported. The people who work for the agency are patriots. They love this country and they die if need be to guarantee its freedoms. They are diligent, deeply committed people who should be revered for what they do rather than scorned by a witless public and held in contempt by unappreciative politicians."

And in all this Emma knew that Charlie Eklund was right. Her experiences with the CIA had not been positive, but she knew that the agency's successes far outnumbered its failures and that lunatics like Eklund were the exception, not the norm.

Eklund placed his hand on Hanover's urn and said, "Thank you, Blake, and may you rest in peace." Then he sat down next to Emma, his eyes shining with tears.

The chaplain stood silent for a moment, not knowing what to do, then he cleared his throat and said. "I think, ah, if it's okay with you I'll skip the reading from the New Testament."

Emma and Eklund both nodded.

"An honor guard will now accompany Mr. Hanover's ashes for interment in the Columbarium Wall," the chaplain said. "I'll, uh, go outside and tell them we're ready." The young priest left the church, his relief evident.

"Thank you for coming today," Eklund said to Emma. "I'm very disappointed that the people who worked with Blake are not here. I'm not surprised, but I am disappointed." He paused theatrically then added, "I'm afraid that my own funeral will one day be equally well attended."

Eklund looking for sympathy was more than Emma could take. "I have to go," she said and rose from the pew. She didn't intend to accompany the honor guard to the Columbarium and hear taps being played for Blake Hanover. Taps made her cry. She'd heard them played too often for too many people she'd cared about.

Eklund looked up at her and said, "You won. Paul Morelli will never be president. And you know something, my dear? I don't care. So I'm not sure how you did it, but I hold no hard feelings against you."

Emma just shook her head and turned to leave.

Eklund sighed. "I'm thinking of leaving the agency," he said. "Voluntarily. The world has just become too confusing a place. It's time for me to go."

Emma looked down at Eklund. "Charlie, you lying little prick," she said, "who do you think you're kidding? You'll never retire."

Chapter 59

A ringing telephone pulled DeMarco out of a sleep so deep he felt as if he were being pulled from the womb. As he reached for the phone, he pried open one eye and checked the luminous hands on the bed-side clock. Two a.m. Christ.

"Joe Bob. How the hell ya doin', boy?"

DeMarco hadn't spoken to Sam Murphy since they had destroyed Paul Morelli almost two months ago. Murphy had tried to contact DeMarco after Morelli's arrest, but DeMarco didn't return his calls. He had no desire to hear Murphy tell him what a great job he'd done; helping the Texan get a step closer to the White House was not something he was proud of.

DeMarco put his head back on the pillow. Keeping his eyes closed, he said, "What do you want, Sam?"

"That young cop, Gary Parker, he was just killed."

DeMarco sat up in bed. "What happened?"

"He was hit by a car. Happened about five hours ago."

"Hit-and-run?"

"No. He had just parked his car near that place you got him on Capitol Hill and he got hit crossing the street to get to his apartment. He didn't cross at a crosswalk and he was a little buzzed at the time he was killed. The guy who hit him stopped and called the medics, and he was as sober as a judge."

DeMarco didn't say anything for a second. He was thinking of how Gary had looked the last time he had seen him on TV, the big grin on his handsome face, the cocky tilt of his uniform cap. A portrait of a man who had the world by the balls.

"Sam, I'm sorry to hear he's dead, but why are you calling me about this at two in the morning?"

"Two? Shit, boy, I plumb forgot the time difference. I was juss sittin' here, having a drink, and thought I oughta talk this thing over with you. It bothers me."

"It bothers me too, Sam, but why call me? Don't you have any friends?"

"You don't understand, Joe Bob. I didn't call to ponder the fickleness of fate. I had my people look into Parker's death, to see if anything looked funny. Well, something did. The guy that hit him is a small-time hood. Has convictions for robbery, car theft, petty shit like that. He's not the kind of guy that stops and calls the cops when he kills somebody."

"If it was an accident, why wouldn't he stop? Particularly with his record, why take the risk of being nailed for a hit-and-run?"

"Because of who he is. This guy would lie even if the truth made a better story."

"What are you trying to say, Sam?"

"I'm sayin', what if Morelli set this up? What if he paid this punk to run Parker down? Since he wasn't drunk, he probably won't even do any jail time. It's a free killin'!"

"Why in the hell would Morelli do that?"

"Revenge, boy! You stupid or still asleep?"

"You're getting paranoid, Sam—a common affliction of a guilty conscience."

"Real funny, partner."

"I'm not your partner."

"Sure you are, boy. And with what we've done together, you always will be."

Before DeMarco could tell him to go to hell, Murphy said, "Look, I want you to check this out. See if Morelli's tied to it in some way."

"Not interested. The only further involvement I want with you is when I vote for your opponent in the next election."

"I ain't told you everything yet, smart-ass. After the cop was killed, I had my people check around and see if anybody else who helped you had any recent misfortune. Well, that photographer, Berg, he had some kind of accident."

"What happened to him?"

"I don't know exactly. I just found this out an hour ago and I don't have all the details yet. All I know is Berg had an accident and he's in the hospital. So now what do you think? Two guys help you and two guys have accidents."

When DeMarco didn't say anything, Sam Murphy added, "I'm telling you, I *know* it's Morelli. I can feel it in my gut."

"Sam, if he wanted revenge, it's me and you he'd be going after, not Gary Parker or Arnie Berg. They just had walk-on parts in this little drama."

"And that's why you better listen to me. You can't get Secret Service protection like I can, boy. So if I was you, I'd be checkin' the locks on my back door right now."

"I appreciate the warning," DeMarco said.

"So help me out. Help yourself out. Find out what happened to Berg. Find out if Morelli was involved in that cop's death."

"Nope."

"Come on, Joe Bob. If we can tie Morelli to this, we can finish him off for good. Now I know that appeals to you."

"Sorry, not interested."

"Listen to me, you smug bastard. I know you don't like me, but this ain't about me and you. You talked that young cop into helping you, and now he's dead. You *owe* it to that boy if I'm right."

DeMarco didn't respond immediately. If Murphy was right and Paul Morelli was responsible for Parker's death, DeMarco did owe him. But he didn't trust Murphy and wanted no further involvement with him.

"Bye, Sam," he said.

Murphy started swearing. The last thing DeMarco heard before he hung up was "sanctimonious fucker." The vocabulary of a wildcatter with a college degree.

———◆———

DeMarco couldn't get back to sleep after the phone call. He put on a robe, went into the kitchen, and made a cup of chamomile tea. When he was a child and had nightmares, his grandmother used to give him chamomile tea; he hoped he had not outgrown its powers.

He sat drinking his tea, looking out his kitchen window at the blue lights twinkling annoyingly on the eaves of his neighbor's house. He wondered why the putz left them on all night. He knew if he'd still been married there would have been a holly wreath on his front door, a decorated evergreen in his living room, and a dozen poinsettias scattered about the place to provide splashes of Clausian red. His ex-wife had been big on Christmas. But his ex was no longer with him, and now, as he looked around his unadorned home, he felt like young Scrooge in the flight path of a Dickens ghost.

Thoughts of Christmas past were soon replaced with present-day concerns of Paul Morelli. A man who would kill his wife and an innocent teenager to protect his career was capable of anything, and Morelli wouldn't be human if he didn't feel the desire for vengeance against those responsible for his downfall. But why kill Gary Parker? As he'd told Sam Murphy, Gary was just a bit player. If Morelli wanted revenge it was DeMarco and Murphy he should be going after—and maybe he would. Maybe he was just saving the best for last.

DeMarco didn't have any illusions that Morelli couldn't figure out he was responsible for his ruin. He was sure a good investigator would be able to prove that DeMarco had met with Sam Murphy twice and would be able to tie him to other people involved in the sting. So although he doubted that Parker's death had been anything other than a tragic accident, tomorrow he'd find out what had happened to Arnie, and maybe he'd call Brenda to see if she'd had any recent close brushes with death. He also decided it might be prudent to find out where Paul Morelli was.

When the senator's doctors declared him miraculously cured after only two weeks at Father Martin's, Morelli made a brief attempt to resume his life but he was hounded relentlessly by the media and became the scornful subject of every hot-air essayist from George Will to Howard Stern. His Democratic colleagues began to push quietly for his resignation from the Senate while his Republican foes cried loudly for his expulsion. But as expulsion took a two-thirds majority, the Republicans had to settle for making impassioned statements to the press about how they found working with a sexual predator disconcerting.

One day after almost breaking down in tears on the Senate floor, Morelli issued a statement saying that he was departing Washington for a brief period. He needed time alone, he claimed, to sort out the curve balls that life had thrown him. All the political commentators jerked a thumb in the direction of the dugout: they were convinced that Morelli was finished in politics.

DeMarco hoped the commentators were right, but knew it was usually a mistake to assume the public had standards. He agreed that Morelli's chances of reaching the White House were nil, but was afraid Morelli might be able to hold his seat in the Senate indefinitely. Ted Kennedy's past had not kept him from getting reelected every six years in Massachusetts, and today he seemed to be the reigning patriarch of his party.

At the time he took his leave of absence, demands for Morelli to resign had reached a screaming crescendo. The Senate Ethics Committee was being urged to at least censure him if they couldn't do more. Oddly enough, by his simply walking away from his post, Morelli's opponents appeared to go into a holding pattern, apparently awaiting his return to the Capitol before taking further action. What fun would it be to stone someone in absentia?

So Paul Morelli was temporarily gone, supposedly off licking his wounds and pondering his future—or maybe Sam Murphy was right, and it was revenge he was pondering.

The tea finally began to do its job and DeMarco began to feel drowsy. According to his grandmother, he should now be safe from the things that went bump in the night.

Chapter 60

DeMarco found Arnie Berg on the fourth floor of Columbia Hospital. He was in a private room, looking out a window, and from his location he could watch the homeless in Washington Circle fight over bottles of Thunderbird wine. DeMarco suspected Arnie was envious of them.

Arnie was in a motorized wheelchair, the kind with a little joy stick that allows the occupant to operate the chair with only one hand, or in his case, a couple of fingers. He was wearing a neck brace, but even with the brace his head lolled forward. DeMarco walked up to him and put a hand on Arnie's shoulder and his head twitched in surprise. He touched the joy stick and the wheelchair spun around so he could face DeMarco.

"Arnie," DeMarco said slowly and softly. "It's Joe DeMarco. Remember me?"

"Of course I remember you. I'm a fucking crip, not an imbecile."

His words were slurred, but his voice was strong.

"What happened, Arnie?"

"I killed myself."

There was nothing DeMarco could say to that.

"Anyway, why do you care what happened to me?"

"I care, Arnie. We weren't friends or anything, but . . ."

"That's for sure."

". . . but I don't like seeing you like this. And I appreciate the help you gave me with Paul Morelli."

DeMarco looked for some sign when he mentioned Morelli's name, but Arnie's face didn't change expression. Maybe it couldn't.

"Since you're so grateful," Arnie said, "I'll let you change my diaper the next time I shit." He tried to smile, but only half his face moved. Spit drooled from the corner of his mouth, down his chin.

DeMarco wanted to take out his handkerchief and wipe Arnie's chin but he knew that would only make the man hate him more.

"Arnie, I need to know what happened."

"Why?"

DeMarco saw a spark flare in Arnie's eyes. Old habits die hard. Arnie was trying to figure out how to get his slice of the action, not knowing or caring what the action was. But the spark died quickly. Arnie Berg was through cutting deals.

"Arnie, please. Tell me what happened."

He looked at DeMarco sullenly for a moment, then said, "I was out drinking with this buddy of mine. We got totally shit-faced. When we got back to my place, I decided to show him my pigeons. I keep—I kept—racing pigeons on the roof of my apartment. Anyway, we go up there to look at my birds, and the next thing I know I wake up in a hospital, ninety percent vegetable. I fell off the fuckin' roof—a two-story swan dive."

"Who was the guy you were with?"

"A bud, another journalist."

Journalist. Now that was a joke, but this wasn't the time to malign Arnie's profession.

"What's his name, Arnie?"

"Phil Morrow. Typical Aussie with a hollow leg."

"Was it your idea to go see the pigeons, or Morrow's?"

"Hell, I don't know. The docs told me I had a .29 alcohol level that night. I can't remember half the evening, much less who wanted to look at the birds."

DeMarco didn't say anything for a moment. He knew the question he wanted to ask, but was trying to figure out a subtle way to ask it. Before he could say anything, Arnie said, "Why are you asking these questions? Most people come to see me, they ask how I'm doin', how I'm feelin', that kind of shit. You obviously don't give a damn how I'm doin', so why are you here?"

It was time to forget subtlety. "Could your friend Morrow have pushed you off the roof, Arnie?"

"What! Why the hell would he do that?"

"Maybe because Paul Morelli paid him to."

Arnie's mouth twisted in a sardonic half smile. "Ah, now I get it, you slick fuck. You're starting to hear footsteps, aren't you?"

DeMarco didn't bother to deny the accusation. "Yeah, Arnie, I am. We did a number on Morelli, and I—"

"*You* did a number on him. I was just hired help."

"Maybe so, and when I heard you had an accident, it seemed like a good idea to find out how it happened."

Arnie snorted a laugh, amused that DeMarco was afraid, then said, "Go over to the closet there."

DeMarco was puzzled, but did what Arnie said.

"There's a gym bag on the floor, with a bottle of vodka in it. And a straw. Bring it here."

"You shouldn't be drinking, Arnie."

"Fuck you. Bring me the bottle or get the hell out of here."

DeMarco found the bottle, put the straw in it, and held it so Arnie could take a sip.

"Now answer my question, Arnie. Could Morrow have pushed you off the roof?"

Arnie laughed. "I was so drunk he could have cornholed me and I wouldn't have felt it. But why the hell would he have wanted to kill me?"

"Money, Arnie."

"No way. Phil's no choirboy, but he's a pal. I've known him for twenty years."

Arnie sucked on the straw again, then said, "And Morelli, he's uptown. You jammed him good, but he ain't the type to bump somebody off. For Christ's sake, he cried when that cop handcuffed him that night."

Arnie Berg didn't know Paul Morelli as well as he did, but DeMarco didn't argue with him. He let Arnie lower the level in the vodka bottle another inch, then over his protests, returned the bottle to its hiding place. He'd let Arnie's next visitor help him reach oblivion.

"What's the prognosis, Arnie?"

"Prognosis?"

"What's going to happen to you? Will you be able to walk again?"

Arnie grinned horribly. "The prognosis is death. I'll be in this chair until I die, and the doc says it'll probably be soon. As a result of being a wheelchair jockey, my kidneys are failing. The doctors in this place have been full of good news."

"I'm sorry to hear that."

"If you're so damn sorry, come back with a gun and blow my head off." Tears glistened in Arnie's eyes when he added, "I'd do it myself, but I can't pull a trigger."

DeMarco returned to his office and called Emma. He asked her to use her contacts to find out about Arnie's drinking buddy, Phil Morrow, and the man who had run down Gary Parker. He wanted to know if these men were the type you could buy to do nasty things. Even if they were, he realized that Arnie was probably right: it was unlikely Paul Morelli would have hired someone to kill Gary or Arnie. Not that Morelli was above such behavior, it was just hard to imagine that he'd do such a thing so soon after what had happened to him.

If all those who participated in Paul Morelli's demise were to die suddenly, someone would make the connection, and Morelli would become the obvious suspect. And a lot of people had been involved: Sam Murphy, Brenda Hathaway, Arnie Berg and Gary Parker. And Emma and himself, of course. DeMarco supposed he should also include Clayton Adams, the ex-congressman who had lied to help Brenda get the job on Morelli's staff. Yes, if Morelli was planning on maiming or killing all the people involved, it was a very long list.

Though not overly concerned about her safety, he decided to call Brenda in California.

"Sorry, meester, she no home now."

"Do you know when she'll be home?"

"Many day. She making peecture."

"Do you know where she's making the picture?"

"In Hollywoods maybe. I doan know."

Shit.

Since he could think of no other excuse for shirking his duties, he turned his attention to the latest assignment from his boss. Mahoney had heard that a freshman congressman was using his connections to make a killing on Wall Street, and DeMarco had spent the last week trying to unravel the young gentleman's finances. He had illegally obtained a copy of the politician's stock portfolio and tax returns, and was comparing them to his appointment schedules, his financial disclosure statements, and his normal committee work to see if there was an illicit relationship between the congressman's rising income and his job. It was like trying to untie the Gordian knot wearing mittens. DeMarco had concluded two days ago he needed the help of a world-class CPA with a minor in computer hacking, but he was still stubbornly plugging away at the records. His eyes were just beginning to cross when the phone rang. It was Emma.

"Berg's drinking buddy, Morrow, is a guy just like Berg. A paparazzo without a conscience."

"Would he kill for money?"

"It's hard to say. He's a photographer, not a professional hit man, but he's a lowlife. My guess is that for enough money, he'd do anything."

"How 'bout the one who ran down Parker?"

"Just what you heard from Murphy: he's a small-time hood who's been in jail half his life, and in trouble all of it. He's definitely the type who would kill if the money was right. The cops who investigated the accident were amazed this guy turned himself in, and even more amazed when they found he didn't have a drop of alcohol in his system. He's a known lush, and they figured it had to be a DWI accident. When the blood tests came back clean, they figured he must have stayed off the sauce for a week to get it all out of his system."

"So it's possible Murphy's right?"

"He could be," Emma said, "but it seems unlikely Morelli would take this kind of risk. Especially this soon."

That was exactly what DeMarco had thought.

"But you better watch your back, Joe," Emma added. "Do you want me to provide you with some protection?"

DeMarco hesitated. Maybe someone to cover him wouldn't be a bad idea. Maybe he should even ask Emma for a gun. "No," he finally said. "I'll be okay."

After he finished talking to Emma, he tried to get back to the congressman's financial records but after five minutes he said to hell with it. He wanted to know where Paul Morelli was.

Packy Morris gave a languid wave as DeMarco entered his office. DeMarco didn't see how it was possible—the human skeleton has structural limits—but Packy looked even bigger than he had the last time DeMarco had seen him. He had the phone to his ear, almost invisible in one large hand, and was nodding every few seconds, saying, "Right. Right."

Packy looked at DeMarco and rolled his eyes in exasperation. Finally he hung up, sat back in his chair, and said, "Morons, Joe, this city is filled with morons. Washington should be floating, the empty heads of its befuddled citizens, like hot-air balloons, tugging it aloft." Shaking his head in mock dismay, he added, "I despair for the republic."

DeMarco waited a beat then said, "Are you through, Packy?"

Packy's small, malevolent eyes twinkled. "So what do you want, little citizen?" he said.

"What's Paul Morelli been up to lately?"

Packy studied DeMarco's face, and as he did, he tapped his front teeth with the eraser end of a pencil.

"The last time you were here you asked about Morelli," he said. "Are you the head of his I-coulda-been-a-contender fan club?"

"I'm just curious about him."

"Just curious, my ass. You're asking for a reason. Would you care to share?"

Packy sat there like an arrogant Buddha, his small eyes laughing. Toying with DeMarco was more fun than plucking the wings off flies.

"Packy," DeMarco said, "would you like me to talk to your born-again boss about a member of his staff who has a thing for hookers made up like kittens?"

Packy started tapping his teeth again with the pencil, trying to gauge DeMarco's sincerity.

"You'd be such a prick?" he asked.

"Without hesitation. Now quit pretending you're Bill Buckley's fat brother and tell me what Morelli's been up to."

"Well, since you asked nice, all right. Senator Morelli has disappeared."

"What do you mean, disappeared?"

"Just that. He's disappeared. His own staff doesn't know where he's at."

"How do you know?"

He gave DeMarco a you've-got-to-be-kidding look.

"Yes, and it's been tres embarrassing for his staff."

"Packy, if you wanted to find him, how would you go about it?"

"You're asking me? I thought you were some kind of investigator. What the hell do you do, Joe?"

DeMarco ignored the question, and said, "I'm not talking about a missing persons search. I'm asking who you'd talk to that would most likely know where he is."

"I've already talked to him. He doesn't know."

"Who?"

"The chief of staff in his New York office. Next to the late Abe Burrows, he was closer to Saint Paul than his confessor. If he doesn't know, nobody does."

"But would he tell you?"

"I've got more on him than you have on me. I mean, if you want to hear about something kinky . . ."

"Uncle Harry, it's Joe."

Harry Foster hesitated before he answered. "Yes," he finally said, "what can I do for you?"

DeMarco was taken aback. Harry was never so formal, not when dealing with him.

"It's about Paul Morelli, Harry."

DeMarco thought he heard a small groan come from Harry.

"Joe," Harry said, his voice serious, "there's a lotta speculation that someone set Paul up. No one believes that this out-of-work actress just decided to become a secretary or that this photographer just happened to be hanging around the Russell Building. Please tell me you didn't have anything to do with that, son. Please."

"Of course not, Harry," DeMarco said. He hated to lie to his godfather, but what else could he say?

There was another lengthy pause while Harry contemplated DeMarco's response. Finally he said, "So what is it you want to know about Paul?"

"I want to know where he's hiding."

"You and every journalist on the planet. But why do you want to know?"

Shit, DeMarco thought. He should have anticipated *that* question. He began to think of a plausible lie, but before he could utter it, Harry said, "It doesn't matter. I don't know where he is. When I heard about his troubles, I called him, figuring he could use a good PR man, but he didn't return my calls. I've tried to track him down, but he's vanished."

"How the hell could he vanish, Harry? He's a U.S. senator with one of the most recognizable faces in the world."

"It's easy to vanish if you've got money. You grow a beard, you buy a hat, and you have a chartered jet take you someplace with palm trees."

Harry was right.

"Harry, if anybody would know where he is, who would it be?"

"Two people, and I've talked to both of them. One's the chief of staff for his New York office, George Burak, and the other's a . . . oh, a relative."

"What relative?"

"Joe, I gotta run now. I have a client waiting." And Harry hung up.

DeMarco spent lunch at the Monocle, drinking martinis, eating free peanuts, and arguing with himself. On the blank page of his mind, he drew a line down the middle. On one side he listed all the reasons why Paul Morelli could be having people killed and maimed, and on the other side, all the reasons why that didn't make sense.

He thought about Morelli, sitting off in some isolated spot, driven over the edge by what had happened to him, using his sick, brilliant mind to plot revenge, but he ultimately rejected the idea. Revenge was an emotional crime, it was about getting even, and Morelli, unless he was drunk, was calculating and totally rational. Killing everyone who had been there the night he was arrested was too risky and not rational at all.

DeMarco finally concluded that the similarity between Parker's death and Arnie's accident—the timing of the events, the fact that both occurrences had involved people with less than sterling characters —was just coincidence. It had to be.

Sticking the swizzle stick from the last martini in his mouth, DeMarco waved a jaunty goodbye to the bartender. It was time to quit worrying about Paul Morelli.

Chapter 61

Eight a.m., two days later, DeMarco stood in the doorway of his house, shaking the rain off his umbrella. He was wearing a raincoat over a wife-beater undershirt and boxer shorts. His slippers were soaked through. In his left hand was the newspaper, the edition that was supposed to be delivered by six a.m., and the paper was a waterlogged mass that he had found under a rhododendron ten feet from the door. DeMarco's Christmas tip to his paperboy would be a note advising him to buy an alarm clock and improve his aim.

He went into the kitchen, still muttering curses at the paperboy, laid the wet paper on the counter, and poured a cup of coffee. Since the first part of the paper was nothing but soggy pulp, he put the national news aside and turned to the local section. On the bottom of the second page, beneath an article on cost overruns incurred renovating the Jefferson Memorial, was a picture of one-time congressman Clayton Adams. The picture of Adams, a headshot taken from his days in the House, showed him smiling; apparently they couldn't find a photo of him when he wasn't smiling. The article accompanying the happy picture said that Clayton Adams was dead.

Adams's obituary did not contain the modifier "distinguished legislator"; no one was willing to state, even posthumously, that America's destiny had been altered in any appreciable way by Adams's five terms of service. The paper did note, for some mean-spirited reason, that Adams had once been investigated by the House Ethics Committee for sponsoring a bill that benefited a construction company owned by a cousin. Regarding the cause of death, the only thing that DeMarco cared about, the *Post* said that the good congressman had died of a heart attack, noting that he had had a quadruple bypass two years earlier.

DeMarco looked out his kitchen window at the rain falling on his untended backyard lawn. He had once read a story—probably in *Reader's Digest* while waiting to have his hair cut—about a man in Arkansas who had been struck five times by lightning. It seemed the poor fellow's head was some sort of knobby lightning rod. The same article mentioned other queer folk, all sounding like the type that aliens preferred to kidnap, who had also been zapped more than once. The point of the story was, contrary to the old cliché, that lightning could indeed strike twice.

And maybe it did, and maybe coincidence against incredible odds was more commonplace than he had ever suspected, but DeMarco did not believe that what had happened to Gary Parker, Arnie Berg, and Clayton Adams was a trifecta of random acts of divine whimsy.

Brenda!

He rushed to the phone in his den and dialed her number. The phone rang five times before she answered.

"Brenda, thank God you're home," he said.

"Sweetie! It's *so* good to hear from you," she said. "I've missed you terribly."

That was a bald-faced lie, but a nice one. Since gaining instant celebrity status for her part in Morelli's demise, Brenda's career had skyrocketed. DeMarco had read that she was currently acting in a Matt Damon movie, not the lead, but a good supporting role. He'd also read she'd been seen recently in the company of another famous actor, but was *definitely* not responsible for him breaking up with his wife.

"Brenda," DeMarco said, "there's something going on that—"

"Joe, I'm just tickled pink you called, but I can't

talk now. The limo's waiting for me. My plane leaves in an hour."

"Brenda, listen to me, you're in—"

"Honey, I'll be in Seattle tonight. At the Sheraton. Call me there."

"Brenda, goddamnit, wait a—"

He was speaking to a dial tone.

Chapter 62

———◆———

At four-thirty that evening, DeMarco was in the lobby of the Seattle Sheraton. Brenda wasn't in her room and he didn't have the slightest idea where she might be. He walked over to the concierge's desk, where he was ignored and forced to listen to the concierge and a bellboy talk about the Seattle Seahawks collapsing in the fourth quarter of their last game. Go Skins. He took a twenty from his wallet and held it up so the concierge could see it in his peripheral vision. The man's head swiveled so fast that there was the pleasing possibility of whiplash.

"Yes, *sir*!" he said. "May I help you?"

DeMarco said he was trying to find a Ms. Hathaway, an actress from California making a movie in Seattle. The concierge had a wandering eye and was able to focus simultaneously on the twenty and

DeMarco's face. He plucked the bill from DeMarco's hand.

"They're filming just a few blocks from here, down at the Pike Place Market. They'll be there until midnight."

Seattle's Pike Place Market is an open-air bazaar, a must-see tourist trap filled with produce vendors, tone-deaf street musicians, and weekend artists. It's a place where fishmongers mong. At six o'clock at night, the vendors' stalls were closed and the smell of rotting sea-life lingered in the air.

DeMarco found the film crew easily. They were on the second floor of a restaurant called Lowell's, surrounded by a small crowd of stargazers. Matt Damon and a busty, dark-haired actress that DeMarco recognized, but whose name he couldn't remember—Kathy, Katy, something like that—were seated at a table, holding hands, eyes locked: Hollywood's portrait of a couple in love. The windows behind them, which stretched the entire length of the wall, offered a magnificent twilight view of Elliott Bay.

DeMarco looked around for Brenda but didn't see her. Walking in his direction was a harried-looking woman with reading glasses half-buried in the nest of her frizzy perm. She was holding a clipboard and two cell phones hung from her belt. She looked like someone whose name would sweep by unnoticed in the credits at the end of the film—second gaffer to the gaffer's boy, third assistant to the cinematographer's toady. DeMarco reached out and grabbed her arm as she passed.

"Do you mind!" she said, glaring at him as she pulled her arm free.

"I need to talk to Brenda Hathaway."

"Tough shit," the lady said. "If you don't wanna get tossed outta here, get back over there with the rest of the looky-loos."

DeMarco pulled out his congressional ID and flashed it in her face.

"I'm a federal investigator, not a fan. Tell me where she is or I'll shut down this whole operation."

"Oh, bullshit," she said. "We've got a permit."

DeMarco pulled from his memory a line from some movie he'd once seen. "Lady," he said, "I've got a badge, a gun, and a bad temper. Now where is she?"

The clipboard lady wasn't intimidated but she said, "Oh, for Christ's sake. She's in the restaurant next door, taking a break with some of the crew." As he turned to leave, he heard her mumble, "Fucking storm trooper."

The place next door was called the Athenian Inn and Brenda was seated at a table with two other women drinking coffee. Before DeMarco could reach her table, a young man built like a bouncer and wearing a blue windbreaker with the word SECURITY on it put a hand in the center of DeMarco's chest. Fortunately Brenda noticed him at that moment.

"Joe!" she shrieked, and rushed over and kissed him on the mouth. It was a nice kiss. "What on earth are you doing here?" she said.

"Brenda, we need to talk. The people who helped me bring down Paul Morelli are getting killed."

"What are you talking about?" Brenda said, unconsciously backing away from him.

"Just what I said. Gary Parker, Clayton Adams, they've been—"

"Gary's dead?"

"Yeah. Brenda, you have to—"

"Brenda, they're ready for you." DeMarco turned and saw the lady with the clipboard. She gave DeMarco a little go-fuck-yourself smile.

"Brenda," DeMarco said, "listen to me. You have to—"

"Stop!" Brenda said and waved her hands in front of DeMarco's face. "I can't handle this right now. I've got a scene to shoot and I don't want this stuff inside my head. Whatever you're talking about, I'll deal with it later."

Brenda turned and walked away before he could stop her. He thought about dragging her out of there, and then realized he was being foolish. She'd be safe with so many people around and the cameras rolling—plus the guy in the security jacket would probably break his neck.

Over her shoulder Brenda said, "Come on, Joe, you can watch my scene."

The crowd of gawkers who'd been watching the filming was no longer paying attention to Matt Damon and his female lead. They weren't paying attention because Brenda had just taken off her blouse, offering fans and camera crew an eye-popping view of her marvelous chest in a push-up bra. She stood there, not the least self-conscious, tapping her foot impatiently until a skinny, bald guy wearing a faded nuke-the-whales T-shirt pushed his way through the ring of spectators and gave Brenda something that looked like a lightweight life jacket. After she had the vest on, the whale-hater reached out and appeared to fondle Brenda's boobs.

Brenda had gotten DeMarco a place to stand near one of the cameramen and DeMarco said to him, "Uh, what's that guy doing?"

The cameraman, a man as big and hairy as a Kodiak bear, grinned and said, "He's the prop guy. Luckiest dude on the set. The vest he's playing with has these teeny radio-controlled charges that explode when Brenda gets shot. They throw fake blood about ten feet so you can get slow-mo gore. Real Peckinpahish. You'll see."

Brenda rebuttoned her blouse and the prop guy handed her a silver-plated automatic pistol. She took the gun from him then turned and quickly exited the restaurant. A moment later someone yelled, "Quiet on the set. Action," and Brenda came back into the restaurant and walked toward the table where Damon and the dark-haired starlet were seated.

Brenda staggered slightly as she walked, feigning either intoxication or some state of advanced psychosis. Her lips were moving, but DeMarco couldn't hear most of what she was saying; he assumed the dialogue would be dubbed in later. Damon and the other actress pantomimed shock when Brenda pointed her gun at them, then stood up and made don't-shoot-me gestures with their hands. When Brenda narrowed her eyes and pointed the gun at Damon's heart, Damon's leading lady jumped forward and grabbed Brenda's arm.

The two actresses fell to the floor and rolled about, wrestling for the gun, the skirts of both women rising nicely to expose sleek, creamy thighs. DeMarco assumed that what would happen next would be the old movie ploy where a shot would be fired as the women struggled, followed by a long, suspenseful moment to allow the audience time to bite their nails and wonder if it was the heroine who'd been plugged—which instantly made DeMarco wonder about the gun. What if it contained real bullets and not blanks?

It turned out DeMarco was wrong: the gun didn't go off while the women were wrestling. Katy, Kathy, whoever the hell she was, put some sort of kung-fu wrist lock on Brenda and managed to win the weapon. Katy then jumped to her feet and backed cautiously away from crazy Brenda, aiming the gun at her—and at that point a man wearing a Yankees baseball cap yelled "Cut."

The damn gun *really* made DeMarco nervous. "Didn't someone get killed with a movie gun once?" he said to the cameraman. "Some actor's son?"

"Yeah," the cameraman said, "Bruce Lee's kid. But that can't happen now. The union gotta bunch of safety rules put in place after that."

The director said something to Brenda then yelled "Action" and the actors picked up the scene from where they'd been when it was interrupted. Kathy-Katy stood, legs apart, holding the pistol, and Brenda backed away from her toward the windows that looked out toward Elliott Bay.

Brenda stood still for a moment, a strand of hair hanging down, partially covering one eye. She looked menacingly from Damon to the brunette, then her mouth began moving as she lip-synced demented things. Damon responded with some words of reason which Brenda apparently found irritating, because she picked up a steak knife from a nearby table and charged toward Damon. The other actress screamed "No!" and fired the pistol three times. The noise in the small room startled the spectators, and DeMarco saw flame leap realistically from the barrel of the gun.

As the cameraman had predicted, bright red movie blood flew in all directions from electronically assisted wounds, then, to DeMarco's amazement—his heart almost stopped—Brenda crashed through the window behind her and disappeared from view. It appeared that she'd been thrown backward by the force of the shots; in reality she had launched herself backward by thrusting off her right foot.

An instant later Brenda's head popped up into view as she looked in through the shattered glass. The director yelled, "Fantastic, Brenda. That's a take." Brenda held her hands above her head in a victory gesture and beamed liked she'd just scored a perfect ten in a gymnastics routine.

Just as DeMarco let out the breath he'd been holding ever since the scene had started, he heard the sound of nails or screws tearing from wood. The smile on Brenda's face was replaced by a look of horror and her hands started to wave as if she was trying to maintain her balance—then she screamed and disappeared from view.

DeMarco stood there paralyzed but the movie people surged en masse toward the window opening. The cameraman who had been talking to DeMarco looked down once then yelled over his shoulder, "Call for an ambulance." DeMarco fought his way frantically through the crowd, over to the window, and looked down.

Because the Pike Place Market is built on a bluff overlooking Seattle's waterfront, it was a six-story drop from the second floor of Lowell's restaurant to the street below. Brenda lay on the asphalt, unmoving, her limbs twisted. Near her was an inflatable airbag, and scattered about were pieces of wood. Cars had stopped on the street, their headlights shining on Brenda's body, and a man was standing, looking down at her. The fact that the man was standing rather than kneeling down to aid her said it all.

It didn't take long for DeMarco to understand what had happened. Staging had been built outside the window, a platform about six feet square, complete with safety rails. Brenda was supposed to have landed on the airbag placed on the platform and the safety rails would have prevented her from rolling off. But something had failed, and one end of the platform had torn loose from its mountings.

DeMarco, his mind numb, an icy feeling spreading through his chest, went down to the street where Brenda's body lay. Her face wasn't marred but her lips were twisted in shock or pain, and the blood from the damage to the back of her head had created a dark puddle that looked black in the light from the street lamps. The cops and medics wouldn't allow him to approach her, so he just stood there, feeling hollow inside, watching helplessly as they eventually zipped her into a black body bag and took her away.

He couldn't believe that she was dead. Just a short time ago, she'd been in bed next to him, warm and bright and lovely and alive. She'd had her whole life in front of her and it had looked as if she was going to finally realize her dreams. DeMarco hadn't known her long and he hadn't been in love with her, but he'd liked her and cared about her and had considered her a friend. And now all the dreams were gone and a beautiful young woman was nothing more than broken, mangled flesh—and it was his fault.

After the ambulance drove away, DeMarco began to walk, not knowing or caring where he was going, just needing to be in motion. His thoughts gradually turned from grief and guilt, and he began to think about the way Brenda had died. *Somebody* was helping Paul Morelli kill people and whoever this person was, he had a long, vicious reach, all the way from D.C. to Seattle. And there are very few people who have the money, influence, and talent to penetrate the security of a movie set and turn scaffolding into a lethal weapon. Since he was certain that Charlie Eklund and the CIA were not involved, he could think of only one other answer: whoever was helping Morelli was someone in organized crime. He knew he was making a leap to come to this conclusion but he was sure he was right: everything that had happened both recently and during Morelli's political ascendancy smelled to him like the mob. But then he also realized that there were major problems with this theory.

Lydia Morelli, the day they had walked along the C&O Canal, had made the strange remark about monsters eating their young. And when DeMarco had asked Harry about Morelli's whereabouts, Harry had said that one of the two people close enough to know where Morelli might be hiding was a relative. But what fucking relative? DeMarco just couldn't imagine how Paul Morelli or a federal judge or his daughter could have mob connections. The Morellis' past had been turned inside out by the FBI—and the Republican Party—looking for ties to the Mafia. There just weren't any—at least none that anyone had been able to find.

And there was one other thing that still didn't make sense: If the mob was helping Morelli kill people, why didn't he use them to kill Lydia? Why did he take the risk of being arrested for her murder? The people who had killed Gary Parker, Brenda

Hathaway, and Clayton Adams had already proven that they could make any death look like an accident. So why didn't they do something similar to remove Lydia Morelli? DeMarco was missing something—something huge—but he didn't know what it was.

Then something else occurred to him, something that if he'd thought of it earlier might have saved Brenda's life. He stopped and pulled his cell phone off his belt and made a call.

"Emma," DeMarco said, "Brenda's dead." He told Emma what had happened and then he said, "I need you to do something for me. Right away."

Chapter 63

It was 11 p.m. when Emma hammered her fist on Charlie Eklund's front door.

The door was eventually opened by Eklund's bodyguard and he was holding an automatic in one hand. Emma had apparently woken the man up: he was wearing only a T-shirt and boxer shorts. She noticed the muscles in his legs, and bet that the guy could do fifty-pound curls with his toes.

"What do you want?" he said in a voice that was surprisingly high for a man his size.

"I need to speak to Mr. Eklund. Immediately," Emma said.

From behind the bodyguard, Emma heard Eklund say, "It's all right, Stan, let her in."

The bodyguard stepped back and allowed Emma to enter.

"Go back to bed, Stan," Eklund said. "I'll be all right."

Eklund was wearing a red terrycloth bathrobe, white pajamas, and slippers. His soft white hair, in spite of his being roused from sleep, wasn't the least bit tousled. Emma wondered how Eklund managed that, to sleep without mussing his hair, which made her think of a vampire lying motionless in a coffin.

Eklund gestured Emma toward a couch in his living room. "Would you like a drink?" he said.

"No," Emma said. "And I'm sorry for bothering you so late." She wasn't, but that sounded like the right thing to say to a man whose help she needed.

"So why are you here?" Eklund said. "I thought our business with each other was concluded."

"Someone acting on Paul Morelli's behalf is killing people," she said.

"Really?" Eklund said. He sounded surprised, but Emma couldn't be certain if he actually was.

Emma told him as rapidly as she could what they had done to destroy Morelli's political career. She didn't want to tell him, but she knew that if she didn't share information, he wouldn't help her.

"What a marvelous operation," Eklund said, completely sincere in his compliment. "But now you say that all the people who helped you are dead or dying."

"Yes."

"Well, that's unfortunate, but what do you expect me to do about it? Why don't you call the police or the Bureau?" Eklund smiled slightly when he said this.

"The police won't do a damn thing and you know it."

"But you think *I* can help? As I'm sure you know, the agency doesn't involve itself in domestic matters." Eklund was having a wonderful time.

"Don't toy with me, Charlie. I'm not in the mood and I don't have the time. I know you were keeping Paul Morelli and his wife under surveillance for some time. I want you to tell me if he's associated with anyone in organized crime."

Eklund didn't say anything; he just studied Emma's face.

"People are dying, Charlie," Emma said. "Civilians. And I think you know who might be killing them."

Eklund just stared at Emma, his little doll's-button eyes bright with mirth. "I think I will have a drink," he said. "Are you sure you won't have one?"

"No," Emma said, struggling to control her temper.

Eklund walked over to a cabinet in his dining room and took out a bottle of brandy and a snifter and poured himself a drink. He returned to his seat, sipped his drink, then swirled the brandy in the glass and pretended to examine its color.

"Goddamnit, Charlie," Emma said, "quit sitting there trying to figure out how this situation can help you and the Company. For once in your life, just do the right thing, the *simple* thing. Paul Morelli's a sexual predator and a murderer and he's finished in politics. He's of no use to you anymore. Now tell me what I need to know, or I swear to God, I'll make your life a living hell."

Eklund's small fingers tapped the side of the brandy snifter.

"Will you give me the photographs of me talking to that reporter?" Eklund said.

"Yes," Emma said, her teeth clenched.

"And will you use your sources to help me find the drug lord who wants to kill me? I'm fond of Stan, but I'm really tired of him living in my house."

"Yes," Emma said again. And if Eklund helped her she'd do what she said, but at some point, somehow, some way, she'd find a way to remove Charlie Eklund from the CIA. He was just too dangerous to leave in place.

Eklund sat there a minute more looking like someone's cuddly old grandpa with his white hair and his twinkling eyes and his red bathrobe. At last he spoke.

"Senator Morelli took a trip to New York after his wife was killed. He went there ostensibly to consult with a doctor about his injured shoulder. While he was in New York, a man named Harry Foster picked him up at his hotel and took him to an office building in lower Manhattan. My men said that Morelli was in the building for half an hour. The meeting occurred late in the evening, after most of the people who worked in the building had gone home for the day. Upon my instruction, my men identified everyone who exited the building after Senator Morelli left."

Eklund stopped speaking and took a sip of his brandy.

"One of those people was a man named Dominic Calvetti."

Chapter 64

The red-eye from Seattle to New York landed at 9 a.m., and DeMarco walked into Harry Foster's office forty-five minutes later. He barged past Harry's blond secretary without saying a word and threw open the door to Harry's office. His godfather was talking to two men and he looked up in irritation at the interruption, but when he saw the look on DeMarco's face he dismissed his guests.

"What are you doing here, Joe?" Harry said.

DeMarco placed his knuckles on Harry's desk and leaned down and said, "Paul Morelli's connected to Dominic Calvetti, Harry. And Calvetti is in some way related to Lydia Morelli. And you, goddamnit, are connected to both Morelli *and* Calvetti." DeMarco paused for a beat and added, "You're going to tell me everything you know, Harry."

"Calvetti? Jesus, Joe, I don't know what the hell you're talking about."

"No, Harry, don't lie to me. People are getting killed, and Calvetti and Morelli are the ones doing the killing. So don't you *dare* lie to me!"

"Getting killed? Who's getting killed?"

DeMarco took a deep breath, struggling to get his emotions under control, struggling to keep from grabbing Harry by the throat and shaking the shit out of him. Then he told Harry how he had set up Paul Morelli and why, and how everybody involved but he and Sam Murphy was either in a hospital or dead. He never mentioned Emma.

Harry didn't interrupt while DeMarco was speaking but he seemed to shrink into his chair, as if he was trying to disappear inside himself. He closed his eyes as DeMarco spoke of Lydia's murder and her allegations against her husband.

When DeMarco was finished, Harry said, "His stepdaughter, Joe? Are you positive, son? Are you absolutely positive?"

"Yeah," DeMarco said. "I'm positive."

Harry rose from his chair and walked slowly over to the wet bar in his office. He moved like he'd aged ten years in the last five minutes. "I need a drink. You want one?" Before DeMarco could answer, Harry said, "Ah, Jesus, Joe. What have you done?"

"Harry, I don't want a drink. What I want is for you to stop beating around the bush and tell me what I need to know."

As Harry filled a glass with crushed ice and bourbon, DeMarco, too agitated to sit, walked to a window and looked down at Central Park. He could see ice skaters on a pond, and from twenty stories above, they looked like mechanical figures on the top of a music box.

"Kid, you've put me a bad place," Harry said. "You can't believe the place you've put me in. If it wasn't for your dad—"

"Harry, I don't have time . . ."

"Joe, what you're asking me to talk about . . . It could get me killed, son."

"Harry, I'm gonna get killed if you don't talk—and there's no 'could' about it."

Harry didn't answer.

"Harry. Please."

Harry stood there staring at his godson, trying to make up his mind, trying to sort out where his real allegiance was. Finally he said, "Dominic Calvetti is Lydia Morelli's father."

Chapter 65

———◆———

Dominic Calvetti was a mobster of mythical proportions.

His criminal domain extended into all the five boroughs of New York and to points far up and down the eastern seaboard. In the forties and fifties he'd been deeply involved with the teamsters—and their pension fund—and as time went on he managed to penetrate virtually every major labor organization that operated in the Northeast. He controlled judges and politicians, and possibly even a few of Mahoney's cronies in Congress. In some places his people managed his criminal operations directly, and in other areas he made alliances with local crime lords whenever he considered an alliance more beneficial than outright warfare.

Unlike the John Gottis of the world, Calvetti avoided publicity and displays of ostentatious wealth.

Even as a young man, he was never seen strutting with bottle-blond showgirls or rolling the dice in Vegas. He lived in a modest home on Long Island, rarely left it, and when he did, he never traveled with an entourage, only one or two bodyguards. Most significantly, other than one brief prison term when he was still in his twenties, he had never been indicted for his activities. In part this was due to his intelligence, in part because he had penetrated every law enforcement agency that might want to indict him, and in part because he was known to be completely ruthless to anyone who might betray him.

Dominic Calvetti was now seventy-nine years old.

According to Harry, Lydia's mother had an affair with Calvetti in the fifties when they were both young and both married. Dominic had been a handsome young man and Lydia's mother a beautiful woman with a bit of a wild streak. How Lydia's mother and Calvetti became involved Harry didn't know, but he imagined that Dominic found it amusing to be screwing the wife of a big-shot lawyer who later became a federal judge. Or maybe they were just two young people who fell in love.

"And Lydia's father, the judge," DeMarco said. "He never knew that Lydia wasn't his child?"

"I don't think so," Harry said. "Why would she tell him?"

"And how would Lydia's mother have known the child was Calvetti's and not her husband's?"

"I don't know that either. Maybe she didn't have sex with her husband all that often or maybe he'd been shootin' blanks for years. All I know is that Lydia's mother knew the child was Calvetti's and she told him, and later Calvetti told Lydia he was her old man."

DeMarco was getting hit with so much new information that he was having a hard time sorting it all out. "So is this why Calvetti's been helping Paul Morelli," he said, "because Lydia's his daughter?"

"No. Dominic never had anything to do with Lydia when she was a child. He didn't have, as far as I know, any emotional attachment to her. When Lydia's mother got pregnant, they stopped the affair, and Lydia's mother went back to her husband and Dominic back to his wife. So, no, Dominic didn't help Paul because of Lydia. He helped Paul because Paul could help him. He helped Paul because he could see Paul's potential. Lydia, she was . . . she was leverage."

Harry said that a few months after Lydia married Paul Morelli, Calvetti set up a meeting with the couple and told them that he was Lydia's real father. He said if they didn't believe him, he'd submit to testing to prove it.

"Okay, so he's Lydia's father," DeMarco said. "So what? Why would Morelli go along with him?"

"Now we get to Paul. Paul's about thirty at this point; he's ambitious but he's going nowhere. He's just another assistant DA. A smart one, a good-looking one, but he's just one of the herd. And his father-in-law, the big judge, a guy who could have helped him, had just retired from the bench in disgrace and if anything, Paul's now tainted by his association with the guy.

"So along comes Dominic. He says he can help Paul, and he says he wants to help his daughter and the granddaughter he's never met. We'll get to Kate later. But the main thing is he says he can help Paul's career. And then he makes a threat. Dominic says that if Paul doesn't agree to work with him, then maybe the word gets out that Paul's related to Dominic through his wife. That would have killed Paul's political career."

DeMarco remembered what Lydia had said the day they walked along the canal: *Then the devil danced in.*

"And it worked for Paul. He and Calvetti made it work. They didn't do dumb things, they didn't try to make barrels of money or get Calvetti's minor hoods out of jail. They focused mostly on advancing Paul's career." Harry laughed. "When Paul was mayor of New York, everybody thought he was a genius the way he kept the unions in line. But it was Dominic who controlled the unions. He'd been controlling unions ever since the days Hoffa ran the teamsters."

"And the other reason Morelli did so well," DeMarco said, "was because Calvetti would destroy his political rivals if they became a problem."

Harry shook his head. "Rarely, Joe. Rarely did Dominic have to intervene. Paul was a good politician. He did most of it on his own."

"So that's it, Harry? That's how Paul Morelli became Calvetti's pet politician?"

"No, Joe, you still don't get it. Paul wasn't anyone's pet. He and Dominic worked together. They were equal partners, as near as I could tell. Paul concentrated on being a good politician and he did good things. Those stories I told you the day we had lunch, they were all true. If anything, Paul turned the mob into a positive force."

"Come on, Harry. Calvetti helped Morelli for the good of the people? Who the hell are you trying to kid?"

"I'm not saying that. Sure, Dominic got some things out of the arrangement. But they didn't do things just to make money. Calvetti was already a multimillionaire when he hooked up with Paul. And if you look at Paul's finances, you'll see that he's not real rich, not Kennedy-rich."

Harry paused. "I'll tell you something I've suspected for a long time," he said. "I think for Dominic this wasn't about money at all. It was a game to him."

"A *game?*"

"When Dominic hooked up with Paul, he already had everything. And I don't just mean money. He had power, respect. He was at the pinnacle of his career. But the idea of making a man mayor of New York, then a senator, then president . . . I think that's what appealed to him. I mean can you even imagine the feeling? *His* guy in the White House. I think for Dominic that's what it was all about: he just wanted to see if he could do it, see how far he could help Paul rise. It would be Dominic's way of giving the finger to the whole system. But for Paul, of course, it wasn't a game at all. The White House was what he had wanted from day one."

A game, DeMarco thought, played with people's lives and reputations.

"And someplace along the way," Harry said, "something else became important to Dominic and that was Kate. He never knew Lydia when she was young, but Kate, he saw her the first time when she was about two and he just fell in love with her. Kate may have been the only person in the world Dominic Calvetti ever really loved. I know he didn't love his own wife or Lydia's mother or even Lydia. And he never had children of his own. But Kate, she was different. Dominic actually cried when she died; I saw him. So I think part of the reason he helped Paul was so he could have some contact with his granddaughter, not that Kate ever knew who he really was."

"Wasn't it dangerous for Calvetti to meet with Paul or his family?"

"Damn straight it was dangerous. If anyone ever tied them to each other, Paul would have been finished. So Dominic and Paul, they've only met face to face maybe two dozen times in the years they've been working together. But when Kate was little, before she was really old enough to know who Calvetti was, she'd be taken to see him sometimes. And these visits, they were set up like . . . like I don't know what. They'd switch cars, meet in remote spots, use helicopters for surveillance. It was like a military operation, every time he saw the girl."

"But at some point when Kate was older she must have been curious about old Uncle Dominic," DeMarco said. "She must have realized he wasn't your average, smiley relative."

"I don't know," Harry said. "I don't know what they told Kate when she got older. And when Paul moved to D.C. the meetings had to stop. The logistics were just too hard and the stakes too high."

DeMarco walked over to the window and looked down at Central Park. He could see a squad car down there now, near the skating rink, its light bar flashing red and blue. The lights of the patrol car blended in with the twinkling lights of a Christmas tree near the pond.

Now everything made sense to DeMarco, including why Paul Morelli had not solicited Dominic Calvetti's help to kill Lydia. Morelli would have been asking Calvetti to kill his own daughter. And there was another thing: if Morelli had asked Calvetti to kill Lydia he'd have to tell him why, and he couldn't tell him that it was because he had molested Calvetti's cherished granddaughter.

There was something else that now made sense as well: now he understood why Lydia had been unwilling to name Calvetti. Lydia had wanted to destroy her husband because of what he'd done to her daughter, but her motives hadn't been entirely pure. She didn't want the world to know that Calvetti was her father and that she'd gone along with all the things that he'd done for her husband.

"Harry," DeMarco said, "what was your role in all this?" DeMarco was pretty sure he already knew the answer to that question.

"I was the go-between for some things Paul did with Dominic. Dominic's known me a long time, since the early days with your dad, and he trusts me. And I knew Paul from before he ran for mayor, and he trusted me too. There were a lot of things that had to be done—people to talk to, deals to make—things that neither Paul nor Dominic could be involved in. And for those kinda deals, Paul couldn't send some snot-nosed kid from his staff and Dominic, he sure as hell couldn't send one of the bent-noses that works for him. So they used me."

And they paid you, DeMarco thought, and they paid you well. Harry's high-rent office made a lot more sense now.

Although Harry looked as he had the last time DeMarco had seen him—carefully trimmed silver hair, manicured hands, well-tailored suit and silk tie—he seemed somehow a bit seedier, a bit closer to the mean streets he had escaped years before. And DeMarco, as much as he loved Harry, knew he'd probably never see him again. Assuming he lived to see anyone again.

DeMarco already knew the answer to the next question too, but he still asked it.

"Harry, what do you think would happen if Paul Morelli told Dominic Calvetti the names of the people who had cost him the White House? Do you think Calvetti would help him get even?"

"In a New York minute," Harry said. "Dominic's big on payback. He might do something even if Paul didn't ask for his help. Like most people, Dominic likes Paul." Harry made the last statement sound like an accusation.

DeMarco stood at the window with his back to Harry. The cops were now putting someone in the squad car and it looked like a guy in a Santa suit. Only in New York.

Now he knew who was helping Paul Morelli and why, and the answer was even worse than he had expected. If Dominic Calvetti wanted him dead, he had the life expectancy of a snowflake.

DeMarco said, "And what do you think Calvetti would do if he found out that Paul Morelli killed his daughter and molested his granddaughter?"

Chapter 66

Harry set up the meeting with Dominic Calvetti in the same small restaurant where DeMarco and Harry had eaten lunch the last time DeMarco was in New York. It had taken DeMarco an hour to convince Harry that he needed to see Calvetti. He had told Harry that he had to do something, because if he didn't, Paul Morelli was going to have Calvetti kill him. It was either meet with Calvetti and make him see reason, DeMarco argued, or leave the country and have his face rebuilt. Harry had said that a meeting with Calvetti was suicide; they had anesthetics for plastic surgery.

When he and Harry arrived at the restaurant there was a CLOSED sign in the window but Harry opened the door and walked in. The only one in the place was the owner. DeMarco recalled that his name was Benny and remembered how he had thanked Harry for all the things that Paul Morelli had done for his son and daughter. Benny didn't look so grateful now.

Twenty minutes later two men walked into the restaurant. The pair looked enough alike to be brothers—scary brothers, the type who quit boxing because it wasn't violent enough. They were in their mid-forties, with dark wavy hair and permanent five o'clock shadows. Not tall, but very broad—52-large jackets and 38-short pants. One wore a blue suit, the other wore gray.

Blue Suit took Benny by the arm and walked him toward the rear of the restaurant to check out the kitchen and restrooms. Gray Suit just stood there, looking at DeMarco and Harry. Blue Suit returned to the dining room, nodded to Gray Suit, and took up a position near the entrance. Benny came back into the dining room with a bottle of wine. He proceeded to clear away the glasses and ashtray that Harry and DeMarco had been using, put on a fresh tablecloth, and placed the wine bottle and three glasses on the table. He stopped a moment to survey his work, then took a vase of flowers from a nearby table and placed it in the center of DeMarco's table. Gray Suit said something to Benny in Italian and he removed the flowers, then left the dining room.

After Benny had disappeared, Gray Suit made a motion for DeMarco to rise. There was something odd about the man's hands, DeMarco noticed. They looked as if they'd been caught in a lawn mower and put back together. After he patted DeMarco down for a weapon, he told DeMarco to unbutton his shirt, then ran his scarred hands over DeMarco's bare chest and back checking for a surveillance wire. As he searched, he stared impassively into DeMarco's eyes. There was no animosity in Gray Suit's face; he was just a man doing his job, going about his trade with as much emotion as the guy who changes the oil in your car. He'd look at DeMarco the same way shoving a knife into his heart.

Gray Suit gave the restaurant one final sweep with his eyes, then nodded to his partner, who turned and exited the restaurant. A minute later, Dominic Calvetti came through the door.

Calvetti ignored Harry and DeMarco while one of his bodyguards helped him with his topcoat and took his fedora. They both rose as Calvetti approached the table. Harry held out his right hand and Calvetti shook it, his grip soft. "Harry," he said, his voice cool and noncommittal.

"Dominic," Harry said, "this is Joe DeMarco. He's my godson."

Calvetti ignored DeMarco's outstretched hand and said to Harry, "I came tonight, Harry, because we've known each other a long time. But I can make you no promises, no commitments, where this man is concerned."

The fact that Calvetti knew who DeMarco was confirmed everything he suspected.

As Harry had said, Dominic Calvetti was old. He was wearing a suit, a white shirt with a slightly frayed collar, and a wide, old-fashioned tie. His hair was white and very fine; his complexion a burnished bronze; and there was a network of wrinkles around his eyes and a single deep furrow on each side of his mouth. He had probably been handsome in his youth but age had elongated his nose and ears and put a slight curve in his spine. His eyes were black and empty, like stellar black holes, absorbing light and life, belying any possibility of mercy.

Gray Suit poured a glass of wine for Harry and Calvetti. He pointedly turned DeMarco's wine glass upside down. Harry gave DeMarco an apologetic glance.

"And how's your health, Dominic?" Harry said. "You look good."

"No, Harry," Calvetti said with a small shake of his head. "No chit-chat. Just tell me what you have to say."

Harry nodded, his face becoming serious. "Dominic, my godson's a good man. An honest man. I want you to listen to him. If I didn't believe him I wouldn't have brought him here tonight."

Calvetti didn't respond.

"He's also Gino DeMarco's son," Harry said. "You remember Gino? He worked for Carmine Taliaferro."

Calvetti raised an eyebrow in surprise. "Is that right?" he said, and Harry nodded.

It was a hell of thing, DeMarco thought, when a blood link to a killer was considered a character reference.

Calvetti glanced at DeMarco and said, "I see the resemblance now. I thought this man was a civilian."

"I am, Mr. Calvetti," DeMarco said. He was tired of this guy not looking at him and speaking only to Harry. "I never had anything to do with the Taliaferro family. I'm just a lawyer who works for Congress."

"Not just a lawyer," Calvetti said, giving DeMarco the full force of his eyes. "You're a man who traps other men using young women for bait. You're lower than a pimp."

"Dominic . . . ," Harry said.

"Mr. Calvetti," DeMarco said, "I'm not going to deny that I destroyed Paul Morelli's career. But you need to know why I did it."

"You did it because you work for some other politician," Calvetti said. "We don't know which one yet, but we'll find out. Maybe we'll find out tonight."

DeMarco had an immediate image of Gray Suit's huge, mangled hands pounding on his face until he gave up Mahoney. It wouldn't take long.

"I destroyed Paul Morelli because he killed his wife, Mr. Calvetti. Your daughter. I couldn't let a man like that become president."

DeMarco had thought that mentioning Lydia's death would have some emotional impact on Calvetti, but if it did, DeMarco couldn't see it. The mobster's face remained completely impassive.

"Why would he murder his wife?" Calvetti said. "If he was dissatisfied with her, he would have divorced her. It's what Americans do."

That was rich: murder was apparently acceptable to Calvetti but divorce wasn't.

"He killed her," DeMarco said, "because she was going to tell the newspapers what she knew about him."

"What did she know? She didn't know anything."

DeMarco hesitated; what he was about to say could get him killed on the spot.

"Lydia was going to tell the press that Paul molested your granddaughter."

Calvetti came out of his chair with surprising speed, and backhanded DeMarco across the face. His bony, old man's hand stung and DeMarco could taste blood on his lower lip. DeMarco noticed that both bodyguards had drawn guns and now waited like Dobermans for the command to kill.

Harry stood up and said, "Dominic, wait. Listen to him. Please."

Calvetti remained standing for a minute, looking down at DeMarco. His thin chest rose and fell from exertion and emotion. Finally he turned to his bodyguards and motioned for them to put their weapons away. He sat back down, lit a cigarette, then said to DeMarco, "You know *Arabian Nights*? Scheherazade?" There was a thin, cruel smile on Calvetti's bloodless lips.

DeMarco nodded. He knew exactly what the old gangster meant: tell a good story or he wouldn't see morning. DeMarco wiped the blood from his mouth with the back of his hand and began by saying, "I had always admired Paul Morelli."

DeMarco told Calvetti everything, everything he learned from Lydia Morelli and why he was certain that Paul Morelli had killed Lydia and Isaiah Perry. While he was speaking, Calvetti was silent, smoking one cigarette after another, staring at DeMarco through half-shut eyes. DeMarco had never been a trial lawyer. He had never made a desperate plea to a jury to save an innocent man's life. This was his day in court—and he would have liked it better if someone else's life had been at stake.

DeMarco finished speaking and Harry said, "Dominic, this thing with Paul and women. There was a woman here in New York . . ."

Calvetti raised a hand, stopping Harry in midsentence. He looked at DeMarco for what seemed a lifetime. DeMarco could tell that Calvetti had not immediately dismissed his story as a self-serving pack of lies. No, he had doubts about Morelli, that much was clear, and now he was obviously trying to come to a decision. It occurred to DeMarco then that

Calvetti was, in his own right, an executive. He made decisions all the time based on the information available and his instincts. He wasn't going to argue or ask for clarification—he had heard all he needed to hear. Now it was just a matter of deciding. At last he spoke.

"Tomorrow morning," he said, "you be standing in front of Harry's apartment at ten o'clock. *Capisce?*"

DeMarco nodded.

"Dress warm," he added.

Dress warm?

Calvetti rose and Gray Suit helped him into his topcoat. Blue Suit left the restaurant first, while Calvetti and Gray Suit waited by the door. Blue Suit gave the all's-clear signal from outside, and Gray Suit opened the door for his boss. Before leaving, while placing his fedora on his head, Calvetti turned to look at DeMarco a final time. Looking into Calvetti's eyes was like looking down the barrels of a shotgun—if you saw any light at all, it meant the triggers had been pulled.

Chapter 67

It was a brilliant December morning, Christmas only two days away.

The winter sun sparkled off the roofs of a million Yellow Cabs and people bustled by with shopping bags in their hands, the season generating smiles for strangers. As DeMarco stood waiting for Calvetti, the old Indian expression about it being a good day to die flashed morbidly through his mind.

A long black Lincoln pulled up to the entrance of Harry Foster's apartment building at exactly ten a.m. The man driving the car was Gray Suit, the one with the deformed hands who had frisked DeMarco at the restaurant. Today he wasn't wearing a suit. He had on a navy peacoat over a plaid shirt and wool pants. On his head was a dark blue stocking cap. He looked like a guy who should be stamping his feet for warmth outside the longshoremen's union, waiting for his name to be called.

The other man in the front seat of the Lincoln wore a black leather jacket over a heavy sweater, tight-fitting jeans, and ankle-high boots. On his hands were lightweight leather gloves the same color as the jacket. He was tall and sinewy, with close-cropped white-blond hair. Wire-rimmed glasses magnified pale blue eyes. The driver, DeMarco guessed, was pure muscle. The other guy was some sort of specialist—and DeMarco didn't want to think about what he specialized in.

The specialist unfolded himself from the front seat of the car and told DeMarco to take his place. He didn't look at DeMarco. Instead his eyes swept the stream of people going by on the sidewalk and the windows above their heads. He was holding an aluminum briefcase in his right hand, and for some reason—too many movies, he supposed—it occurred to DeMarco that the suitcase could contain a rifle, one that came apart in sections, the pieces fitting neatly into felt-lined indentations in the case. He wondered if he would subconsciously feel the tickle of the cross hairs as they moved up his face, to a spot in the center of his forehead.

As DeMarco entered the Lincoln, he glanced at Calvetti, who sat in the rear seat, directly behind the driver. Like his driver, Calvetti was dressed for cold weather: a heavy parka, wool pants, and on his feet, thick-soled boots. The parka was zipped up to the neck even though the temperature inside the car was hot enough to grow orchids. The old Sicilian looked at DeMarco without expression, his black eyes giving away nothing.

The driver told DeMarco to take off the too-tight ski jacket he had borrowed from Harry. He made sure the pockets of the jacket were empty, then prodded the fabric with his fingers to verify nothing was hidden in the down lining. Finished with the jacket, he had DeMarco kneel on the seat so he could frisk his body above the knees, then had him sit back down and stretch his legs out so he could complete the search. Finally satisfied, he said, "He's clean, boss. You want him to sit up here or there in back with you?"

"Up there," Calvetti said. "Mr. Loomis will sit in the back."

DeMarco didn't like having Loomis directly behind him with his damn aluminum case.

As soon as Loomis shut his door, Calvetti said, "Take off, Eddie," and the black Lincoln merged into a stream of Manhattan taxis like a shark parting a school of tuna.

DeMarco turned to look back at Calvetti, and said, "May I ask where we're going?" He was proud that he sounded calm and nothing like the way he was really feeling.

"Shut up," Calvetti said. "I'll talk to you when I'm ready."

They left Manhattan via the Henry Hudson Parkway and continued north on Highway 9, parallel to the Hudson River. As they drove, DeMarco tried to convince himself that he had made the right decision. He could have tried to hide from Morelli and Calvetti, but eventually they would have found him. He could have gone to the authorities and asked for protection but he had little confidence in the police's ability—or desire—to protect him. So he had put his fate in Dominic Calvetti's hands, hoping the gangster's love for his granddaughter would prevail over his loyalty to Paul Morelli.

DeMarco had thought about calling Emma last night to ask for her help and knew that if he had, she'd have been on the next shuttle to New York. He could have had the comfort of knowing that she was following Calvetti's limo, heavily armed, lethally able, and would be there to kill Calvetti if he needed killing. But in the end he had decided not to call her—and he didn't return her phone call when she called him. As far as DeMarco knew, Morelli, and therefore Calvetti, had no knowledge of Emma's involvement in the operation, and that being the case, DeMarco didn't want to expose her. Enough people had died because of what he'd done. He'd face this situation on his own.

He glanced back again at the man to whom he had consigned his life, and saw that Calvetti was staring impassively out the tinted windows of the

Lincoln at the river. A few minutes later, Calvetti closed his eyes, his head dropped onto his chest, and he began to snore gently. DeMarco's fate was obviously weighing heavily on his mind.

They crossed the Hudson River at Poughkeepsie and headed west on Highway 44 until they entered Catskill Park. Calvetti woke up a few minutes later, lit a cigarette, but remained silent and brooding. As the car gained in elevation, the amount of snow piled up on the sides of the road increased until it seemed they were driving through a white tunnel. They passed a dam near a small town with the silly name of Lackawack, and just beyond a whistle stop named Sundown, at the base of Sampson Mountain, the driver pulled off the main road. They drove a few minutes more and came to a stop near a stand of evergreens. No houses were in sight; there were no people around. It was a good place to kill someone, DeMarco thought, but he was sure they hadn't driven this far just to kill him. They could have found a fallow field in New Jersey if that had been Calvetti's intention.

Calvetti continued to sit silently, staring out at the snow-covered forest. After what seemed an eternity, he said, "Now here's what you're gonna do." As he spoke, DeMarco was again struck by the absence of warmth in Calvetti's eyes. He couldn't imagine a man with eyes like that loving anyone, not even a granddaughter.

"You understand?" Calvetti said, and then he added, "It's either you or him."

DeMarco nodded. He understood perfectly; he just didn't like it. This wasn't the course of action he'd expected.

"Give it to him, Mr. Loomis," Calvetti said.

Loomis wordlessly handed DeMarco a holster that contained a small-caliber automatic. It looked to DeMarco like a .25, the same caliber weapon that Morelli had used to kill his wife. The holster was designed to clip onto a belt. As DeMarco accepted the weapon, Eddie, the driver, took out his gun and pointed it at DeMarco's face. DeMarco noticed that Eddie's gun was bigger than his gun; Eddie's gun would blow a hole in his head the size of a grapefruit.

"If you take that peashooter out of the holster while you're anywhere near the car, you're dead," Eddie said.

DeMarco clipped the holster to his belt, opened the door, and stepped from the car. Before shutting the door, he looked at Calvetti. The Mafia boss had pulled a blanket over his knees and another across his thin shoulders. He looked cold and uncomfortable. A snow-covered forest in the mountains was not a natural hunting ground for an old urban predator.

The enigmatic Loomis exited the rear of the Lincoln, holding the ominous suitcase in his hand. He pointed and said, "Up there about fifty yards, you'll see a driveway on the left. And do this quick. Mr. Calvetti doesn't like it up here."

DeMarco made sure his ski jacket concealed the automatic, then stood a moment, looking at the woods around him. It was a scene peeled off the front of a Christmas card: evergreens dusted with snow, the ground covered with a soft white blanket, a twenty-foot holly tree on his right decorated with bright red berries.

Loomis set the aluminum case on the hood of the Lincoln and DeMarco heard the latches click open. He wondered how long it would take to dig a grave through four feet of snow. He wondered if the corpse would be cold for eternity.

———◆———

The cabin was made of logs and had a cedar-shake roof and a stone chimney. Nearby was a firewood shed stacked with at least two cords of wood. Smoke drifted skyward from the chimney; the cabin windows were glazed with frost; icicles hung from the eaves. It was the perfect haven: an escape from the stress of the city, a hidey-hole to come to with your lover—a snowy Elba for a self-imposed exile.

DeMarco walked quickly toward the cabin. With the frost on the windows, he couldn't see anyone inside, nor, he assumed, could anyone see him. When he reached the door, he partially unzipped his jacket so he'd be able to reach the gun, then raised his hand to knock. Before his knuckles struck the door, a voice said: "Why hello, Joe. It's good to see you again."

DeMarco turned and saw Paul Morelli standing less than four feet away. Morelli was smiling—he had a beautiful, infectious smile—and DeMarco almost smiled back. Morelli was holding an axe in his right hand and in his left hand was a cloth sling holding several pieces of firewood. DeMarco's lips moved in a silent curse. Morelli must have been behind the firewood shed when DeMarco arrived.

DeMarco glanced down to make sure the weapon on his belt wasn't visible and when he raised his eyes, he noticed that Morelli wasn't looking at him. Instead he was scanning the nearby woods, apparently checking to see if DeMarco was alone. DeMarco thought of pulling out the pistol at that moment but was afraid that Morelli might cave in his head with the axe before he could draw the weapon. He'd wait until Morelli put down the axe.

"Where'd you park?" Morelli asked. He seemed completely relaxed; if he was surprised that DeMarco had found him, he didn't act like it.

"Up on the main road," DeMarco said. "I wasn't sure I'd be able to get down your driveway."

Morelli laughed, and said in a perfect Yiddish accent, "You've never heard of four-wheel drive, chickie?"

Morelli's hair was longer than he normally wore it, touching his collar, partially covering his ears. He was wearing a blue plaid shirt over a cream-colored turtleneck sweater, and gray corduroy pants were tucked into boots with fur lining around the tops. He had to be the handsomest beast ever seen in these woods.

Morelli scanned the forest a few more seconds, then said, "I don't know why you're here, Joe, but let's go inside. It's too cold to talk out here." He put down the firewood sling he was carrying, but kept the axe in his hand. He reached past DeMarco, opened the unlocked cabin door, then waited for DeMarco to enter the cabin ahead of him. When DeMarco hesitated, Morelli said, "Come on, Joe. You become mindful of heat loss when you chop your own wood."

DeMarco stepped into the cabin, heard the door shut behind him—then felt the barrel of a gun at the back of his head.

"Aw, shit," he muttered. It had never occurred to him that Morelli might be armed. Then he realized, too late, that his frame of reference was completely wrong. He wasn't dealing with a United States senator—he was dealing with a murderer. And when you killed people as Morelli had done, you began to expect others to act the same way. Or maybe there was something else going on. Maybe Calvetti had set DeMarco up. But if that was the case, why had he given DeMarco the gun?

"Stand still," Morelli said. "Don't even twitch. I need to see if you're armed or wired. Remove the coat, please. Slowly."

DeMarco hesitated and Morelli prodded him with the barrel of his gun. DeMarco shrugged out of the ski jacket and when Morelli saw the weapon in the holster on his belt, he said, "Now what have we here? Was it assassination you had in mind?"

DeMarco didn't answer. He was fucked without that gun. He needed that gun.

Morelli took DeMarco's weapon and tossed it to the other side of the room, then completed frisking him. Satisfied that DeMarco didn't have another weapon and wasn't wearing a recording device, he patted DeMarco affectionately on the shoulder and said, "Let's go sit over by the fire and have a little chat. I've been alone up here so long, it's good to have someone to talk to."

There were two rocking chairs near the fireplace and DeMarco sank down slowly into one of them. Morelli took a seat in the other chair and began to rock gently—but the gun in his hand remained steady, pointed at the center of DeMarco's chest.

DeMarco looked around the cabin. There was a bed along one wall and a small kitchen area with a propane-fueled stove. In the center of the room was a table with a rough-plank top. On the table was a laptop computer. Behind the table was a free-standing whiteboard, and the board was filled with terse phrases, such as: philanthropic support, hydrogen research, nuclear power, Detroit resistance. There were a number of names on the board. DeMarco recognized a few of the American names—all billionaires—but there were other names he didn't recognize, including some that looked Arabic, and DeMarco had no idea who these people were. There were lines connecting some of the phrases to some of the names. None of it made any sense to him.

"How did you find me?" Morelli asked. His tone was conversational, not the least bit hostile.

"Your wife told me about your relationship with Dominic Calvetti," DeMarco said. Actually Lydia hadn't, but she could have.

"My God, that woman was a liability," Morelli muttered, speaking more to himself than DeMarco.

"When people started dying, I realized Calvetti was helping you, and I figured you had to be someplace like this. So I started checking property records—yours, your wife's, then Calvetti's."

Morelli shook his head. "I don't think so, Joe. Dominic's too smart to have this place in his own name."

"It's not. It's owned by a corporation he controls."

Morelli didn't say anything for a moment as he considered DeMarco's answer, then apparently satisfied, he said, "Who else knows you're here?"

"Several people," DeMarco said.

Morelli smiled and shook his head. DeMarco

amused him. "I don't think so," he said. "If you were planning to assassinate me, you wouldn't have advertised the fact. And you did come to assassinate me, didn't you?"

That was the third time Morelli had used the word "assassinate." Heads of state were assassinated, common folk merely killed. And Morelli's calmness infuriated DeMarco.

"Why in God's name did you kill Brenda? And that young cop and Clayton Adams? If you wanted revenge, why didn't you just kill me?"

"Clayton Adams?" Morelli said, appearing puzzled. "I didn't have Clayton killed, Joe."

The way he said it, DeMarco believed him. So Adams had died of natural causes just as the papers had said.

"And you're wrong about something else," Morelli said.

"Wrong about what? Are you saying that you didn't . . ."

"Those people didn't die because I wanted vengeance. They died so I could reclaim my destiny."

"Your destiny?"

"The presidency, Joe."

"You're out of your fucking mind. You're finished in politics."

"Wrong again, Joe. Doesn't it bother you to be wrong so often?"

Before DeMarco could respond, Morelli said,

"Do you know what's in that computer, and on that board over there?"

"No."

"A road map to the White House. Al Gore gave me the idea. Poor Al loses to Bush, crawls off with his tail between his legs, and we all thought he was finished. But then what happens? He gets an Oscar and a Nobel Prize. And what did he do? All he did was make a movie, for Christ's sake, and not even a very good one in my opinion. But the point is, Al took an issue like global warming, became the poster boy for the cause, and the next thing you know he's an international hero and people are saying he should run for president again.

"And that's what I'm going to do, Joe. I'm gonna do an Al Gore—except I'm going to go *way* beyond making a movie. What I'm going to do is make this country oil-independent."

"You're what?" DeMarco said.

Morelli laughed. "Now I can see by the look on your face that you think I'm crazy, but I'm not. I can do it. I have the whole thing figured out."

Morelli then launched into an animated speech explaining that it wasn't the lack of affordable alternatives that kept the U.S. dependent on oil. It was instead a complex conspiracy between oil companies, automakers, OPEC, and, of course, Congress all doing whatever they could to maintain the status quo. But according to Morelli, he knew how to break this conspiracy apart. He'd drag the whistleblowers out of the closet; he'd apply leverage—with the help of Dominic Calvetti if needed—to get laws changed; he'd convince billionaire philanthropists to fund start-up companies that would show that fuels like hydrogen were cheap, feasible alternatives to oil. Much of what he said was too complex for DeMarco to follow, and it occurred to him that Morelli's energy plan may have been nothing more than the delusional ramblings of a madman—but DeMarco didn't think so. Paul Morelli may have been a murderer but he was also a genius.

"I'm going to resign from the Senate, Joe. I'll say that even though I'm innocent I'm resigning because my circumstances are distracting the legislature from doing its job, but the real reason I'm resigning is to shift the media's focus. Then in a couple of months, I'll launch my campaign. I'll tell the press that I've given up on politics to devote myself to a far more noble cause." Morelli's dark eyes gleamed when he said, "Joe, I promise you that in less than ten years I'll be a hero to the average citizens of this country. They'll be buying cars that don't pollute the skies and that cost pennies per mile to drive. And as a nation, we'll never again have to pander to some Muslim dictator just because he was lucky enough to be born in a place with oil beneath his feet."

Morelli sat back in the rocker and made a face that seemed to say: Now do you get it? And in case

DeMarco didn't, he said. "Joe, I'm only forty-seven years old. By the time I'm fifty-seven, I'll be president."

DeMarco laughed. "Do you really think it'll be that easy? Ted Kennedy never made it because of Chappaquiddick and you'll never get there because of what you did to Brenda. Your political career is dead." It made DeMarco feel good to say that.

Morelli shook his head, as if he was disappointed that DeMarco was such a dunce. "You're standing too close to the problem, my friend. You need to step back to see the picture clearly. Now pay attention. Please.

"In a few months that video of me and Brenda, and the copy that crooked detective made, will be destroyed. Dominic will arrange for a fire or an explosion in the police evidence locker; knowing him, he'll probably destroy the whole building. And keep in mind that the *public* has never seen the video that Berg took. Oh, I know a lot of people saw it—but how clear do you think their memories will be in a few years? And with the video gone, and if I say events happened a certain way, who's going to be there to contradict me? No one, Joe, because all the witnesses to what actually transpired that night will be gone. Now do you understand? I wasn't killing people for revenge. I was eliminating *witnesses*."

"You can't possibly believe . . ."

"And very soon, the next phase of my resurrection will begin. While I'm ripping apart the oil conspiracy that's enslaved this country for a century, a report will surface showing that the tea that Brenda gave me that night contained a small amount of PCP mixed with Rohypnol. Yes, Joe, angel dust and a roofie. It's no wonder I acted so bizarrely, so out of character. The technician who analyzed the tea will confess that he hid the report because he was forced to do so by the diabolical Gary Parker."

"But the tea was never analyzed," DeMarco said. "The papers said so."

Morelli smiled. "A brazen lie, Joe, fabricated by Gary Parker." Before DeMarco could say anything else, Morelli said, "Very soon, a few well-paid, credible people will begin to destroy the reputations of Parker and Arnie Berg and Brenda. In Berg's case, it obviously won't be hard to smear his image. The man was despicable. Parker, it will turn out, was a cop on the take, had been one all of his short career, and people will come forward to substantiate this. Your little actress will require some effort. I haven't worked out all the details yet, but don't worry, I'll come up with something.

"Now do you understand, Joe? Now do you see the picture? It's five or six years in the future. The video is gone and all the people who conspired against me are dead, and all have tarnished reputations. There's irrefutable evidence that I was drugged and entrapped by a group of treacherous people to keep me from reaching the White House. And by that time, I'll be the darling of the Western world, Time's Man of the Year, the one who broke the shackles of Big Oil and who *really* did something to stop global warming." He winked at DeMarco. "I believe, sir, that my plan has . . . potential."

"Don't you think," DeMarco said, "that someone's going to notice that *everyone* who was involved is dead?"

"Of course they'll notice, but so what? Parker died in a simple traffic accident. Berg got drunk and fell off a roof with a friend as a witness. And poor Brenda, she was just the victim of an unsafe stunt. And did you know, Joe, that the man who built the staging for Brenda's last scene, a man with terminal cancer and four kids still living at home, has already admitted that it was his fault the staging fell apart?"

"Jesus Christ," DeMarco said, "You killed your wife and an innocent kid. You raped your *stepdaughter*. You belong in an asylum, not the White House."

DeMarco expected that Morelli would get angry but he didn't. Instead he nodded his head as if agreeing with DeMarco. "You're right," he said. "I have weaknesses. All men do, even great men."

"You consider killing your wife a 'weakness'?"

"No, that was a necessity. She was about to destroy everything that I'd worked for. I was talking about Kate. I really do regret what happened to her; I feel terrible about it." Morelli paused before he added, "But she did overreact a bit."

"She overreacted?" DeMarco said.

"Well, yes. She didn't have to kill herself. At any rate, and I certainly hope this makes you feel better, I've sworn never to drink again."

DeMarco had never known anyone so brilliant yet so totally devoid of humanity. He was sure there was some clinical term for Morelli's condition, but "monster," as his wife had called him, was easier to understand.

"I've got some bad news for you, Senator," DeMarco said, "Dominic Calvetti knows that you killed Lydia and molested his granddaughter."

DeMarco could tell that he'd finally managed to surprise Morelli, but not for the reason he thought.

"*You* figured out that Lydia was Dominic's daughter? I guess you're brighter than I thought you were. But Dominic doesn't know I killed her and he never will. The police haven't figured it out, so how would he?"

"Because I told him," DeMarco said.

Morelli laughed. "Ah, Joe, you run a terrible bluff. If you had ever talked to Dominic, you wouldn't be sitting here. But Dominic was the reason I killed Lydia. I was worried, of course, that the public might believe her about Kate, but my real fear was that Dominic would. And Lydia had also threatened to tell the press about my relationship with him. That could have had a greater impact on my political career than an alcoholic's unsubstantiated charges of rape.

"You know the real irony, Joe? I could have been another Dominic Calvetti. I was raised with kids who ended up as wise guys working for him, but I chose the higher road. I've given my life to public service, not to lining my own pockets. And still you don't respect me." Morelli made a little tsk-tsk sound with his tongue, and said, "You're a hard man to please, my friend, and I guess you'll go to your grave that way."

While Morelli was still smiling at his own joke, the door to the cabin swung open. Morelli's gun hand jerked in the direction of the door, but when he saw who it was, he said, "Lord, Eddie! What on earth are you doing here? You practically gave me a heart attack."

"Mr. Calvetti's outside, Senator. You need to give me the gun so he can come in. You know how it is."

"Dominic's here?" Morelli said.

"Yes, sir," Eddie said. "So give me the gun."

Morelli hesitated, momentarily confused, and maybe frightened, but then he regained his composure. He rose from his chair and walked over to Eddie and handed him the gun. "Thank God, you're here. You must have followed this lunatic up here," he said, gesturing toward DeMarco. "He was planning to kill me."

Eddie said nothing; his face had the mobility of the figures on Mount Rushmore. He put Morelli's gun in the pocket of his peacoat—and then he hit

Morelli in the left side with one of his huge, disfigured hands.

DeMarco heard Morelli's ribs break.

The breath exploded from Morelli and he collapsed to the floor and curled into a fetal position, clutching his side.

"All clear, boss," Eddie said.

Calvetti walked into the room alone; Loomis must have remained in the Lincoln.

Calvetti looked down at Morelli. His face was unreadable. His lips were compressed into a thin, unyielding line.

Calvetti had heard every word that Morelli had spoken. DeMarco's holster had contained a wafer-thin transmitter; the receiver had been in Loomis's aluminum suitcase. Loomis was a surveillance expert who worked for the FBI—and for Dominic Calvetti. Calvetti had given DeMarco the gun to compel Morelli to admit that he had molested his stepdaughter although Calvetti had believed, that even under the threat of death, that Morelli would never confess to such an unspeakable sin.

"Dominic, what are you doing?" Morelli said. He was in such agony from the pain in his side that he could barely speak.

Calvetti didn't answer him. He just looked over at Eddie and Eddie kicked Morelli in the side, in the same place where he'd hit him before, and Morelli passed out from the pain.

Calvetti studied Morelli's prone form for a moment then said to Eddie, "Call your brother. Tell him to come up here." Turning to DeMarco, he said, "Go back to the car. Loomis will take you back to the city."

DeMarco just nodded his head. He couldn't speak because he was holding his breath.

"You know what will happen if you talk about any of this," Calvetti said.

DeMarco nodded again.

Calvetti looked at DeMarco for what seemed an eternity, apparently wanting to be sure that DeMarco understood what he meant, that if DeMarco ever talked he would die. Then Calvetti's gaze shifted back to Morelli, and with his unblinking stare and his lined, ancient face and his long, bony nose, he looked like a vulture about to dine on something dead.

DeMarco hadn't thought it possible to feel any sympathy for Paul Morelli, but at that moment, he did. And then he turned and left the cabin and walked down the snow-lined road back to the Lincoln.

He didn't look back, not once.

Chapter 68

———— ◆ ————

It was the afternoon of Christmas Eve.

Congress was in recess and the Capitol was quiet, seeming more like an empty cathedral than a government structure. DeMarco loved the building when it was this way, when it was empty of tourists and lobbyists and politicians. His footsteps echoed throughout the rotunda as he made his way across the floor toward the steps leading up to the Speaker's suite.

He opened the door to Mahoney's office and was greeted by the sound of a party in progress and Bing Crosby singing "White Christmas." He had forgotten, with everything else on his mind, about the Speaker's Christmas bash. Two desks had been turned into buffet tables, and thirty or forty people milled about, sipping doctored punch from plastic glasses. In one corner stood a small Christmas tree decorated with red-and-white-striped bulbs. Mistletoe dangled from light fixtures in a dozen places. Mahoney loved mistletoe.

And there was Mahoney, at the center of the crowd, the center of attention. Covering his white hair was a red Santa's hat with white fur trim and a small bell on the top. In one meaty paw he held a glass of spiked eggnog; his other paw rested paternally on the shoulder of a young blond intern.

Mahoney was in the middle of an old and raunchy joke, something involving a priest and three goats. He delivered the punch line in an authentic Irish brogue and his staff all laughed because the boss was laughing. The face of the intern turned pink enough to match her well-filled sweater. The only one not laughing was Mahoney's chief of staff, who had looked over in alarm when DeMarco came through the door, terrified that he might have been a reporter.

Mahoney saw DeMarco—and the expression on his face. He motioned DeMarco toward his office and proceeded in that direction himself. He stopped once to top off his eggnog with a shot of Jamaican rum, then stopped again to buss a woman standing within the target radius of a mistletoe sprig. The woman was in her forties; Mahoney was an equal-opportunity lecher.

On the drive back to New York with Loomis, DeMarco wondered why Calvetti had decided not to kill him. It could have been because of his relationship to Harry Foster, but he also suspected that somewhere in the lump of anthracite Calvetti had for a heart, he felt remorse for the things he had done on Morelli's behalf. Whatever the case, he was alive. He was certain that Paul Morelli was not.

He did, however, ignore Calvetti's warning not to talk to anybody about what had happened at the cabin in Catskill Park. He told Emma. He told her because she had a right to know, and he knew that he could trust her with any secret. Emma's whole life was a secret. And now he told Mahoney.

"Jesus," Mahoney said, when DeMarco finished speaking. "What do you think happened after you left?"

"I think Calvetti killed him. Morelli destroyed Calvetti's plan of placing his own man in the White House, and he killed Calvetti's daughter and was responsible for the death of his granddaughter. There's no way Paul Morelli's still alive." DeMarco paused, then said, "But I'll bet we never find the body. Someday, somebody's going to walk into that cabin where Morelli was staying and see the things he had written on that whiteboard, the vision he had to resurrect his career, and then they'll think that he realized that it was futile, that he had no chance for a comeback. They'll think he walked into woods and made himself disappear."

Mahoney nodded, apparently agreeing with DeMarco's reasoning. "I think I'm gonna eventually tell Dick Finley what happened," he said. "He should know why his son died."

"I guess," DeMarco said, not sure that that was a good idea.

Mahoney shook his head sadly, making the bell on the Santa hat jingle. "Ah, Joe," he said, "the things Morelli could have done, the things *we* could have done."

Mahoney and DeMarco both sat in silence for a while, reflecting morosely on all that had happened. DeMarco's morose thoughts were mostly about himself. He felt as if God had decided to make a sequel to the story of Job, and that he'd been cast to play the lead. In the last year he'd lost another lover, almost been killed by a madman, and been manipulated, as always, by his boss. He was responsible for the deaths of three people: Gary Parker, Brenda Hathaway, and, very soon, Arnie Berg. If he had never set about to ruin Paul Morelli, they would all still be alive.

Maybe he was even responsible for the deaths of Lydia Morelli and Isaiah Perry. If he'd never met with Lydia, maybe they wouldn't have died. And Marcus Perry—if he hadn't talked to him, maybe he would not have tried to avenge his brother's death.

Maybe. His conscience was sodden with maybes.

Mahoney tipped back his head and polished off his eggnog. "Well, that's that," he said, his tone indicating that he was through ruminating about Paul Morelli. "I think I'll call this kid in New York I know. He's the attorney general up there now. I think I'll see if he's interested in bein' a senator."

DeMarco knew that the "kid" in New York was at least fifty.

"He's kind of an idealist," Mahoney said, "always tiltin' at one fuckin' windmill or another, but I think he's coachable."

One thing DeMarco had always admired about John Mahoney was his optimism. Politics was a tough game, and even with Mahoney's clout, he probably lost half the battles he fought. But each day he got up, put on his armor, picked up his lance, and climbed onto his trusty, sway-backed steed. Mahoney also jousted with windmills.

Yes, the Speaker was through mourning Paul Morelli—it was time to find his replacement, time to fight another battle. DeMarco wished he had Mahoney's ability to shrug off life's blows so easily.

And Mahoney must have been thinking the same thing because he said, "Get your chin off your chest, son. You did what you had to do."

"I know but I was just thinking . . ."

"There's a gal here this afternoon, my secretary's niece. I'll introduce you. I swear she looks like Gina

Lollobrigida, Joe. You're too young to remember Gina, but this gal . . . well, she's the spittin' image of her."

The bell on the Santa's hat jingled as Mahoney rose unsteadily to his feet. "Come on, Joe. We're missin' the party."

"I love Christmas," Mahoney said.

Chapter 69

———— ◆◆◆ ————

Paul Morelli was barely conscious when Eddie and his brother took him out of the trunk of the car.

Eddie had busted him all up inside. His ribs on both sides were broken, and his kidneys were horribly bruised. He wouldn't be surprised if his spleen had ruptured. Every time the old man had asked him a question, and every time he had hesitated, Eddie had hit him. He hit him with a fist that felt like a wrecking ball slamming into his body. And in the end, he admitted to every lie. He confessed to everything.

They put him down on his back on a damp, concrete floor. His hands were tied behind him and there was duct tape over his mouth. His eyes took in the building, some sort of circular, concrete structure. He thought it might be a grain silo, and he had this vivid image of tons of wheat pouring down on him, crushing him, smothering him.

He heard something behind him then, metal scraping on metal, like rusty hinges being forced open. Eddie and his brother, two men build like a matched pair of oxen, were grunting with the effort. If *they* were grunting, it had to be very heavy. As frightened as he already was, it frightened him even more not being able to see what they were doing.

Eddie suddenly came into his field of vision. He bent down, grabbed him by an ankle, and with one hand, dragged him across the concrete floor. He flipped him over onto his belly and cut the rope binding his hands behind his back. Thank God! If he could get the tape off his mouth maybe he could reason with Eddie. But before he could remove the tape, Eddie placed a foot against his shoulder and shoved and he felt himself falling.

He didn't fall far, maybe six feet. He landed on his back, the breath knocked out of him, waves of pain coursing through his body. He lay there for a minute with his eyes closed, willing himself not to pass out. He couldn't pass out. He wondered if his back was broken or if one of his fractured ribs had punctured a lung. He finally opened his eyes and looked up.

Calvetti was standing there on the edge of the opening that he had been thrown through. A short, frail, white-haired old man—a man who at that moment seemed as old and as terrifying as death itself. He just stood there, looking down at Morelli, studying him, his face expressionless. There was *nothing* there: not anger, not regret, and certainly not pity.

Morelli reached up to scrape the tape off his mouth so he could talk to Calvetti. He ripped at the tape so frantically that his fingernails scratched grooves into one of his cheeks. "Dominic!" he screamed when the tape was finally off. Then, struggling to control his fear, he lowered his voice and said as calmly as he could, "Don't do this. Please. I can still be president. I can still achieve our dream."

Calvetti just shook his head—one time, slowly, from side to side—and then he looked over and nodded to Eddie.

Morelli watched in horror as Eddie and his brother began to lower a heavy concrete door. The door was on massive hinges and was three inches thick. Morelli struggled to get to his feet but with his injuries he was too slow. By the time he got up, Eddie and his brother had closed the door, sealing the space he was in. The last thing Paul Morelli saw before the door closed was Dominic Calvetti's black eyes silently condemning him to hell.

Morelli raised his hands. He was tall enough that he could touch the door. He pushed against it but knew that even if he hadn't been injured, he wouldn't have been able to move it. Then he heard something click, as if some sort of mechanism had been engaged to lock the door.

He sank to the floor in pain, his injuries aggravated by straining against the door. He bit down on the knuckles of his right hand to stop himself from screaming, to force himself to think.

He was now in the dark, but while the door had been open, he'd gotten a brief look at his surroundings. He knew he was in a hidden space beneath the floor of a building that he thought might have been an empty grain silo. But just then he realized it wasn't a silo. He could hear liquid splashing onto the floor above him. A lot of liquid, as if it was being pumped into the building through several large-diameter pipes. He realized then that he was in a tank, a tank normally filled with water or some other fluid, and when the tank was full, the door above his head would be invisible.

Once again the panic began to wash over him and once again he held it back, suppressing his fear. Think, he told himself. Calm down and think. Why didn't Calvetti just shoot him and bury him in the woods near the cabin? Why go to the trouble of transporting him to this place? And Eddie hadn't hit him in the face. He'd battered his body something awful but had never touched his face, and that *had* to mean that Calvetti hadn't wanted to mar his looks. Yes, that had to be it. Calvetti was just going to leave him here for a while, thinking he'd scare him so badly that he'd never fail him or lie to him again. He wouldn't throw away all their years of work, not for a daughter he hadn't loved or a granddaughter that had only been a small part of his life. Yes, the fact that Dominic hadn't killed him meant that there was still hope.

He searched his pockets. They were empty. No, wait. He felt something. It was a small disposable cigarette lighter. Where had that come from? He didn't smoke and he'd used wooden matches to light the fire in the cabin. He flicked on the lighter and raised it above his head and looked around. The concrete walls were complete bare, no other openings or outlets that he could see, but just as the heat from the lighter began to burn his thumb he saw something in the shadows on his right-hand side. He crawled on his knees in the dark in the direction of whatever he'd seen, and flicked the lighter again.

Oh, Christ! It was a skeleton. And it had been there a long time. There was no flesh or hair on the bones, just a few tattered bits of cloth and leather. He noticed, just before the lighter began to burn him again, that there was something near the skeleton's right hand.

He waited impatiently until the lighter cooled a bit, then spun the wheel again with his thumb. The object he'd seen near the skeleton's hand was a pair of rusted nail clippers, the file blade of the clippers sticking out. What was the man doing with the file blade? Had he figured a way out?

He let the flame die again and took a few shallow, rapid breaths. He told himself not to panic. He ignited the lighter once more to see what the dead man had been doing with the nail file—and then he screamed.

He screamed until his throat was raw. He screamed for Calvetti to release him. He screamed for God to save him. But even as his screams were echoing throughout the chamber he knew that the likelihood of Calvetti returning for him was less than the possibility of God reaching down from heaven and opening the door above him.

Now he knew why Calvetti hadn't simply killed him. And he also knew why Calvetti had placed the cigarette lighter in his pocket. Calvetti wanted him to die slowly and painfully, and he wanted him to know *while* he was dying that there would be no last minute rescue, that no one was going to find him and save him. Dominic Calvetti wanted him to suffer a slow, horrible death knowing—with absolute certainty—that there was no hope.

He knew this because scratched into the concrete wall above the skeleton were the words:

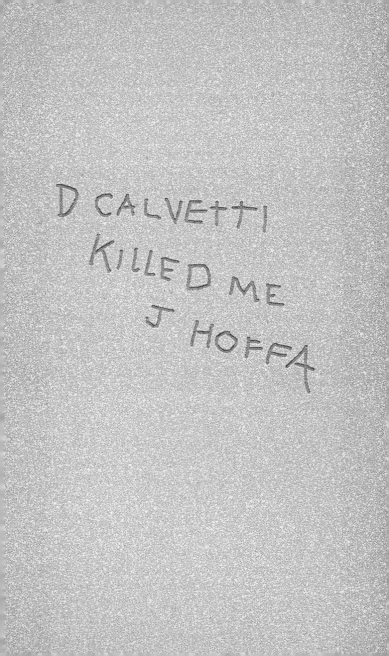

Read on for the opening pages of *House Justice*, the next Joe DeMarco thriller.

"Sleazy legislators, CIA spooks, Russian gangsters, assorted hit men, a misanthropic billionaire, a SoCal surfer/computer gamer/millionaire, and a mysterious man hell bent on avenging a murdered spy. [*House Justice* is] a superb example of the post-cold war espionage novel."
—*Booklist*, starred review

Available now!

Prologue

***

The battery was dead.

For six years she had evaded discovery. For six years she had lived in their midst and endured everything she had to endure but now, after all her sacrifices—now, when it was time to go home and accept the medals no one would ever see—now, when she would be given a job where she wouldn't wake up shaking every night, terrified that the next day would be the day she'd be caught—now she was going to die because a car wouldn't start.

She overcame the urge to scream and pound the steering wheel in frustration. She needed to stay in control. She needed to think. But she couldn't stop the tears leaking from her eyes.

She couldn't understand why Carson had waited so long to tell her to flee. As soon as the story appeared in the newspaper she knew she was vulnerable but Carson had told her not to panic, that too many people had attended the meeting. Then, four days later, he sent the text message to her cell phone. Just a single word: eclipse!

Eclipse meant: run. Run for your life.

For the last two years she had been begging Carson to let her go home, and he kept saying that he would but he needed her to stay just a little bit longer. Just give me six more months, he said—and then it was six more after that, and six more after that. The manipulative bastard. If he had kept his word, she would have told her lover that she had to visit a fictitious dying aunt in Bandar-e Maqam and taken a routine, commercial flight to the coastal city, after which a navy SEAL team would have picked her up on the beach. But now she couldn't do that; there was no way she would be allowed to board a plane. So she had to use the backup escape plan, the plan they had never expected to use. And maybe that's why the battery was dead: because someone had forgotten to check on the car they'd parked in the garage so long ago. Or maybe, because Carson waited too long, no one had time to check.

She had fled from the ministry as soon as she received Carson's message and immediately called the four people in her network to alert them. None of them answered. That was bad. If they had been picked up they may have already talked. She knew they'd talk eventually because everybody talked in the end, no matter how strong they were. All she could do was hope they hadn't talked yet.

The backup plan had been for her to pick up a car hidden in a small, private garage two miles from the ministry and then drive to a house twenty miles east of the city. There she would be hidden, for weeks if necessary, until they could transport her safely across the border into either Afghanistan or Kuwait. When she left the ministry, she had wanted to sprint the entire distance to the garage but had been afraid that she would call attention to herself. So she had walked as fast as she could, knowing each minute she spent walking was one more minute for them to get the roadblocks in place.

But now the roadblocks didn't matter. Without a car she had no idea how she would get to the safe house. She couldn't take a bus: there were no bus routes that went near the house. And as for walking or taking a cab . . . the police, the military—and, of course, the brutes from the Ministry of Intelligence and Security—would all have her picture. They'd be showing it to cabdrivers and stopping every woman walking alone—and here, few women walked alone. And if she took a cab, and if the driver remembered her, not only would she die but so would the family who hid her at the safe house.

She forced herself to take a breath, to suppress the rising, screaming panic. Did she have any other options? Any? Yes, maybe one: the Swiss Embassy. The United States didn't have an embassy in Iran but the Swiss did. Moreover, the Swiss were designated as a "protecting power" for U.S. interests in Iran, meaning that if some visiting American got into trouble the Swiss would do their best to help him out. But what she wanted the Swiss to do went far beyond helping some tourist who had lost his passport.

The Swiss Embassy was close, less than a mile from where she was, and if she was careful—if she used the alleys and ducked through buildings—she might make it there and she might live. They would know if she entered the embassy, of course, and it would cause the Swiss enormous political problems, but maybe they would provide her sanctuary until her own people could get her out of the country through diplomatic channels. God knows what sort of trade they'd have to make for her and she couldn't even imagine the international uproar that would ensue, but she didn't care about any of that. She was too young to die.

The way she'd lived the last six years, she'd never had the chance to experience the joys of being young. Her youth had been stolen from her—so they owed her, and to hell with the political fallout that would occur if she ran to the Swiss. She had done her job—

and now the diplomats and the damn politicians could do theirs.

Her mind made up, she exited the useless car, ran to the side door of the garage, and threw it open—and was immediately blinded by the headlights of two vehicles. Men armed with machine pistols closed in on her.

She just stood there, head bowed, shoulders slumped in defeat, unable to move. She could feel something draining from her body—and that something was *hope*. There were no options left. There was no place to run or hide. She wished, more than anything else, that she had a gun; if she had had one she would have killed herself.

It was over.

She knew what was going to happen next.

She knew how she was going to die.